"I read and reread *On Strike Against God* when I was in my early twenties, riveted by its strange amalgam of coming-out story, campus novel, cri de coeur, and vertiginous Nabokovian stand-up routine. Russ was both enlisting me in her struggle and, I see now, throwing me a rope so I wouldn't have to struggle quite as much as she did. Alec Pollak's critical edition offers up an utterly delightful array of historical, contemporary, and personal context that I hope will assure this curious and powerful revolutionary work the recognition it merits."

—**ALISON BECHDEL, author of** *Fun Home:*
A Family Tragicomic

"Joanna Russ's work is a gift and so is everything else in this deep little volume. *On Strike Against God* is a beautiful historical document that shows us, today, what it looks like to create language for a world of experience that we have not yet managed to articulate. Plus it's funny, if you're cool."

—**IMOGEN BINNIE, author of** *Nevada: A Novel*

"Joanna Russ possesses a ferocious, formidable intelligence, so blazing you almost expect the page to burn to ash as you read it. To engage with her is to become aware of the ways in which the world wounds us and our own ability to, in turn, imagine and then demand that the world change for the better. Russ's nonfiction, her novels, her short stories are essential, singular works, and I have wanted with all my heart for a very long time to see them back in print again."

—**KELLY LINK, author of** *Get in Trouble: Stories*

"Angry, funny, sharp, and intense, *On Strike Against God* captures the feel of the feminist revolution of the 1970s with unusual brilliance."

—**KIM STANLEY ROBINSON, author of** *Red Mars*

"What a delight to be reading Joanna Russ again. *On Strike Against God* showcases her stylistic brilliance, the intimacy and courage of her voice, the warp-speed flights of her brain. Excellent supporting materials an added bonus."

—**KAREN JOY FOWLER, author of** *We Are All Completely Beside Ourselves: A Novel*

"An immensely important, subversive book that's as hilarious and deliciously fun to read as it is deadly serious. Russ reckons with the confusion and heartache of claiming identity and love in a world that refuses to acknowledge her existence—a reality present-day lesbians and queer people might find familiar. Paired with several of Russ's field-shaping essays, the book examines the nature of pleasure, friendship, conversation, and self-knowledge and offers a window onto a world in which the narrator—and the reader, by proxy—might finally be allowed to exist."

—**JENN SHAPLAND, author of** *My Autobiography of Carson McCullers: A Memoir*

"A powerful, witty, revelatory meditation on culture and identity as only Russ could do it."

—**KAMERON HURLEY, author of** *The Light Brigade*

"This is a miracle of a book! *On Strike Against God* is Joanna Russ's mainstream masterwork—warm, angry, brilliant, wise, and laugh-out-loud funny. As was Joanna herself. I urge you to read it with all appropriate emotions."

—**MICHAEL SWANWICK, author of** *The Iron Dragon's Daughter*

"The Feminist Press's new edition of Joanna Russ's realist lesbian novel *On Strike Against God*—a creatively significant but underappreciated piece in Russ's oeuvre—productively nests the original story within a well-curated selection of essays (including two by Russ herself!), interviews, correspondence, and other archival documents. These additions provide richly illustrated context for *On Strike Against God*, as well as Russ's broader 'transhistorical and multi-genre appeal,' which should delight both familiar and fresh readers."

—**LEE MANDELO, author of** *Summer Sons*

"*On Strike Against God* is not only a long-overlooked essential work of feminist and lesbian awakening—told in Joanna Russ's inimitable mix of wild humor, acid commentary, and fierce humanity—but also a vulnerable reflection on her own coming-out experience. I know of few novels that are as tender, radical, and wonderful as this one."

—**NICOLE RUDICK, editor of *Joanna Russ: Novels & Stories***

"Fearless, funny, and quirkily honest about homophobia, lesbian desire, and being a decent human being upon whom much patriarchal stupidity is unloaded. *On Strike Against God* is a brilliant novel, and so remarkably prescient. It confirms without a doubt the importance of Joanna Russ as both an ancestor and a compatriot. This edition provides an insightful introduction by Alec Pollak and essays by Jeanne Thornton and Mary Anne Mohanraj which locate Russ in her time, assert their own presents, and show us how profoundly relevant Russ's work is to theirs. The interview between Alec Pollak and Samuel R. Delany gives us the necessary connections we need to understand how writers and communities can and must evolve their thinking and social orientations in order to draw into the present the true power our forebears have bequeathed us. I laughed, I sympathized, and I was deeply moved."

—**LARISSA LAI, author of *The Tiger Flu***

"An invaluable edition of Joanna Russ's iconic work of queer rage and self-making. Students of Russ's work will rejoice in these excellent essays and contextual materials that illuminate Russ's life and political concerns. This is a rich scholarly resource and celebration of one of the twentieth century's great literary rebels."

—**ANNALEE NEWITZ, author of *Stories Are Weapons: Psychological Warfare and the American Mind***

ON STRIKE
AGAINST GOD

JOANNA RUSS

EDITED BY ALEC POLLAK

THE FEMINIST PRESS
AT THE CITY UNIVERSITY OF NEW YORK
NEW YORK CITY

Published in 2024 by the Feminist Press
at the City University of New York
The Graduate Center
365 Fifth Avenue, Suite 5406
New York, NY 10016

feministpress.org

First Feminist Press edition 2024

 This book is made possible by the New York State Council on the Arts with the support of the Office of the Governor and the New York State Legislature.

First printing July 2024

Cover design by Sasha Staicu
Text design by Drew Stevens

Library of Congress Cataloging-in-Publication Data is available for this title.
ISBN 978-1-55861-314-0

PRINTED IN THE UNITED STATES OF AMERICA

CONTENTS

1 Introduction: I'm Not A Girl I'm A Genius
by Alec Pollak

39 **On Strike Against God**
by Joanna Russ

169 Author's Note by Joanna Russ

CONTEMPORARY COMMENTARY

173 On Lightning, and After Lightning
by Jeanne Thornton

189 Nothing Too Frightening
by Mary Anne Mohanraj

209 The Other Axis: An Interview with
Samuel R. Delany by Alec Pollak

FROM THE ARCHIVES

231 What Can a Heroine Do?
or Why Women Can't Write
by Joanna Russ

253 Not For Years But For Decades
by Joanna Russ

279 Correspondence between Marilyn Hacker
and Joanna Russ

291 Alternate Endings to *On Strike Against God*

299 Notes

307 Acknowledgments

309 About the Contributors

I'M NOT A GIRL I'M A GENIUS

ALEC POLLAK

A groundbreaking writer of science fiction's "New Wave," Joanna Russ has been lauded as "one of twentieth-century [science fiction]'s greatest writers"[1] and the "most influential writer of feminist science fiction the field has ever seen."[2] If you've heard of Russ, you've probably heard of her most famous novel, *The Female Man*, published in 1975. Science fiction aficionados may be familiar with her other award-winning genre works, including *We Who Are About To . . .*, *The Two of Them*, and the Alyx stories. But *The Female Man*, which thrust Russ into the public eye and sold half a million copies by 1987, is Russ's primary claim to fame. The novel has become a staple of feminist science fiction curricula alongside Ursula K. Le Guin's *The Left Hand of Darkness*.[3]

Joanna Russ was a lesbian, a socialist, an author, a teacher, and a scholar; she was also a "brilliant, impossible person"[4] and a "difficult character."[5] According to some, she was a "raging man-hater"[6] and "lady militant."[7] She was a mentor and teacher to countless rising stars of science fiction—at the time, Samuel R. Delany, Sally Miller Gearhart, and Octavia E. Butler—and she nurtured complex, decades-long friendships with other established authors, including Ursula K. Le Guin, James Tiptree, Jr., and Philip K. Dick. She is, according to Samuel R. Delany, "one of the finest—and most necessary—writers of American fiction."[8] However, today, much of Russ's full multigenre corpus of writings—works of fantasy, drama, and realism, not to mention a wide-ranging body of nonfiction feminist criticism—remains a relatively well-kept secret.

Throughout her life, Russ faced cultural and institutional headwinds: a lesbian adolescence in the 1950s, the travails of higher education for women in the 1950s and 1960s, the rise and fracturing of the feminist movements of the 1970s, and the punishing misogyny of the publishing industry in the 1970s and 1980s. Born in the Bronx in 1937 to a newly but staunchly middle-class Jewish family, Russ was a precocious, outgoing child unfortunate enough (she would say later) to come of age in the 1950s. Russ spent her adolescence and young adulthood struggling and failing to find fulfillment according to the social mores of the era. According to her elementary school teachers, psychologists, and friends' parents, she was too loud and too assertive; her romantic and sexual relationships with other women were a "stage" ("Not For Years But For Decades," page 254). Her sexuality evolved in "profound mental darkness." "It wasn't real," she finally accepted at age sixteen, and "it didn't count, except in my own inner world" ("Not For Years," page 260). In high school, Russ was selected as a finalist for the Westinghouse Science Talent Search—a rare feat for a female student at that time—and went on to attend Cornell University from 1953 to 1957, where she majored in English and developed her writing craft under Vladimir Nabokov. The English Department urged her to apply for PhD programs, but she declined, disgruntled that she was being encouraged to pursue an academic career "by a department that had never employed a woman."[9] Instead, she enrolled in an MFA program in playwriting at the Yale School of Drama, where she wrote experimental plays on the inner lives of department store mannequins, satyrs, and unruly, monstrous children.

After graduating from Yale in 1960, Russ moved to

New York City's East Village, where she spent seven years trying and failing to make her living as a playwright while working a rotation of thankless day jobs. She moved through her time in New York in a fog, deeply closeted. She married a man because, "bitterly ashamed" as she was to admit it, she was "running out of money" ("Not For Years," page 263). She wanted to work, and she wanted to write, but psychologists urged her to embrace domestic life—to be less ambitious and more easily satisfied, less assertive and more deferential. Russ's writings from this time document at length the havoc wrought by midcentury psychoanalytic practice on the lives and minds of women, queers, and otherwise "deviant" patients. They reveal a woman deeply frightened and confused, her intelligence, ambition, and desires distorted into uncertainty, listlessness, self-loathing, and, eventually, the clinical depression and anxiety that would dog her throughout her life.

An instructorship at Cornell rescued Russ from a life in pieces when in 1967—the same year as her traumatizing divorce—she returned to teach English at her alma mater. In 1969 she attended the now-renowned Cornell Conference on Women, an unprecedented gathering of feminist leaders that resulted in the nation's first accredited women's studies course, offered at Cornell that same spring.[10] Russ left the conference "feeling that the sky had fallen" and that "'English literature' had been badly rigged" ("What Can a Heroine Do?," page 231). In response, she wrote a nonfiction essay about literary sexism, "What Can a Heroine Do? or Why Women Can't Write," included in this volume, and the short story "When It Changed," which would become her legendary 1975 novel *The Female Man*.

An experimental, gut-wrenching tour de force detailing a woman's lesbian coming-to-consciousness, *The*

Female Man broke ground on multiple fronts. Russ's "frank, sensuous descriptions of erotic scenes between women" were shocking at the time, as were her "controversial depiction[s]" of women's rage.[11] The novel gave voice to decades of Russ's own gender trouble, repressed lesbianism, familial estrangement, and voracious ambition. As a "tall, overly-bright and overly-self-assertive" reader of "Great Literature" in America's repressive 1950s ("Not For Years," page 255), Russ had become "convinced that [she] had no real experience of life."[12] Everywhere she turned, women (and especially queer women) were doomed: "It was always (1) failure (2) the love affair which settles everything," she wrote to her friend and award-winning poet Marilyn Hacker, in life and literature alike (page 287). The women characters she encountered in books and in movies were never people with complex motives, desires, and inner lives, capable of growth and creation, but rather "depictions of social roles women [were] supposed to play," such as "maidens, wicked temptresses, pretty schoolmarms, beautiful bitches, faithful wives, and so on." "Look at them carefully," Russ would later write, "and you will see that they do not really exist at all" ("What Can a Heroine Do?," page 234). So she was "left with the contradictions," she explained, between her "real experience, undefined and powerful as it was" and what the world afforded her the language to describe.[13]

By the end of the 1970s, the Women in Print movement—an amalgam of feminist publishers, bookstores, distributors, and periodicals—would establish a "women's market" and transform commercial publishing nationwide. "Feminist fiction" would emerge as a recognizable, publishable, and marketable genre unto itself. But in 1969, when Russ reached for fiction to help her reconcile the "contradictions," her models for feminist and lesbian literature were few and far between. Mainstream presses rarely published books by women, to say nothing of lesbians. And so Russ turned to science fiction, an established commercial genre, as an "escape from the equation Culture = Male," as she had in her adolescence when she inhaled books about women dressing like men, men dressing like women, and aliens desiring aliens and exploring the stars ("What Can a Heroine Do?," page 247).

Throughout her writings, Russ sought to answer the guiding question of her life: "How can you write about what really hasn't happened?"[14] For Russ, it was a feminist question—one about the relationship between life and literature for people whose identities, desires, and ambitions were ignored, erased, and denounced by mainstream cultural imagery and storytelling. "Make something unspeakable and you make it unthink-able," Russ wrote, and in pursuit of the unspeakable, her writing traversed science fiction, fantasy, realism, and nonfiction feminist criticism alike ("What Can a Heroine Do?," page 246). Science fiction provided an especially potent alternative to "great" literature, with its "profound bias" against women's lives as "proper mate-rial" for fiction.[15] Writing science fiction, Russ could authoritatively "write of things nobody knew anything about,"[16] which in 1969 included queer desire (the American Psychological Association classified homosexuality as a disease until 1973), women's economic freedom (women couldn't open bank accounts until 1974), and sexual safety (marital rape didn't become illegal in all fifty states until 1993). These topics weren't the stuff of realistic fiction, let alone of "Great Literature"—but they could be addressed safely within the realm of science fiction. As Russ explains in "What Can a Heroine Do?," the "plot-patterns" endemic to science fiction concern themselves not with "accepted gender roles" but with the creation and navigation of new worlds, within which gender roles can be either peripheral, malleable, or both (page 247). She embraced speculative fiction not only out of a love for cyborgs and interstellar travel but because she saw the genre's potential as a "vehicle for social change"[17] and a tool for escaping the "profound mental darkness" that engulfed her youth—a consequence of hearing repeatedly that her self-conception, desires, and ambitions "weren't real" and "didn't count" ("Not For Years," page 260).

The Female Man was Russ's first deliberate, concerted attempt to use science fiction to speak the unspeakable and think the unthinkable, and it worked. Science fiction's old guard (mostly men) disparaged it, even as a new generation of readers (mostly women) "breathed the name Russ and spoke of *Female Man* . . . as holy writ."[18] By 1987 the novel had sold over five hundred thousand copies, securing Russ's name for posterity. The tropes and tools of science fiction allowed Russ to build fictional worlds around her own "undefined and powerful" internal life—a life that "didn't count" by any external metric, but thrived within her fiction. On Whileaway, for example, *The Female Man*'s feminist utopia, men don't exist and lesbianism is the norm—no mind games or repression or coming out needed. At the same time, over in Manland, *The Female Man*'s dystopia, characters' rage isn't an overreaction to "real" society's courtship rituals, but rather a reasonable reaction to life amid the ever-present threat of gender-based violence. And indeed, although *The Female Man* is heralded widely as a work of science fiction, its allure lay not only (or even primarily) in its use of parallel worlds, cyborgs, and parthenogenesis—all conventional science fiction tropes. What was most groundbreaking about *The Female*

Man, and what spurred its market success, was its ability to validate readers'—mostly women readers'—inner lives as *real*, despite everything they'd been taught to believe. "*The Female Man* is all reality," one reader wrote to Russ in 1977. "I felt I was (or had been) all the principal characters in this life alone."[19] "I remembered how nice it was to feel All Right, Real, Valuable, Valid," wrote another.[20]

Written immediately after Russ completed *The Female Man*, *On Strike Against God* was Russ's second attempt to use fiction—this time, "realist" fiction—to speak the unspeakable. It is a deliberate, explicit, and potent continuation of the work Russ had done in her earlier novel. "It's like the other axis of *The Female Man*," wrote her good friend Samuel R. Delany, "The two of them should be published in one volume."[21] Russ concurred: she herself described *On Strike* as doing "what [she] couldn't in F.M."[22] She turned from science fiction back to "realistic" fiction because, as useful and necessary a thought experiment as *The Female Man* was, it was nevertheless a concession to the impossibility of reconciling her inner life with her external "real" world. Jeanne Thornton's essay "On Lightning, and After Lightning," included in this volume, speaks poignantly to Russ's continuity of purpose from one novel to the other: "In *The Female Man*," Thornton writes, "the charge between Janet and Laura requires a Whileaway, an alternate-dimension feminist utopia, as catalyst." But in *On Strike Against God*, "to come out, to become radical, is something you might actually go out and do" (page 181). Thornton asks, "What does desire look like among equals? And what if you didn't have to wait for a portal to Whileaway or Womanland to open in order to demand it? What if you had to be brave right now?" (page 185). *On Strike* was Russ's attempt to insist upon the possibility of love between equals (and between women) without an alternate-reality portal to aid her. It was her attempt "to be brave right now."

In her essays "Not For Years But For Decades" and "What Can a Heroine Do? or Why Women Can't Write," also included in this volume, Russ speaks to the autobiographical stakes of her oscillation between genres—to why she embraced science fiction in the first place, and why she turned back to "non-genre" or "realistic" fiction when she did. "What Can a Heroine Do?" explores speculative fiction as a "vehicle for social change,"[23] while "Not For Years But For Decades," written sometime between 1976 and 1978 (at a safe remove from the rawer emotions of Russ's early thirties), fills the interstices of Russ's enthusiasm in "What Can a Heroine Do?" with Russ's experiences as a "tall, overly-bright and overly-self-assertive" child who struggled amid the punitive gender mores of the 1950s. "Not For Years But For Decades" is especially relevant to *On Strike Against God*: ultimately published as a stand-alone essay in Julia Penelope and Susan J. Wolfe's *The Coming Out Stories* (1980), "Not For Years" was initially written as *On Strike Against God*'s afterword. Readers are welcome—encouraged, even—to take their cue from this relationship and to interpret "Not For Years But For Decades" as *On Strike Against God*'s autobiographical accompaniment. Together, these essays avow something transformative and undoubtedly controversial for Russ's legacy: that science fiction was, for Russ, a means to an end. Nothing can detract from *The Female Man*'s scintillating brilliance, but we owe it to Russ, and to ourselves, to recognize *On Strike Against God* as what came next in Russ's feminist quest to tackle in fiction "what really [hadn't] happened" in life, and to rethink Russ's legacy accordingly.

Although it was published after Russ achieved celebrity with *The Female Man*, and although it received stellar reviews, *On Strike Against God* quickly went out of print and became largely lost to contemporary readers.* Russ hoped *The Female Man* would improve *On Strike*'s chances: "I suppose I ought to keep the ms. until FEMALE MAN is out and see if a paying market opens up," she wrote to Delany in 1974.[24] But not only did *The Female Man* not open up "a paying market" for *On Strike Against God—The Female Man* only narrowly avoided this same fate itself. The earlier novel's survival, let alone its ascent, was a rare deviation from that quick descent into oblivion typical of feminist books.

The Female Man was ill at ease within the established markets and genres of its day, and Russ struggled for years to place it with a publisher. That it was, ultimately, legible as a work of science fiction was the novel's saving grace: in 1975, science fiction was a mainstream commercial genre with willing publishers and eager, established audiences. And so, when Russ finally placed *The Female Man* with commercial publisher Bantam Books, she secured a far larger reading audience for her controversial feminist novel than she could have otherwise, had she published through an independent (let alone feminist) press. Yet by 1977, Bantam Books had allowed *The Female Man* to go out of print and "had no plans to re-print [the] title."[25] Why? Because despite feminist

---

*Because Russ struggled to find publishers for both *The Female Man* and *On Strike Against God*, their publication chronology does not reflect the chronology of their composition. Russ finished *The Female Man* in 1971 and began *On Strike Against God* in 1973. She began writing her next novel-length work, *The Two of Them*, in 1974. *The Female Man* came out in 1975; *The Two of Them* came out in 1978; and *On Strike Against God* came out in 1980, with the longest lag between composition and publication of the three. Because of this lag, readers have no way of knowing that Russ wrote *The Female Man* and *On Strike Against God* in rapid succession. *The Two of Them* is the last novel-length work of fiction Russ ever wrote. *On Strike Against God* is the last novel-length work of fiction she published.

readers' "great demand" for *The Female Man*, the novel had not, according to Bantam, "performed well enough to be kept in print."[26] *The Female Man* would have stayed out of print, too, had feminist bookstores not coordinated letter-writing campaigns and inundated Bantam with inquiries and requests. By 1978, *The Female Man* was back in print—not because Bantam Books had miraculously seen the light, but because the burgeoning feminist movement made the novel impossible to ignore.[27] At the same time, if *The Female Man* hadn't been published with a publisher of Bantam's caliber, it's unlikely that the novel's initial distribution—how many readers it originally reached—would have been big enough to capture the attention of the feminist readers and booksellers who saved it from oblivion. In 1986, Beacon Press licensed rights to the novel and has kept it in print ever since.

I raise the curtain on *The Female Man*'s uphill battle to help present-day readers understand the difficulties that faced feminist books—even the ones that we take for granted as inevitably successful today—before the feminist publishing revolution of the 1970s and 1980s. Feminist authors' tendency to flout the status quo (whatever it may be), challenge literary norms, and tell uncomfortable truths has long disgruntled mainstream culture's gatekeepers—those largely male editors, publishers, booksellers, critics, and others empowered to deem writing "good" or "bad" and act accordingly. And so these feminist writings are often misunderstood, maligned, and out of print before their insights, wisdom, and pleasures can reach eager readers. Whether a book finds a publisher, sells well, and stays in print often has nothing to do with whether it is "good" or "bad" according to *readers*. "I remember the answers we kept getting [to *The Female Man*]" recalled Russ, in 1990, "usually along the lines of, 'We've already published our feminist novel this year, so we don't want another.'"[28] Publishers couldn't wrap their heads around the possibility that a "difficult" feminist book could sell—and sell well. Once *The Female Man* was finally "allowed to cultivate an audience," writes literary critic Larry McCaffery, it "acquired an ongoing readership" and sold phenomenally; the trouble was getting the novel past publishers' disbelief and into readers' hands—not once, not twice, but multiple times.[29] This was the founding principle of the Feminist Press—the publisher of the book you're holding now, the oldest continuously publishing feminist press in the United States: that feminist books need and deserve more than one chance to reach the readers hungry for them, and that their readers deserve that same chance.[30] *The Female Man* got this chance, but many of Russ's other writings—fiction and nonfiction alike, similarly unconventional and incendiary—haven't been so lucky.

As Russ's only novel-length work of non-genre (read: "realist" or "literary") fiction, *On Strike Against God* has been regarded and dismissed repeatedly as an outlier within Russ's larger science fiction corpus, despite critical acclaim. The novel has its devotees, certainly: enthusiastic readers include Samuel R. Delany, Kim Stanley Robinson, and Alison Bechdel, who wrote to Russ in 1986, "I've never read any of your science fiction, but I do re-read with punctual regularity *On Strike Against God*."[31] But, originally published by a tiny independent feminist press—Brooklyn-based Out & Out Books—*On Strike* reached only a fraction of the audience of *The Female Man*. The novel went out of print after its 1987 reissue and stayed out of print until 2023, when the Library of America published it in *Joanna Russ: Novels & Stories*, alongside a host of Russ's science fiction works.*

---

*Open Road Media issued an ebook edition of *On Strike Against God* in 2021.

During that interim, *On Strike Against God*'s anomalousness—its status as "minor" Russ—compounded, to its detriment. As a result, decades of readers have discovered, read, and appreciated Joanna Russ without access to this work, and so when readers praise and cite Russ's writings, and when publishers look to reprint them, it's not *On Strike* they turn to—it's Russ's science fiction. The cycle repeats. *On Strike* stays "minor," outlier, obsolete Russ. As a result, Russ has been perceived for decades as a one-hit science fiction wonder, with minimal recognition of her significance as a groundbreaking, wide-ranging feminist writer.

The fact that *The Female Man* was, for nearly fifty years, Russ's best-known work speaks not to the extent of Russ's skills or the worthiness of her other writings but to the timing and context of Russ's entry into the literary marketplace. Over the course of a four-decade career, Russ wrote and published works of fantasy, science fiction, realism, and nonfiction criticism, as well as the occasional poem and play. But because she entered the literary marketplace when and how she did, thrust into the public eye by *The Female Man*, Russ remains frozen in time, remembered for a sliver of her science fiction writing, hailed and criticized as a noteworthy historical artifact rather than a prescient interlocutor from whom we, in the present, stand to gain. She sorely needs (and deserves) the chance to emerge as the wide-ranging, ambitious, multigenre author that she was—and readers deserve the chance to encounter the full scope of her capacious, durable feminist vision. Quarantined in science fiction, Russ's legacy remains safe but stagnant.

And yet, despite history's best efforts to dismiss and pigeonhole her—despite her sequestering in science fiction and her work's widespread unavailability—Russ pops up persistently as a source of provocation, reassurance, and permission for contemporary readers far outside her prescribed wheelhouse of science fiction. Russ's corpus is vast, and readers of all stripes find something useful in it. As a long-time scholar and reader of Russ, I'm struck by decades of readers' appreciation for her non-science fiction and out-of-print works, preserved in fan mail, literary magazines, and defunct blogs—evidence of readers' enthusiasm, affection, and engagement that indicates Russ's transhistorical and multigenre appeal. When you start looking out for Russ, she shows up everywhere. Her reputation as a founder of feminist science fiction is well established, but her legacy is more pervasive and elastic than that. She appears in interviews and articles and works of fiction; she informs the thinking of Larissa Lai, Torrey Peters, Sophia Collins, Deepika Arwind, and others. Mary Anne Mohanraj's essay "Nothing Too Frightening," included in this volume, recounts Mohanraj's own early encounter with Russ's wisdom: "She was telling me that I had options," writes Mohanraj, "that there were a host of other lives I could live, if I dared to reach for them" (page 195). Imogen Binnie credits Russ's essay "What Can a Heroine Do?" with "giving her permission to structure" her groundbreaking work of trans fiction, *Nevada*, the way she did.[32] *How to Suppress Women's Writing*, Russ's darkly funny investigation into literary sexism, has, since its 2019 reissue, bolstered Russ's legacy and exposed her to a general audience for the first time in decades. "There is a mourning in the celebration," writes Amal El-Mohtar of discovering *How to Suppress* after a lifetime of struggling with—well, the suppression of women's writing.[33] "In a just world," writes Carmen Maria Machado, "[*How to Suppress*] would be required reading in all the humanities."[34] More popular now than it was in 1983, *How to Suppress* has stricken contemporary readers with its uncanny, devastating prescience, and it's only one of dozens of Russ's nonfiction works that await republication and reconsideration after spending decades out of print.

Russ was a stunningly incisive, elegant, and persuasive writer of nonfiction criticism, but her primary objective as a feminist author wasn't to analyze, diagnose, and argue. "It's very rare to be convinced by discussion," she wrote to Delany, "I never am." "I'm convinced by recognition," she continued, "I mean above and beyond a level of sense and common, logistical consistency."[35] Nonfiction was for "discussion," fiction, for "recognition." Russ sought, through fiction, to curate experiences and simulate emotions that changed how readers felt about themselves and related to the world around them. "I really do sail by my gut," she wrote, and, in pursuit of "recognition," she pursued readers' guts, rendering their demons and desires, hopes and fears, lusts and disgusts so palpable that readers felt they were living—or had lived—through Russ's plots.[36] Science fiction made this process straightforward; it allowed her to design societies to validate the inner lives of her and her readers (take Whileaway and Manland, again). *On Strike Against God* stands out amid Russ's writings because it is her sole novel-length "realist" effort to catalyze for readers that same potently feminist moment of recognition she modeled in *The Female Man*—that moment of recognition whereby the unthinkable becomes thinkable, the unspeakable becomes speakable, and the contradiction between disavowed internal life and "objective" external reality is reconciled. Furthermore, although *The Female Man* is undoubtedly a masterpiece, its dense, experimental prose can flummox and deter first-time readers. This stand-alone edition of *On Strike Against God* will, I hope, reintroduce Russ to a new swath of readers for whom Russ's insights spark recognition, but for whom *The Female Man* is not a feasible point of entry into her oeuvre.

Within the context of the Old Boys' Club of mid-twentieth-century science fiction, Russ remains an undeniably significant feminist innovator. Outside it, though—and specifically within feminist discourse—Russ has become troublesome, dated, taboo—disclaimer-worthy and "problematic." Searching for a publisher to reissue *On Strike Against God*, I encountered the same feedback again and again: "I love it, but it's so second wave." Meaning not "I love it, but I love it less because it's 'so second wave,'" but rather "I love it, but I shouldn't." *The Female Man* is "second wave" too, of course—staggeringly so—but the novel is simply too important to cast aside. As a founding work of feminist science fiction, it remains noteworthy, radical, worth grappling with and preserving. It also has an alibi—the buffer of genre. *On Strike Against God* has no such buffer; its second wave rhetoric is undiluted, not obfuscated by the trappings of science fiction. *On Strike Against God* affords an opportunity to readers that *The Female Man* does not—an opportunity to face the fact that Russ's appeal persists not despite but because of her legacy as an incendiary second wave writer.

By "second wave feminism," I mean the fractious, transformative amalgam of people, institutions, and beliefs that comprised the feminist movements of the 1970s. Second wave feminism contained contradictory multitudes: assimilationists and separatists, gender abolitionists and transphobes alike. Second wave feminism was Betty Friedan, author of *The Feminine Mystique* and cofounder of the National Organization for Women (NOW), with her designs on assimilationist uplift for white, straight, middle-class women, *and* activist group Radicalesbians, which stormed NOW's Second Congress to Unite Women to denounce the institution's homophobia. It was both Radicalesbians, with its predominantly white membership, and the

Third World Women's Alliance, a group of, in Patricia Romney's words, Black women, *and* Latinas, *and* Asian women, *and* Middle Eastern women who "were deeply involved" and who "asserted [their] rights in vocal and active ways."[37] It was Janice Raymond, with her transphobic screed *The Transsexual Empire* (1979), and Margo Schulter, whose writings on trans lives and rights predate Raymond's by at least five years.

But today the phrase "second wave" retains none of this nuance. "Second wave" has become a kind of shorthand for "bad" feminism—a catch-all for the mistakes, oversights, and evils contained within feminism(s) of the late twentieth century. And yet, despite the shortcomings and offenses of second wave feminists—their incendiary rhetoric and problematic obstinance—second wave attachments and pleasures live on. Second wave feminist writers were a prolific bunch: some writings ring true today, others (often by the same author) embarrass and offend. Their uncompromising, unapologetic screeds still strike a chord, even as they unsettle us; their sweeping categorical claims intrigue, even as they infuriate us. These reactions aren't logical or rational, beholden to definitions of feminism or analyses of gender. We're drawn to their incendiary rhetoric despite intellectual disagreement. By "we," I mean readers who find themselves provoked and ignited, begrudgingly or not, by second wave feminists and their rhetoric—those present-day Russ readers I listed above, as well as the second wave recuperators that I'll list below. Are the readers who invoke Russ in the present familiar with the full scope of Russ's oeuvre, all her -isms and phobias, her missteps and retractions? Maybe, maybe not. Either way, the fact of the matter remains: Russ still sparks interest, pleasure, even courage—all emotions that attest to some enduring relevance at her writings' core. But as shorthand for "bad" feminism, the description "second wave" discourages readers from making sense of these persistent attachments—from inquiring into moments of recognition that might offer insight into indignities, aspirations, betrayals, and desires that aren't, it turns out, wholly past, even as they remain bound up in the fraught legacies of a bygone era.

Russ is squarely "second wave," in good ways and bad. Her oeuvre has plenty of pejoratively second wave features. As a white, Jewish, middle-class lesbian writing political, polemical, autobiographical fiction in the 1970s, when new languages for naming identity, making sense of experience, and building coalition were rapidly evolving, the language Russ gravitated toward to describe her experiences and her rage were organized around her own personal experiences—often to a fault. In *The Female Man*, we see Russ embrace bioessentialism to describe her experiences of sexist oppression (she would later recant her derogatory comments about trans women), and readers have accused *The Female Man* of misogyny.[38] But Russ's greatest intimacy with the second wave was, arguably, stylistic: she was a polemicist *par excellence*. Feminist polemic was the second wave's primary rhetorical export, a genre driven by a sweeping, authoritative "we" that, in the words of Breanne Fahs, "tells us how to think, assumes we agree with them, and imagines no possibility for refusal or resistance."[39] (In)famous polemics of the era contain statements like "Lesbians are not women"[40] and "*Violation* is a synonym for intercourse"[41] and "A lesbian is the rage of all women condensed to the point of explosion."[42] These statements are potent, absolute, and incendiary; they do "not invite us to carefully piece [them] apart," but pursue an "emotional response," aspiring to leave readers "raw and exposed."[43]

"You can't unite woman and human any more than

you can unite matter and anti-matter," Russ writes in
The Female Man, a statement that wrecked me for years.[44]
Read literally without context (and arguably in bad faith),
the statement is, of course, a misogynist one. "Women
aren't human," it reads. But considered autobiograph-
ically, the message is different: Russ's world foisted a
contradiction between "woman" and "human" upon her,
a contradiction that threatened to define her out of existence, and *The Female Man* was her exploration of it. (By
"Russ's world," I mean the 1950s of her coming-of-age
but also those homophobic parts of the woman's movement in the late 1960s and early 1970s that prompted
many lesbians to disavow the category "woman" in defiance.) But in *The Female Man*, Russ's claim isn't couched
in autobiography or history; it is absolute, categorical, universal—it purports to speak for all and leaves no
room for nuance or dissent. The conviction of Russ's
claim is a measure of the grief of her failure: "[Woman
and human] are designed not to be stable together," she
writes, "and they make just as big an explosion [as matter
and antimatter] inside the head of the unfortunate girl
who believes in both." Implied: "I know. I tried." There's
power in claiming authority previously denied, but there
is also the risk of doing harm. The danger and power of
polemics go hand in hand; this duality is a hallmark of
the second wave.

When I, as a twenty-year-old college student, read
Russ (*The Female Man*) for the first time in 2013, I didn't
need a tempered, qualified, autobiographical version of
her claims. I needed exactly what she gave me: a scathing,
unapologetic statement of fact, a moment of recognition that placed me at the center of the cosmos, exalting
my own uncertain experience as true. Russ's words are
not prescription but diagnosis; they are an attempt to
articulate the experience of being barred, as a woman

(and especially a queer person), from the empowering fantasy of universal experience, reserved by default for (white, straight) men. At twenty, I needed something totally unlike the cellophane-packaged "Girl Power" and corporate have-it-all womanhood of the aughts, through which I had moved uninterested and unphased for a decade. I had no fealty to girlhood; the only moments I claimed it for myself were moments of protest. Tall, shorn, and outspoken, with a boy's name and a creative, extraordinary mother, mine was a boyhood, not a girl-hood, which is to say, it was a childhood. And let me tell you: it was better. Boys get childhoods; girls get girl-hoods. "Girl Power" was irrelevant—in Russ's words, "What has any of this to do with me!" If anything, "Girl Power" was an alienating attempt to redeem something that wasn't mine to begin with.

By college, "woman" was an ill-fitting nuisance—but I didn't have the words to say so. By that age, writes Johanna Fateman, "the insults have accumulated" and "the double standard has doubled."[45] She's right. For Fateman, second wave feminist Andrea Dworkin presented "a feminist literature empty of caveats, equiv-ocation, or the endless positing of one's subjective limits";[46] for me, Russ's polemic presented the same. My college campus was teeming with assailants and harassers of every kind (aren't they all?), which, amid nationwide upheaval over Title IX, was an opportunity to experi-ence firsthand that bureaucratic "feminism" designed to minimize university liability under the guise of protect-ing undergraduates from sexual violence. I encountered cooing, equivocating Title IX administrators who would look students dead in the eyes and encourage them to remember those same "subjective limits." They loved the word "valid"—"Your experience is valid"—so much that, to me, "valid" still presages inaction, always followed by "but." My response? Get your equivocation away from me. You'd have me equivocate myself off the side of the earth.

Let's put the disclaimer right up front to get it out of the way. Russ's words *were* subjective, which is to say they're a commentary on her personal experience, but she stated them as pure, authoritative fact for a reason. There's something eerie to me about how seamlessly the rhetoric of contemporary feminism, with its mandate to qualify, qualify, qualify, can veer into the apology and caveat of gendered self-erasure. "You can't unite woman and human any more than you can unite matter and anti-matter." Or, as Russ writes elsewhere, "I'm Not A Girl I'm A Genius" (Russ to Marilyn Hacker, page 280). Obviously women are human. Of course girls can be geniuses. But surrounded on all sides by apology and caveat, I needed those words exactly as written, lest they wither away into more empty affirmations. Reading Dworkin, Fateman "decided to be more arrogant and hyperbolic." "I decided to push my feelings and ideas to their logical extremes," she writes, "in order to find the exact point at which they became untrue."[47] Russ pushed me to that extreme: my visceral, bodily response to Russ's unequivocal claims granted me insight into myself, my place in society, my relationship to gender. It would have been dangerous and misogynist indeed to entertain "woman" as a violent, stupid, and degrading category *and stop there*, at that logical but untrue extreme. Instead, I kept living, reading, and growing. I learned shortly thereafter that what was true for me wasn't true for others, that the points of entry into "woman" can be joyful and various, and that my desperate need for alternatives wasn't a referendum on anyone else's gender attachments. But Russ's absolutes made me whole and secure enough to get there—to appreciate the differences between "me" and "you." Better to push one's feelings "to their logical extremes" and locate the point of untruth, I think, than to languish in nonexistence. "I'm not a woman," writes Russ in *On Strike Against God*. "Never was, never will be. I'm a something-else." Me? I'm a something-else, too.

And it's not just me. It's not just Joanna Russ. If it were, this project wouldn't exist. A number of second wave figureheads have been reexamined and recuperated in recent years, and their recuperators all narrate evolving, ambivalent attachments—to the era, to their subjects, and to their subjects' incendiary rhetoric. Take Andrea Dworkin, author of *Woman Hating*, known for her anti-rape, anti-pornography, and, arguably, anti-sex activism. Johanna Fateman recalls encountering, at eighteen, Dworkin as a "bloody revelation," who she subsequently spent a "whole career . . . disagreeing" with.[48] Or take Shulamith Firestone, author of the best-selling *The Dialectic of Sex* (1970), known for her call for women's emancipation from reproductive biology. Sophie Lewis "disagree[s] with more of Firestone's individual points than not," and yet, "I see something of my late mother in her biography," she muses, "and I love—sometimes to the point of weeping—her book's absolute negationism, its horniness, and its sincerity."[49] There's a formula at play in these recuperative writings: avowal, disavowal, qualified historical appeal, all narrated from the first-person point of view. Speaking from the first-person point of view—from personal testimony, from the "I"—recuperators take care to set themselves apart from their subjects, whose sweeping, unqualified claims about gender, violence, and ethics "imagin[e] no possibility for refusal or resistance," and to speak only for themselves.[50] "What is true for me needn't be true for you," Fateman and Lewis seem to say, "but it's worth considering because it's true for some."

This is the work of second wave recuperators: to reframe polemic as a "reasonable response"[51] to lived experience, rather than "an attempt to discipline real people."[52] To do this, we work to create context, to restore links between the movement's incendiary rhetorics and the experiences, sensations, and feelings that gave rise to them. We explain why speakers would have wanted to make such drastic and absolute claims in the first place. We rend the rhetorical veil to reveal the very reasonable goings-on behind, hardly "hyperbolic" or "incendiary." Before critics made Dworkin's rhetoric a scapegoat for anti-sex dogma, for example, it was her attempt to "restore [her own] sense of reality" in the aftermath of a lifetime's worth of sexual violence.[53] The "great payoff," writes Sam Huber of *My Name Is Andrea*, Pratibha Parmar's 2022 documentary film, "is that Dworkin's most incendiary rhetoric, so often lampooned or dismissed as excessive, instead appears inevitable: we encounter her words as a reasonable response to what she lived through."[54] Context contains and defuses that hegemonic "we" that claimed individuals who did not claim it back, recuperating polemic's usefulness for the present day.

But this restoration of context, however necessary today, must coexist with a crucial rhetorical fact. Polemics are most potent when context—that same context we now labor to restore—is set aside and polemical feeling is empowered to exist, albeit fleetingly, unencumbered by historical context or caveat. "While there were legions that would charge [Andrea Dworkin] with hyperbole," writes Fateman, "there was also a growing feminist army who found, in her electrifying indictments of male supremacy, the truth at last."[55] Readers who found in Dworkin the "truth at last"—Fateman, even, who encountered Dworkin as a "bloody revelation"—did so precisely because of Dworkin's "hyperbole," her "incendiary rhetoric." Against a dominant culture that disbelieves her, the individual "I" falters, comes to disbelieve her own experience and doubt her own reality. The polemic's purpose is to posit a "we" able to contend *at scale* with that status quo, to speak with the ferocity and authority needed to override it. To claim this authority—to establish that "we"—polemics sever ties with context, purporting to speak for all and for all time. This authority is a necessary fiction, one that emboldens the "I" to withstand disbelief and avow her reality and, therefore, herself. Thus, the second wave's extravagant self-assurance isn't itself a mistake to be corrected, but rather a necessary stopover en route to individual self-assurance. The enduring appeal of second wave "hyperbole" attests: as messy as these polemics may be—and as in dire need of context and qualification as they are today—they endure as catalysts for "nascent feminist rage" that *continue* to serve readers, even as each reader will move beyond that rage, beyond that moment of revelation, in their own way.

This is the lesson—both the experience and the argument—that *On Strike Against God* preserves. *The Female Man* is a "pre-feminist, pre-political" acceleration into feminist consciousness that "ends with the beginnings of integration," as Russ wrote in a letter to Delany, but doesn't move beyond the initial revelation of feminist consciousness, packaged as the polemical second wave "we." "I couldn't then," Russ continued, "put the whole thing together. [*On Strike Against God*] does that, I think."[56] And indeed, *On Strike Against God* picks up where *The Female Man* left off—not in terms of plot, but in terms of Russ's personal quest to tackle in fiction "what really [hadn't] happened in life." *On Strike Against God* is Russ's do-over, her second attempt at what she tried to do in *The Female Man* but didn't quite achieve. "It's the whole radicalization business, step by step," she wrote. "What I couldn't do in F.M."[57] Sequel or rewriting—either way, the books share a bond. *On Strike Against God* isn't just, or simply, polemic. As fiction, it achieves something that polemics don't (and can't) achieve on their own: the bold authority of polemical self-creation *and also* what comes after—the self-assured but tempered "I" laboriously deployed by recuperators of second wave writers, able to carefully consider and appreciate the differences that separate "me" from "you." *On Strike* manages to contain both second wave potency and the tempering commentary that has followed.

On Strike Against God's unique duality—potent polemic and retrospective commentary—reflects Russ's struggle to write "what really [hadn't] happened" during the novel's composition. The work required to translate her allegedly unreal and "trivial" inner life from the familiar terms of science fiction into the terms of the "real" world was immense. Writing in 1973, Russ's models for feminist and lesbian literature were still few and far between, and without the trappings of science fiction, she had to find other ways to make her characters' internal lives external, to make her readers feel the ambitions, desires, and fears of characters who were, according to her present "reality," impossible. The result? A realistic amalgam of satire, autobiography, and second wave polemic, all with an "implicit s.f. perspective" that, Russ wrote, "gives [the novel] much of its fun."[58] "My God it is *hard*," she confessed to Delany, "like ice-skating or walking a tight-rope; there are times I stop in mid-air, close my eyes, and scream because I *know* it's impossible, but I go on anyway."[59] As a result, *On Strike Against God* tells two stories: (1) the coming-out story of its main characters, Esther and Jean, and (2) the story of the strife of its creation.*[60]

Story #1: The story of Esther and Jean's brief love affair, which Russ summarized as follows: "(1) heroine has happy Lesbian love affair, after lots of initial worrying and reluctance (2) heroine 'tries out' her feminism—integral to the affair and in fact what produced it—on 2 sets of friends. (3) is repulsed by both (4) is radicalized (5) gets lover back (who has been going through the same process) (6) prepares for Ultimate Revolution by learning to shoot rifle" (Russ to Marilyn Hacker, page 286). This story is noteworthy in its own right: it introduces characters and events for which Russ had no models in the "real" world—characters and events that didn't and shouldn't have existed according to the "Great Literature" of her youth. As Russ wrote an unconventional plot for her unconventional, real-world heroines, the gravitational pull of "workable myths" was immense: "The pressure of the endings I didn't write—the suicide, the reconciliation, the forgetting of the feminist issues . . . kept trying to push me off my seat as I wrote," she confessed to Marilyn Hacker (page 286). She asked herself again and again: "How can one write about success in a situation in which success and the implications of it are still unrealized and fluid in actuality?" (page 284). She had boldly set *On Strike* in the "real" world, and yet she still did not know how Esther's story ended—let alone succeeded—in that "real" world, where there were still no models of success for women like her. Did Russ successfully evade the "plot-patterns" that threatened to derail

*On October 7, 1974, Russ wrote to Delany, "The only way to write 'a good novel with good politics . . . and good, well-rounded women' when you can't, is to write a novel about how you can't write a novel about . . . &c. (and why)."

her? For the most part. Neither heroine dies. Neither marries. But the novel's plot certainly isn't Russ's "most memorable."[61] The book's potency lies in what of its process it preserves, something far and away beyond the characters and events that mark it as an early work of coming-out fiction.

Take, then, Story #2: the story of *figuring out how to tell* Story #1, or, the story of *On Strike*'s creation, which made Russ want to scream. Story #2 is the story Russ told repeatedly throughout her science fiction, fantasy, realistic fiction, and nonfiction criticism: it is the story of recognizing and reckoning with the phenomenon of "split consciousness," something that, she explained to Delany, "exists in the life of almost every woman I know, whether she has succumbed to the demand that she evaluate herself in double terms . . . or not."[62] Story #2 is *The Female Man*'s raison d'être: in *The Female Man*, one woman's consciousness is so split by the contradiction that "woman" cannot equal "human" that her single psyche appears as four separate characters that Russ could not manage to integrate within the confines of that earlier novel. In *On Strike Against God*, Story #2 manifests as a "split attitude in the central character," "well concealed" by the novel's content but still there.[63] Russ uses satire and polemic to effectively dramatize this split without literally splitting Esther into multiple people.

The appeal of Story #1 has waned with time: by 1985, at the peak of the Women in Print movement and amid a wash of other works of coming-out fiction, one reviewer called *On Strike Against God* "cliché."[64] The novel's durable appeal lies, I think, in Russ's meticulous attention to Story #2, which is a story that defies, and to some extent transcends, both summary and historical context. Story #2 is the story of inhabiting "split consciousness," not so much about external events as it is about psychological experience. *On Strike Against God* is less a story about coming out than it is a story about the difficulty of writing about what really hasn't happened yet—of speaking the unspeakable and thinking the unthinkable when the unspeakable and unthinkable entity in question is *you*. It is a story about the agonies of cognitive dissonance, the collision between internal certainty and external denial, and the difficulties of knowing that you live in an unjust world while business goes on around you as usual. It's about facing down the mystery of an unknown, uncreated, unsupported future—and the terror of facing it down alone—on your own doorstep.

In *On Strike Against God*, Esther's brief love affair with her friend Jean turns her world upside down. Up until the moment they kiss, Esther doubts Jean's feelings—"People do not do things like [this] in reality," she thinks, "reality doesn't allow it"—and when Jean reciprocates, Esther's "reality [tears] itself in two, from top to bottom" (page 99). Then, shortly after they sleep together, Jean skips town without a word. The horror of Jean's departure is worse than simple heartbreak because their affair has rent Esther's reality—her core beliefs about herself and the world and other people—asunder. On the one hand, it happened: "You don't ask the whole world if it's really doing what it's doing," Esther thinks (page 99). On the other, maybe it didn't: Esther keeps wondering if she "invented the whole love affair" (page 115). Like Jean, Esther flees their small college town—Ithaca, New York, although Russ never names the town explicitly in *On Strike*—to reconcile these contradictions.

At the end of *On Strike Against God*, Esther returns to Ithaca, radicalized. Jean returns, too. She apologizes: "Sorry I got scared and ran away." The two reconcile and eventually part (Jean gets a job in New Zealand).

There's no "love affair which settles everything," hetero-sexual or otherwise, and there's certainly no "failure" (madness, death). The story's climax is Jean's return and everything that brings with it: confirmation that Esther's revelation, her courage, her crisis of faith, all really happened—and what's more, that they *happened to someone else, too*. With Jean, early in the novel, Esther has a rare and precious moment of "believing [her] ears and eyes"—something she'd spent a lifetime not doing. After Jean leaves, Esther loses her precious "right of private judgement," her burgeoning self-belief; without Jean, "you can't think of yourself," Esther says, "you have to be thought." But with Jean back, professing acquaintance with "other Lesbians," Esther's "right of private judge-ment" is restored. She can "think of herself" again. A world of possibility opens before her, one in which she unequivocally exists. For Esther, and for Russ, it takes only two to be a "we," but one "we" is both necessary and enough to take on the world. "The 'we' is . . . the crux of the story," wrote Russ, "a little unit of 2, 20, 200, 2000 [that] is beginning to form."[65]

On Strike Against God's revelations are simple: "I exist." "We exist." "Maybe it can be better than it is." "What I want to say is, it's not just me," says Esther. It is a novel born of a contradiction: "How can I be a Lesbian when there aren't any?" Russ wrote to Delany.[66] In *On Strike*, Esther resolves this contradiction by wresting from an "inhospitable" world "the tools to change herself and, hopefully, it."[67] It's a significant feat indeed, especially considering the "profound mental darkness" Russ clawed her way out of as she wrote the novel. But she struggled to end *On Strike* because there was no formula for taking "what [actually] happened" and turning it into the aesthetically pleasing ending she wanted the book to have. "I kept saying to myself 'That's banal. That's propaganda. That's *obvious*,'" Russ explained as she wrestled with the novel's ending. "But there was simply nothing else to do—anything else would have been false" (Russ to Marilyn Hacker, page 286).

"Authors do not make their plots up out of thin air," Russ writes in "What Can a Heroine Do?" They work with familiar, well-worn attitudes, beliefs, expectations, events, and character types—which Russ called "plot-patterns"— that are already available to them, modeled for them by extant works of art. These plot-patterns are difficult to avoid; creators reproduce them, often whether they mean to or not. The problem with these plot-patterns, Russ explains, is that they reflect "what culture believes to be true—or what it would like to be true" (page 233). Russ was torn: she found that the "unities and conclusiveness and dramatic resolutions" that would make *On Strike Against God*'s ending "tidy," "dramatic," and "good," and toward which she was instinctively drawn, were "embodiments of accepted moral ideas" that she hated: "the love affair which settles everything" (comedy) and "failure" (tragedy) (Russ to Marilyn Hacker, page 287). Neither ending was true to "what happened" to Esther and Jean. Russ *had* written about what happened—Esther and Jean's consummation, Esther's revelation, Jean's return—but what happened wasn't a "proper" ending. "How," she asked, "can one write about success in a situation in which success and the implications of it are still unrealized and fluid in actuality?" After much back and forth, revision, and resistance, Russ concluded: "One just can't. . . . You can only write about how it might or it should [end], meanwhile confessing: this is the best I can do at the moment, this is the moment, this is me, my eyes, my ears, &c."[68] And so, instead, Russ dramatizes the "real uncertainty of real issues" by "dumping [the story] into the reader's [sic] laps" (page 284).

ALEC POLLAK

For Russ, polemic was the path forward. Polemic was a way to pass the baton to the reader—to enlist the reader in the work of creating that defiant, as-of-yet nonexistent ending. "Polemics ought to end with a kind of prayer," she wrote (Russ to Marilyn Hacker, page 285), to "end up in the readers' laps, with the author saying (in exasperation or censure or inspiration or whatnot) Here: YOU finish it."[69] A polemic was, for Russ, *an appeal to the future*" (Russ to Marilyn Hacker, page 283), an ending that says, "This is the beginning."[70] And so, as *On Strike Against God* dumps itself into readers' laps, readers find themselves facing down the notorious, authoritative "we" of second wave polemic. But, because it is fiction, *On Strike* does something that nonfiction—whether polemic proper or second wave commentary—cannot do: it presents a polemic that explains its own motives and catalogs its effects. It places polemic's contextless freeze-frame alongside the historical particulars and human (albeit fictional) faces that lurk behind polemic's authoritative "we." I've argued that the erasure of context is a requirement of the polemic form, and that the present-day restoration of context, necessary as it may be, shouldn't overshadow polemic's particular strategic utility. *On Strike Against God*, written in 1973, anticipates and excerpts this dialogue, decades in the making. It confirms the strategic utility of second wave polemic—that, to speak at all, the "I" must first become a "we." It doesn't matter if that "we" is "a little unit of 2, 20, 200, [or] 2000"; the singular, anomalous "I" comes into existence only by association with others—real or fictional.[71] But *On Strike* also intervenes, mediates between second wave polemicists and recuperators. Restoring much-needed context to second wave polemics needn't be done in the spirit of apology or "progress," but rather in the service of completing a necessary cycle of feminist self-creation.

On Strike Against God ends twice—once with the polemical fiction of universality and then again, beyond the "we." The novel's first ending is a wretched cliché: Jean and Esther shoot a rifle in Jean's backyard so Esther can learn how to "kill a man." But this ending, cliché as it may be, is crucial. The coming-out story that *On Strike Against God* tells is also the story of Esther "putting herself at the center of the cosmos," writes Marilyn Hacker in her 1981 review of the novel, "not in comparison to, or instead of [other women] but simply, centrally, unequivocally, there."[72] "I wondered what it would feel like to be, everywhere, one among many, the basic, emblematic human integer," Hacker continues, and concludes: "It would feel like power."[73] Russ's first ending realizes the fantasy of existing at "the center of the cosmos," where it is safe enough, finally, to *be*, free from the burden of equivocation and caveat. Esther and Jean have each other, and they have a weapon, which they name "Blunderbess" and, in one of the novel's more dated scenes, use to shoot tin cans, which stand in for the encompassing boogeyman "you"—the psychiatrists, parents, and friends who have long angered and injured them. With Jean and a rifle by Esther's side, awash in the "amazing peacefulness, the astonishing lack of anger, the sweetness and balm of being at last on the right side of power," the novel ends (page 160). It's pure polemic. Maybe not the "astonishing lack of anger," but certainly the "we," the "you," and the revelation of self-creation in the aftermath of discovering others like yourself.

But how can one be "the basic, emblematic human integer" and *not* exist in comparison to, or instead of, others? How can one exist "at the center of the cosmos" without forcing others to the periphery? One can't. It's the work of polemic to thrust a burgeoning "we" into the "center of the cosmos" and leave it there, to bask in the "balm of being at last on the right side of power." Russ's polemic brings Esther to the "center of the cosmos," but because *On Strike Against God* is fiction and not polemic proper, it doesn't simply leave her there. Even as Russ indulges Esther's flight to the "center of the cosmos," the novel preserves the context that brought her there—and then takes Esther beyond that point. And with her, readers encounter Esther's moment of empowered recognition as a necessary stopover en route to a more capacious, more patient, and more practical future—the novel's second ending.

But before I discuss the novel's second ending, you should know that, once upon a time, *On Strike Against God*'s first ending was the novel's *only* ending, and it was even more polemical than it is in the published novel. It was as polemical an ending as Russ could muster. Amid rifle practice, Esther turns to the reader and says,

I'll kill you.
If you're my enemy.
Are you?

And that's where it ended—the first draft of the novel, at any rate.

When I discovered this ending in Russ's archive, I was surprised—it's so uninspired, so unlike Russ. When you think of second wave feminism, what are the clichés that come to mind? "Bra burning" is probably the second wave's most identifiable trope. Lesbians killing men, or antagonizing men by doing them some type of bodily harm, is, I think, a close second. A whole class of misogynist pejoratives—man-hater, ball-breaker, castrator, etc.—pay homage to it. Russ eschewed the plot-patterns

available to her via mainstream publishing in 1973—
death, marriage—but her original ending to *On Strike
Against God* was a near miss of precisely the same kind.
Lesbian rifle practice and a threat to kill? It was 1973,
and so the trope was likely still emerging—but in a
decade's time, it would be a well-established subcultural
plot-pattern in its own right, as trite and meaningless
as the myth of the bra burner (which Esther scoffs at
in *On Strike Against God*: "Oh, that never happened,"
says Esther, "That was invented by the newspapers").
I'm grateful that Russ didn't keep the original ending
because it's hardly an end to *this* novel; instead, it's a
prefab scene airlifted in, nonspecific and unoriginal,
generically signaling "feminist rage," hardly better, in
my opinion, than death or marriage. Russ wanted an
appeal to the future, and "I'll kill you" isn't one.

Fortunately for Russ (and for this novel, and for us),
Marilyn Hacker didn't like Russ's original ending. In
a letter, she noted that it was discordant with everything that comes before it. "Why are [the last pages]
addressed to *men*?" she asked. "I wanted this one to be
for us, women." "I can see," she continued, "that the
book must end on a note of challenge . . . but there is still
the implication that The Man is still so important that
even *this* book, even in defiance, in hatred, in challenge,
is addressed to *him*, that the person you see reading it is
not a woman or a girl thinking here is something at last,
but a *man* being Affronted" (pages 289–290).

Russ pushed back. "I'd be lying if I said I myself could
just disregard The Man," she countered. "It has to end as
it does, the story is a sort of progress-report-from-the-
front, state-of-things-now, certainly not Utopian, and I
know my limits."[74] Russ aspired to write "an appeal to
the future," but she could only muster a "progress report
from the front." She simply wasn't ready to bridge the

divide between her fictional, homogenous "we" and her antagonist "you." Her back was up against a wall. Nevertheless, Hacker had planted a seed. By 1976, Russ was ready to write the ending that she ultimately published, the one that ends the novel you hold in your hands.

Remember: we've just spent an entire novel in Esther's head, confined to her consciousness, suffering with her through confusion, disappointment, and heartbreak. Between Jean's departure and her return, Esther struggles to steel herself against inner demons that tell her she's an aberration, that her experiences don't count. She flees her friends, too existentially precarious to withstand their doubt and dismissal. Without a strong sense of self—a grip on her own inner life—Esther cannot entertain the inner life of anyone else. She struggles to be a "me," an "I," to trust in the evidence of her eyes and her ears. She conceives of the world, and herself, in the simplest possible terms: "me" vs. "you."

> (I'll kill you.
> If you're my enemy.
> Are you?)

But with Jean back, after their excursion with Blunderbess, as Esther basks in the peace of being "on the right side of power," she exists for the first time, irrefutably and irrevocably, and a world of possibility opens before her. And with Esther nurturing a meager "we"—just herself and Jean, to start—the novel ends again.

"You'll recognize us," begins the novel's second (and final) ending. Is "you" the "hapless liberal"? Is "you" the enemy? We're not sure. Sometimes Esther identifies "you": you're Stevie. You're a teenage male student. You're Rose. You're my Polish grandmother. You're my friend Carolellen. But mostly she doesn't. Mostly she describes "you": what you think, what you've done, what you need, what you love. "You" could be—well, anyone. The possibilities multiply. "You'll meet us." "You can't recognize us in a crowd." "You're alone." "You say nasty things about women." "You breed cats." "You can't stand my mother." "Sometimes you are my mother." And on, and on. There's no clear through line, no one "you." "I'll kill you" is nowhere in sight, even as "you" isn't always Esther's ally. "What can I say to you?" she says. "You're more various than that. How can I love you properly? How can I praise you properly?" (page 165). Esther doesn't "tell us how to think, assume we agree with [her], and imagine no possibility for refusal."[75] She assumes disagreement, in fact—she imagines refusal. But from the right side of power, Esther can endure. The novel's second ending—this affectionate, open-ended appeal to diverse "you"s—accomplishes what its first can't: it launches Esther onward, from the self-assured center of the cosmos into a universe where, on the other side of self-creation, multiple "basic, human integers"[76] can harmoniously and unthreateningly coexist.

"I'll kill you" is no appeal to the future. It's the "gutsy language" of self-creation—the powerless claiming power.[77] It's a fantasy designed to help usher Esther's "I" into existence. It's necessary for Russ, and it fulfills the purpose of polemic, but it is not a "you" that can finish Esther's story—that can write about what really hasn't happened yet, which is what Russ ultimately wanted. "I'll kill you" is an abrupt ending, not a beginning. But the "you" of the published novel's last line—"[The book] is for you"—*is* an appeal to the future. Because the fact of the matter is, it's not just Esther. If it were, her story wouldn't exist, and neither would she. She's not sure who "you" is, but she knows you're out there, and she wants to find you. She doesn't care who "you" is, she says, "as long as you love [her]." "As long as I can love all of you," she says. "What I want to say is, we're all in it together," she says. "What I want to say is, it's not just me" (page 167).

I've discussed only one of the novel's alternate endings; Russ entertained at least two others before she composed, in 1976, what would become *On Strike Against God*'s published ending. If you flip to the back of this book, to the section entitled "From the Archives," you'll find all three alternate endings, ordered chronologically. You'll also find Russ's correspondence with Hacker, in which Russ agonizes over the problem of feminist endings and Hacker urges Russ to conclude the book with an address to women, not men. According to materials in her archive, Russ wrote and revised the ending of *On Strike Against God* in 1973, 1974, and 1976. Together, these endings document yet another instance of the process of feminist self-creation I've described. The process that *On Strike* compresses and simulates in fiction, and that second wave recuperators have undertaken through intergenerational dialogue with their feminist forebears across reviews, annotations, and front matter, occurred within Russ herself as her feminist politics evolved and she settled into her identity as a feminist and a lesbian—and the novel's alternate endings preserve this evolution. "I wasn't altogether a Lesbian when I wrote [*On Strike*]," she mused in 1976.[78] She considered rewriting the entire novel but settled for rewriting the ending. Across three years' worth of endings, we see Russ's beleaguered "report from the front" become an appeal for coalition. Her gutsy, polemical "we" gives way to a self-assured "I"—an "I" that is unassuming, appreciative, and capable of forging a path through difference.

Imagine: a polemic is lightning, to borrow Jeanne Thornton's brilliant metaphor (turn to page 173). It strikes when the conditions are right, and when it strikes, it illuminates the world around it—the world of the affected "we," the reading "we" alerted, enlightened, and even sometimes created by that lightning's strike. Now, lightning stays lightning. There will always be conditions ripe for it, but those conditions change. Settings change. The affected "we" changes. This "we" isn't the same hegemonic "we" lurking behind "Lesbians are not women," or "Violation is a synonym for intercourse," but rather a "we" that carefully considers its existence, takes seriously the multitudes it contains, and works diligently to understand the through line uniting each disparate "I." When lightning first struck, in the form of Andrea Dworkin's "oracular voice," it "helped shape the grassroots feminist organizing of the late '70s and '80s."[79] In the 1990s, it struck again, fueling Fateman's "nascent feminist rage."[80] No doubt Fateman saw something different from what others saw ten and twenty years prior, but she saw *something*, because she, like her predecessors, experienced the lightning's strike. The lightning may or may not strike you as you read, and only you will know if it does. But if it does strike, what does it illuminate? What do you see? The power and fate of these polemics lie with their readers. The question is whether you, the reader, retrieve from the lightning's strike insight into yourself, into your surroundings, into history—and use that insight to move into the future.

Sometime between writing *On Strike* in 1973 and composing its final ending in 1976, Russ swapped the "us"/"them" of second wave polemic for a genuine appeal to all her readers. One can only "en[d] up in the readers' laps," she wrote to Delany, "saying (in exasperation or censure or inspiration or whatnot) Here: YOU finish it."[81] The "you" of "I'll kill you" won't finish *On Strike Against God*. It won't live through and then write that hopeful future of "what really hasn't happened" yet; it won't successfully appeal to or activate another human "you." It can't, because it's a faceless, impersonal "you," held at arm's length, homogenous and scorned. But perhaps the "you" who breeds cats, fixes cars, lives on unemployment, teaches introductory biology, has wonderful memories of World War I, writes awful stories—maybe that "you" *will* move into the uncharted future and finish the novel. Any meaningful, future-oriented appeal for justice must involve other people—other real, living, breathing people. In *On Strike Against God*, Russ writes her way up to the very precipice of impossibility—as far as she can go with her mettle alone. Living and writing what hasn't happened yet takes more than just one person. It takes more than just two people. Esther needs "you," with all its heterogeneity, just as Russ needed her readers as collaborators. And she still does. Do you find yourself in the novel's final pages? In the novel's final line—its final word? If you do, then this book is for you.

—Alec Pollak
Ithaca, NY
March 2024

On Strike Against God

JOANNA RUSS

"You are on strike against God"—said by a nineteenth-century American judge to a group of women workers from a textile mill. He was right, too, and I don't wonder at him. What I do wonder is where did they get the nerve to defy God? Because you'd think something would interfere with them, give them nervous headaches, hit them, muddle them, nag at them (at the very least) and prohibit them from daring to do it, just as something interferes with me, too, tries to keep me away from certain regions. As I write this the cold March rain is turning the new growth of the trees and bushes an intenser yellow and red, a sort of phantom fall in the tangle of weeds and bramble outside my window. But something doesn't want me to think about that. It's too beautiful. I once had a friend called Rose, whom I'd known for years, who lived in a slum that no matter how she painted the walls, it still looked rotten. The last time I ever saw her was just before I started teaching; I was twenty-nine. I went to visit her in East New York (Brooklyn) where she still lived with her mother and we talked, as we always did, about art and about the college professor she'd been in love with for years, a man much older than she. Rose and I went to high school together. It's this long-drawn-out business of interpreting his glances, his casual remarks, how he shakes her hand. She's got it all elaborately figured out. When I visited her she was putting away her three suits, her two scarves, her one sweater, her two changes of junk jewelry—all Rose has.

She lays it out exquisitely in her bureau drawers and enjoys the sensation of living light. It's cheap but she takes endless time choosing it and laundering or cleaning it. (She works as an accountant, but not often, so she hasn't much money.) Whenever Rose decides to renounce the world she feels so good that she goes out to the movies and calls friends that very night. When I was there her mother had the TV on in the living room of that very little house—they live in a section of dilapidated clapboard houses, iron gates over all the storefronts at night, lots of weeds. Her mother's great pride was a pink, plastic tablecloth and matching plastic curtains in the living room, a vinyl-topped table for the TV. Rose had just repainted her own room with quick-drying paint; she was arranging her clothes, she who never goes out (hardly) and telling me in great detail about her fantastically complicated, draining, difficult, unhappy love affair with this man, which would be consummated (I suppose) in about twenty years when he was seventy and she almost fifty. She's very, very fat and good-looking, with a fat woman's strange and awesome smoothness, her monumental (and fake) physical serenity.

I said, "I'm in love, I'm in love again. Rose, did you hear me?"

She went on talking, folding and re-folding her clothes, turning toward me her witty, careful, pointed glance, so imitative of happiness. She knew I didn't mean it. At that time I didn't, and I don't know why I said it. Rose was preparing to leave the world again, which meant she would be very unhappy in a week or so. She didn't even listen to me. She was telling me how her mother had once seen her walking in front of a speeding car when she was a child and hadn't warned her.

I left her wallpapering her much-loved, much-tended little corner of hell.

Not really being in love then. Heavens, no. Not even thinking about it. Without love there's nothing to bring into focus what's outside oneself, like (let us say) the soul of things non-human as manifested in the quiet clearness of a hillside in late winter, the place I live now, from the yellow grass-stems to the pebbles to the cut made for the road to pass through—all this in the misty graying-out of the Pennsylvania hills, the regular, rocking line of the ancient flood-plain, the occasional fountains of yellow-green where the willows are coming alive, red where it's some kind of bush, all these harmless, twiggy nerve-centers, the animate part of the great World Soul. Harmless until now, anyway. Landscape has a dangerous and deceiving repose, unlike cats or dogs who have eyes with which they can (gulp!) look right at you and sometimes do just that, as if they were persons, looking out of their own consciousness into yours and embarrassing and aweing you. Wild animals are only mobile bits of landscape. Until you learn better, you think that a landscaped world can't hurt you or please you, you needn't bother about its soul, you needn't be wary of its good looks.

Until you learn better.

I went out one night last August to look for my friend Jean, who's a graduate student in Classics here. The small town I work in (I teach English) has a collegiate appendix stuck on one end, two small streets on the hill down from the University, and in the more important block, the one restaurant that stays open throughout August, even after summer school has closed, the kind of place that's called Joe's, Charlie's, or Kent's; you know what I mean. Earlier in the evening there had been clouds sailing across the moon, up there in that deep inky blue; so it was obvious to everyone that it was going to get much warmer or much colder by morning. I passed the melancholy parking meters (unused now), the pizza carry-out, the electronics parts store (closed), the laundry, the drugstore, the Indian boutique, the piano somebody has stuck on a sturdy pole and painted aluminum-color to advertise a private house that sells pianos—this looks very odd under the streetlights and is really the damnedest thing I have ever seen. I'm going to look for Jean, the Twenty-Six-Year-Old Wonder: the eternal shield of her large sunglasses, her absurdly romantic long dresses (mauve or purple), her beautiful, square, pale, Swedish face, the tough muscles in her arms from three months on crutches (after a skiing accident in which she smashed her kneecap).

But she wasn't there. Nobody was, I mean nobody I know. There was someone I'd met at a faculty cocktail party, if you can call it met, but I ignored him because I really had thought that Jean would be there, or somebody. And I might have seen him in a play, not met him, I mean he might have been one of the Community Players; that's embarrassing. So I jumped when that fellow came over right after I'd sat down, I mean the unfriend, smiling suavely and saying, "Waiting for someone?" And what can you say when you jumped, when you thought you didn't know him, when you *don't* know him, not really? Are you going to turn down the chance? That's a lovely way to end up with no chances at all. And I'm thirty-eight. He frowned and said uneasily, "Um, can I sit down?" I'm not going to be mean. Four years ago—but it's different now—four years ago was my Israeli graduate student whom I picked up here out of sheer desperation right after I'd moved here (from another college five hundred miles away), sheer desperate loneliness (and because I knew I had to learn how to pick up men in bars)—he approved of my not wanting car doors opened for me like most demanding American women (but none of that pierced my ghastly haze of distress) and told me his views on America and the politics of campus revolution and what he was studying and why and what I should be studying and why. I said yes, yes, yes, oh yes, not even telling him I was a teacher, gibbering like anything out of sheer terror at existence (I had just got divorced, too) and later blew up at him when he tried to kiss me "because you're so understanding." Because it was a fake. Because he wasn't there. Because I wasn't there. Because he didn't know that I knew that he didn't know what I knew and didn't want to know.

Yes, dear, oh yes yes yes.

Why do men shred napkins? Three out of four napkin-shredders (rough estimate) are male. Female napkin-shredders are really napkin-strippers, i.e., they tear napkins into little strips, not shreds. But men who tear napkins tear them to shreds.

My new napkin-shredder sat down, a little dark fellow in Bermuda shorts and knee socks, and Goddamnit there went his hand out for the very first napkin. Blindly, appetitively seeking. Do you think I could ask him? Do you think I could say: Please, why are you tearing that there napkin into shred-type pieces? (Or pieces-type shreds, possibly.) Why? Why? Why? Oh, put your hands in your lap and leave the napkin alone!

Now, now, he's as nervous as you are, dear.

I said, "Your napkin—"

"What?" he said, alarmed.

I shook my head to indicate it was nothing. First we'll talk about the weather, that's number one, and then I'll listen appreciatively to his account of how hard it is to keep up a suburban home, that's number two, and then he'll complain about the number of students he's got, that's number three, and then he'll tell me something complimentary about my looks, that's number four, and then he'll finally get to talk about His Work.

"I've got an article coming out next May in the *Journal of the Criticism of Criticism*," he said.

"Oh, congratulations!" I said. "It's such a fine place. They don't keep you waiting, do they? Like *Parameter Studies*."

(My analyst and I often discussed—years ago—my compulsion to always have the last word with men. We worked on it for months but we never got anywhere.)

"They didn't keep *me* waiting," says Napkin Shredder (thus neatly dodging any mention by me of my seven articles in *Parameter*); "Perhaps you saw my articles there—the imagery of the nostril in Rilke?"

I made myself look frail and little. "Oh, no," I said. "I just can't keep up, you know."

(So far, so good.)

He then told me what his article in *C of C* was about and how he was going to make it into a book, none of which I particularly wanted to hear—nor did I want to talk about mine, which I also find extremely boring, why inflict it on strangers?—but it's a sign they like you, so I listened attentively, from time to time saying "Mm" and "Mm hm" and watching the front window of the restaurant in the hope that Jean might walk by. *Why are you telling me all this?*—but that's a line for the movies. Besides I know why. And, as usual, the burden of maturity, compassion, consideration, understanding, tolerance, etc. etc. is on me. Again.

"Oh my, really?" I said. (I don't know at what.) He beamed. He began to tell me about a grant he was going to get. He told me this in a confidential way (leaning very close across the table) and I thought in a confused fashion—or my manners must have been slipping—or I'd been watching the front window too long—anyway, one ought to help, oughtn't one?—so I answered without thinking (my analyst and I worked on this too but we didn't get anywhere):

"Don't do it. Just don't do it. They make you work too hard for your money. I know; I've gotten grants from them twice."

There was a strained silence. Perhaps I'd discouraged him. He told me the names of his last four articles, which had been published in various places; he told me where, and then he told me what the editors had said about them (the articles). He was talking with that edge in his voice that means I've provoked something or done something impolite or failed to do something I should've done; you are supposed to show an intelligent interest, aren't you? You're supposed to encourage. So I analyzed the strengths of all those separate editors and journals and praised all of them; I said I admired him and it was really something to get into those journals, as I very well knew.

"I often wonder why women have careers," said Shredded Napkin suddenly, showing his teeth. I don't think he can possibly be saying what I think he's saying. He isn't, of course. Never mind. I'll stand this because Reality is dishing it out and I suppose I ought to learn to adjust to it. Besides, he may be sincere. There is a human being in there. At least he isn't telling me about something he read in the paper on women's liberation and then laughing at it.

"Oh goodness, I don't know, the same thing that makes a man decide, I suppose," I said, trying to look bland and disarming. "Cheers."

"Cheers," he said. The drinks had come. He opened his mouth to say something and then appeared to relent; he traced circles with his forefinger on the table. Then he said, leaning forward:

"You're strange animals, you women intellectuals. Tell me: what's it like to be a woman?"

I took my rifle from behind my chair and shot him dead. "It's like that," I said. No, of course I didn't. Shredder is only trying to be nice; he would really like me best with a fever of 102 and laryngitis, but then he's not like everybody, is he? Or does he say what they only think? It's not worth it, hating, and I am going to be mature and realistic and not care, not care. Not anymore.

"At least you're still—uh—decorative!" he said, winking.

Don't care. Don't care.

I said quickly, "Oh my, I've got to go," and he looked disappointed. He's beginning to like me. I am a better and better audience as I get numbed, and although I've played this game of Impress You before (and won it, too—though I don't like either of the prizes; winning is too much like losing), I'm too tired to go on playing tonight. Will he insist on taking me home? Will he ask me out? Will he fight over the bill? Will he start making remarks about women being this or that, or tell me I'm a good woman because I'm not competitive?

Oh why is it such awful work?

Shredder (coloring like a schoolboy) says he hopes I won't laugh but he has a few—uh—odd hobbies besides his work; he's always been tremendously interested in science, you know (he tosses off a frivolous reference to C. P. Snow and the "two cultures") and would I (he says, shyly) like to hear a lecture next Thursday on the isomeric structure of polylaminates? As I would, actually, but not with him. (His ears turned pink and he looked suddenly rather nice. But will it last?) I don't want to make a bafflefield—sorry, battlefield—of my private life. Bafflefiend! Goodbye, Mr. Bafflefiend. I will leave Shredder and go look for a Good, Gentle-but-Firm,

Understanding, Virile Man. That's what my psychoana-lyst used to keep telling me to do. To avoid quarreling I let Shredder pay for the drinks (a bargain for him but not for me); to avoid endless squabbling insistencies I let him walk me around the corner to what I said was my home; and to duck the usual unpleasant scene ("What's the matter with you? Don't you like men?") gave him my—entirely fictitious—telephone number. I waited inside the building until he'd vanished uphill and then slipped out into the street and started off in the opposite direction. Spoiled, spoiled. All spoiled. My psychoanalyst (who has in reality been dead for a decade) came out of the clouds and swooped at me as I trudged home, great claws at the ready, batwings black against the moon, dripping phos-phorescent slime. Etcetera. (All the way from New York.)

You will never get married!

All right, all right, Count Draculule.

You fear fulfillment.

Buzz off, knot-head.

Your attitude toward your femininity is ambivalent. You hope and yet you fear. You attract men, but you drive them away. What a tangle is here!

I giggled.

You do not like men, Esther. You have penis envy.

They have humanity envy. They don't like me.

Come now, men are attracted to you, aren't they?

That's not what I said, kiddo.

He comes back every once in a while, very stern and severe; then he goes back up into a cloud to clean his fangs. We get along. After a while you tame your inte-rior monsters, it's only natural. I don't mean that it ever stops; but it stops mattering. I trudged down the hill and up the hill to home (then up the stairs). My kitchen is always a greeting; I don't know why. I don't like to cook. Yet my apartment always strikes me—after each small absence—as something I've created myself, with my own two hands, something solid and colorful and nice, like an analogue of myself. It greets me. You can see that this is going to require an awful lot of (naturalistic) padding while I walk home, climb steps, sleep, or go from one room to another. But in recompense I will tell you what I was thinking all the way home in that chilly, fragrant, August night: I was thinking that I felt sexually dead, that I was perpetually tired, that my body was cold and self-contained, that I had been so for eleven years, ever since my divorce, and that nothing I had done or could do or would ever be able to do would ever bring me back to life. I didn't like that. Not that it was a tragic feeling; it was only something mildly astonishing (in the middle of all the things I do like and enjoy). It amazed me. As I threw the windows open to the night I thought that at least I had fed my showy, neurotic, insecure, exhibition-istic personality to the full over the last few years, that in this one way (and many others) I was very happy, I enjoyed myself tremendously, but there was something else I didn't have, another way in which I was deprived. Yet a mild feeling, believe me. At least so far.

I'll tell you something: my psychoanalyst (I mean the real one) used to ride around Manhattan on a motor-cycle. It was his one eccentricity. I think he was secretly proud of it. Whenever patients in our group (what a word, *patients*) got audibly worried about this rather dangerous habit, he would (I think) be secretly delighted; he would beam without apparently being aware of how pleased he was, and then this tall, balding busi-nessman would say, "O let us analyze your anxiety." He never analyzed his own liking for the motorcycle. He was thrown from it in a collision with an automobile and died in the street, leaving behind a widow (badly provided for) and two small children. He was younger than I am now. You may gather that I didn't entirely like the man and that's true—but when he comes zooping down from his black cloud, fangs aquiver, I think of his death and it warms me. It pleases me. The man was such a fool. I try to make myself sorry by thinking of his wife and children—there's his poor wife, compelled to believe all that nonsense, yes, and live it too (don't tell me she never sneaked a peek in Freud, just to see). Did she have the wrong kind of orgasm? Did she succeed in renouncing her masculine protest? Hypocritically I try to make myself cry, thinking that I should feel sorry for anyone in such an accident, all that blood over the street, etc., the twisted motorcycle, etc. Then I'm not pleased. Then I have a very different reaction.

Snoork! I laugh.

To be sexually dead. . . .

Well, people pretend to be better than they are. That used to mean frigid, but now it means something else. The truth that's never told today about sex is that you aren't good at it, that you don't like it, that you haven't got much. That you're at sea and unhappy. When I was married I never lay back and opened my knees without feeling (with a sinking of the heart, an inexpressible anguish), "Here we go again," a phrase I couldn't explain to my analyst and can't now. I think it was because my thighs hurt. I did get some mild pleasure out of the whole business, I don't want to misrepresent that, but not much; I could never get my feet down on the bed when I put my knees up (my tendons were too tight), so after a few minutes my knees and thighs would begin to hurt; then they'd hurt a lot and if I turned over and we did it the other way my face would get pushed into the mattress and I didn't like that. I couldn't move at all that way. And if I sat on top it was lonely and I couldn't relax and I knew I was supposed to relax (all the books said it) because if I pushed or tried to take control, then I wouldn't come. But my husband never seemed to know what to do. *To be made love to*—that was the point. Only I was no good at it.

What I cannot convey is the intense confusion I felt when I tried even to think about it.

Cures: my analyst told me not to try for orgasm at all, so I knew I was wrong to be hung up about it because it wasn't important; or rather it was so important that you had to treat it as if it wasn't important (or you would never have it); so for a long time I could never think of myself sexually at all without intense confusion (as I've said) and great personal pain.

Have masochistic fantasies—but that's much too close to real life.

Pretend you're a man—I did that when I was fourteen. But that's forbidden (and impossible). I used to daydream (twenty-four years ago, can you believe it was so long? I can't) that I was a man making love with another man. Which still strikes me as fairly bizarre, if you start thinking about the transformations of identity involved. I told my analyst.

He: In this—ah—daydream, are you the active or the passive partner?

Me: What?

He (patiently): Psychology knows that in homosexual pairs, one man is always the active partner in love-making and the other man is always passive. Now which do you imagine yourself being?

But here an abyss opened beneath my feet. I still am not really sure why. The truth is that I felt the coming battle without being able to name a thing about it; was it that I wanted to say one thing and would be made to say another? Or ought to say another? Or must say one thing and must not say it at the same time? I didn't know. I knew one thing only and that was crystal-clear: *I was going to lose.* So it was with the simultaneous sense of sneaking home safe and yet being intolerably—oh, just intolerably!—coerced that I replied very haltingly:

Me (blush): Um . . . passive. The passive one.

He (delighted): Ah! So you really are the woman, you see.

Which is not so. It's just not so.

"You know," said my analyst, "there's no reason you can't tell your husband what you'd like him to do to you. Women ought to be aggressive in bed."

Me: Lost again. I always lose. (But I didn't say it. I smiled a sick, feeble, little smile and agreed.)

What else could I do?

I remembered summer camp at the age of twelve when I necked with my best friend (we all did) but wouldn't touch her breasts because I was too embarrassed. The next summer everyone had apparently forgotten what we had done the summer before. (A point of peculiar integration from which everything has gone most definitely downhill.)

I desired my husband—but it didn't work. I experience the same muddle-headedness when I try to remember *what* didn't work. I have no words for it.

Having a heartfelt crush on beautiful, gentle, helpless, intelligent Danny Kaye at age twelve and a half. I seem to be going through the right phases at the right times. Still, I keep wanting to rescue him from things. Can that be right? (Is it sadism?)

The best solution (and the one I pursued after my divorce): Not to think about it at all.

Jean dropped over for breakfast the next morning, which was Sunday, bringing with her black cherry ice cream and bacon, both of which we ate. This is an honor;

she seldom spends money for luxuries because she lives
on a fellowship in a co-op downtown. Sat around the
kitchen, loath to leave (the most crucial room in the
house), drinking endless cups of tea until the memory
of the black cherry ice cream became unpleasantly dim.
There was a wonderful surfeit of odds and ends on the
table. I had been trying to plan the day's affairs to avoid
the premise that I had absolutely nothing left to do, for
a three-months' vacation (my vacation, an academic one)
is like the jungles in H. Rider Haggard: first your little
traveling party goes through the harmless fringes of the
first few days, everything looking only mildly sinister;
then there's the thickening growth and the awful feeling
that it'll never end, and then you start losing people—
beating the bushes for them, holloa-ing for them (but it's
no use)—and finally all those early glimpses of prehistoric
monsters and strange footprints (or arrows or axe-heads
buried in tree-trunks) pay off, so to speak; I mean that
your camp is attacked in the brief tropical dawn by Beast
Men or a Phagocytus Giganticus who eats the native
guide, the heroine's father (a scientist), his assistant, and
all the maps, leaving our heroine alone in the jungle she
now knows contains almost two months more of vacation and nothing whatever to do. There I was. With the
hope that I could eventually walk in a sort of trance to
the foothills (I mean that you will get used to it) and
begin to climb. But my apartment's been burnished to
a high gloss (including cutting fuzz off the rug with a
nail scissor, honest) and I've also decided not to move
to another apartment. The dinosaur's eaten the map.

I told all this to Jean.

"Look!" she said, and she drew three interlocking
circles on her napkin (like the beer ad).

"Mimetic," she said. "Didactic. Romantic." And went
off into something I couldn't follow.

"This morning I dreamed I saw Death at the foot of my bed," she said. "He was reading a newspaper. Hiding his face in it. Banal, really."

"Work is a real blessing," she said. (She's right.)

I stirred my tea. I played with my food. Brightening up, she told me how the cooperative's dog had caught a rattlesnake, courageously biting it in two although it made him vomit. So-and-so had made noodle pudding. So-and-so was trying to fix the phonograph. It's a loose practical association, nothing very striking; I mean you must not think of it as any close, mystical, hippie-dippy sort of thing because it's not. Jean studies mathematics for fun, makes her own clothes as a recreation, can do anything, is ferociously private. Stupid Philpotts (the cooperative's dog) is a cross between an Afghan and an English sheepdog; first he chases the sheep, then he knits them into sweaters. I couldn't stop laughing. Jean, whose arrogance toward other people is often terrifying, was staring dreamily ahead, one hand curled in her lap. Stupid Philpotts (she told me) is large and skinny and covered with immense amounts of curly white hair (which quite conceals his face); if you lift the hair, you see his beautiful, intelligent, long-lashed eyes, which gleam at you like lovely jewels. He was missing for eight days last winter and came back with ice-balls the size of golf balls frozen into his hair. And diarrhea from eating garbage.

"Those damned bastards," said my friend, thinking of something else entirely.

In the summer, in my apartment, you can always go into the living room and look over the hills. Actually you can do it in winter, too, because the setting sun—in the course of one year—describes an arc that stretches from the Southernmost window of the living room (in December) to the Northernmost end of the study window (in June). You can watch the sunset every day of the year through my enormous windows. Overhead the third-floor tenants were walking about, a nuisance that somewhat dilutes the pleasure I take in my windows. Jean had sat here exactly eight months ago, basting the lining of a coat; she often hauls her sewing around with her. But don't think of this as anything domestic or feminine in the ordinary sense; Jean's sewing is part of her perfectionism. It's armor plate.

"Those—!" she said again. Some teacher of hers (she told me) making passes at her in spite of her saying no; some teacher's wife (at another time) badmouthing women graduate students with that venomous sweetness that shows you how very "feminine" the woman is—she can't get angry openly, not even at another woman. Pathetic and awful, both of them. And the men in the collective not wanting to do certain kinds of work.

"Men run the world," said Jean. "Men are people; therefore people run the world."

"Evil people," I said. "Are you a man-hater?"

"Don't be silly" (absentmindedly).

Am I a man-hater? Man-haters are evil, sick freaks who ought to be locked up and treated until they change their ideas. If you think (under those conditions) that I'm going to admit *anything*, you're nuts. Let's just say that I don't like to sit still and smile a lot. And I would rather not hate anyone (virtuous me!); that is, I would rather there was no reason for it.

"Jean," I said, "did I ever tell you about my friend Shirley?" (Shirl the Girl who went into an expensive private mental hospital in New York and came out insisting *she had to wear stockings* or they'd get her again. "You gotta conform," she'd said to me grimly.)

"Yes. Many times."

"Oh," I said, shaping the O sound very purely (but silently) with my lips. Playing. Bored.

"I would rather not hate anyone," said Jean, pausing in her work (she had brought a pair of white gabardine slacks with her, to hem by hand). The Duchess Look: objective, dispassionate, not pleased. I told you that last night was very clear, active, and cold; now huge black clouds are rising on the Southwestern horizon, the place our weather comes from through a pass in the hills. Leaves, twigs, and bits of detritus are being blown all over the place. The light's turning green. I went about shutting windows and wondering if the rain gutter would fall into the garden again—not that we have a real garden, I'm talking about the rather elementary piece of lawn the landlady pays the boy next door to mow once in a while and our two unkempt forsythia bushes. The house is old, and besides providing a sounding-board for footsteps, it has trouble with some of its trim. Jean and I sat and watched the faraway part of the town (in the valley) disappear under rain; there was a *crack!* and you could see the streets darkening one by one. Sound of machine-gun fire or round-shot in buckets. Myriads of dashes on the screens first, then on the windowpanes. Pockmarks on the porch roof. Then with another rattling slam the windows became invisible and the whole house ran with water, a real summer storm. The air in the living room was already getting stuffy. Stupid Philpotts (said Jean) would be hiding under somebody's bed now, although what all this meant to him, deep in his doggy mind, nobody could tell.

"Ah! *he* knows," said I. Jean giggled. She fiddled with my radio and then turned it off. Our storm withdrew down the valley and along the lake, grumbling and muttering. Eight minutes after it had begun we opened the windows; the temperature had dropped fifteen degrees during the rain, but the sun was coming out, straight overhead and very hot. It was noon. No, it was high noon, sun-time. I don't know if a clearing storm can ever be followed by a rise in temperature unless it's hot beforehand, but that's what happened. Summer was back again. Proper August: humid air and puddles. I looked at Jean again, wanting to say something-or-other and expecting she'd be back at her work, but she was looking past me, the Duchess look gone from her face, all the cynicism gone, the laziness, the bitterness. Through my bedroom window, where the sun rises in December, through the Southeastern window just opposite the direction of the departing storm, was a double rainbow which the Australians call mother and daughter. So rare, so lovely. Everything a vivid emerald green in which the mailbox on the corner shone like 1940s lipstick. Those strange, aniline hues you never see anywhere in nature, and at the earthly end (guaranteed or your money back) King Solomon's Mines. (I'm in the foothills at last.) It's not possible to stay unhappy. I took Jean's hand and we waltzed clumsily around the room. We said, "Isn't it lovely?" as people do, but we really meant more than we could say: this double rainbow, a completely circular ice-bow on Cape Cod, a seagull against the sun, cherry trees in the Brooklyn Botanical Gardens, being wheeled there when I was a child, times like these.

We meant: It's a sign.

Even if it were permissible to hate men, I don't think I would. You can hate some of the men all of the time and you can hate all of the men some of the time. Tell the truth or bust! (We shall not bust.) I remember walking down the city streets years ago and being suddenly amazed into a stab of love and admiration for my beautiful, gentle husband with whom (as I told you) I could not make love. Why did we ever separate? Something must have shown on my face, for people stared. I remember being endlessly sick to death of this world which isn't mine and won't be for at least a hundred years; you'd be surprised how I can go through almost a whole day thinking I live here and then some ad or something comes along and gives me a nudge—just reminding me that not only do I not have a right to be here; I don't even exist. Since I crawled into this particular ivory tower it has not been better, hearing about the typical new man in the department and his work and his pay and his schedule and his wife and his children (me? my depart-ment), well that's only comedy, but what goes right to my heart is the endless smiling of the secretaries where I work, the endless anxiety to please. The anxiety. Like my husband, coming home on the bus with me from my shrink and blurting out, "There's only you and me, what does he mean, *the* marriage!"

Still, sex was no good with him. Seeing a double rain-bow with Jean and waltzing around the room (clumsily but solemnly) has somehow enabled me to remem-ber that sex with my husband was in fact very bad, the badness of it being (as I remember) a good measure of the truly vast number of things I could not—then—manage to remember. Or rather, I labored so conscientiously to remember to forget them; if only I'd had a worse memory! But I didn't. I am a good, earless, eyeless girl who walks past construction workers without hearing or seeing anything and the last time I hung upside down by my knees from the top of the jungle gym I was five years old. I wonder what I made of that upside-down world. Already dainty and good, not liking to have smudges on my dress (when I remembered) and setting my dolls to school like my elementary-school teacher aunt, dress-ing them in appropriate costumes for the season (which practice I continue with myself, by the way), and spend-ing a lot of time fussing over which of them was the tallest and which the shortest because they had to be put in a row of graduated height for school. I wrapped up my best doll and took her downstairs once to see a hailstorm. But I got dirty, too. And I liked the world upside down (having bat blood) and longed fiercely to get up in the clouds, which you could only do if they were "down"—i.e. hanging on the jungle gym. I would swing my way absentmindedly to the top like a monkey and then hang there, stern and sensible, full of cosmic awe. There's a picture of this dead little five-year-old woman looking at the inside of her first post office, rows and rows of post-office boxes right up to the ceiling; she's hanging on to the knobs of two of them with an indecipherable—perhaps stunned—expression. I'm looking at a jail. The Rose-Growers' Association gardens where we went every week-end was my mother; my father was the post office (because he worked in an office); I myself was the stone lion outside the post office. There's a picture of me sitting astride it, looking uncomfortable and exalted. In the earliest family snapshot of all (I mean after the wet-lump stage, which does not show personality, at least in a kodak) I am peeking dramatically around the corner of a city fire hydrant, my face smeared beautifully all over with chocolate ice cream. It all looks so good: don't give a damn about anybody and having a good time. I am told that these short people are still alive somewhere, possibly inside the great, grand palimpsest of Me, and somewhere at the center (like a kernel in a nut) the archaic idol, all red wrinkles, who got wrapped screaming in a blanket (covering her enlarged vulva—this is true, you know, for a few days after birth) who sucked in foodstuff at one end and squirted product-stuff out the other, like a sea anemone. But this I don't believe. You're supposed to break your teeth on this archaic center if you bite too deeply into things—but I find the howler monkey, the wanter, the hater, the screamer, far too modern and present to think of her as the leftovers from a baby. And who could call a wet lump *she*? You might as well call it Irving. What has truly never left me is the post-office boxes (which I rather liked; they certainly looked powerful and important) and the jungle gym. Witches do everything upside down and backwards; they go in where they should go out, and out when they should go in. Or flat. Like all women. So get used to seeing everything upside down as you read this.

But the name is bad. The name is awful. I mean that everyone I've met, everyone I know well (unless they're lying, as I always am in a social situation—you don't think I want to get locked up, do you?)—anyway, every female friend of mine seems to have accepted in some sense that she is a woman, has decided All right, I am a woman; rolls that name "woman" over and over on her tongue, trying to figure out what it means, looks at herself in a full-length mirror, trying to understand, "Is that what they mean by Woman?" They're ladies. They're pretty. They're quiet and cheerful. They want a better deal, maybe, but they're easygoing, they have a certain serenity, they're *women*. Perhaps they've lost something, perhaps they've hidden something. When they were sixteen they could say, "I'm a *girl*, aren't I?" and not be stupefied, stunned, confused, and utterly defeated by the irrelevant idiocy of the whole proceeding.

I'm not a woman. Never, never. Never was, never will be. I'm a something-else. My breasts are a something-else's breasts. My (really rather spiffy) behind is a something-else's behind. My something-else's face with its prophetic thin bones, its big sunken eyes, my long long bones, my stretched-out hands and feet, my hunched-over posture, all belong to a something-else. I have a something-else's uterus, and a clitoris (which is not a woman's because nobody ever mentioned it while I was growing up) and something-else's straight, short hair, and every twenty-five days blood comes out of my something-else's vagina, which is a something-else doing its bodily housekeeping. This something-else has wormed its way into a university teaching job by a series of impersonations which never ceases to amaze me; for example, it wears stockings. It smiles pleasantly when it's called an honorary male. It hums a tune when it's told that it thinks like a man. If I ever deliver from between my smooth, slightly marbled something-else thighs a daughter, that daughter will be a something-else until unspeakable people (like my parents—or yours) get hold of it. I might even do bad things to it myself, for which I hope I will weep blood and be reincarnated as a house plant. I do not want a better deal. I do not want to make a deal at all. *I want it all.* They got to my mother and made her a woman, but they won't get me.

Something-elses of the world, unite!

Do you think Jean is—might be—a something-else?

Sally, Louise, Jean, and I were watching a bad movie on TV. Behold a handsome, virile, football-player actor pretending to be an eminent scientist. It was one of those movies in which a computer takes over the world and you jolly well wish it would—anything's better than the people. I notice that the Amurricans are all glamorous mesomorphs under thirty-five but the Rooshians are fat and middle-aged. So I'm in trouble with art, too. Sally and Louise are visiting—old acquaintances of Jean's, not really friends, for they're much older than she is (she's twenty-six)—with a dog named Lady who barely got into the apartment before she zipped frantically under the sofa and stayed there for the entire visit, at the end of which she came out very stiff and stretching herself as if she'd had rheumatism. Lady's afraid of new places. Lady, I was told, is a Belgian sheepdog with a tendency to herd strange children—that's funny to tell about if nobody takes you to court over it; nor is it funny or pleasant for the children who have their heels nipped, I imagine.

What are Sally and Louise like?

Well, they look like—well, like anybody. They aren't glamorous. From a distance they look young (that's the blue jeans); but they're grown women in their late thirties, even as you and I; Jean knew them when they were English teachers here. I don't know them. Louise is the chunky one who wears huge, fashion-model sunglasses and tried very patiently to coax Lady out from under my sofa (Lady growled and retreated). Sally is the skinny one and talks a lot. If she weren't so friendly and civilized, one feels, she'd be into your refrigerator instantly, or examining your drapes for blister rust or your cupboards for teacup blight. Not that she's pushy; she's just interested. Truth to tell, Louise is not so plump nor is Sally so skinny; it's only that there's little to say about women who don't project themselves dramatically by way of make-up or dress. And there was the weariness of their eight-hour drive from Virginia. In both ways totally unlike my friend Jean, who was being very WASP college-girl fresh and beautiful: her hair caught back by a green ribbon, her bell-bottomed green pants, a man's white shirt tied together in front. All of us, I think, had the academic drabness in which everything has run to voice, so I remember Sally's quick, brilliant, insistent hammer-blows (the voice of a short woman who's on her way to becoming a time bomb because nobody ever takes her seriously) and from time to time Louise's slow, deeper, ironic, Southern interruptions, one hand going down to rub the dog's nose. Lady didn't say a word. And Jean is always just Jean.

What did we talk about?

I don't remember. We talked so hard and sat so still that I got cramps in my knees. We had too many cups of tea and then didn't want to leave the table to go to the bathroom because we didn't want to stop talking. You will think we talked of revolution but we didn't. Nor did we talk of our own souls. Nor of sewing. Nor of babies. Nor of departmental intrigue. It was politics if by politics you mean the laboratory talk that characters in bad movies are perpetually trying to convey (unsuccessfully) when they Wrinkle Their Wee Brows and say (valiantly—dutifully—after all, *they* didn't write it), "But, Doctor, doesn't that violate Finagle's Constant?" I staggered to the bathroom, released floods of tea, and returned to the kitchen to talk. It was professional talk. It left me grey faced and with such concentration that I began to develop a headache. We talked about Mary Ann Evans's loss of faith, about Emily Brontë's isolation, about Charlotte Brontë's blinding cloud, about the split in Virginia Woolf's head and the split in her economic situation. We talked about Lady Murasaki, who wrote in a form that no respectable man would touch, Hroswit, a little name whose plays "may perhaps amuse myself," Miss Austen, who had no more expression in society than a firescreen or a poker. They did not all write letters, write memoirs, or go on the stage. Sappho—only an ambiguous, somewhat disagreeable name. Corinna? The teacher of Pindar. Olive Schreiner, growing up on the veldt, wrote one book, married happily, and never wrote another. Kate Chopin wrote a scandalous book and never wrote another. (Jean has written nothing.) There was M-ry Sh-ll-y who wrote you know what and Ch-rl-tt- P-rk-ns G-lm-n, who wrote one superb horror story and lots of sludge (was it sludge?), and Ph-ll-s Wh--tl-y who was black and wrote eighteenth-century odes (but it was the eighteenth century) and Mrs. -nn R-dcl-ff- who wrote silly novels and M-rg-r-t C-v-nd-sh and Mrs. -d-n S--thw-rth and Mrs. G--rg-- Sh-ld-n and (Miss?) G--rg-tt- H-y-r and B-rb-r- C-rtl-nd and the legion of those who, writing, write not, like the dead Miss B--l-y of the poem who was seduced into bad practices (fudging her endings) and hanged herself in her garter. The sun was going down. I was blind and stiff. It's at this point that the computer (which has run amok and eaten Los Angeles) is defeated by some scientifically transcendent version of pulling out the plug; the furniture stood round us unknowing (though we had just pulled out the plug) and Lady, who got restless when people talked at such length because she couldn't understand it, stuck her head out from under the couch, looking for things to herd. We had talked for six hours, from one in the afternoon until seven; I had at that moment an impression of our act of creation so strong, so sharp, so extraordinarily vivid, that I could not believe all our talking hadn't led to something more tangible—mightn't you expect (at least) a little blue pyramid sitting in the middle of the floor? But there wasn't anything. I had a terrible shock, something so profound that I couldn't even tell what it was; for nothing had changed—the sun sank, the light breeze blew through my enormous open windows. The view over the hills was as splendid as ever. I looked for the cause in Lady, who had eased herself stiffly out from under the sofa with a plaintive whine of discomfort, I looked at the lamps, the tables, my floor-to-ceiling bookcase, my white walls, my blue rug and red curtains, my black-framed pictures of roses and robots. But nothing has exploded, or changed color, or turned upside down, or is speaking in verse. Nor had the wall opened to reveal a worldwide, three-dimensional, true-view television set playing, for the enlightenment of the human race and our especial enjoyment, a correct, truly scientific (this time) film about a runaway computer in Los Angeles in which all the important roles were played by grey-haired, middle-aged women. That would violate everything. (The other way only we are violated.) Perhaps in the days of the Great Goddess (before everything went wrong) creation was both voluntary and involuntary, in the mind and in the body, so to bear the stars and planets—indeed, the whole universe—She had not only to grunt and sweat with the contractions of Her mind, but think profoundly, rationally, and heavily with Her womb.

Then the spontaneous remission. The healing. The Goddess's kindly and impatient gift. I started thinking again and the first thought was very embarrassing: I realized I had been staring very rudely at Jean, who was sitting in front of the window and whose breasts were silhouetted through her blouse by the late afternoon sun. I tried to tell all this to the others, but I think they were only amused. "We're brilliant," I said. "We're the great ones." (I meant: what those others say about us isn't true.)

"Sure," said Louise.

I wanted to say to Jean, I'm embarrassed because I saw the outline of your breasts and you're running around without a bra. But my head hurt.

"I'm dying of hunger," said Sally. "Let's go out."

(You see, we're the real people. We're the best. I don't mean that we're "as good as men" or that "everyone is equal" or that "people should be judged as individuals." I'm not referring to those others out there at all. It's a question of what's put at the center. See Copernicus and Galileo. I know you know all this, but indulge me. Listen to me. The roof has just come off the world and here is the Sun, who took Her broad, matron's face down behind the last, the Westernmost hill, and here is baby Night, who's leaning Her elbows on the cool sill of the East. She carries a fishing rod so that She can dangle the bright bob of setting Venus over the brow of the Sun. Something has vanished from the top of the sky, some lid or lens or fishbowl that's been closed oppressively over my head as long as I can remember and nobody ever even remarked upon it or criticized it or took the trouble to suggest that it might not be a good thing, that it might even be better if it were removed. I trailed after Jean to the door, thinking that I was making some other decision, too, but something I didn't understand, and that it was unsettling to feel voluntary action taking place in a region you can't even reach. Anyway, it's just one of my fantasies. And it doesn't matter. Not that it's something in me; it's only something strange in the way the world is put together, something about the way foundations of the world are arranged.

(But what is "it?"

(I don't know.)

My fantasies. Oh lord, my fantasies. The human bat fantasy about mating in midair. The Super-Woman fantasy (before the comic book). The hermit fantasy. The Theda Bara fantasy. The disguised lady as reckless hero fantasy (Zorra). I have a million of 'em. One of us who is writing this (we're a committee) was told by her mother that she was named Joan after Juana la Loca or Crazy Joanna, a poor Spanish Queen bereft of her wits who followed her husband's embalmed corpse around An-da-lu-*thee*-ya etc. for eighteen years. It's in the encyclopedia. Now this is a hell of a thing to put on your daughter. I found out last week that her real namesake was in fact the spiritual leader of the entire Western World and somebody who scared everyone so much they had to rearrange the succession of Popes (with two years left unaccounted for and one Pope John), efface her from the history books for four hundred years, and demand a physical examination of every candidate for the Papacy thereafter, lest they again get stuck with a woman (Brand X). I mean, of course, Pope Joan—or John VIII, Joannes in Latin. Not to mention the saint who came after her, which makes this particular name very powerful indeed.*

That poor mother was deceived. She had become abject.

It is very important, Boadicea, Tomyris, Cartisman-dua, Artemisia, Corinna, Eva, Mrs. Georgie Sheldon, *to find out for whom you were named.*

Queen Esther, my namesake, got down on her knees to save her people, which is no great shakes, but Ruth—whose name means Compassion—said Whither thou goest, I will go too.

To her mother-in-law.

Big news for all the Esthers and Stellas in the audience—your name means "star." Forget Hollywood. Stars, like women, are mythologized out of all reality. For example, the temperature at the core of Y Cygni, a young blue-violet star of impeccable background (the main sequence), is thirty-two million degrees Centigrade. This is also Epsilon Aurigae, that big, cool, unwieldy red giant, whose average temperature is a bare seven hundred degrees C but whose outer edges are as big around as the orbit of Uranus. And the neutron stars, denser than white dwarfs (20,000 times the density of water) and those even more collapsed but poetical persons who are supposed to disappear entirely from the known universe, at least to the eye (their immense gravitational fields trap the light trying to escape from their surfaces) but

---

*d. 855, anathematized *1601*. Oops.

who remain at the center of an unexplained attraction—
the disturbing center at a lot of nothing, you might say.
Sylvia did this once or twice. If you're really ambitious,
you might try to be a nova, which (says George Gamow
in *The Life and Death of the Sun*, Mentor, 1959):

> *will blast into an intensity surpassing that of its normal state
> by a factor of several hundreds of thousands and, in some cases,
> even of several billions.*

(p. 155)

Or

> *an essentially different class of stellar explosions* [with a] *maxi-
> mum luminosity on the average 10,000 times greater than that
> of ordinary novae and exceeding by a factor of several billions
> the luminosity of our Sun.*

(p. 157)

This part of the book is full of italics; I think even the
author got scared. Moreover, a supernova is visible from
Earth every three centuries and we're about due for one.
Just think: *You might be it.*

Did you hear that, Marilyn? Did you hear that,
Natalie, Darlene, Shirley, Cheryl, Barbara, Dorine, Lori,
Hollis, Debbi? Did you hear that, starlets? You needn't
kneel to Ahasuerus. You needn't be a burnt offering like
poor Joan. Practice the Phoenix Reaction and rise perpetually from your own ashes!—even as does our own quiet
little Sun, cozy hearthlet that it is, mellow and mild as
a cheese, with its external temperature of 6,000 degrees
Centigrade (just enough to warm your hands at) and
its perhaps rather dismaying interior, whose temperature may range anywhere—in degrees Centigrade—from
fifteen to twenty-one million. The sun's in its teens,
fifteen to twenty-one. The really attractive years. The
pretty period.

And that, says *my* bible, is what they mean by my name. That's an Esther. That's me.

Jean and I went to a party. It was given by Jean's parents, with Jean acting as a social slavey along with her younger sister, her younger brother being exempt and her older sister having married a tree manufacturer in Oregon—sorry, a lumber manufacturer. (Only God can make a tree and She seldom tries, nowadays.) It was mostly academic people, friends of Jean's parents, who are both biologists at the university agricultural and veterinary school, her father a full professor, well paid, her mother a part-time researcher, unpaid. (Their work is far too esoteric for me to understand, let alone explain.) The first thing that happened at this party was that someone started a contest between the men and the women—there was one way in which women were physically superior to men, which involved standing two feet from a wall, putting your forehead against it, and then trying to raise a chair. It was something to do with leverage. Whatever the damned thing was, I wouldn't do it. They coaxed me but I wouldn't. "Aren't you interested in the differences between men and women?" they said. I said I thought we ought to judge people as individuals. What I really wanted to say was that if we were having a contest of physical abilities, I'd like to see some of the men give birth, but if you do that (I mean say it, not do it) you spend the rest of the evening fending off some extremely respectable character (sometimes, but not always, from the Middle East) who has been looking all his life for a free, independent woman to Talk Dirty With. Jean's parents had made her put on stockings so she was scratching herself as ungracefully as possible whenever anyone looked at her. She was sulky. The talk next turned to push-ups, which the men got very excited about (but I can't do push-ups either) and then to the more usual things, like weather, so it appeared that we might be getting out of the woods, but then somebody leaned across the coffee table (dropping ashes on the family's expensive but sturdy-and-practical rug—why is it that the only aesthetic people in science are the physicists?) and remarked, looking rather pointedly at me:

"I hear someone's giving a paper on menstruation at the next MLA." The MLA is the Modern Language Association, a sort of English-teacher monopoly.

O giggle giggle giggle (all over the room).

Probably a eunuch, said I. Aloud I said:

"Come on, you're just making that up to tease me."

"Oh, no," he said. "Honestly. I wondered what you thought about it."

"Be serious," said I, brightly.

"But I am!" And he writhed a little, like Uriah Heep. "I want to know your opinion of it."

I wanted to say that I could hardly have an opinion of it, not having read the blasted thing, but something took it out of my hands.

"Why are you telling me this?" I said.

He winked gallantly.

I went to the bathroom.

Twenty minutes later when I figured it would all be over, I came out. I was right; they were talking about chowders or clowders or fish parts or something. The trick of doing this is to insinuate yourself carefully into the group by stages in a dimmed-down sort of way so that the inevitable liberal in the group can't come up and apologize for the bad behavior of the first nut, because then you have the problem of whether or not to dress him down for not having come to your aid earlier, whereupon he gets a little snappish and says he thought that a woman fighting her own battles was what women's liberation was all about. Another way to avoid this is to eat a lot. I saw that Jean was attempting to slouch as disgustedly as possible in the kitchen (stomach out) because she does not like her father's friends. Her parents have very good, unimaginative food at their parties, which is a relief after you've been exposed to a lot of bad attempts at curry, or the kinds of things graduate students do under the romantic impression that nobody's ever cooked before. Jean's mother has a maid who comes in every day to clean up and everyone in the family (but Jean) thinks the maid is a very serious cross to bear because she talks a lot. I suspect the maid has crosses of her own. (She's white hill-people with bad legs: varicose veins and swollen ankles.) Jean's mother stayed home with her four children until the youngest was eleven, as was only right (she said); then when she went out to work after eighteen years she had, of course, to get household help. "My mother has too much energy," says Jean. There was the usual nervous discussion about Them (Blacks, who else?) in which Jean's father maintained with desperate, unhappy passion that They were better off than Black people in other parts of the world and the whole company (including me, I am sorry to say) jeered at him most cruelly; Jean's father is a kind of eccentric knickknack in his friends' eyes. They're liberals and they won't stand for anything biased or unfair. I have in me a demon who had slept all through the previous really rather personally painful exchange (I mean the MLA article) and which was now beginning to wake up—to keep it down I started talking with my female neighbor about the clothes you can't buy for summer any more, and the old trolley-cars (which we both remembered) with the woven sides that went halfway up. My mother's summer shoes used to be similarly woven, with some sort of holes in the straw-y fabric, and her rayon dress (the first synthetic) also had little patterns of holes. I used to think summer was made of little patterns of refreshingly aerated holes. Also putting away the winter drapes, if you remember, and the rug, and putting slip-covers on the furniture, although I do not know why anyone ever did or (for that matter) stopped. Mysterious. I love women—I mean I just decided that, talking to her; I mean women don't come up to you and go sneerk, sneerk, menstruation ha ha. You can have a simple, lovely conversation about 100% polyester double knit and what do they *think* they're selling for summer fabrics these days!—it's like astronomy, like zoology, like poetry—without taking your life in your hands, as I seem to do every time I talk to a man. The men, by the way, were deep in international politics (of a rather amateur kind) at the other end of the table. The one Continental thing Jean's parents do is to serve a good deal of wine with their formal meals, so I think my neighbor was getting a little zonked; she was telling about how it had been, going to a woman's college twenty years ago, that if you wanted to be a scholar you had to wear lisle stockings, Oxfords, and mannish suits or nobody would take you seriously. Wasn't it wonderful now (she said) that we could all be *feminine*? She said this over and over, like a life-raft. I said, Yeah, I guess. Faculty wives (she teaches part-time—freshman courses) tend to dress for parties like a rather weird version of TV talk-show hostesses, as if they had tried but hadn't got it quite right—and this nice lady, my table-mate, was wearing a long red silk skirt slit up one knee and a white organdie blouse with ruffles down the front of it. Dangling ivory earrings, I believe. Very strange. I mean all those things that glittered and all that stuff *put* on her (on her face) and inside all that the real face, looking sad. She said *she* wasn't a woman's-libber, she wouldn't burn her bra, but with such a frightened look that I wanted to put my arms around her. Blonde hair carefully combed down her back (dyed). Not what you'd call freely blowing in the breeze, exactly (like in the ads) but that was the idea, I suppose. "Oh, that never happened," I said. "That was invented by the newspapers." (And this is so.) Then she began to tell me what a rotten life she had—at every faculty party there's a faculty wife who ends up with me in a corner, crying over what a rotten life she's had (but it's always a different woman)—and then when I started talking about babysitters, free time, husbands doing housework, etc., she said: "I have a very rich life. I love my husband and children," and retreated into the fruit salad. "What a beautiful child Jean is!" said my neighbor. "You know," she went on, "family life is not dying, as they say," and here, in an assumed tone of immense superiority, started to talk about how her children needed her because they were fifteen and seventeen respectively. "Yes, dear," I said; "Isn't the salad nice?" (Sometimes they begin crying at this stage.)

Don't imagine, she said, *don't imagine that anything I've told you indicates—is—the slightest—shows that I'm—means shows the slightest—*

"What are you two gabbing about!" cries her husband with uncharacteristic heartiness and jollity from the other end of the table.

"Patterns," I said.

"I think," said my neighbor, her chin *very* high in the air (and still spiffed, I am glad to say), "that women who've never married and never had children have missed out on the central experiences of life. They are emotionally crippled."

Now what am I supposed to say to that? I ask you. That women who've never won the Nobel Peace Prize have also experienced a serious deprivation? It's like taking candy from a baby; the poor thing isn't allowed to get angry, only catty. I said, "That's rude and silly," and helped her to mashed potatoes.

"*You* wouldn't know," said she, with a smirk.

"It's rude, Lily," I said in a considerably louder voice, "and if you go on in this way, I shall have to consider that you are both very foolish and very drunk. Eat your potatoes." Scenes bother ladies, you know. Also she thought her husband might be listening in. Do you know who her husband is?

The liberal!

"Phooey," said Lily dimly, into her plate. (Oh dear, but she had had a lot to drink!) "*You* can't catch a man."

"That's why I'll never be abandoned," said I. Fortunately she did not hear me. Did I say taking candy from babies? Rather, eating babies, killing babies, abandoning babies. So sad, so easy.

Something is changing within me. Did I mention my demon? It goes to sleep at its post sometimes, but it was back now and now I didn't mind it; when we got up for dessert and coffee in the living room (and then the screened-in back porch, for it was a hot night and everybody was sweating from having eaten so much) I decided I liked my demon. It has possibilities. Conscientious clawlets out, a-lert and a-ware, prowldy, prowldy, woman's best friend. Maybe I was a little drunk myself. Something in the back of my mind kept coming up insistently and I kept irritatedly shoving it away; I don't want to think of that now. Did you know that the Liberal is a tall, athletic type with everything except a straight backbone and the original Hartyhar is ginger-moustached, older, shorter, redder, a little plump as if he were going to burst his clothes, which are imitation British? He's one of those academic men who imitate English dress under the impression that—well, I don't know under what impression. It's idiotic, especially in summer. They're not such big deals; they're just fools. Oh, I know they're fools; I've always known. Stay with me, demon. Somebody started a discussion about the mayor we're all going to elect in the fall because we're politically conscientious (though his winning certainly won't change my life). I was asked what my politics were.

"Menstruation," I said, with a bit of a snarl.

"Oh come, come, come," says slick-and-suave, "I really do apologize for that, you know." (But he never looks sincere, no matter what he says; he always looks greasy and lying.)

"My politics," said I in a glorious burst of idiot demonhood, "and that of every other woman in this room, is waiting to see what you men are going to inflict on us next. That's my politics."

"Well, you can't get along without us, now can you?" says piggy, with a little complacent chuckle. This is my cue to back off fast-fast-fast—and Jean was looking at me from inside the living room—was it warningly? I couldn't tell. She was too far away to be anything but sibylline. I said crossly that they could all go stuff themselves into Fish Lake; it would be a great relief to me.

He twinkled at me. "Disappointed in love," he said.

I think he thought that I thought that he thought that I thought I was flirting. This is unbearable. I'm absolutely paralyzed.

"I can see that you like spirited wenches," said the obedient puppet who lives inside me.

Everybody roared appreciatively.

"What you don't understand," said our fake Briton (why do they always say this?), "is that I'm not against the women's liberation movement. I believe in equal pay for equal work. But surely you ladies don't need equality when you can wrap us around your little fingers, now do you?"

The Liberal was looking at me with his eyes shining, as if I were going to stand up and sing Die Walküre. Afterwards he will come up to me and say in a *very* low voice that he thinks I was *very* brave.

"Leave me alone," I said leadenly. I should never have started.

"Ah, but that's just what we don't want to do!" cried piggy. "We love you. What bothers us is that you're so oversensitive, so humorless, of course that's the lunatic fringe of the movement—I bet you thought I didn't know anything about the movement, didn't you!—but seriously, you've got to admit that women have free choice. Most women do exactly what they want."

"Just think," said someone else, "how much good the women of this community have done lobbying for a new school."

The demon got up. The demon said Fool. To think you can eat their food and not talk to them. To think you can take their money and not be afraid of them. To think you can depend on their company and not suffer from them.

Well, of course, you can't expect people to rearrange their minds in five minutes. And I'm not good at this. And I don't want to do it. It's a bore, anyway. Unfortunately I know what will happen if we keep on; I'll say that if we are going to talk about these things, let us please talk about them seriously and our fake Britisher will say that he always takes pretty girls seriously and then I'll say Why don't you cut off your testicles and shove them down your throat? and then I'll lose my job and then I'll commit suicide. I once hit a man with a book but that was at a feminist meeting and anyway I didn't hit him really, because he dodged. I have never learned the feminine way of cutting a man down to size, although I can imagine how to do it, but truth to tell, that would go against what I believe, that men must live up to such awful things.

Dead silence. Everybody's waiting. What do you do after you blow up, nitwit? I could already hear them twittering, "Didn't you notice? She's unbalanced." There's a solution to this problem. The solution is to be defeated over and over and over again, to always give in; if you always give in (gracefully) then you're a wonderful girl. I am terribly unhappy. I smiled and got up, and I made my way out in that ghastly way you must after a defeat, while Piggy-brit said something or other which I didn't even hear, thank God. Like being eight again on the playground; I will *not* let them see me cry. I walked through the living room and out the front door; after all, I can go back in another twenty minutes. I can ask to help Jean in the kitchen, to avoid all those others. My mother used to tell me not to hurt people's feelings, but what do you do if they hurt yours? But it's my own fault. The worst thing is that you can't kill that kind of man; I imagined very vividly hitting him with a plate or the punchbowl. Then I imagined pulling his ear off with my fist. I called him a shit-head and a stupid, filthy prick. I knocked him down. After I had sort-of hit the man with the book, I had trembled all day and cried. You can't kill them; they grow up again in your nightmares like vines. I thought I would feel better if I stepped out on the lawn and smelled the good night air, which doesn't care that I'm crazy. Somewhere there is a book that says you ought to cry buckets of tears over yourself and love yourself with a passion and wrap your arms around yourself; only then will you be happy and free. That's a good book. I stood inhaling the scent of the ever-blooming roses on the corner of the lawn and thinking that I was feeling better already. God, had I been a liar when I'd said we ought to judge people as individuals? Of course not! I'd had a bad analyst—well, there's no guarantee. I'd had a nice, crazy, bruised husband. Well, he'd had a bad family. There's no reason to spend time with people you don't like. Jean doesn't like her father's friends, either (her mother is very quiet and doesn't initiate social things much). I said to my demon that there are, after all, nice people and nasty people, and the art of life is to cultivate the former and avoid the latter. That not all men are piggy, only some; that not all men belittle me, only some; that not all men get mad if you won't let them play Chivalry, only some; that not all men write books in which women are idiots, only most; that not all men pull rank on me, only some; that not all men pinch their secretaries' asses, only some; that not all men make obscene remarks to me in the street, only some; that not all men make more money than I do, only some; that not all men make more money than all women, only most; that not all men are rapists, only some; that not all men are promiscuous killers, only some; that not all men control Congress, the presidency, the police, the army, industry, agriculture, law, science, medicine, architecture, and local government, only some.

I sat down on the lawn and wept. I rocked back and forth. One of those awful drunk downs. (Only I was sober.) I wouldn't mind living in a private world and only seeing my women friends, but all my women friends live in the middle of a kind of endless soap opera: does he love me, does he like me, why did he say that, what did he mean, he didn't call me, I want a permanent relationship but he says we shouldn't commit ourselves, his feelings are changing towards me, ought I to sleep with him, what did he mean by that, sex is getting worse, sex is getting better, do you think he's unstable, I'm demanding too much, I don't think I'm satisfying his needs, he says he has to work—crisis after crisis and none of it leading anywhere, round and round until it would exasperate a saint and it's no wonder their men leave them. It's so unutterably boring. I cannot get into this swamp or I will never get out; and if I start crying again I'll remember that I have no one to love, and if anyone treats me like that again, I'll kill him. Only I mustn't because they'll punish me. Certain sorrows have a chill under them, a warning-off from something much worse that tells you you'd better leave certain things unexplored and unexplained, and it would be best of all if you couldn't see it, if you were blind. But how do you blind yourself once you see enough to know that you ought to blind yourself?

It was at this point that I heard behind me a formal, balanced sentence, an Ivy Compton-Burnett sentence, hanging in the air in front of the house. The kind of thing written in letters of fire over the portals of the Atreidae. Such language! It was in Jean's voice. It was elegant, calm, and very loud. The words "stupid prick" recurred in it several times.

She came up behind me in a great rush and flung her arms about me. It occurred to me that although we'd shaken hands and made those rather formal, ritualized cheek-kissings that one does, otherwise we'd never touched before. It was a bit startling. Also she's bigger than I am.

"Oh you good girl!" she cried. "Oh you splendid good girl!" She added, more conversationally, "Did you hear what I said?"

"But your mother—" I said. "Your father—"

"That!" said this unbelieving Valkyrie with scorn, and hugging me as if I had acted like a heroine, which you and I know I most certainly had not. "Look, Esther, I don't have to come here. If they want to keep up the family pride by having me visit once in a while, they treat me right. Otherwise I stay away." She laughed.

"A secret ally," I said.

"Oh," she said, "you should have seen their faces when I told them you were right!"

Her last words, she said, before she had informed the whole company that they were a bunch of cowards. ("You don't know the effect that has on the liberal types," she added, making a face.) Jean is an aristocrat who believes in good people and bad people (mostly the latter) but not in class warfare; I reminded her of this.

"Exactly," she said comfortably. "They're bad. They deserve to be told so. Besides, I already have my money for next year. My last year."

"You can cope and I can't," I said. Then I said, "I thought you weren't a feminist. Not really."

"I'm not," said Jean, squatting on the lawn and smiling at me. "I'm a me-ist."

"Let us," she added, with a look at the house and in a tone of profound disgust, "go somewhere else, for heaven's sake."

We went to Joe's and had a beer and French fries, sitting so we didn't have to face the television set directly. It went from a Western to a hockey game to a fight. Then Olga Korbut, the Russian gymnast who is only 4'10" high, came on and started doing beautiful and impossible backflips; but just then one of the men from Jean's co-op waved to us and came over. He began talking earnestly about Jean's commitment to social revolution and Jean said lightly, "Oh, you'd be amazed at the number of things I'm not committed to," but he wasn't going to take it as a joke—which (unfortunately) reminds me of all the circumstances under which I have behaved in exactly the same way. He said again that he hadn't seen any evidence of Jean's being politically committed, and she said furiously that the next time she came out of the library with a fifteen-pound foreign-language dictionary, she'd drop her commitment on his foot. He said, "You're selfish." (Some of the things Jean is not entirely committed to in his opinion: Communism, Third World peoples, the workers, ecology, and organic foods. The one thing she is absolutely not committed to: white middle-class young men who suffer.)

I gathered X's shirtfront in one hand and brought us nose to nose. Oh I had cool! I said the following, which I am going to quote you in full because I am proud of it, very proud of it indeed, and it embarrassed him. Radicals shouldn't be embarrassed. It went like this:

"You a radical? Bullshit. Radicals are people who fight their own oppression. People who fight other people's oppression are liberals or worse. Radicalism is being pushed to the wall. Would you dare to tell Sawyer" (a Black acquaintance of his) "that he's selfish because he's committed to himself? Yet you tell us. Do you dare to tell a little country with bombs being dropped on it that it's selfish? Yet you dare to tell us. You're white, male, and middle-class—what can you do for the revolution except commit suicide? When the sharks start swimming around our raft, *you're* gonna get Daddy to send a helicopter for you; you could shave your beard and cut your hair and in five minutes go right back to the enemy. Can Jean cut off her breasts? Don't say it, pure soul. You a revolutionary! You just want to purge your sins. If you're still a revolutionary in ten years I'll eat this tablecloth."

Isn't that stunning? (Even if it wasn't *quite* as good as that.) Then I added, for the poor thing looked as if it might speak, "No, don't say it. Go away gracefully. Anything either of us does now is bound to be embarrassing."

He said that we couldn't make him leave because he had a right to be there, so I said *we'd* leave, but on second thought we didn't want to leave, so he'd better go because if he didn't I could do all sorts of unpleasant things, like shouting in my trained teacher voice (current suburban children can't speak above a whisper), or wringing his nose (which hurts awfully and looks silly into the bargain), or yanking at his ears, or throwing water all over him, or hitting him, which I might not be good at but oh, would it be embarrassing. He got up.

"No," I said seriously. "Don't say it. Think again."

He went away.

I felt sorry for him. It's that tender, humane compassion you feel right after you've beaten the absolute shit out of somebody. I suppose if he feels so bad somebody must be doing *something* to him, but this, of course, is exactly what our walking Jesus Christs never admit. I could have mentioned this is my magnificent rhetorical performance, but it's a fact I cleverly concealed out of sheer brilliance.

Why does Jean look now as I looked before? Why did I look then as she looks now?

"Jean, dear," said I, "tell me about God," for religion is the one thing we really have in common. Jean's religion is this: that somewhere (or rather, everywhere) in the universe there is a fourth dimension, and that dimension is the dimension of laughter. Eskimos, finding themselves stuck in a blizzard for the fifth day, foodless, on a piece of ice insecurely fastened to the mainland, burst out laughing when that piece of ice finally moves out to sea, thus dooming them (the Eskimos or whoever they really are) to a slow, painful, and horrible death. They laugh because it's funny; Jean and I understand that. On the Day of Judgment, Jean says, when we all file past God to be judged, He will lean down and whisper into our ears the ultimately awful joke, the ghastly truth, something so true and yet so humiliating, so humiliating and yet so funny, that we will groan and rock back and forth and blush down to the bone. "I'll never do it again," (we'll say) "never, never. Oh, I feel awful." Then they'll let you into Heaven. There will be long lines of sinners giggling and snurfing and bending double with shame.

"What will Christ do during all this?" I said.

Jean said Christ was a liberal and would stand around looking sort of upset and helpless, saying, "Oh, Dad, don't."

I've talked of God as She. Perhaps it's the He-God who repeats the joke. The She-God *is* the joke.

But Jean had a toothache, a mental toothache. She didn't want to stay. It's a dreary subject, whom you outrank and who outranks you, and I pull rank on him and she pulls rank on them, and this plane leaves for Bergen-Belsen in fifteen minutes, not that we really murder each other, Heavens to Betsy, no, not yet.

Jean didn't like Joe's anymore.

Leaning her silly, beautiful, drunken head on my shoulder, she said, "Oh, Esther, I don't want to be a feminist. I don't enjoy it. It's no fun."

"I know," I said. "I don't either." People think you *decide* to be a "radical," for God's sake, like deciding to be a librarian or a ship's chandler. You "make up your mind," you "commit yourself" (sounds like a mental hospital, doesn't it?).

I said Don't worry, we could be buried together and have engraved on our tombstone the awful truth, which some day somebody will understand:

WE WUZ PUSHED.

Many years ago, when I thought there was no future in being a woman, I awoke from a very bad dream and went into the bathroom, only to find that I had just got my period. I was living in a small New York apartment then, so there was barely room for me in the bathroom, what with the stockings hung over the railing of the bathtub and the extra towels hanging on the hooks I'd pounded into the wall myself. I stared at that haggard 2 a.m. face in the mirror and had an (imaginary) conversation with my uterus. You must imagine my uterus as being very matter-of-fact and down-to-earth and speaking with a Brooklyn accent (I grew up there).

LITTLE VOICE FROM DOWN BELOW: Look, I'm not doing anything. Whaddaya want from me anyway?

I lit a cigarette from the pack I kept on top of the toilet tank. (I used to smoke a lot in those days.)

LITTLE VOICE: If you're mucked up in the head, that's not my fault. I'm just doing the spring cleaning. You clean out the apartment once a week, right? So I'm doing it once a month. If you wanna be fertile, there's certain ways you gotta pay. It's like income tax. Don't blame me.

Silence. I smoked and brooded.

LITTLE VOICE: I want a hot water bottle.

So I got the sensible little thing its hot water bottle, and I went back to bed and fell asleep.

I accompanied Jean for days, looking sideways at her and admiring her romantic profile, her keen eyes, the large fake railroad-engineer's cap she wore in imitation of a famous French movie star in a famous French movie. I followed my shield-maiden all over campus as we rambled through libraries and gardens. I wanted to open doors for her. I do think Jean is one of the seven wonders of the world. My shrink once told me that I would stop envying and resenting men when I had made a satisfactory heterosexual adjustment, but I think he got it backwards. We had an awful fight about it. Jean and I sat in the hidden garden behind the art museum and told each other horror stories.

". . . and, as any connoisseur of the subject might imagine, a disembodied Hand came creeping round the bed-curtains like a large, uncomfortable spider. Lady Letitia screamed—"

"—and screamed—" (said I).

"—and screamed—but not very loud because I have to finish the story. The Earl, awakened by he knew not what formless bodings, stumbled out of his room and down the great staircase—"

"—but quietly, because you don't want to wake anyone else up—"

"—where he was found dead the next morning, a look of nameless terror stamped upon his perfect British features. Meanwhile, back in the pantry, a slithering, rugose tentacle investigated ranks upon ranks of jelly jars. Could the pet octopus have got loose? Alas, it seemed not likely since—"

Oh, the numbers and numbers of slithering, rugose tentacles I've met in my time! And the squamous abominations and nameless cravings from beyond the stars and accursed heaps of slime in ancient, foetid cellars, and the opened crypts lit by hellishly smoking torches whose filthy punk (that's wood, lunkhead) give out an odor of the charnel house whilst succubi vanish into mouseholes in the fourth dimension (located in old New England attics) and strange figures celebrate blasphemous rites with unspeakable howlings and shocking sacrifices to nameless eidolons of hideous basalt mounted on . . . well, on Singer sewing machines, I suppose. And my eyelids sink in a luxurious, lovely droop. Why are horrors always nameless? Does that make them worse? It certainly puts you to sleep faster. The names things do have to put up with sometimes—for instance this secret garden (hidden behind the old museum, which was some trustee's mansion in 1875) is called the Emily

M. Mapleson Planting after the lady who left it as a bequest to our institution. Poor woman! I would have called it Emily's Garden. For some reason every flower in it is white; at different times of the year different white blooms are potted in (though I've never caught anyone doing it; perhaps Ms. Mapleson endowed it with elves, too). Emily's Garden is completely hidden from the outside view by a dense stand of evergreens; inside are two stone benches, and in the middle of the flower beds a plaque with the name I've mentioned and a rather lumpish bronze faun with silly teeth. The whole thing is no more than fifteen feet across. At this time of year, in mid-August, very little is flowering; there's a lot of groundcover, small white blossoms (like Baby's-breath or Sweet William), with swaying Cosmos just inside the borders and a lot of disheveled Phlox in the middle, shedding like mad. Someone has put a few Shasta daisies (which are—or look—greenish in the shade) behind the benches. It's not yet time for the Aster family and last week's white snapdragons have failed and been taken away to mourn themselves. Late summer is a difficult time for gardens because so little happens. Jean has got to "a terrible slithering splash in the old attic" and I tell her for Heaven's sake, how can you splash in an attic?

"In the cellar," she says. "Besides, they keep an old washing machine in the attic." Helpless laughter from both of us at the idea of the Lurker from the Stars hobbling about in the family laundry. I ask her will she finish the thing off, for goodness' sake.

"All right, a great number of shots rang out and everyone dropped dead. The end," said Jean.

It was very quiet in Emily's Garden. Flowers make no noise. Beautiful little plant genitals swaying in the breeze and surrounded by vast evergreens; earlier in the year yellow hemlock pollen had drifted on to the spring flowers, the ground, the benches. Even the now-disgraced snapdragon bells made no noise. I was trying to concretize all this "blasphemous," "rugose," "nameless" stuff in the person of a clump of hysterical Phlox at my feet, each plant looking like a mad prima donna: Ophelia, perhaps, scattering used-looking white flowers in all directions. Phlox blossoms are insecurely fastened to their stems at best, so the flower-spire always gives the impression of letting its hair down. Phlossoms. The phlossoming Phlox. The phantasy of the phlooms of the Phlox.

I looked up into Jean's face, about to tell her about the Phlooms of the Phlox, but I was dazzled. Absolutely dazzled. All this happened before I had words for it, before I could even identify it; I felt the blow, the astonishment, the thing-in-itself. Something transmitted, something endured with a gasp. Unspeakable. Unnameable.

Elves got your tongue? said the swaying white Cosmos.

"'Rugose' only means 'red,'" I said to Jean.

She agreed.

It's all right as long as it's nonsense, just fantasy. I'll understand in a moment. It's ridiculous to say that I'm in love with Jean, because Jean is a woman, and besides she exasperates me too much for that. I know her far too well. It's all fantasy and admiration, just as the blooms in Emily M. Mapleson's Planting are not Lucia di Lammermoor (a heroine of the patriarchy who went mad when deprived of her lover, stabbed her husband—with the overhand, or opera grip, not the proper underhanded tennis-racket one—and died, presumably from too many high C's). How can I giggle about Lucia and yet not be able to keep my eyes off Jean? It's all right if it doesn't mean anything. The memory of seeing her breasts silhouetted beneath her blouse went through me, went right through me, with such a pang that the horizon ducked as if I'd tried to hit it—ducked like a boxer while I clung to Emily M. Mapleson's cement bench because I was falling down. There's no excuse for it. I must make my heterosexual adjustment, as Count Dracula told me when together we chased the Big O, that squamous, rugose, slithery little man with his techniques and his systems and his instructions about what "wives" do for "husbands" and what "husbands" do to "wives"—what did he think *we* were doing, running after love with a butterfly net?

It's all right if I don't mean it. If I never tell Jean. If I never tell anybody. If I do nothing.

I accepted it on those terms.

What you do sordidly, in cellars.

"What?" said Jean. It seems that I had spoken aloud. She then informed me that she had already finished that silly horror story. I decided I must babble of something so that she would think I was behaving normally, while the sun shot arrows through my bones—although I do not look like a truck driver with a ducktail haircut, do I?—while my sex radiated lust to the palms of my hands, the soles of my feet, my lips (inside), my clumsy, eager breasts, while they radiated it back to between my legs and I very obligingly thought I was going to die.

What is lust?

A permission of the will.

Jean began to talk about tenth-century Icelandic proper names—but that's all I heard, for she was walking in front of me and I watched her tapering back fit into the vase of her behind as if I'd never seen such a miracle before—which I hadn't, because I swear on my foremothers' bones that this is the first time since the age of twelve that I'd even thought of such a thing. And who doesn't, at twelve?

Count Dracula told me I was blocked. He told me I

must Try. How to Feel Lustful Against Your Will. He never told me how it goes in waves from your belly up to your chest, and then into your head, and then down again; when I felt nothing above the belly-button he seemed to think that was A-OK—the Lurker in *his* Attic was "genital insufficiency," which the ladies seemed prone to (said Count D.), the poor ladies who wanted a lot of all-over skin contact, he with his screwdriver or power-lathe approach.

"Are you sure you're all right?" said my suspicious friend, turning around and frowning with concern. "You look funny." Telepathy? Two can play at that game.

I told her I was very, very depressed. About the snapdragons.

We both screamed with laughter. I thought I could risk a look at her again, blazing with beauty with her Swedish chin and her beautiful behind, but again it happened: the pang, the blow, the astonishment.

Why, oh why didn't anyone tell me?

"Jean," I said, tottering at my own daring (but I won't tell her, oh no, not in a million years), "do you think one ought to go to bed with one's friends?" She looked at me with her wry look—beautiful, of course, for everything my friend Jean does is beautiful. And intelligent.

"With who else?" she said dryly. "One's enemies?"

I tried to be a good girl, honest I did. I looked in the mirror and told myself I was bad. (This worked at the age of five, why not now?) But the self in the mirror loved me and laughed and blew kisses. I went about, cheerfully bawling popular songs in a very graceless manner; I sang "All Of Me, Why Not Take All Of Me" and "Love Is A Many Splendored Thing." I sang a bad country-and-Western ballad with lots of twangy accompaniment between the lines, like this:

Ah hev a never-endin' luv fer yew,	(bloing, bloing)
And mah never-endin' luv is trew.	(bloing, bloing)
Ah luv yew so, whut kin ah dew?	(more bloing)
Ah hev a never-endin' luv fer yew.	(final bloing)

I'm lean, moody, prophetic. I'm aging well. (That's what the mirror tells me.) I want very much to sit in Jean's lap. Count Dracula and I have a long conversation about what is happening to me:

COUNT D: Now, Esther, let us discuss your perwersion.

ME: Sir, sirrah, ober-leutnant, sturmbannsfeuhrer, wherefore is it that you speak with a Viennese-Polish accent, whilst you are as Amurrican-born as you or I? Could it be that you have been reading too much Freud?

COUNT: No diwersionary tactics, Miss Frood. We must nip this abnormality in the bud before it flowers into something orbful. Do you realize that your present daydreams and style of life might lead to—gasp!—Lesbianism?

ME: Oh sirrah, tee hee, haw haw, you jest.

COUNT: I do not, indeed. What will you do when you are pointed at by The Phallic Phinger of Scorn? When your vile secret is exposed and your landlady throws you out of her apartment? When you lose your job? When rocks and sneers are thrown at you in the street?

ME: Who's going to tell them? You? I'll bust you in the fangs.

COUNT (complacently): Mordre wol out.

ME (mockingly): God will punish.

COUNT: But seriously, Esther, don't you realize that your sexual desire for women is merely an outpouring of your repressed and sublimated desire for Mommy? How can I stand to think of my dear little girl, who might have a repressed (and therefore normal) desire for Daddy if she so chose—missing out on all the good things of life? You too could have a baby—

ME (aside): Little does he know that I could have a baby anyway.

COUNT: You could have a home in the suburbs, a floor to wax, a dear hubby all your own, a washing machine, a ouija board—

ME (sotto voce): I think I *will* have a baby.

COUNT (unheeding): Of course I know you have an automobile already, Esther, but think what an old, cheap automobile it is. It's the wrong make. You could have a nice, new, expensive automobile if you were heterosexual, especially if you were heterosexual with the right sort of man, i.e. men who have high salaries, like stock exchange brokers. Men make so much more money than women do. Think, Esther! all this and penis, too. But you prefer squalid, inconclusive embraces in basements, disgusting scenes with big, fat, low-income women in ducktail haircuts—

ME: What's wrong with being big and fat and having a ducktail haircut? What's good for Marlon Brando is good for the nation!

COUNT: Yes, you prefer doing things like in *Esquire* or *Playboy*—only backwards—all this instead of mending your hubby's sox and seeing the love shine thru his eyes.

(He thinks for a minute. This business about *Esquire* and *Playboy* is obviously not getting to me, perhaps because it has nothing to do with me. He thinks that I think that he thinks that I think that I *really do* read girlie magazines. Then he finds it.)

COUNT: Esther, have I ever lied to you?

ME: Yes.

COUNT: Then listen to me now. Don't you realize that your desire for women is merely a repressed and sublimated desire for men? If you could get men, you wouldn't want women and we could forget all about this dreadful nonsense. You're not a real homosexual. Real homosexuals have horns. Your pseudo-homosexual desire for your friend springs from an insist complex whereby the great mother-figure stands at the doorway of your libido, making nasty, negative gestures and warning you back from the promised land of your father's womb.

ME: My father's—?

COUNT: If only you were able to realize that the penis is equivalent to the breast and the breast to the penis, you would understand that the great reality of normal sexual intercourse (which includes fellatio) lies in its ability to simultaneously allow the male to express his own maleness and the female to possess the male's maleness through her passive receptivity of his penis, thus transcending her own receptivity-oriented passivity (or passivity-oriented receptivity) and for the moment making the two one. And that one is the husband. People who suck each other off with their mouths or fingers are evading this great, primordial identity crisis (in which everybody becomes male) and remaining their sexually undifferentiated, irresponsible, pathologically pleasure-seeking selves. How do they know what kind of shampoo to use? What kind of deodorant? What color of comb? In such terrible cases a male might put on a flowered Band-aid or a female a shirt that buttons from left to right instead of from right to left. I might wake up one morning and find that my wife had bought for my birthday a belt with daisies embossed upon it. The heavens would fall!

ME: That is a better birthday present than strychnine, Count D, which otherwise your poor wife might assuredly get for you. Count D., Count D., I hereby dub thee not Count Dracula but Cunt Dracula. Come back, oh D., to the womb, come back to the head, come back to the cunt and fingers and feet which once called thee forth. You died long ago in reality; so what is not-me I hereby reject and throw out with the weekly garbage; what is me I reappropriate.

Go away.

HIS PARTING SHOT: Esther, you are *bad* (because you don't like men).

Ah! that's a weak spot. I don't. But if what I feel for Jean is a substitute, then I had better never meet the real thing because I would certainly die from it. As it is, every time I have to wipe myself after going to the bathroom I bend double. Years ago, after our group therapy time was over, we would go to a coffee shop in the east seventies of Manhattan, a district full of embassies, of private schools, of luxury high-rise apartment buildings, one of the most expensive neighborhoods in any city in the world. Here Dr. D. had his office, despite the cost (for which we middle-class white people paid, even though we loathed writing copy for catalogs or putting out industrial newsletters) so every Thursday night post-mortem we would go and have "coffee"—this means hamburgers, pastries, late dinners for some, what-have-you. I liked these gatherings. I didn't like the sessions themselves; no matter how they went I didn't want to be there. Every week the woman who was afraid of staircases came in to report that she had gone up and down two steps or she hadn't and we commended her or blamed her; every week the man whose marriage was breaking up came in and told us how he was "working at the relationship" and we said Good for you. And every week for three years a little voice inside me said *Get out of here!* although I could never explain it. I liked the people. It was like that book on the power of positive thinking: *Every day in every way I am getting better and better*. There seemed to be no way to measure anything except by the book. Sometimes people in psychoanalysis were really cured and got normal—although there was no way for them to tell when they were normal, the doctor told them, I guess—and then (presumably) you just stopped coming because you Measured Up. Nowadays "relationship" is a euphemism for fucking or having a love affair, but then it meant something different, something grim, hard, central, and unrewarding, something you had to do anyway, whether you wanted to or not. You had to *work* at it. My husband, to the intuitive marrow of his bones, knew it was bad.

"How do you know when you're happy?" I said once.

They said impatiently that they weren't talking about that and besides of course you knew. The doctor added that a bag of heroin could make you ecstatically happy, if you wanted to function at such a low level. That sounded fine to me and I thought about it quite seriously, but in the end was scared away by the law (and my own inexperience).

I liked the coffee shop; that was where we really talked.

One night a new patient showed up: a cute ugly woman with a huge hooked nose and a receding chin who knew (she said) that if she'd only been born beautiful, she wouldn't have any "problems." Beauty was what mattered in this world.

"Oh, no, it's not important," we said with one voice— imagine, we in our high heels, nylons, girdles, wigs, padded brassieres, make-up, false eyelashes, painted fingernails, tipped and permanent-waved hair, and costume jewelry!

I never came back. Oh not melodramatically, not like that, but within a few months. It was an odd kind of religious cult like the Flat Earth people or the Shakers; in a hundred years they will still be sitting around the coffee shop (it will still be 1963, it will still be the most expensive part of the world) waiting for the tooth fairy to zap down from the ceiling and endow them with the suburban substitute for bliss. Just as the suburbs are a bad imitation of the country and I and my husband were bad imitations of—well, would you believe angels? I do not mean to make light of the suffering, which was real enough and which at least brought us all face-to-face with something real, whatever it was and however frightening it might have been—but oh the muddle, the mystification, the nonsense, the earnestness, the silliness of the whole wretched business! It was without dignity, courage, or sense. It helped with some things—the gross things—if there'd been no return at all, how could the doctor have stayed in business?— but all the same it reminds me of nothing so much as Ravel's "Bolero," which is the middle-brow substitute for music, that ghastly mock-Spanish piece you hear on every Muzak-bedongled elevator; it and the elevator and the people in the elevator go round and round to infinity without ever getting anywhere, like a snake eating its own tail.

I hope somewhere they've all gotten out of 1963 and are thinking the same things about me.

I used to go home futilely to my sad, mad (but never bad) husband—who knew his own sickness too well to meddle with it—and admire his broad, knotted back, the muscles in his shoulders and arms, his lovely vulnerable belly, that pelvic crease of Greek sculpture that comes out in a man only when he stands on one leg, his funny little round-flat ass, his rubbable, bristly chin, that indescribable line from rib to hip, so subtle and so different from a woman's. Men have straight knees and elbows; women's go in. He would stand—wistful and banana-flowered—and I'd say tiredly over and over again (to an absent Dr. D.) that I had no troubles with sex, only with men, and that my trouble with men did not come from what was between their legs but from what was between their ears. My husband envied me my brain, that Bear of Little Brain. But I cannot cannot think of myself as the Nut Brown Maid or the Pretty Lady, truly I can't. And we only multiplied each other's angry clinging, he and I.

An awful thought:

What if Jean . . . won't?

I had two dreams that night and woke up scared; in one I was falling—nothing to see, just the sensation—and somebody giggled and told me, "You're in free fall." In the other I was very sick, being taken to the hospital on a stretcher and feeling so awful that I started to pray to get well, but that made me feel more helpless; so I prayed only that She might grant me endurance. That's all. "Give me my Self," I said. Then I woke up, with a sense of the dream over and (along with the fading of the dream) the sense of something being over for good. That's all the guilt I ever felt. I think I had it out somehow that night; it's like going through an electric fence where the worst point is just before you touch it and your nerves jump, but once you go through, it's O.K. I thought in my innocence: *Now I can be friends with men.*

Another marvelous discovery, in one of my waking periods at about 4 a.m., a vision of the local Howard Johnson's (east of the campus, on the superhighway) full of healthy, comely young women. *There are others besides Jean!* For the first time in my life I felt free. In fact, I felt perfectly wonderful.

So I went happily back to sleep.

Jean came over for breakfast the next day, bringing some inferior lox, which is the only kind you can get in a small town like this. We ate it and made a face. I was wildly excited. I finally got up and did an imitation of Jean's last—latest?—boyfriend who was somewhere in Canada slaving away at a doctoral thesis.

"Absent lovers are the best kind," she said.

I can't wait. Can you?

The trouble is, if I make a pass at Jean or tell her anything, she'll just push me away. It'll ruin our friendship. And suppose she tells someone? (Though I don't think she'd do that.) It would be awful to have to have such suspicions. My kitchen had never seemed friendlier. We sat and talked about one thing and another—she was telling me nasty, funny stories about her professors (my colleagues!) and I had to decide there was nothing I could tell Jean, even though I'm looking over her shoulder at her math textbook (a course she's taking just for fun). I've pulled my kitchen chair so close that I can smell her, which makes me want to cry.

I will have to keep it a secret.

Unhappy. Miserably unhappy. Why? Because people do not do things like that in reality. Reality doesn't allow it. In books or movies or maybe newspapers, yes, but real life is not like that, and in real life if I were to throw my arms around my friend and kiss her, she would only wonder at my madness; she'd say, "Esther, stop it!" very sharply, and the heavens would re-form; reality—in which, by the way, I have as considerable a stake as anyone else—would simply remain itself. If I ever try anything I will be struck dead from on high anyway. (Some of the other things real people just don't do, according to my family: get divorced, become drug addicts, murder someone, kill their children, kill themselves, expose themselves in subways, get raped, fail in business, go mad.) So I can't do it. Of course I can't.

Clumsily I put my arms around her, twice-clumsily I kissed her on the neck, saying hoarsely, "I love you." (Which was something of an oversimplification, but how are you going to explain it all?)

She went on reading.

She blushed delicately under me, like a landscape, I mean her neck, she just turned red, it was amazing.

Reality tore itself in two, from top to bottom.

"Jean," said I, not believing my ears and eyes, "do you really—" but I guess she did! because she continued to pretend to read, only reddened like a tide, a forest, an entire planet. You don't ask the whole world if it's really doing what it's doing. I felt her skin get hot under my mouth. She closed her book deliberately, turned to me, and put her arms around me. *People* get divorced, *people* kill, *people* go mad. Saying I loved her might not have been so untrue, really—well, here was something worth dying for! When I think of those times that I did it to oblige, or because it was my duty, or to get affection, or because I couldn't refuse, I am ashamed. When I say "dying for" I mean the poems and the stories, the jokes, the obsessions, the terror, the wonder. I am dreadfully ashamed of my past.

We sat back and looked at each other (frightened) at the same moment. Not because it was wrong but because it was an overcharge, like the copper wire you unwittingly overload and it's going urp! help! eek! aargh! oop! (in Wire) and you don't even know why the poor thing is jumping and twitching so. Better if calmer. Men think that once you admit your desire you have to fall down and fuck on the floor right-away, but women know better; I helped her to some inferior lox and A&P cream cheese and she did the same for me. We munched away at our bagels together. Suddenly she laughed and choked on hers.

"Shame on you," she said, "making love to someone you've known for only three years!"

I said, "Well, I can't get you pregnant, can I?" feeling very daring.

We laughed until we cried, partly out of nervousness. We were both (I think) rather wary of touching each other again. So much more is at stake now. Jean went back to explaining her book, only she reached out now and again and stroked my hand. I was blind, deaf, overwhelmed. I kept wanting to put my fingers through the central hole of the last bagel because it struck me as such an extraordinarily good joke; there was a sort of divine giggle somewhere in the room.

"You don't mind?" I cried suddenly.

She caressed my hand again. The nearest part of Jean to me (once she sat back and continued reading) was her foot, for she had crossed her legs and one foot kept advancing toward me and then retreating. Now feet are not as compromising as hands and not so close to the person, so I grasped Jean's individual, very expressive foot and admired her arch, which is so much higher than mine. I was terrified. (She looked pleased and a little embarrassed.) I explained about feet and that I was not a foot-fetishist, really, but hands were too vivid for me right then, so she let me hold on to her ankle; I kept imagining that she would change her mind at any moment, that she was merely being charitable, that she was intimidated, that she'd "mind."

I know too well what can really be going on when women are silent.

We talked about how everybody was bisexual, and how this was only the natural result of a friendship, and how we had better take our time, and then—like virgins—began to whisper, "When did you first—?" and "When did you—?" "I knew instantly by the way you looked at me," she said, and I turned red from head to foot at the thought of being so transparent, in veils and waves of heat.

Jean "screwed" the last bagel with her forefinger, looking very severe and haughty.

I gingerly picked up the ends of her dark hair, where they lay on her shoulder. It was like picking up something living, with nerves in it, and it used to annoy me when men told me I should grow my hair. Though I would never tell anyone what to do.

"I have to go," she said.

Relief.

"My job," she said. "You know." (She has a part-time job at the university library, checking out books or something.)

"You won't—" I said.

"I'll tell *everyone*," said my friend, making a face, and I was really ashamed. I knew and she knew—and she knew that I knew—that really it was too much and we'd better both recover a little. Better to be calmer. She said she would come that night—no, tomorrow night, but tonight come down to the co-op and help bake a cake if I wanted—she would turn up tomorrow night with some pot.

"It hurts my tonsils," I said. (But the idea was to keep from getting scared or anxious.) "Poor little thing," she said, and then bent down and kissed me on the mouth for a few seconds. Oh dear. They never tell you your clitoris is connected right to your stomach. I was terribly frightened that sex would be just as bad with her as it had always been with a man but at the same time I didn't care because it was such a glorious opportunity to fail, you see. I didn't really care. (I think I had better stop saying "really.") But if it turned out badly, what would I do then? I kissed her back on her velvety cheek.

Women's faces are covered with fine, almost invisible down. I said to myself that whatever happened, we'd still be friends, but I knew that was the talk of a fool; I didn't want to be friends. I didn't actually know what I wanted, being too much involved in her individual odor, and the smoothness of her skin, and her heavy, utterly lovely behind, to care about what had not yet happened. I kissed Jean on the cheek and said a trembly goodbye.

And staggered to the bedroom, kicked off my shoes mechanically, sat down on the bed. Pulled the curtains to, pulled down my pants, reached in the bottom drawer of the bureau for the vibrator.

A little voice cried, *You'll wear yourself out!*

But ah, that was impossible.

I didn't go to the co-op that night because my soul was already in too many pieces. Spent that day and the next wandering around: gardens, swine pens, the lamb barns with the lambies and their mommas (I was sobbing a little at everything because it was all so sweet). Just up and down the usual goldgreen lawns and under the lovely trees with their dark-goldgreen shadows, and some day we will all go to the great Multiversity in the sky. Beamed at all the men in the street. By 6 p.m. was convinced she wouldn't come, but every time I heard footsteps on the stairs I jumped. Something about keeping windows open (in the summertime) makes electric light very bright indoors. When she did come I was in the living room dusting the tables and didn't even hear her knock until she repeated it (Jean almost beats doors down). I had the weirdest fancy that Rose (you remember Rose; she's buried way back on page 1) was sitting in the shadows outside the lit circle of the living-room lamp. I walked from the dark room into the lit one, a progress to which all creation moves, one of those moments in which the shape of your house or your life takes on all the meaning in the world. I opened the door with no nerves at all, and Jean waved a bottle of wine at me. She's old-fashioned, she's decided, and doesn't like pot. It felt like any other visit. What's the etiquette for this sort of thing? I haven't tried to get drunk for love-making in years, but this is going right back to adolescence, so we solemnly took two glasses of medicine (feh) and then I ruined it by remembering a pound of ice cream I had in the freezer, which of course we had to share, more or less.

"I can't make love; I'm too full," said she.

I stroked her hand, then her arm. I put my arm around her and kissed her on the cheek.

"Do you want to?" I said. She nodded. We went into the living room and carefully pulled the curtains shut, then dragged a quilt from the bedroom. There isn't enough room on a single bed; besides, I like to feel that my whole house is my home. We put the wine on the floor near the quilt and lay on our stomachs, fully clothed. There is this impalpable barrier between every-day life and sex, perhaps to be connected up with that lack of etiquette I spoke of before; anyway there's some sort of gap you have to jump with your eyes shut, holding your nose (so to speak) as if you were jumping into water. I remembered, with fear of exactly what, I can't specify—that Jean is, after all, twelve years younger than me. Before we brought in the quilt I had trotted into the bedroom and brought out my vibrator, hiding it shyly between the couch cushions because it is really a gross little object, about eight inches long, made of white plastic and shaped like a spaceship. Contrary to popular belief, most women use vibrators on their outsides, not their insides. Unfortunately the batteries are wearing out and instead of going bzzzz it just rattles—the truth is I'm afraid Jean will find it repulsive or possibly that she will find me repulsive. She's down to her slip by now. I've always assumed I was reasonably good-looking—to men—but why should a woman have the same standards? Jean has finally taken off her clothes and so have I; to me she looks beautiful but very oddly shaped; I suppose there's the unconscious conviction that one of us has to be a man and it certainly isn't me. Jean says she wants to put a record on the hi-fi but I don't because it's too distracting. So she bursts into angry tears. I put my arms around her and rock her back and forth, which kept me from looking at her, so although she might have still looked odd (it was wearing off) she felt beautiful. Who doesn't look odd? Men look odd. God looks odd. We smooched a little, then put a record on the player (I don't remember what. Baroque?); then lay down and necked a little more, less timidly. I love Jean. She's a vast amount of pinkness—fields and forests—but with my eyes closed it feels more to scale and it's nice. The way you measure the genuineness and goodness of an experience is this: what does it do to reading an ordinary magazine? If *Life* looks inexplicably silly to you, then life is doing its stuff. This is what I use myself and I recommend it (undoubtedly there are other tests). My friend is snowfields and mountains. Another world. Her odor (everyone has a particular, own smell) is a complicated key, one among millions. I don't understand her. For example, I don't know why she's still upset now—so I said, "Oh, phooey, turn over and I'll give you a back rub." Phooeys we doubt ever got phooeyed. She lay mistrustfully on her stomach and I knelt between her legs, gaily pounding away at her shoulder blades, very professional though I don't know a massage from a message. So soft, so soft. Back rubs are sneaky, low-level trickery because there's something in our mammalian ancestry that signals Good good good when your back is rubbed and you wouldn't dream of not being trustful (like scratching a dog's ear or rubbing under a cat's chin). It's taking advantage. After I had busily kneaded her shoulders for a while, I sneaked down to the small of her back and started kissing her neck; she said, "This isn't fun for you, Esther, is it?"

"Oh no, not a bit," I lied. And slid down to the rose between her legs. That's exactly what it is. Amazing. (Medieval stories.) I have the advantage of knowing where everything is and more or less how to do it. And feeling the strangest sympathetic pangs. Besides, you cannot bite men's backsides because they haven't any. Jean began to breathe hard, which made me want to cry; I kissed her on the neck where I know that sensitive place. To be the cause of so much pleasure to someone else!—as the book says, *to make a difference.* I knew that when Jean came, I would burst into tears.

"No—wait a minute—stop!" she said, rolling on her side and angrily pushing me away. She's very fair-skinned. From neck to groin my friend was covered with pale-red spots like an interesting variety of measles; I had never seen what the book calls "the sex rash" before. You know, just before climax. Utterly fascinating. You can only see it on very fair-skinned women and Jean is the eighteenth-century Irish ideal: dead-white skin, blue eyes, black hair. "Stop," she said. "I can't feel anything," she said. Wild roses and milk. The first time I came with a man (fooled you, didn't I? I bet you thought I never came with a man) I shouted "I can't! I can't get there, God damn it!" and proceeded to go into internal waves that surprised me because I thought you lost your mind when you did it. And there I was, thinking away as usual.

"Oh, Jean!" I said. She stalked angrily into the kitchen—to the window that was hidden (thank Heaven) by the branch of a tree—she drank a glass of water and came back into the living room. For those of you I am confusing by the "internal" in "internal waves" (above) I will tell you my own, recently-developed theory of sexuality, proven by years of experimental masturbating: i.e. you feel your climax most whenever you are being most stimulated. This opens surprising fields of research to those of us with suckling infants or three hands or other situations like that. Honest.

"I guess I can't," said Jean. "Or I don't want to. I mean I do want to but I suppose I can't—can I—if I'm behaving like this."

"If you don't want one, I don't want one," said I promptly. I thought, *Behave any way you like. Stand on your head. Keep your clothes on. Make it with the electric toaster.* If I had to choose between always pleasing her but never myself and always pleasing myself but never her—well, I'd choose the former. At least for a while. I can always please myself afterwards. An orgasm is an orgasm, but how often is there a Jean?

"Never mind," she mumbled. "I never come with anyone."

Now this is really surprising, considering how many men she's been with. I suppose this is the time to whip out the vibrator and attack her with it, but somehow I have doubts about the whole proceeding. I think we began this wrong.

I tell her so. There should be no failure and no success.

Blushing very deeply, she asked me if she could do something. I said yes, of course. She averted her face and moved my hand on to her rose (sorry to be so kvetchily sentimental).

"Let me—ah—um—do it myself."

"Oh my goodness yes, is *that* all!" I cried. Trying to memorize the motion, an odd sort of diagonal one. Jean seems to like things done lightly.

She came in the usual way about three minutes later, not very satisfactorily, it seemed to me. She said I couldn't put my mouth down there because she hadn't had a bath for days. I said that sounded reasonable to me, although we might be wrong. She said her wrist hurt, and rubbed it. Then I lay down and Jean gave *me* a back rub and I was hung up on the edge of it forever. Finally, with not much satisfaction, I flipped over.

"That was awful!" said Jean, sitting up, tears in her eyes.

"Well," said I reasonably, "you know what they say in Swedish movies about the first time."

"What do they say in Swedish movies?" (rather sharply)

"Oh, dear, I don't know."

We sat for a while, had a glass of wine, and then began to cuddle. The formalities were over. (Thank goodness.) She kissed me and whispered to me that I was beautiful. I blew in her ears. I fulfilled a daydream of twenty years' standing and nibbled along her hairline, under her temples and around her ears. We lay on the quilt and got mildly potted, feeling—as is usual, I think, with people who take off their clothes—that nudity is the only pleasant state. The living room was a garden. We locked big toes and had a toe fight, then began to throw couch pillows at each other, but stopped guiltily when we knocked over my floor lamp.

"My big toes are bigger than your big toes!" hissed Jean, raking her toenails up and down my back.

"Ooooo!" I said. "Oo, I like that."

"She likes that muchly," said Jean.

Now what is the trouble? That sex doesn't commit you to anything, in spite of our tradition about it? That love doesn't give you a code of behavior? I think so. She could go away now and never come back. I saw already

JOANNA RUSS

what the pattern of my love affair would be—worrying each time she was away, relieved each time she came back—or does that mean that Jean and I don't really love each other? Anyway, it's awful.

Jean got up and said Oh feh, she had to go. She put on her clothes regretfully and I put on mine; we rooted in the ice cream container for the rest of the ice cream (Hail, Hearth and Home! Hail, O Great Food Goddess!). Then Jean went to the door. We said in unison:

"When will I see you again?"

A great relief, after years of being the only one to say it! I can't come to see her because of the co-op gang and Stupid Philpotts (though we could tie him to a peg on the back lawn if we had to) but there wouldn't be enough privacy in the co-op, though Jean has brought men there many times before. There's a difference. She kissed me on the edge of the chin and I watched her as she went downstairs, swaying like a snake standing on its tail. The Snake of Wisdom? Something embodied. Jean will surprise me some day and perhaps not nicely; there's the chill of finding out that I didn't know her as well as I thought, that there's something in her sexuality, even, that I didn't know about. Though I like it that she never came with a man, I love it that she came with me, however awkwardly, and I will love it no matter what she uses: my hand, her own hand, my glass paperweight with the private snowstorm over the New England Church (with the spire, kiddies). As the real Jean waned, the mythical part of Jean came back into my kitchen, flooding the waxed floor and the refrigerator and the little study I'd fixed up in the kitchen around the corner of the L; I tasted Jean, saw Jean, thought Jean, breathed Jean. The Jean I can keep in my head.

Bonny, bonny Jean.

George Eliot never ended her books properly. There's so little for heroines to do; they can fall in love, they can die. As the story begins, you wonder whether the heroine will be happy, but by the middle of it you're beginning to wonder if she will be good. Such is George Eliot's sleight-of-hand, i.e. cheating. We still think this way a hundred years later. I've been reading wretched-housewife novels written by women and they all end the same way; either the awful husband has a mysterious change of heart (offstage) on the last page but one or the wife thinks: Yes, but I really loved him so it was all right. You would not believe the suffering and wretchedness in these books. (And one of the characters is called Sophia, too, which means Wisdom.) I spent two Jean-less days reading these books and making marginal notes for some article or other I was going to do next winter if I ever got around to it, and then, like the heroines of these stories, I had a great "realization," a pious illumination (they're always having these, like their children really love them or they adore housework or they are really happy even though their husband ties them to a newel post and beats them with a goldfish). Progressing by a series of flat denials of the evidence. My pious illumination was that I did not want to do the article. But everything in print is sacred, as we all know, including this sentence. All words are sacred. (Unless written by a computer, in which case the *computer* is sacred.) Some astonishing things are sacred, really; thus we have the Pain Goddess and the Sleeping-late-in-the-morning Goddess, the Trip Troll (who makes the transmission fall out of your car fifteen miles from your destination), and the Mayonnaise Deity, who presides over gourmet cooking. Love is like sleeping late in the morning; you dive down through layer after transparent layer, utterly content, farther and farther until you reach the sea floor. But it's bottomless.

Waiting for Jean is pleasant: one anticipates her arrival.

Waiting for Jean is useful: perceptions are sharpened.

Waiting for Jean is educational: it teaches you that even good things must be waited for.

Waiting for Jean is fortunate: that she will come at all makes you feel blessed.

Waiting for Jean is exasperating: I can't wait much longer.

On the superhighway at night, doing sixty-five in my old rattletrap; the wet, cloverleaf roads twist and turn under the city lights like shining black snakes. It's just rained: brilliance and darkness. I'm coming home from the art museum in a town sixty miles away.

The world belongs to me. I have a right to be here.

Two days later, by mutual agreement, Jean came "just to visit." She came trotting up my stairs—or rather, dragging behind her the stately hem of a long, mauve-paisley dress. She always puts on long skirts and her shades when she wants to go in disguise. I sat with my feet curled under me, timid as a mouse, on my corner of the couch (where I was prepared to sit until Doomsday, if necessary) while Jean retailed gossip. Her gossip has one extraordinarily redeeming feature: she makes it all up. None of it is ever true. In the middle of an impossible detail about something the Dean's wife had said to the salesgirl, she looked at me long and hard and then narrowed her eyes, for I had cleverly drawn the curtains *before* she came. Just in case.

Then she took off her sunglasses and smiled at me, so that tears rose to my eyes. She unhooked her dress (homemade so no zipper) and let it drop to the floor, then with crossed arms shucked her slip and did a little victorious dance around the room, waving the slip in the air. We took off all our clothes, very soberly, and then had a cup of tea, sitting politely on the couch, naked; I went into the kitchen to fetch it in my bathrobe. We looked each other over and I showed Jean the mole on my hip; so she lifted her hair and showed me the freckles on the back of her neck. We compared our "figures" like little girls. We sat on the two ends of the couch, our knees up, feet to feet, and talked about the ecstasies and horrors of growing breasts at twelve, of bouncing when you ran, of having hairy legs, of being too tall, too short, too fat, too thin. There is this business where you think people end at the neck; then gradually as you talk, as we talked, as we reconstituted ourselves in our own eyes—how well we became our bodies! how we moved out into them. I understood that she felt her own ribs rise and fall with her breathing, that her abdomen went all the way into her head, that when she sat, she felt it, I mean she felt it in herself, just as I did. Until she looked—as she had felt to me before—all of one piece. Why is it impossible to talk about women without making puns? When you fuck someone, you are fucking with their eyes, too, with their hair, with their temples, their minds, their fingers' ends. (If we didn't wear clothes all the time we'd see personality all over, not just the face.) We sat side by side, holding hands and quite naked; then Jean put her arms around me and it felt so good that it made me stammer. Such astonishing softness and everything shaped just right, as if thirty years ago we had been interrupted and were only now resuming. I'd been worried, but it turns out to fit some exact shape in your head that you never knew you had, fits it with the perfection of a Swiss watch. As close as we blurry human beings can ever come to instinct. I had been worried about Jean, as I said, but now I didn't care, although I think she disliked the awkwardness of having to break apart in order to get up and go into the bedroom. I stroked her back to let her know I would do anything for her, set fire to the rug if she wanted, lean out the window in my skeleton, make a gift to her of all my insides, my pulsations, the electricity in my hair, the marrow of my bones. That's what they mean when they say your bowels yearn; something tries to move out through your skin. We lay down on the bed in each other's embrace but didn't do much; only I tried to explain how lovely it was for her to have long hair. She stopped me. "I don't mean to be sexist about it," I said; "It's just fortunate." It came to me as an inspiration, an astonishingly fine and surprising idea, that we should fuck each other now, for the excitement (although spread all over) did seem to be centering in one particular place and I was so beside myself with aching that I thought she must be too. And I must say the only disadvantage to its being Jean was that there weren't more arms. Anyway at the end you don't care if you are fucking a rhinoceros; you just want to go on and do it. She half did it and I half did it, moving against her hand, and because Jean knows what a woman feels she didn't stop at that moment but a little after, as soon as I had stopped. Then she said, "Hey, I took a bath this time," so I slid down and very cleverly (I read this in a book) sucked at her, this being something I would never think up all by myself because you can't very well practice on yourself, now can you? And we tried a little of this and a little of that, Jean being as inexperienced this way as myself, until we ended sitting up in bed with Jean in front of me, my left arm around her waist and my right hand between her legs, a very beautiful, statuesque pose. I think the other takes practice. She came once a little bit but told me to keep on, which I did; she came again, awesomely.

Like someone who's speaking in tongues, crying out, seeing visions.

"I'm noisy," she said. "I'm sluttish."

"Oh, do it again," I cried admiringly, "do it again!"

"Don't want to," said Jean.

"I hope I feel like an armchair," I said. I think what I always missed about men was breasts. Jean's are the usual shape—don't laugh, I mean they're not conical, the way some of us are—round enough, small enough; pulled down by gravity to be fuller underneath. She has one oddity; light circlets of hairs round her aureoles. Dreadfully sexy. How odd, to carry these empty milk cartons in front of us for sixty years, whether we use them or not. I think my own body has imperceptibly got to be some kind of standard for me; yet it was fascinating to see her so different. Not a line of her was imperfect. My bowels yearned with gratitude because I wanted to give her something, not for any reason, but for my own relief, for something that wanted to transfer itself out of me. My true love hath my heart and I have hers. Nothing I can name. This may simply have been a second grand idea that we should do it again, but at this point Jean got up and went into the bathroom in my sleazy pink rayon kimono (this is not my bathrobe because I own both).

"Madama Butterfly," I said.

When she came back, she sat down on the bed and started putting on her shoes. I said, "You're not going!"

She gave me a look which I recognized, having once been on the other side of the fence myself.

"I'm not?"

"Oh, of course you are," I said, "but please, please, don't. Please stay."

"I want to think about it," said my friend. She began to put on her underwear. This is the part of the movie or TV special where he speaks to her authoritatively and she obeys, or he tells her how she's got to be honest, so she bursts into tears and reveals her problem, which he then solves. But you and I know better; I'm not going to give Jean an excuse to pick a quarrel with me. And I didn't even try to look forlorn and waif-like; I was much too happy. And I could think of nothing except her. I begged her to wait until I had dressed so I could accompany her to the door, so she did. And I did. We both got decent. Standing at the door with no premonitions, waving goodbye as if we'd been having a late tea, with our clothes on all the time, quite respectably, in as false a position as possible. I saw her descend the stairs, me shutting my own door before she reached the bottom and went into the street. There would be something too final about the other way. I sat at the kitchen table, not to think (there was nothing to think about) but only to feel her all over my skin, to wonder what had gone wrong, how long it would take to set right. Twenty minutes later the phone rang.

"Hello?" I said, wondering who on earth could be calling now.

"Jean here," said she (a habit she'd picked up on a visit to England two summers before. Jean is a sponge to other people's mannerisms).

"Oh, *Jean!*" said I, pleased.

"I forgot to say goodbye."

"You what?" I said.

"Goodbye," she said distinctly.

And she hung up.

I let a day go by. I didn't do anything because I knew what would happen if I did. It came—I called the cooperative and they said she'd left the day before with all her possessions. Her family didn't know where she was. I said, "You don't *know*?" over the telephone, trying to make them feel as guilty as possible. That's it. This is the painful part. I'm subject to thinking that I've invented things, so for a while the thought kept coming back to me that I'd invented the whole love affair, though that isn't possible, and then the idea that unrequited love is ghastly because it turns into a cult or phantasmagoria, something poisonous, too private a puppet show to exist. I wanted to call the family and tell them I was her wife (or husband) but I didn't think they'd enjoy that. Then I called the co-op again and got the same message—they very obligingly provided me with a second person to talk to, so nobody knew I had called twice. Like calling the weather on the telephone. Nothing but machines left between people. Telephones, taxis, letters, the discarded automata of the modern love affair. I thought perhaps I'd made the whole thing up. This is an awful despair. After the first shock you think, "Well, *that's* over," but what do you do then? The news that kills is the news that makes everything else impossible; you can't sleep or go out or read or watch TV because you can no longer enjoy anything; I had never before realized what a substratum of pure pleasure there is in just going to sleep, for instance. Just eating. All spoiled now.

And I can't tell anyone. I can never tell anyone.

I decided to take a walk, thinking that perhaps I might meet Jean, but I faltered at the bottom of the stairs. Stood for a while on the last step. What a push it takes to get out of the house! Having only imagined it would be—somehow—worse than anything—better to be unhappy—so I forced myself out into a world where everything was lovely (there was a full moon) like a Jean who said "I didn't really mean it, you know" from every black bush, from every gilded housefront. It was a beautiful and horrible sight. I thought of going back to my apartment and writing to Sally and Louise, but they weren't friends. I didn't know them well enough. Besides, what could I ask from them? If I went to visit friends (and I do have other friends) I would have to tell them I'd had a love affair with a man who'd fucked and run; then they'd say, "Oh well, men do that," and I'd say it wasn't like that, we were old friends; so they'd say "Why did he leave?" Because he was a homosexual? Then (they'd say) I was well rid of him and if I kept on grieving I was a fool. There's no equivalent and I can't tell the truth. With each step it got worse, as if I were walking through molasses, my nerves all exposed, what will I do if I meet anyone? (Spies.) So I went back home, hastening all the way. Though I have no home, really. And remembered my past "depressions" when I'd thrown a screen out the window in the powerful, vague fear that otherwise it would be me. All long, long ago, sadly. The rule now is for the wounded to recite, like Scarlett, oh tomorrow will be another day. I can't get back to my old symbolic craziness. I wished for Count Draculule, but he's dead; all my imaginary monsters are dead. It occurred to me that if Jean had called while I was out, I wouldn't have been able to hear the phone ring, so I ran the last block and up the stairs.

It was quiet. Everything was exactly the same. Everything was just as I had left it: the gleaming refrigerator, the red-and-blue curtains, vinyl table, cupboards, white sink. I thought it would have changed somehow. Oh, the dreariness of that place! I tried to persuade myself that there was still some enjoyment to be got out of it, but it looked dreadful. Nothing there. Nothing elsewhere; my other rooms were equally intolerable. Ditto the outside. People always tell you you'll get over things (and they're right) but what do you do while you're getting over it? The old joke: your wife is buried, you weep on her grave, your friends tell you in a year you'll forget it, you'll go out, meet someone else, get married again. "But what'll

I do *tonight*?" I first heard this told about an Italian and it was supposed to show how sex-crazy Italians were (I think), Italian men anyhow, but you know what I mean. In graduate school I'd envied the cats who came into my back yard and rubbed their fat, whiskery faces on the stems of the lilac bush. They had it easy. I lay down on the couch because it hurts less in the horizontal (the old lesson of a seasoned veteran of grief) and I thought I would begin a letter to Sally—no, Louise; Louise looked kinder. But what can you say except "Help me?" They won't fly up here to be my lover. I could be cunning and tell them Mommy and Daddy never loved me. Mummy loved me but she died (weak giggle). I got up to write some sort of letter to them, but realized I hadn't any idea how to begin. Jesus, I didn't want to write anybody. I wanted to feel better is all. Once years and years ago I tried getting drunk when I was miserable; I only became drunk and miserable. What is so astonishing is to realize that not only the people who love you but also husbands and wives, I mean people bound together by a legal tie as real and impersonal as the one that keeps me in classes and pays my salary every month, even these people can just disappear like soap bubbles. And do. But my money will keep coming in every month. That's why money is more reliable than love—people become misers this way. I thought of my work and therefore, grief-drunk, sat down to work; I dusted books and looked through some magazine articles I'd kept to throw away duplicates. I couldn't do anything less routine than that. There's always work to do. Jean called work a blessing.

I sat down at the kitchen table, leaned my face and arms on the cold plastic tablecloth (but it's pretty, it is, it's an unusual deep, pleasant red) and began to weep. No more can I sing: I love my kitchen, my kitchen loves me. There's nothing so awful as being (coming) alive.

They call this mourning, that is: grief work.

George Eliot depicts suffering very well: her heroines just sit in a room and hurt. They don't have the money to do anything else. In lousy novels heroines with broken hearts plunge into "a mad round of dissipation" about which I have only one question, i.e. where do you find it. One academic party A.J. (After Jean) and I was out the door after ten minutes with "a bad headache." You can drive around a lot but a beat-up old station wagon is no Duesenberg (*The Green Hat* 1920s). Ah! they smoke cigarettes, too, in those books. I called writer friends in Watertown, NY, in whose house I've always felt at home, and asked for permission to visit them; I was going to stop over in New York City.

Fine, they said.

My New York friend—only one of them but the one to the purpose, for I wasn't going to see any of those people left over from college, i.e. the amateur Thespian who'd married and moved into the suburbs and who did nothing now but pick up after an immensely destructive two-year-old, or the thirty-year-old insecure spinster who worked for an opera magazine and thought marriage would solve everything, or the Phi Beta Kappa poet who works at a secretarial job, getting drunk on week-ends and wishing she were back at school— as I said, my real, live friend is a gay man a few years older than me. We met after a ballet matinée which I had sat through in such complete, implacable, hostile silence that I had caused several of the people around me to become acutely nervous, at least I certainly hope so. High art doesn't neutralize misery, far from it. And ballet combines obsessively romantic, heterosexual love stories with athletics and you-know-what. (Rose and I after *Swan Lake*, crying into our coffee.) It's ridiculous. I met Stevie at an expensive chain restaurant place on West Eighth that serves nothing but French crêpes; you know, fake wooden beams, fancy Breton costumes on the waitresses, the menu hand-calligraphed in two languages, and right out in the middle of the room (where you could watch the crêpes being made) a large griddle with the fake ménagère of this fake tavern and vats of the stuff they put into their pancakes: spinach, cheese, ham, chestnuts, whipped cream, jam, all that. It's not bad food, really. I was in love with Stevie years and years ago, when I was twenty-one and believed that dreams came true. Thinking of those days—there was my old friend Rose (remember her?), there were splendid pink sunsets in midwinter when I was coming to group therapy, or summer evenings with the dirty air turning a delicate rose and blue and the trees on Park Avenue (almost dead of the dust) smelling fresh, but only when you were very close to them.

Stevie's a good friend now: willful, tense, hardworking, good to lots of people, extraordinarily well informed and well read. He could no more live where I do than a fish could migrate to Death Valley. I saw him before he saw me, and waved; catching sight of me, he patted the place setting opposite him, meaning of course that I should approach and sit down. He beamed at me. He was wearing one of those dreadfully recherché things he loves; this time it was a rhinestone pin in the shape of a pair of kissing lips. Stuck on a fishnet shirt. Which, with leather shorts and sandals, and a Viking beard, gives you some idea why Stevie would be stoned to death in (say) Watertown, NY. I sat down and we made nice and kissed each other and exclaimed a lot, and asked about everybody's friends and relations, like the people in *Pooh*. I complimented him on his beard, which had squared off since the last time I'd seen him. I had suddenly and very intensely the feeling that Stevie is smarter than I, braver, stronger, better, more knowing; I admired him and feared him.

I was going to tell him about Jean.

He ordered spinach-and-cheese. I got greedy and ordered chestnuts and whipped cream.

"Well, love, how's the world been treating you?" he said.

I got shy. I described in melodramatic detail the head-aches of marking papers, summer cleaning, getting the car fixed, my academic-ugly neighbors.

"Ah, you're a New Yorker at heart," he said.

I told him it wasn't so bad being away if you stayed glued to the TV. We both snickered. I told him my survivor's instincts had become atrophied after such a long time away; I wouldn't be able to function any more. He laughed and shook his head. Then I began hesitantly to tell him that I'd had a bad love affair, using phrases like "the person" or "the other person." It occurred to me that I could even use Jean's real name because people would confuse it with Gene, a man's name.

Finally he said, "Darling Esther, this fellow is *no good.*" He had rested his chin in his hands, listening intently.

"He's not a fellow," I said, confused. "He's my best friend."

He tsked and demurred. He smiled and a wry look came into his face. "Would *I* like him?" he said. We'd had a running joke for years about the similarities of our taste in men. I looked down. Red-alerts everywhere. Don't say it; he won't like it. But why not?

"It's a woman," I said.

Stevie said nothing. I guess he's thunderstruck. Surprised, anyway. Despite (or because of) the china collection, his affectation of hating politics, his desire to be a nineteenth-century Russian aristocrat, the rhine-stone pins, etc., Stevie is a very good-looking man, and sitting here, trying to cover my embarrassment or my stiffness at his embarrassment or his embarrassment—I feel an eerie return of that love of ten years ago. How I had liked him! (I like him still.) I wanted him because he was unattainable—that was the official version. No. I liked him because he was on my side.

He looked up, his face closed. He said:

"When one gets to a certain age, there's the desire to experiment. You know, to try everything." A year ago I would have agreed.

"No," I said.

Opportunely, the food came.

It was disapproval; it was also a kind of shrinking. Perhaps he wants straight friends. I don't know. When I first met him I was shy, amazed, and very put off, but Stevie doesn't mind middle-class people who are put off; he thrives on it; I've seen him handle roomfuls of middle-class people who disapprove of him and do it so well that everybody went away glowing with conscious virtue. But now I've done something wrong.

We ate silently.

Then he said, rather affected all of a sudden, for Stevie can turn himself inside out like a glove:

"Dear me, this *is* a surprise!"

I began to explain that I had tried to be good but I just couldn't take men any more. Straight men, that is. He said, making a face:

"Oh, I see. Lady's lib."

Now I've asked him before not to call it that. This is Stevie's malicious side: get-away-from-me-or-I'll-scratch. The next step is for me to remember that he's suffered worse than I, that he has been—or could be—beaten up in public, that he could be killed, that nothing I've gone through can hold a candle to what he has. Things always go well after this stage.

"Don't use that word," I said. "It's belittling."

His eyes narrowed. He's going to drawl. He put his chin in his hands, and leaning his elbows on the fake fancy oak of the restaurant table, said deliberately:

"Little Esther's going in for the militant marching

and chowder society. You're losing your sense of humor, dear."

I stared.

He said, "You're not gay. You're just being programmatic. For Lady's Lib."

"Women are oppressed," said I suddenly. (What can one say?)

"Oppressed!" cried this sudden stranger in a cracked voice. "You don't know what the word means, darling! Oppression in your happy, sheltered little life?"

He said I was a parasitic, self-indulgent, petty, stupid, bourgeois *woman*.

He said I should try being beaten up by the police.

"Breeders!" he muttered, the color coming back into his face. Breeders is Stevie's term of contempt for the straights.

I told him—but I didn't. I said, "Oh, never mind." The restaurant cuckoo clock struck five. A Bavarian cuckoo clock of carved wood, the wrong thing in the wrong place.

The whole quarrel had taken three and a half minutes.

I left my food—and with wonderful, unconscious cunning, also the check—and hailed a taxi. Leaning my head out the window to refresh myself with the gasoline fumes. Getting my breeder's body sick. I know I can't tell my writer friends about Jean but I'll tell them about feminism because that cuts across everything. When I was seven years old I had a best friend called Yolanda who was Black; I didn't know what being Black meant and I certainly didn't know what being a homosexual meant, but I jolly well knew what being a girl meant. In a then-current Fred Astaire movie called "Yolanda and the Thief," the thief (who was probably Fred Astaire, thinking back on it) danced over the skyline of New York while Yolanda watched him. When Yolanda and I grew up (we planned it that way) we would do the movie over again, only this time it would be Yolanda and me dancing over the tall buildings. Yolanda not only had a wonderful name, she was very independent; she got a quarter from her father every week for mopping the bathroom floor. I tried that but my parents wouldn't let me. They preferred to give me things.

I—the old me who's just got Stevie so mad at her— began to cry in the taxi. It's all such a tiresome puddle of failure. There's this horrible insistence (just as if somebody were riding in the cab next to me and nagging me) that I ought to understand Stevie, that I ought to make allowances, that I've behaved badly, that I'm selfish. I thought of asking the cab driver to take me to a gay bar, but was interfered with by a memory from a book: woman asks cabbie to take her "where women go." He says "Right, lady," and lets her off at the YWCA. Years ago a painter friend of mine was stopped on Eighth Street by a small, dark foreign man with a monobrow who hissed at him from behind one hand, "Where are the secret places?" My friend, of course, did not know. As he said: If you can't make it with the people you know—

Then what?

Anyway it's got nothing to do with me; I'm not a Lesbian. Lesbians. Lez-bee-yuns. Les beans. Les human-beans?

I'm a Jean-ist.

A nasty little tune I couldn't place followed me into the cab, to my hotel, through the Metropolitan Museum the next day, out to the airport, like a snail leaving disgusting little tracks on the European paintings, the Middle Eastern carpets, the fancy airport luncheon, the jets taking off, everything I am supposed to enjoy. It was about somebody looking for a job in the last century and never getting one because (here the refrain would come in):

> I asked the reason why.
> He said, Now don't you see that sign?
> *No Irish need apply*.

Though it was about a man looking for a job, not a woman. Always a man.

Pain is boring. That's the worst of it. I cried so much in those two days that I had to put on dark glasses in self-defense. I won't bother you with the details: the sobbing in the public restroom, the haughty, injured look you put on to conceal the fact that you've been crying. I flew up to—sounds very sophisticated, doesn't it?—but my plane was a tiny one of a line I won't mention, a sort of flying Toonerville Trolley that carries baby chicks and live lobsters as often as people (and airmail) and sits out on the field as if in flat denial of the laws of aerodynamics: You mean I'm going to fly in *that*? Half the stops are made in ports that don't have central towers or ground-to-air radio; you just come in for a good look and take the chance that nobody else wants to land on the same patch of grass. I found myself next to a little old Italian lady who was carrying vast quantities of bundles: bread, salami, cheese, wool, sausages, sweaters, God knows what. It seems this was stuff her relatives had given her. She explained in bad English that she'd come in on the morning plane and was going back on the afternoon one. We spread her bundles on the seats behind us (Toonerville is never full) and then I hid behind a book. The affront of all that upstate New York scenery—blue sky, white clouds, mountain-colored mountains (as the Chinese say). Promises, promises. A young unmarried couple (no ring) across the aisle was reading a copy of

Life magazine, sort of leafing through it and looking at the pictures. They were working-class Appalachia, I suspect, covering bad nutrition and lack of means with lots of make-up in her case and lots of self-assertiveness in his. She wore a beehive hairdo and sneakers with her pink dress, he, some sort of sleazy, green rayon suit. She looked around the plane slowly and wonderingly (it was almost empty except for us and a family in back), apparently rather bored, and said:

"I bet this next election will be different because—" (here she named a current government scandal).

"No it won't," he said. "Why should it? It won't be. That's full of crap." And he went back to reading. She looked around again, a little desperately—it's not boredom, just the last-ditch, lip-wetting, oh what shall I do now. They leafed through the pictures.

"Oh hey," she said, "look at that. Isn't that weird? It says we're all descended from fish. Just imagine, a million years ago your great-great-great-grandaddy was a fish." I thought this rather imaginative. He twitched the magazine page out of her fingers, saying sharply:

"Jesus, you'd believe anything."

Again the glance round, to hide her embarrassment. She was radiating dumbness in all directions. We all know that self-deprecating uh-oh I put my foot in it. She got stupider and prettier as I watched (from behind my book). Finally she wet her lips and with an exaggeratedly casual air, slipped her arm under his and made a little kissing face at him. This he liked. So they began to neck. Imagine forty years of this. Think how girls like that idealize men who "act like gentlemen." I attempted to disappear into my seat and meditated why beautiful always means expensive, why in order to be "naturally beautiful" you need the clever haircut, the skin conditioner, the good diet, the cod liver oil, the dental work, the fashionably-fitting clothes, the expensive shampoo, the medical bills, the exercise. Always money. The voices of my inarticulate, radical young students are full of money.

Then I thought of Jean, who radiates not only money but a frightening personal force, a truly terrifying, unconscious determination—she thinks everybody has it. I drifted away, pleased at first, then remembered she didn't want me. Bad.

I was rescued by a thunderstorm, water shivering across the windows and blue glare you wouldn't believe. The plane dropped twenty feet and left our stomachs on the ceiling. The pilot (chuckling on the intercom) told us he'd gotten careless heh heh and it was only a little local storm heh heh and we'd be out of it in a minute and into Watertown. Wow, a joke, right?

It got better but not much; there was a bad, bumpy descent and I began to get airsick.

The pilot is amused. Someone has placed that abominable young couple right in my way when we all know such scenes of mutual neurosis and degradation are few and far between in this our free, modern, sexually liberated land.

Is somebody trying to tell me something?

Hugh and Ellen Selby live in Watertown, NY, near the Canadian border, in a vast, rambling Charles Addams mansion—there is a story that a leak in the roof once had to be repaired by helicopter. Their place has been a mecca for their friends for years. The Selbys, because they are writers, know what nobody else does: I mean, why writers need quiet, why they keep odd hours, why people can't always stay where they're born, why publishers are no good at all, why sitting still and thinking is hard work. He edits various kinds of specialized technical books; she writes children's fantasies, very good ones. Ellen grew up in Kansas, in some Fundamentalist sect (which I never got quite straight)—no cards, no dancing, no movies, no make-up, no drinking. She takes children and what children read very seriously. Hugh comes from a more ordinary small town but when asked about it he will only giggle and light wooden matches with his feet (honest); but I understand that they both left their respective homes as soon as they could. Ellen is the steady one; Hugh is short, fat, and wears old-fashioned striped bathing suits in the summer, over which his uncut grey beard floats like Spanish moss. The Selbys, in addition to planting the delphiniums in their front yard in a hammer-and-sickle pattern, have inside their house a vast portrait of Grandfather Mao—this is a joke but the neighbors can't be trusted to understand it.

Ellen cooks—plainly but well. Hugh has water-fights and greenpea-fights in restaurants (sometimes).

There are in the Selby mansion four fireplaces, a tank of tropical fish, statuettes of monsters from outer space, a living room thirty feet by thirty feet, and a miscellaneous collection of Victorian plush furniture: green and rose-red are the predominant colors.

Some of the furniture is falling apart.

You find manuscripts everywhere, sometimes even in the (separate) garage.

My friends' one fault is that they don't believe names run in cycles and that the name of their infant daughter—Anya—is part of the new wave of fashion after Sherri, Debbi, Dee, and Leslie. Little Ivan, little Anya, little Tobias, are the names of the future. The Selbys think they picked out their daughter's name all by themselves.

Aside from that, it's the best of all possible worlds.

I took a taxi from the airport and walked in; Ellen was in the kitchen. When she heard me, she came out and put her arms around me.

"Mm," I said. "What do I smell?" (Something cooking, that is.) My insides know that the Selbys are my real momma and poppa. They themselves often mention young writers who want to be adopted by them, but I've never presumed so far. I went out at Ellen's direction into the back yard to get lettuce from the kitchen garden. I'm such a bad cook—or rather a non-cook (I often get interested in reading and let the food burn)— that I eat well only when at friends' houses. Years ago I used to be very embarrassed at the awkwardness of my first hour with the Selbys, each time I visited—I used to think it was my fault—but now we all seem to accept it. It's one of those things that happens with friends one sees only twice a year.

I gave Ellen the lettuce to wash—she insists she knows where everything is and I'd only be in the way—and watched while she chopped it into the salad. Ellen is forty-five and trim rather than pretty; nonetheless her gestures and attitudes have that extraordinary interest or glamor or beauty or what-have-you that some people radiate. One might call it authority or one might call it love. I don't mean that I love Ellen in the ordinary way or that I'm sexually attracted to her. I mean she's a blessing.

Hugh is a mad, plump owl (his round glasses) who hangs from ceilings, wiggling his bare toes. (He has actually been known to do this when parties occur in houses with exposed beams.)

Ellen took clothes out of the washer and put them in the dryer. She let me help her set the dinner table in the next room: i.e. she handed me the dishes and I took them in. The Selbys have a dinner table that seats fourteen, though there are seldom that many people in the house at one time.

"No, four," said Ellen.

"Anya?" I said. (Anya is two months old.)

"Somebody else," she said. She went down into the cellar for canned goods and preserves. (She puts up preserves, too.)

Just before dinner Hugh descended from the higher regions of the house, glasses and all, and started poking into the oven (after saying hello to me, of course). Letters and packages were scattered all over the kitchen; he started opening some of them and making interested noises: chuckles, mimed disbelief, sounds of wonder. I took paper napkins into the dining room and laid them in a heap on the table. (The Selbys are not formal.) We trooped into the dining room, where Ellen had laid out everything on those heatproof pads.

The bell rang.

"There she is," said Ellen. She and Hugh looked guard-edly at each other; they had apparently been trapped into having dinner with someone they didn't like. We don't want that one here. I saw "that one" in the old pier glass opposite the coat rack in the hall—a series of blue-and-white reflections spotted and stained by the leprosy of the old glass—and then I saw her come in through the kitchen.

"Leslie," said Ellen, "this is Esther."

"Esther, Leslie," said Hugh, satisfied.

Leslie was a tall twenty-two-year-old with long fair hair like Alice Liddell's, long legs in impeccable, flared white trousers, white wedgies, and a blue, clinging, frilly nylon tank top that kept pulling up above her belly-button. I had never seen such expensive clothes. She was an ex-student from Richmond, VA who "wrote" and who had come to Watertown only God knows why; she had taken a small house outside of town, she said. As she ate her salad, she kept pulling languidly at the tank top to get it to meet her trousers, but you could see that this was only a gesture; her heart wasn't in it.

Ellen helped her to some canned pâté.

"Merci," said Leslie, with an impeccable accent. I had a sudden yen to announce that I could understand only Yiddish. Leslie talked for a while about her family's maid in Richmond and how the maid was phobic about snakes in the garden but had to go there every day to get flowers for the dinner table.

They had a wonderful dog named Champion, a malemute who had to stay indoors in the air-conditioning most of the year. Leslie went right on, all about Mother and Father and the maid and the cook. She thought her own girlhood was fascinating.

Leslie had been the most beautiful girl in Richmond.

Ellen was getting annoyed at being addressed in snippets of French, I could tell. The way she shows it is that she gets very steady, very controlled, and her voice becomes perfectly civil.

Leslie said, "Georgie and I think we'll go to Greece this fall. When I go back home in September, I'll just have to leave, you know. I couldn't stand the winter." She started talking about this island they'd gone to the year before which nobody else had discovered yet; you had to get there by water taxi. Georgie (she explained) was Georgette, the teacher Leslie had been living with ever since she'd graduated from the University of South Florida. Georgie had an awful lot of money. But the owner of the apartment building where she and Georgie lived in Richmond wouldn't let them take Titi to the swimming pool on the roof. Wasn't that awful? Titi was a silver Siamese with marvelous blue eyes. Their building had a swimming pool, a boutique, a doorman, a sauna, a private TV system, and a quartz solarium. Their apartment had eight rooms. Leslie started to talk about a science fiction story she was going to write (about "a girl of the future") but at this point Ellen remembered something she had to go get in the kitchen. (Or the attic or the cellar). I excused myself and followed her. Ellen, of course, was not looking for anything but simply standing over the kitchen table and trying to control her temper.

"That—that *girl* never writes anything!" said Ellen.

"Look on the bright side," I said. "If she did, you'd have to read it."

"They live in two rooms," said Ellen vehemently, "she and that—that teacher of hers." (Georgie, it turned out, was a solid, middle-aged former Bostonian who had maddened Ellen by coming up once to visit her protégée and lecturing the Selbys about literature for two and one half hours by the clock. I assumed it was the usual collision of bad academic with real writer.)

"Do you think they're—" I said, embarrassed.

"I don't care," said Ellen, "I don't want to know. It's bad enough as it is." I remembered another young writer friend (male) who had come into Ellen's kitchen three winters before, having returned from his first European tour, and said, "Ellen, darling, I've found out the most astonishing thing about myself," while both Ellen and Hugh listened with weary patience, everybody else but the young writer having guessed it all long ago.

They don't really understand, of course.

We went back to the dining room and finished dinner—plain, fine food. Leslie didn't eat much; she never ate much. After the cherry pie she jumped up (did she know what we wanted of her?) and said she had to go, she'd almost forgotten, she was so sorry but she had to meet somebody who had a motorcycle. He was going to take her some place for a drink. I regarded Alice Liddell's pretty Anglo-Saxon face, her marvelous blue eyes, and foresaw the day when she'd burst into tears in the Selby's living room, begging them, "How can I change!"

She went out, and three carefully-scheduled minutes later Hugh whooped. (Out of hearing, I suppose.) He told me that when they'd first met, she'd asked him his name and he'd said, "Just call me Hugh," whereupon she'd said, bewildered, "But what's your name?" He fluffed his beard with his fingers like actors in Chinese opera do to indicate rage. He blew into it, too.

We took our coffee into the living room, in front of the empty fireplace (summer nights near the Canadian border can be cold) and Ellen began to talk about the current ruin of the world in general and New York State in particular. Since the last time I'd seen her she'd become passionately involved in ecology—not the organic foods kind, the all-over kind. I know that bitter, hopeless desperation—the petitions, the radio appeals, the placards, the letter campaigns, the demonstrations. It's like trying to move a locomotive with your bare hands. Hugh nodded amiably and vanished upstairs to edit something; I yelled after him, "But Hugh—what does an editor *do*?" He chuckled. Ellen talked, hunched over, her hands trembling with continual anger; swamps were being drained all over the country, forests were being covered with asphalt, fish and algae were being killed. I said, "I know how you feel. There's something—"

"Tomorrow," I said. "I'll tell you tomorrow."

The Selbys' guest room is on their third floor, with a tiny mirror tacked to one wall, an old farm sink (iron) from which you can get cold water only, and the real bathroom a long flight of stairs down. I took a good look at my face in the bathroom mirror that night because I knew I wouldn't get to see it again until morning (would it change? I wonder!). I have a melancholy Jewish face, big-featured, lean, and hungry. A prophet's face. In some novel somewhere there's a Jewish character, a big fat man who fled Germany in the late '30s and who says Why travel? Wait, and they'll chase you around the world.

I kept the subject successfully at bay for most of the next day. Hugh and Ellen worked in the afternoon, so after browsing in their library, I walked into town to visit the local florist (who sold mostly garden plants—tomatoes, started green peppers, that sort of thing) and then on to the five-and-ten, browsing through the drugstore magazines, having a soda, and so on. There aren't many possibilities in Watertown. I had lunch in a hamburger place (gummy cottage cheese, tired fruit) and walked back to the Selbys', scuffing my feet in the dust at the side of the highway, watching the white Queen Anne's Lace which blossoms everywhere at this time of year. Wild carrot.

I knew I would have to tell Ellen. Otherwise why be friends? I mean if it's not to be unreal.

There was another guest for dinner.

For a moment I thought it might be Leslie's friend who'd taken her out the night before—there was a motorcycle outside the house—but anyway inside it there was a friend of the Selbys called Carl, and I will call him Carl Muchomacho. This may be unfair. I remembered a satire he'd written in which there was (presented with unique completeness) the fantasy woman of a certain kind of freak male: I mean the sexy, earthy chick who loves motorcycles (because she has orgasms on them), who makes pottery, who balls all the time, who isn't uptight about anything, and who never gets pregnant. So Muchomacho is a satirical name. Carl has an attractive swagger, a pleasant, lean face, a dark moustache, and what is called a sense of humor.

But I wasn't in the right mood.

When I came in he got to his feet (he'd been having a drink with Hugh) and—with a flourish—offered me one of the old, plushy, green, Victorian chairs. They're hard things to push across a rug, by which I gather that Muchomacho was turning his sense of humor against himself. I said:

"Oooh, thanks, but I didn't know you were into that sort of thing."

"What sort of thing?" said he.

"Gallantry," I said.

"Well, I hope you were pleasantly surprised," says Carl, rocking back and forth a little on the balls of his feet. He's one of those restless, springy types who can never stand still.

"Surprised, anyway," I said. He smiled. The conversation is picking up. Here is a witty lady with whom he can fence. He said, "You don't dig it?"

"Well, no, not really," I said.

"Why not?"

"Oh, never mind," I said. "It's not worth—I don't want to talk about it all *this* much!" And I laughed. Hugh and Ellen exchanged happy glances of marital complicity: See-it's-working-out-I-told-you-she'd-like-him.

"But why not?" said Muchomacho, sincerely interested.

"It's not important," I said, so he supplied what my modesty would not or could not; he said:

"You mean you don't want to be a lady?" (smiling)

"That's right," I said. He looked interested and expectant. I squashed the suspicion that he and the Selbys were putting me on. I really don't think so.

"Well then," said Carl logically, "how *do* you want to be treated? Would you rather I ignored you? Or pulled the chair out from under you?" Hugh chuckled. Witty Hugh.

"Don't be silly," I said, controlling myself and trying not to sound like a governess; "Just treat me—well, decently. Like anyone."

"Like Hugh?" said clever Muchomacho. ("Please!" exclaimed Hugh happily.) Ellen looked as calm as if nothing were happening. I said, a little sharply:

"I'll tell you, the one thing I do not want to do is continue this discussion all through dinner." This time Ellen looked up. "Sorry, but I didn't start it," said Carl pleasantly.

I got up, excused myself with a smile, and went to the bathroom. I figured that five minutes later they'd be talking about something else and so they were; then I got sneaky and introduced the topic of food additives so we had ecology all through dinner. Everybody listened respectfully. Carl, I am quite sure, did not care for the topic, but he honored it. After dessert we all moved back into the living room while Hugh started a fire in the fireplace; then Carl Muchomacho came over and stood at the back of my chair, saying lightly:

"At the risk of incurring your savage, feminist wrath, can I ask you out with me tonight?"

"Huh?" I said (and jumped).

"Can I take you out and show you a good time?" he said, adding, "I'm really harmless, you know."

"Oh, thanks," I said, "but—" (trailed off, trying to think of an excuse. I just washed my hair?)

"Frankly, I feel rotten," I said. "I don't want to go anywhere or do anything; I just want to sit."

"You can sit on my motorcycle," he said.

"I don't feel up to it," I said.

"Come on," he said, "It'll do you good. Get a little wind in your hair." The Selbys glanced at each other again. They too seemed to think it would do me good. I shook my head. Carl shrugged. We did not go on to have one of those endless arguments about whether sitting on a motorcycle is the same thing as sitting at home and when I said I didn't want to do anything, what did I mean by "do" and what does "mean" mean. Perhaps he's just getting too old to be persistent. He turned to Hugh, saying "See? I do treat you two alike," and proposed they go out somewhere to have a beer.

Which they did. (Though he didn't promise to show Hugh a good time.) Ellen said nothing but she looked at me disapprovingly.

I said, "Ellen, I just can't face it. Not again." (Which was only a small lie.) Then I burst into tears. They were unsympathetic, angry tears and they didn't get me any approval.

I can't tell her.

She said dryly that Carl was a good friend of theirs.

I said wasn't I?

She said softly and exasperatedly, "Oh, Esther!"

"Never mind," I said; "I'll call him tomorrow." (That's what dating's all about; it's to please your Mother. Darling, he looked like such a nice boy. But he's impotent, Mother.)

"You've changed," said Ellen gravely.

I said that yes, I had; I'd gotten a lot into feminism since I'd seen her last. Ellen knows better than to believe in bra-burners; she thought for a minute and then said carefully, "I suppose I've always been a feminist. You know, where I grew up it was impossible for a woman to have a career at all; she could only be a wife and mother, but here I am with both."

I said Yes, wasn't that wonderful.

She smiled.

"And Hugh does half the housework," I said, "and takes care of the baby." (Anya was at the babysitter's because I was there.) "Ah! that's unusual."

"He helps," said Ellen. Then she said, "I don't mind doing it." They all start out by assuming you mean somebody else: third-world women, welfare mothers, Fundamentalist Baptists, Martians. We went through all that. I told her that I meant us both, that I wouldn't have my job at all if I hadn't been twice as good as my colleagues.

"Make the world safe for mediocrity," I said.

She said she didn't care to know mediocre people and she certainly hoped I didn't.

I said, "That's not the point." (But I didn't know what was the point, not then.) I said, "Ellen, when you were with your first husband, when you were trying to write and had two children, wouldn't day care have helped? You couldn't have afforded a babysitter then. And wouldn't it have helped if your family and the clergyman and all those people hadn't tried to shove you right back into your old place? I mean if they thought it was O.K.? My God, you lost your voice for two years."

"That's Fundamentalism," she said.

"Oh no it's not," I said, "look at TV, look at the magazines, look how convenient it is to have a wife, look at the ads."

"Esther, no one I respect believes what they see on TV or in the ads! For goodness' sakes, neither do you."

I said ha ha the things we took least seriously might affect us the most (T.S. Eliot). Clincher.

"Besides," I added, "you told me once you had to get up at 5 a.m. for four years to write because there wasn't any other time."

"If one wants something, one makes sacrifices," said she.

I asked if Hugh had made sacrifices.

"We are different people," said Ellen.

She added, "He may have made other kinds of sacrifices. I'm not going to defend him to you, Esther. The point is that we have to make our individual choices and lead our lives, man or woman, and everybody suffers one way or another. Life is compromise. And that's something none of us can evade. Whether man or woman."

I said furiously that I'd had quite enough of all this literary book club tragic-sense-of-life as an excuse for other people's privileges.

"You're bitter!" said she.

"Sure," I said. "Malcolm no-name saw his daddy killed before his eyes at the age of four and that's political; but I see my mother making a dishrag of herself every day for thirty years and that's personal."

Ellen said my mother was responsible for that, if it was true, and we didn't have to repeat our mother's mistakes.

I said didn't we just!

She said, "I've seen you overreacting to all sorts of trivial, harmless things. If your ideas—"

"It's not trivial or harmless. It happens too often. It's just part of the whole damn thing. And don't tell me he didn't do anything that bad, I know he didn't, but the code of manners is only a symptom of the whole damn thing."

A long silence.

"As far as I can see," said Ellen steadily, "you want people to treat you according to some strange and special code of behavior that only you understand. That's hardly rational, Esther." She was looking down at her hands. As far as Ellen is concerned, this whole subject is finished because Ellen is Superwoman; if Ellen's responsible for everything, that's because it's her choice; Ellen still exists on five hours' sleep a night. I said nothing of this, only that I wasn't alone in my beliefs. I wasn't a Saucerian or an occultism nut, and I guessed it was the old argument about the cup being half empty or half full. We'd never settle it. Anyway, George Bernard Shaw said there is no great art without some fanaticism behind it, so I was starting ahead of the game, right? Her, too. Look at her and ecology.

Ellen said very quietly and distinctly, "I am not a fanatic."

I said, "No, no, I don't *mean* that." But she said again: "I am not a fanatic."

"Oh well, all fanaticism means," (said I) "is a truth somebody else won't accept. So we're both fanatics."

Ellen's anger only makes her more controlled. She changed the subject. Far be it from me to suppose she picks her beliefs for their acceptability to her husband's friends. She told me about a mutual acquaintance of ours who had become—God save us!—a Satanist and had sacrificed goats in the back of occult bookstores.

"Where on earth did he get the goats?" I said.

Ellen said it wasn't funny; he'd ended up in a mental hospital.

"You meet the best people there," I said.

"Esther, he's in a *mental hospital*." Not understanding my lack of understanding of her understanding of my understanding. I said I was sorry; I hadn't meant to be flip.

"Look, Ellen," I said, "I feel as if I'd been flayed, I mean I'm all nerves. I never should've come. I'll go tomorrow and call back in a few months. When I'm human again."

She said, looking right at me, "If this new belief of yours has such a bad effect on your relations with others, I think you ought to re-examine your belief."

(Years ago, when I was in group therapy, I wore "Bohemian" clothes: cheap Indian-print shifts, cheap Mexican dresses, lots of color, big old copper jewelry. This was long before such things became fashionable. The group didn't like the way I dressed; they said I only did it to get attention. They said, "You're trying to be different." This was also the standard explanation for juvenile delinquency that year. I said I dressed that way because I liked it and not because I wanted attention, because I did get gawked at and teased in the street, and that I definitely did not enjoy.

(They smiled.

(They said Oh, so you don't like looking different?

(I said I didn't like being teased.

(*Then why*, said they triumphantly, *do you dress the way you do?*)

I said goodnight and went upstairs. My friend Ellen with her endless work and her earnest assurances to an interviewer last year that *her* children always took preference over her work in emergencies (Hugh is a hit-and-run father) and that she hoped more and more women would experience the fulfillment of both work and motherhood. "No one must go beyond me," she said. Do you know the last time the percentage of women in the professions and women PhDs and women entering colleges was as high as it is today?

In nineteen-twenty, that's when.

And you'd think friends—but Carl is her friend; the truth is that she prefers Carl to me.

There's this club, you see. But they won't let you in. So you cry in a corner for the rest of your life or you change your ways and feel rotten because it isn't you, or you go looking for another club. But this club is the world. There's only one.

"Why do you people go where you're not wanted?"

"Why do *you* go where you're not wanted? *I* don't want you." (My maternal uncle, at a resort that didn't like Jews.)

If Jean had stayed with me I wouldn't have cared, but now I must put on my putrid ankle sox and my cheerleader button because there's no right of private judgment and you can't think of yourself; you have to be thought. By others. Why did Ellen forget the classic exchange? I mean the one where they say But aren't you for human liberation? and you say Women's liberation is for women, not men, and they say You're selfish. First you have to liberate the children (because they're the future) and then you have to liberate the men (because they've been so deformed by the system) and then if there's any liberation left you can take it into the kitchen and eat it.

Oh, I must be bad. I'm hostile. I'm bitter. I'm hideously wicked. I must be crazy or I wouldn't suffer so. Taking things personally—! (Persons shouldn't take things personally.) I stood in my traveling pajamas over the iron sink, brushing my teeth and crying—how could she, how *could* she!—and when I straightened up, somebody else looked out at me from the tiny mirror tacked to the wall.

Who is that marvelous woman!

I was so pleased, she's so cute, with toothpaste around her mouth like a five-year-old. I like her, really. She's Esther who loves everything systematic and neat but it's all moonshine; she has elaborate schemes for traveling with a traveling iron and a collapsible miniature ironing board (which is too heavy to carry), and a traveling sewing case (which is *very* small), and traveling clothes which don't need ironing (so why take the iron!), and shoe trees made of plastic so they'll be light, and a collapsible toothbrush with a marvelous plastic case, and airmail stamps which she never uses.

Wonderful, silly Esther.

So my reflection comforted me and blew me stars and

141

kisses. I thought of Jean—who'd left me—and Ellen—who hated me—and my own crazy nastiness, which is that I don't like men and I'm giving up on them and I don't care about them so I'm a monster and God will strike me dead. Sleeping with women is all right if it's just play, but you must never let it interfere with your real work, which is sleeping with men.

The mirror didn't believe it.

So I slipped into triumph in spite of everything, like an Eskimo lady in a nine-days' blizzard on an ice floe. And very humble (but giggling) I went to bed.

I pray that She my soul may keep. (snf)

Thinking how nice it was to be horizontal when you're tired, and that after a noncommittal, guilty, bland breakfast with the Selbys, after my rather lame excuses about catching a virus or not feeling well or something, after Hugh drives me to the airport and they say "Goodbye" and I say "Goodbye" and after I write a very nasty letter to my New York glamorous media friends who think bisexuality is groovy (but only for women and only if you're married and only if you like men better) there is something else I must do, an option Ellen didn't think of.

What do you do when the club won't let you in, when there's no other, and when you won't (or can't) change? Simple.

You blow the club up.

(The mystery of courage. The mystery of enjoyment. One moves incurably into the future but there is no future; it has to be created. So it all ends up totally unsupported, self-caused, that symbol of eternity, The Snake Biting Its Own Tail. I'm strong because I have a future; I have a future because I willed it; I willed it because I'm strong. Unsupported.

(Ezekial saw the wheel
(Way up in the middle of the air—
(O Ezekial saw the wheel
(Way in the middle of the air!

(Now the big wheel runs by faith
(And the little wheel runs by the grace of God—

(The above made up by professional hope experts, you might say, because willful, voluntary, intentional hope was the only kind they had in anything like long supply. Faith is not, contrary to the usual ideas, something that turns out to be right or wrong, like a gambler's bet; it's an act, an intention, a project, something that makes you, in leaping into the future, go so far, far, far ahead that you shoot clean out of Time and right into Eternity, which is not the end of time or a whole lot of time or unending time, but timelessness, that old Eternal Now. So that you end up living not in the future (in your intentional "act of faith") but in the present. After all.

(Courage is *willful* hope.)

Summer is dying. The airfield's still rank with Queen Anne's lace—its flowers look like white parasols—but the goldenrod's coming out too, and even a few blue asters, which means the beginning of the end. On a sunny afternoon you know summer will last forever, all that iridescent blue and green, but the nights are colder now. Three hours after sunset you can smell autumn. The pilot came in by sight after circling our cow pasture (we don't have ground-to-air communication here either) and I walked to my battered old heap in the parking lot. Home along the roads I know so well: butter-and-eggs (that's like tiny, yellow-and-white snapdragons), purple chicory, which I've heard called corn flowers or flax flowers, and the very few last (battered but game) black-eyed Susans. Everything was growing up through the hay like hair. We'll have hot weather again before October. I went through the town and up the hill, parking in my old place at the top, which is so awful to get into in winter because of the ice, and then hauled my suitcase upstairs, picking up on the way a note my landlady had slipped under my door. I forgot to pay the rent before I left. I opened the windows, disconnected the timer from the living-room lamp, ran water in both sinks until the faucets stopped spitting at me, all the things you have to do when you come back. You know. I was putting clothes away with one hand (mostly the laundry bag which hangs on the inside of the bedroom closet) and carrying the note in the other, with that unaccountable, feverish efficiency that comes over me whenever I come home and have to get everything put away and fixed up again. My suitcase gaped open on the bed and I kept having to step over a pair of shoes. The note said:

". . . how you buy a gun. You giggle a lot and tell the clerk your boy friend wants you to go hunting with him so you have to get a hunting rifle. You say Oh gee he told me to ask *you;* he said you'd know—"

I started again:

"Dearest Esther,

"Now I'm in town and you're not. I'm at 14 Tighe Street, number in the book under Anderson. Sorry I got scared and ran away. I went to Boston, to some friends, and learned a lot. Then I came back and just messed around. Do you remember three years ago, after the bomb scare, the University was going to keep lists of students who took suspicious books out of the University library? But the best bomb handbook turned out to be the Encyclopedia Britannica.

"This is how you buy a gun. You giggle a lot and tell the clerk your boy friend wants you to go hunting with him so you have to get a hunting rifle. You say Oh gee he told me to ask *you*; he said you'd know everything. Then you keep your ears open. You'll pay too much the first time but that's O.K. Don't try to pretend you had it all written down on a piece of paper but lost it; they'll only send you out to get your instructions again. I know. And remember: *you're only a girl*.

"As soon as your lights stop going on and off so regularly, I'll know you're back. I'll call or you call me; I want to talk to you.

Love,
Jean.

"P.S. I hope you're not mad at me.
"P.P.S. I keep Brown Bess in her wrappings in the kitchen. I can take her apart, clean her, put her back together again, load and unload her, and pot a tin can at fifty feet. When nobody's around I talk to her because I love her. I call her Blunderbess.
"P.P.P.S. I love you, too."

I reread Jean's letter. I read it until it didn't make sense any more. I brewed myself a cup of tea, then threw the tea in the sink. I don't want to go through that again, whether she loves me or doesn't love me, whatever "love" means. It's all spoilt. When I was very young—I mean eighteen years ago—I fell in love with a man who didn't know how to drive a car properly; when we hit a patch of ice on the roadway once, he steered against the skid and we went half-way across the road in a sort of figure-eight; he told me complacently that this was the right thing to do and I knew it wasn't but I didn't care because

I adored him. Twenty-five years ago we had parties to which the boys didn't come, or if they did they wouldn't dance or talk or do anything. Twenty years ago I went to college and began to recognize that I was invisible; having dressed for a date (dates were absolutely crucial then) in my low heels, my nylons, my garter belt, my horsehair petticoat, my cotton petticoat, my taffeta skirt, my knit jersey blouse, my circle pin, my gold earrings, my charm bracelet, my waist-cincher, my lipstick, my little bit of eyeshadow, my heavy faille coat, my nail polish, my mohair scarf, and my gloves, I went into the dormitory garden to wait for him. The garden was full of late spring flowers. I had already admired myself in the full-length mirror on the back of my closet door—and that was very nice indeed, proving that I could look good—but standing between the stone walls on the stone-flagged walk, watching the flowers grow ever lighter and more disembodied in the blue twilight—and sitting on the stone bench under the Gothic arches and all that ivy—and we were supposed to get A's and use the library—we were supposed to write papers— we were supposed to be *scholars*—I wanted to take off all my clothes and step out of my underwear. And then take off my hair and fingernails and my face and my flesh and finally my very bones. Just to step out of it. All the way out of it.

My date said, "There you are!"

If I was dying, my mother'd give me a cup of tea. So many times we've sat in the kitchen and fiddled with the tea things and talked inconsequential nonsense; then Daddy came home and admired us both, carefully urging Mother not to be so afraid of so many things, and Mother said she felt better and would go put on something nice.

But never did. Out of some furious, sullen instinct, she never did. She'd always ruin the effect somehow. And about most middle-aged women, don't they always ruin the effect somehow—too childish, too drab, too careful, too flamboyant, too frumpish, too expensive, too something? A genuine Picasso on which someone has scrawled at the bottom, "This is a fake"—or even more cleverly, "This is *not* a fake!"—so of course it's a double fake.

Did I tell you that my mother was the child of immigrant parents and that she taught herself to read English before she went to school? She never worked (I mean outside the house) so she had lots of time to make up fairy tales for me. They always began, "There was a little girl who—" I was immensely flattered. In her middle age she got fat, as if on purpose, gave up reading anything but historical novels because she said she couldn't understand what was written nowadays ("my poor brain"). She died at seventy, keeping to the end her invincible stupidity and her defiant, uncanny, extraordinarily thorough bad taste. That woman could make a shroud look tacky. I wish she'd come back and show me so we could have a good talk about it.

My father, about whom I'm sure you've been wondering, was a nice, ordinary man who did not have that intuitive understanding of feminine psychology always attributed to nice men in novels written by nice women for nice women. He didn't believe in the pretty, mindless muffin who's the style now—that wasn't in his time and it would have offended his sense of propriety anyway—nor did he believe in the busty roll-in-the-hay type (which was the thing in my teens)—to tell you the truth, I don't know what type of woman he did believe in. He used to read Sunday newspaper editorials about science (he thought of himself as an Informed Layman) although he tended to enjoy the physics most and to be skeptical about psychology. He praised and encouraged my mother, rather (I'm afraid) on the assumption that she was a kind of invalid, trying to cure her of her phobias, her daydreams, her distaste for people at parties, her insistence that she was stupid, her sleeping eleven hours a night, her love of gardens, her fairytales, her disbelief in science, her inability to learn to drive a car. He once remarked to me that he'd married her because she was "different"—then I suppose he had to change her back again. Or maybe he got more difference than he'd bargained for. I don't know. It's hard to tell what he thought of women because he always spoke of us with great formal deference.

"What Man can conceive, Man can achieve!" my father would exclaim, looking up from his Sunday-supplement article or his book of popular science.

My mother once confided in me that she didn't believe in atoms. I asked her what the world was made of, then. She thought for a minute.

"Elves," she said.

If she came back into my kitchen now, severely silly, dumpy and deliberately dowdy in her grave-clothes, how could I explain to her that it wasn't all her fault, after all? What could I say to her?

"Mama, how good it is to see you! What's it like being dead? Never mind, I know. Come have a cup of tea." We putter about. I put on the kettle. I gossip and chatter a little. I apologize for going over to Daddy's side when I was in my teens; after all, what else could I do? I was terrified he would think of me as he thought of her. Besides, the world isn't made of elves, not really. She cries a little. Then she shrugs. I say, "Mama, I'm going to tell you a fairy tale.

"It's about a middle-aged scientist who was also a politician and an army officer and a revolutionary and a judge and in Congress and a genius mathematician and a poet. And she—"

Why bother, why bother. I want the matriarchy. I want it so badly I can taste it. I *should* put a rug on the bedroom floor (which is all bare wood); I *shouldn't* have these thoughts. There's an actor on the Late Late Show I'm in love with—is that going to be my love life for the next thirty years, watching 1:30 a.m. TV? Suppose he wears out. Suppose I don't like him anymore. Suppose they show other things. O idiocy! "Sorry I got scared and ran away." So you pick yourself up as if nothing had happened. Easy to say!

I don't want her.

I went about my business for the next two days, and if you're wondering about what I'm going to feel when Jean turns up, well so am I.

I spent my time in the library, picking out obscure references to memoirs written by bad ladies two hundred years ago and novels by worse ladies who, though personally blameless, wrote bad books. *A Romance of the Pyrenees, Marianna, or The Puritan's Daughter*. Weird, icky stuff. I've lost my awe of the library completely: this vast, defunct megalith over which we little mammals wander, nipping and chewing bits of its skin. I rip away at a little pocket: some authoress who wrote five romances (five!) under the pseudonym *By A Lady*. Domestic sentiments. Gothic castles. Purity. If only I can reduce this pulp to pulp and spread it out into some kind of shape. Dead voices, haunting and terrible: *I want. I need. I hope. I believe.* Where'd they live? Who did their cooking? Did they expect to get pregnant every year? (See Mrs. Defoe's journal.) The awful constriction, the huge skirts. Mrs. Pepys's dress allowance ("the poor wretch" her husband called her). "How are we fall'n, fall'n by mistaken rules!" "Women live like Bats or Owls, labour like Beasts, and die like Worms." "Anyone may blame me who likes." "How

good it must be to be a man when you want to travel."
"John laughs at me, but one expects that in marriage."
"It had all been a therapeutic lie. The mind was power-
less to save her. Only a man. . . ." "I / Revolve in my /
Sheath of impossibles—"

Scholars don't usually sit gasping and sobbing in
corners of the library stacks.

But they should. They should.

In my dream the Tooth Fairy stood at the foot of my
bed, wearing an airy, blue, nylon net gown and glitter-
ing rhinestone jewelry, with a little rhinestone coronet
on her head. Her magic wand was star-topped and she
looked just like a Tooth Fairy should. She was going to
give me three wishes.

But I woke up.

Bad weather brought Jean. A cold and blowy day with
bursts of rain, a premature autumn. Her umbrella made
a puddle on the landing outside my door. Tragic. Dark-
eyed. Hands in raincoat pockets.

She smiled sweetly.

She said, "Ick, what weather." I had to let her in. She
shed her coat, her umbrella, her packages, and her boots
outside, then came into my kitchen. She was no answer
to anything. She said, "Do you want to—?"

"No," I said.

"Do you want to sit in the living room?"

We sat in the living room and Jean gave me a look that
said *So you're not a Lesbian any more, are you?*

I said aloud, "That's not—" and then nothing.

"Shall I tell you about Betty Botter?" she said. "You
know: 'Betty Botter bought a bit of bitter butter. Said
Betty Botter, This bit of bitter butter, It will make my
batter bitter. So Betty Botter bought a bit of better butter
and it made her batter better.'"

"What on earth—" I said.

"Blenderblunder. Betsy Batter. Batterburger. My rifle. She's in your kitchen, all wrapped up."

I said, "Who were you staying with in Boston?"

"Other Lesbians," said Jean comfortably.

Now I had done something terrible the day before that I haven't told you: I had been attracted to somebody else. I had been walking towards the library when I saw this twenty-year-old coming the other way in hip-hugger jeans and a funny little knitted top that left her bare from her ribs to her belly button. A silly, ruffled sort of blouse. That's what I saw first. Then I thought *Isn't she cold?* (It was raining.) Then I just knew there was nothing so interesting in the world as that midriff; my palms yearned for it. I wanted every little girl in the world.

That's different, that's very different. That's being a you-know-what.

She said, "'Tis with our judgments as our watches; none / Goes just alike but each believes her own."

"You're mad," I said. Dumb with rage. Her absolutely inexplicable cheerfulness.

"I got you a present," she said, hauling a little brown-paper package from somewhere in her jeans (I don't see how she could have avoided sitting on it). Generously she held it out to me. "Go on," she said.

So I took it and untied the string (some present— brown paper and string!) and unwrapped it, holding in my hand a little white box. A dead mouse? A snakeskin? A bird's skull? These would be just Jean's style. Or, more conventionally, a flea-market ring, or the female symbol with the equals sign or the clenched fist, all done in lousy embroidery.

It was a watch sitting on a folded bit of paper. It wasn't cheap; I know the kind. I don't mean jewelry-expensive, but a good one. Perhaps twenty-five dollars. An awful lot, for her.

"You always say you lose the expensive ones," said Jean the liar, "so I got you a bad one. Here." And the bit of paper—unfolded—turned out to be an advertisement for a watch set about with diamonds, with a silly lady in false eyelashes, false hair, false everything. She was wearing a Jean Harlow slip—dress, I mean—and looking adoringly into the eyes of a handsome, shadowy man whose features you could hardly make out because he was the one giving the two-thousand-dollar watch; and I suppose if you have that kind of money to buy ladies (or to buy ladies presents with), you don't need a face.

Something awful is happening. Rising. I don't think I can live through it. Also the ad is making me laugh. (I mean why not eat diamonds if you want to possess them? Only they'd come out the other end in a couple of days, wouldn't they?) Jean's watch has nice, big numbers I can read and no diamonds. I started putting her present on the white strip left on my wrist by my old watch, but something terrible was happening to the room. I've had an awful shock. Like a poor worm with a pin through it. And I wish to God Jean were somewhere else. Seeing her through what they call "scalding" tears, screaming tears, hurting dreadfully.

I wept, I wept, crying against her shoulder, nasty bilious tears, aching tears; don't ever let anyone tell you it's easy. And they didn't ease me. Is it like having convulsions? I didn't want to be touched, but I did; so she put her arms around me, saying "There, there" and "Now, now" and I put mine about her, feeling the shock of allowing it all to happen, knowing I could trust her. We held each other until I stopped crying; then I said, "I want to make love right now."

She said, "Your face is all runny," wiping it with a kleenex. Then she said, "I know, but you won't come; you'll just keep having these tremendous surges of feeling. It's too distracting."

"Huh!" I said sulkily, blowing my nose. To cheer me up, she told me about a letter some poor woman had written in a newspaper advice column, asking about how could she do away with her terrible deformity because she had this secret shame, this awful thing she couldn't let anybody know: *that she had little hairs around the aureoles of her breasts*. This, of course, is exactly what Jean has. Jean thought the letter very funny, but I turned away, groaned, wrapped my arms around my stomach—a pang of desire so keen I could barely sit up. Jean roared, which is exactly what you'd expect from a heartless, sadistic Lesbian. They all chew tobacco and cuss like truck drivers. Next thing, she'll be putting out lit cigarettes on my breasts, just like a character in a book I read by C. S. Lewis who (after all) must know. She put her arms around me and gave me a fluttery kiss, such a close one, such a loving one, such a just-light-enough one that I began to understand pornography. Do you? I said, "Help, I can't wait!" so good-natured Jean pulled the curtains to and made love to me on the living room rug. We—uh—"did things," we—uh—"endured" and we—mm—"with our"—

See?

I trembled from head to foot, I really did. I didn't lift a finger, just like all those ladies in peignoirs in vampire movies. I have never been so utterly abandoned in all my life. Or so sorry when I came. (She was wrong about that.) After the third orgasm—three, count 'em, three!—but that's nothing, for a woman—I was content to lie there and throb, admiring beautiful Jean, who now wanted the same things done to her, now that I was spryer and she more languid, another kind of pleasure. So I did, trying not to laugh at the persistent memory of that poor woman so tormented by her shameful deformity that she had to write a newspaper about it. Sex, when it's good (but how often is it that?) is like nothing on earth. So silly, so grand. So indecent, so matter-of-fact.

Much later I said, peering through the curtains, "It's stopped raining. Nasty, though."

Jean said, "Get dressed and come into the kitchen, O.K.? I want to show you Blunderbess."

She added, "You ought to learn how to shoot."

The next day I was as paranoid as ever, smiling nervously at the men in the library, trying to keep my eyes off the women. I-know-they're-all-laughing-at-me-because-even-if-they-aren't-I-deserve-it.

Sex doesn't last.

That night I had a conversation with the Tooth Fairy. She came and sat down on the end of my bed, looking very benevolent, spreading out her blue nylon net skirts, and recalling to me (even in the middle of my dream) where I had seen her before—she was somebody I saw in a live stage show when I was eight and I'd swear it was the Ice Follies because I remember her in ice skates.

THE TOOTH FAIRY: Good evening, dear child. I am here to help you.

ME: Mmmmpf! What?

THE FAIRY: Tell me what you want and I shall get it for you.

ME: Thanks but no thanks ha ha. (My standards of wit are pretty lousy in dreams.)

THE FAIRY: Shall I restore to you your lost heterosexuality, so that you may once again adore on the Late Late Show handsome actors such as Buster Crabbe, Dirk Bogarde, James Mason, and Christopher Lee?—leaving it to you to determine what common characteristics (if any) animate this rather peculiar list because, my dear, (to be perfectly frank) you have the damnedest tastes I ever saw.

ME: Not on your life.

THE FAIRY: Shall I give you the gift of sixty million dollars?

ME: You haven't got it.

THE FAIRY: Shall I give you the gift of being attracted to real men?

ME (sitting straight up in bed, in terror): No, no, no, no, no!

THE FAIRY (crossing one leg over the other, thus revealing that she was indeed wearing ice skates, great big clumpy white ones): Well, what *do* you want, for goodness' sakes! Don't be difficult. Tell me your heart's desire.

There was a long, puzzled silence in my by now very symbolic bedroom. What do I want? Health? Riches? Fame? Beauty? Travel? Success? The Respect Of My Colleagues? Do I want to become a saint? (God forbid.) I've wanted all those things in my time. Like the news of the day that runs round and round the top of that building on forty-second street in New York, so little sneaky tags and proverbs ran over the ceiling, now in neon lights, now in electric lightbulbs: It is better to marry than to have a career, Somebody lovely has just passed by, Always give Daddy the biggest piece of steak, It is Woman's job to keep the stars in their courses. None of this helps, of course.

I said, "My dearest desire—"

I said, "Some time in my life—"

I said, "What I really want—"

I said, "I want to kill someone."

Then I amended it. Not a woman. Certainly not a child, not of either sex.

I said: *I want to be able to kill a man.*

I said to Jean, "Why is wanting to be able to kill a man so bizarre? *Men* kill men. Watch TV. Men kill *women* on TV."

"Monopolistic practices," said Jean.

We were in her back yard, standing in the premature autumn leaves, shooting at tin cans. I hoped the neighborhood cats would have sense enough to be warned off by the noise, unlike the two-legged kind of cat, who is so often attracted by sounds like that. No rabbits, either. Just tin cans. I once ran over a dog with my car—not meaning to, of course—I was driving into the sunset and hardly saw him until he was right in front of me. I slowed down to twenty and he went right between the wheels; I felt him bumping against the floorboards (and heard him yelping) but he limped away fast, so perhaps he wasn't killed. It was an awful, hateful thing, worse in some ways than hurting a human being because animals can have no intentions toward you. Not real ones.

Bam! Jean is patiently trying to correct a tendency she has to pull to one side. Inherited from archery practice, probably. A strange, respectably dressed Professorial type appeared in the gap in the front hedge only half an hour ago, saying, amused—as if it were any of his business!—"What are you girls doing?" (As I told you, I'm thirty-eight.)

Jean had swung the gun round, quite coldly. And pulled back the safety catch. "Get out!" He turned pale and backed away, vanished behind the hedge. As if it were his business, you know, as if everything women did was naturally his business.

Against the wire fence at the back of the yard one early maple sapling flames up—pure scarlet. Such useless rage. I used to think I felt like a failure because I was neurotic, because I was over-sensitive, because I'd had a bad childhood (who hasn't), because I lacked that seventh outermost layer of skin that everyone is supposed to have; I said it was the price I paid for being an intellectual. I cried over it. I used to hate you so; I used to dream of killing you over and over again. I used to wonder, with an awe beyond all jealousy, what it was you had that protected you so, that made Rose fall in love with you (over and over again!), what peace, what blessing, what infinite favor in the eyes of God.

Bam!

Jean is, I suspect, holding it.

Bam!

(Any sensible rabbit would have fled long ago. The tin can jerks mechanically.)

"I'm pulling to the left," Jean says.

"Oh Jean, *symbols!*"

There's no sillier activity, practically speaking (or so it seems to me) than shooting tin cans in one's own back yard. Tin cans aren't alive. I don't want to get tin cans out of my way. Yet if men take to it like ducks to water (as a sign of the position in life to which it has pleased God to call them) I think I will practice anyway. I have been shooting all afternoon; my back hurts, my elbows hurt, my skirt's damp and stained from the leaves. Even long, lovely Indian skirts won't do for this sort of activity; first you "break" it, then you eject the used cartridge, then you put it back together again (like a stapler, see?), then you flop down on your stomach, then you push off the whatchamacallit (safety catch), then you brace it against your shoulder, which is going to hurt like blooming blazes before the day is over.

The Tooth Fairy floats down out of the crowded gray heaven, flops on a pile of leaves, and remains there, so shocked as to be nearly invisible. She watches us, bereft of words.

"Jean," I said, "what d'you do with a man you've shot?"

"Leave him alone, dear; he's not much good dead. Nobody is."

"Would you bring him back to life?"

"Dunno. Maybe. Maybe not. I'd probably have to shoot him again."

Bam!

Jean says angrily, "Oh damn, this blasted Bettybop's doing the Charleston. I'm tired." She sits up. "Will you do my shoulders?" So I kneel over her, trying to make like a backrub the best I can, and composing in my mind the following letter to my ex-friend Rose (see p. 1 paragraph 1) which I will entrust to the Tooth Fairy to deliver when it is finished:

"Dear Rose,

How are you? Do you still commit psychic incest with persons bigger, brighter, stronger, richer, more successful, and in every way better than yourself? Do you look for hours at lipsticks in store windows? Are you beautiful?

"My friend and I have just finished viciously murdering 4 rabbits, 3 tree stumps, 8 pieces of paper, and 6 unwary cats with a rifle called Bloodyborebingle. It is a bloody bore (bingle). It sings magically when we take it out of its wrappings and howls every time we shoot it. It wants blood. It wants us to shoot MEN and hang their stuffed intestines on our wall. My friend and I spit on the ground and cuss a lot. We have cut our hair. We flex our muscles in public and wear leather jackets. Are we revolting? You bet!

"The weather here is fine. Winter is coming. Soon it will be too dark to shoot most of the time, so I am concentrating on reading, though frankly there isn't much I can stand, so I am sticking to the diary of Mrs. Daniel Defoe. Mrs. Daniel Defoe is not to be confused with Mr. Daniel Defoe; he has the names and is the man, so don't get them mixed up. I am also writing my own history, which is about how an unstable (tho' pretty) young girl beset by Indefinable Rapture can be corrupted (due to the lack of proper guidance) into a hopeless, happy, neurotic feminist militant invert. You may not know what "invert" means so you had better look it up. It is actually a word used to describe sugar and is synonymous with levulose or dextrose, I forgot which. My story is a warning to all parents, all children, and all psychiatrists.

"Do you still fear to dress in velvet because it is sensuous?

"Do you still think Shakespeare is all about fathers and daughters?

"Do you still think your breasts are ugly?

"I have beautiful breasts but you would not like them, so don't visit. The weather here's too bracing.

Surrealistically yours,
Esther.

"P.S. We are on strike against God."

TOOTH FAIRY: I refuse to deliver that ghastly, obscene communication.

ME (coarsely): Buzz off! You were undoubtedly demoted from Fairy Godmother because of sheer incompetence.

TOOTH FAIRY (spitting on her ice skate blades): Never! Never!

ME: Off! Or I will have you sent back to painting goldenrods.

Jean said, "What are you whispering about?"

"I'm creating," I said.

"Would you stop creating and put your rugose tentacle here, eh?" said Jean, indicating her shoulder under her collar. "It hurts." She's begun to purr.

I said, "Jean, I am willing to come out, but not in the back yard under the eyes of the neighbors."

"Then let's go in," she said.

The amazing peacefulness, the astonishing lack of anger, the sweetness and balm of being at last on the right side of power.

You'll meet us. I'll tell you that the invisible stars I talked about earlier are called Black Holes—but that's too-heavy symbolism; we think I'll keep that to ourselves.

You're Stevie. I'll write you. We're still old friends, at least for a while. Are your friends like you? Are your lovers like you? I just don't know. (I must write Sally and Louise, too, but at greater length.)

You can't recognize us in a crowd. Don't try.

You think Jean and I will go away like ladies and live in the country with Stupid Philpotts and the cats. We won't.

You think we're not middle-aged. You think we're not old.

You even think we're not married. (We might be, even to you.)

Worst of all, you think we're still furiously angry at you, that we need you, that we hate you, that we scrabble desperately at your sleeve, crying "Let me go! Let me go!" We've seen you smirk a little over this, sometimes in public and sometimes secretly in the mirror when you thought no one was looking. You're right, because there is an Esther who still hates and needs you but she never liked you (that was the giveaway) and every day she fades a little more. She cared horribly when you said guns were penises so she couldn't have one, that pens were penises so she couldn't have one, that checkbooks were penises so she couldn't have one, that minds were penises so she couldn't have one. (It astonishes all of us, this monopoly on symbols.)

When I smile flatteringly at you, we're a liar.

When we hate and need you, I'm dangerous.
When they become indifferent, run for your life.

At this point some hapless liberal sees the end-papers approaching and has started looking frantically for the Reconciliation Scene. It (the liberal) is either cursing itself for having got entrapped in what started as a perfectly harmless story of love, poignancy, tragedy, self-hatred, and death, or—rather smugly—is disapproving of me for not possessing Shakespeare's magnificent gift of reconciliation which (if you translate it) means that at this point I must (1) meet a wonderful, ideal man and fall in love with him, or (2) kill myself.

You write it.

The way to do it is this: (1) give up your job, (2) become impotent, (3) go on Welfare, (4) crawl on your hands and knees both to the Welfare people and your sex partners, and (5) just for the hell of it, turn Black.

Now you can write a *perfectly beautiful* reconciliation scene.

You are the liberal who might concede (if pushed into a corner and yelled at by twenty angry radicals) that morality does indeed begin at the mouth of a gun (though you'd add quickly, "It doesn't end there") but do you realize what does end at the mouth of a gun? Fear. Frustration. Self-hate. Everything romantic. (This depends, of course, on being at the proper end of the gun.)

You are the teenage male student who comes to us saying O teachur teachur why teachest not thou Conan the Conqueror, Brak the Barbarian, and Douglas the Dilettante, they are mightye of thewe and arme, O teachur, teach yon mighty heroes of olde, pray pray. To which we answer, Sirrah student thou jestest tee hee ho ho what interest hath a Woman of Reason in yon crappe? To which thou sayest, That is not crappe,

O blind teachur, but Great Art and Universale; it is all about Myghty Male Feats and Being an Hero, appealing alike to yonge and old, hye and lowe, Blakke and Whyt. To which we reply Buzz off, thou Twerp, thou hast of sexism and acne a galloping case feh feh.

You—oh, what a *nuisance* you are!—will someday soon see us on TV asked at a demonstration, or someone like me until she turns round (you can't pick them out of a crowd)—

Interviewer: Who are you?

We (smiling): Oh, somebody. A woman.

Interviewer (he's getting insistent): But what's your name?

And we'll say very lightly and quickly: My name is Legion.

My father once taught me to shoot the same way he taught me to play chess—badly, so he could beat me. He showed me Fool's Mate (so I could avoid it, he said) and then insisted that I play before I'd even memorized what the pieces were supposed to do, before I felt comfortable with them. He then gave me Fool's Mate twice.

I'm a quick learner. We all are. We never played again. Just as we never shot again. Just as we never challenged him again.

Until now.

Jean went to New Zealand. She got her degree, got a job there, and left.

I went to my first Lesbian bar.

It's a gloomy place converted from an old garage and has been bombed twice, not by bigots but by the Mafia, who run the other gay bar in town. They did it late at night when there was nobody in it, which was thoughtful of them, sort of.

I met a big, fat, low-income woman with a ducktail haircut.

I *really do* object to the low income and so does she.

I was introduced to her by a nervous, wide-eyed twenty-year-old who'd never finished high school and who told me a long, complicated story (cracking gum) about an English teacher who accused her of plagiarism when she was writing an essay about religion, which she felt very keenly because at the time she'd been planning to become a nun. When she found out what I did for a living ("An English teacher!" she said in dismay) she was very kind anyway; she insisted on playing a game of TV ping pong with me and then took me around and introduced me gravely to everyone in the bar. I ended up sitting next to the big, fat, &c., with whom I cried a little, about Jean's leaving, but then I perked up when she asked me to dance. I felt like an awful fool, dancing, because I hadn't done it since I was twelve in summer camp (and then we only learned to rhumba, for some peculiar reason) but she felt so good. So lovely and blessed, as upholstered people do. Which surprised me. So we wandered around the floor for a bit and then went to my place because a converted garage with dim lights is pretty depressing (she said it first) and I cried some more.

She showed me her great lavender hat (a cap with a visor) and told me what it's like to drive a taxi. I cheered up.

We made love, nervously.

You know, I am an awful snob. Or I have been an awful snob, but if it's possible to be miserable once and then not, one doesn't have to stay a snob, either.

It was all you, you, you (poor you!), secret guerilla warfare and I won't let you play on my affections; I'm allowed to joke about it but only on my back, this wicked, deadly, ghastly, losing, murderous folly you so genially, so cheerfully, and so jokingly insist on.

But there's another you. Are you out there? Can you hear me? We're going to meet a dozen times a day. You'll

be in my c.r. group and you'll say you can't stand Lesbians, Lesbians are terrible, they're horrible, and I'll say (in
a small voice, trying not to crawl under the sofa), "But
I'm a Lesbian," and you'll say, "Oh," so much in an "Oh,"
so many worlds in an "Oh."

We'll joke across a store counter, eyes meeting, across
a mimeo machine, talk haltingly in a laundromat, saying,
"Yes, I didn't think it would go up to eighty today,"
or "Yes, it's awful to drive in snow," meaning, "Yes, I
know." Women who'd hate me if you knew; you don't
want to hear about libbers and you certainly don't want
to hear about the other thing, either, but still there's
that amazing bond, following each other around the
office tentatively, primitive Democracy, bits of words
exchanged in the margins of Serious, Important, Public
Life, little sympathies, women with silly gestures, women
with self-deprecating laughs, women with too many
smiles, women who wear white gloves, and under it all
the most amazing toughness.

Once a week I get an airmail letter with an efflorescent
stamp, a koala bear or a rhododendron, New Zealand,
of all places.

Students who follow me with slitted eyes, with their
private journals, with handkerchiefs balled in their fists,
because they must talk all about Charlotte Brontë or die.

You're alone. You've had a bad time. You'd rather not
talk to anyone, it's much safer, and yet somehow—impru-
dently—you do, every chance you get. You say the most
amazing things to virtual strangers. You know whom
you can trust.

You say nasty things about women and laugh, get
tense and furious in the presence of women intellectuals, career women, man-haters, un-Christian harpies.

You give me cookies and tea anyway because I look
like a nice lady and you don't know it but you're right;
I am a nice lady.

You have wonderful memories: a hat with a striped ribbon at age eight, waving at a troop train in World War One, being carried in a parade holding a sign that said Votes for Women, having to wear knickers and being forbidden to play with the neighbor cat, a baleful Persian tom with green eyes, whom you loved.

You breed cats. You ride. You fix cars. You can't stand my mother. Sometimes you are my mother. You write awful stories in my classes about women who work in factories (you know less than nothing about them) and whose husbands beat them and who are simple and elemental and who forgive everyone, and in the middle of these stale and dreadful fictions you put your own frightening, beautiful, terrible, vivid dreams.

You're Rose.

You go quietly mad in little backwaters, worry about your kids, tell everybody what's wrong with today's children, hate your mother, mutter aloud in department stores, say awful things in public to my friend's crippled daughter, drag yourself out at thirteen (one leg in a brace) to learn to ride horses. You're the radical so ready to destroy yourself that you intimidate me. You write letters to local papers in which you condemn all the working women in the world, all the Black people in the world, all the pot-smoking students, and all the radicals who would defile the promise of America, and you sign them, "A Christian American Anti-hippie Mother."

What can I say to you? You're more various than that. How can I love you properly? How can I praise you properly? How can I make love to you properly? How can I tell you never to kill for pleasure, never to kill for sport, never to kill for cruelty, but above all, don't play fair, because when they invite you in, remember: we aren't playing.

You teach introductory university biology, cry "Pull yourself togethah!" to your less-than-Spartan friends, and charge up mountains at forty-three, working like ten women, carrying a baby while you teach five classes, running a farm, dyeing your stiff British hair, and intimidating everyone with that upper-class British voice in which you tell us all—so thrillingly—to be Strong.

You live on unemployment, keeping gas money in a cut-off milk carton in the front of your car, fixing four or five cars for a hobby, getting full of grease most of the time, wearing your hair curled above your square jaw like Anna Magnani, whom you say you look like (and you do), and spending brow-knotted hours braiding macramé plant holders for geraniums.

You smile a lot and retreat a lot and discover strange things about mesons, very quiet, very shy, always losing things out of the pocket of your lab coat, deferential to your husband, deferential to everybody, always looking as if you had just said, "What?"

You're my Polish grandmother, bad-tempered and selfish, an immigrant at seventeen to a country that was not paved with gold after all, throwing dishware at your two daughters in a rage until they hid out of range on the porch roof, yet calmly taking a hot iron away from a crazy countrywoman, saying, "Sophie, dolling, you don't mean it. Give me the iron."

You're my friend Carolellen, who dressed as a Russian Maiden in summer camp when we had the costume party, fascinated by lipsticks and blue-tinted stockings at twelve, short-tempered, crying once because you thought somebody was letting a pet salamander die (you were so theatrical about that!), not wanting to hear about sexual intercourse from the camp counselor because you knew married people just felt each other up, and falling in love with your cousin who, to my mind, resembled a long, lanky newt, but insisting that sex had nothing to do with it; it was his beautiful soul.

You write me letters about my books, saying, "Do you know what it's like to find yourself in literature only as a bad metaphor?" and you sign them "Empress of the Universe" and "A Reader" and "A Struggling Poet" and "A Married Woman." You say, "I liked your book and am sending it to my daughter, who is a telephone lineman in Florida."

Hello. Hello, out there. Have you met Jean in New Zealand? Did you meet somebody you thought might be Jean? That's enough. Did you think you had no allies? What I want to say is, there are all of us; what I want to say is, we're all in it together; what I want to say is, it's not just me, though I'm waving, too; I've hung my red petticoat out on a stick and I'm signaling like mad, I'm trying to be seen, too. But there are more of us.

You once sent me a poem. I have an awful feeling you may send me thousands of poems. I can't read them. I'll have to put them in my waterbed. (I haven't got a waterbed.) I'll have to feed them to my camel. (I haven't got a camel.) It's too many poems for one woman to read, but we should all trade poems, we should all talk like mad and whoop and dance like mad, traveling in caravans and on camelback (great, gorgeous, sneery eyes, haven't they?) and elephant-howdah and submarine and hot-air balloon and canoes and unicycles and just plain shanks' mare towards that Great Goddess-Thanksgiving Dinner in the sky; Jean can roughhouse with Stupid Philpotts and tie his hair back with a red ribbon and then roll up her sleeves and make her batter better.

We must all get some better butter; that will make our batter better.

The shirtwaist workers who went on strike started just by going on strike, but then they discovered things; they discovered picketing and unity and museums and *Les Miserables* and Marx and journalism and racism* and parks and love and work and how to cook and each

*Well, they *began* to. Some of them. Sort of.

other. I like to think they had fights about whether trade unionism meant feminism and feminism meant Lesbianism and Lesbianism meant trade unionism and so forth.

So hello. It's beginning. I don't care who you sleep with, I really don't, you know, as long as you love me. As long as I can love all of you. Honk if you love us. Float a ribbon, a child's balloon, a philodendron, your own hair, out the car window. Let's be for us. For goodness' sakes, let's not be against us. Somebody (female?) scrawled on a wall at the Sorbonne the most sensible comment of the twentieth century and it must have been a woman; I will bet a postage stamp (with a koala on it) that it was a woman.* She looked around her and she knitted her brow** and then she wrote what I think we should all follow, not to excess, of course,*** but to excess, because the Road to Excess leads absolutely everywhere, William Blake, q.v. (who was sort of one of us but not nearly enough, not to excess, not to wisdom).****

She wrote:

Let's be reasonable. Let's demand the impossible.*****

---

*I do not have in my possession at the moment a postage stamp with a koala bear on it. I do have, however, a postage stamp with a picture of the New Zealand rhododendron on it (stylized). I'll bet that one.

**Actually she may not have done this; she may simply have written it. You don't have to make a face, though it helps.

***Heavens, no.

****He proposed to his wife, one hot summer's day, that they take off their flesh and sit in the garden in their bones. She did better. She knew better. She sat in the garden in her naked soul.

*****Right!

******A foot note without a referent.

*******Another.

********And another. By far the best kind.

*********Yet another.

**********A perfectly blank footnote.

***********This one is special. It's for Jean.

************This one is *very* special. It ends the book. It is for you.

AUTHOR'S NOTE

JOANNA RUSS

My apologies to friends whose houses, dogs, gardens, mannerisms, clothing, and landscapes I have stolen for this book.

I have also stolen literary quotations. "Indefinable rapture" comes from Mary Ellmann's *Thinking about Women* (Harcourt Brace, Jovanovich, New York, 1968, p. 95). The various quotes from literary women are as follows: "How are we fallen! fallen by mistaken rules"— Anne, Countess of Winchilsea; "Women live like Bats or Owls, labour like Beasts, and die like Worms"—Margaret Cavendish, Duchess of Newcastle, both quoted by Virginia Woolf in *A Room of One's Own* (Harcourt, Brace, & World, New York, 1957, pp. 62 and 64). "Anyone may blame me who likes" is the beginning of the famous feminist outburst in Charlotte Brontë's *Jane Eyre*; "How good it must be to be a man when you want to travel," is quoted by Tillie Olsen from Rebecca Harding Davis's letter to a friend in Olsen's biographical essay on Davis in *Life in the Iron Mills* (The Feminist Press, Old Westbury, New York, p. 101). "John laughs at me but one expects that in marriage" occurs in Charlotte Perkins Gilman's *The Yellow Wallpaper* (The Feminist Press, Old Westbury, New York, p. 6). "It had all been a therapeutic lie. The mind was powerless to save her. Only a man—" is part of Mary McCarthy's story "Ghostly Father, I Confess" in *The Company She Keeps* (Harcourt, Brace & World, New York, 1942, p. 302). The last quotation, "I/Revolve in my/ Sheath of impossibles—" is part of the eleventh stanza of

"Purdah" in Sylvia Plath's *Winter Trees* (Harper & Row, New York, 1972, p. 41).

Some of the above have undergone minor revisions, but there are no major ones.

For those interested, the strike referred to in the title is the shirtwaist-makers' strike of 1909–1910 which occurred in New York and Philadelphia. It was the first general strike of its kind and the first large strike of women workers in this country. It involved between ten and twenty thousand working women, most between the ages of sixteen and twenty-five. They held out for thirteen weeks in midwinter. One magistrate charged a striker: "You are on strike against God and Nature, whose prime law it is that man [sic] shall earn his bread in the sweat of his brow. You are on strike against God." Details may be found in Eleanor Flexner's *Century of Struggle* (Atheneum, New York, 1970, pp. 241–243).

Contemporary Commentary

ON LIGHTNING,
AND AFTER LIGHTNING

JEANNE THORNTON

Most critical references to *On Strike Against God* frame it as period piece, time capsule, "Minor Russ." "Generally considered autobiographical and thus often treated as out of the bounds of the Russ science-fictional canon"[1]—"late-twentieth-century radical satire that aspires to be revelatory to heterosexual women."[2] In other words, a lapse. Samuel Delany calls it "a book that has been all but ignored."[3] Why?

The idea of the lost, outlier work is compelling to me: the stylistic experiment, the supposed wrong turn. Sometimes it really is a wrong turn, but sometimes it's a transit not completed. A dark room lit, at the moment of capture, by a flash before again falling dark. What was Russ imagining in this mid-career (which would retroactively, due to health concerns and publication difficulties, be seen as late-career) turn from genre? What was this book the prologue to?

Russ biographer Gwyneth Jones describes reinvention and new beginnings as "the only pattern in [Russ's] career."[4] Per *How to Suppress Women's Writing*, Russ's initial movement into science fiction was itself reinvention: "Convinced that I had no real experience of life, since my own obviously wasn't part of Great Literature," she wrote, "I decided consciously that I'd write of things nobody knew anything about, dammit. So I wrote realism disguised as fantasy, that is, science fiction."[5] Throughout her career, Russ moved between science fiction and realism but kept her lived experience close as a motive and source of inspiration. "I'm always afraid someone will find out that my fiction is 75% Self + 25% Me Too," she wrote.[6] In her realist short fiction, the autobiographical strain is clear: 1965's "Life in a Furniture Store," 1976's O. Henry Award–winning "Autobiography of My Mother," the 1982 novella "The Little Dirty Girl," and 1970's "The Precious Object," whose plot is in direct continuity with *On Strike*'s. Russ's most famous novel, *The Female Man*, is science fiction, but consciously blurs this with the autobiographical, bringing an authorial-insert character, Joanna, into contact with three alternate-reality selves. Russ completed work on *On Strike Against God* in 1973,[7] after *The Female Man*'s composition but before its 1975 publication date. She consciously conceived of this book as an extension: "what I couldn't do in F. M."[8] Given this, we can read *On Strike Against God* as a reversal of Russ's early-career pivot to science fiction. It's yet another reinvention, but this time, it's also a homecoming.

On Strike's plot can be summed up in a question: "What I do wonder is where did they get the nerve to defy God?"* The speaker is Esther, a professor of English at a pastoral college sometime in the 1970s (likely Cornell, where Russ once taught). God, to Esther, is the patriarchal order, which is ubiquitous and unrelenting. ("'What's it like to be a woman?' I took my rifle from behind my chair and shot him dead. 'It's like that,' I said.")

In *On Strike*, as in *The Female Man*, the war is inescapable: Esther is crept on at bars by napkin-shredders, demeaned at faculty parties. The war extends even into her mind, where her deceased therapist, Count Dracula,

---

*All quotes not otherwise attributed are from *On Strike Against God* or *The Female Man*—I have to hope it is clear which.

lives rent free. He berates her for her marriage's failure, attacks her body, tells her she suffers from penis envy. "They have humanity envy," she replies. Then, to herself: "Pretend you're a man. I did that when I was fourteen. But that's forbidden (and impossible)."

The war leads to a declaration of independence:

> I'm not a woman. Never, never. Never was, never will be. I'm a something-else. My breasts are a something-else's breasts. My (really rather spiffy) behind is a something-else's behind. . . . I have a something-else's uterus, and a clitoris (which is not a woman's because nobody ever mentioned it while I was growing up) and something-else's straight, short hair, and every twenty-five days blood comes out of my something-else's vagina. . . . They got to my mother and made her a woman, but they won't get me. Something-elses of the world, unite!

"Heroine #1," Russ calls Esther in her letter to Delany.[9] Jean is "Heroine #2," Esther's opposite number, the "twenty-six-year-old wonder" graduate student who lives in a local cooperative. In 2004, Samuel R. Delany quotes memoirist Jane Gallop's description of Joanna Russ at Cornell in 1971:

> One of the campus's best known feminists, an early leader in the national movement for women's studies, a published writer over six feet tall, this teacher was a woman whom I looked up to in every way. She walked into the dance accompanied by a beautiful girl I had seen around and knew to be a senior. The teacher was wearing a dress, the student a man's suit; their carefully staged entrance publicly declared their affair. I thought the two of them were the hottest thing I had ever seen.[10]

Jean "studies mathematics for fun, makes her own clothes as recreation, can do anything": a figure of raw force. Esther thinks Jean is "one of the seven wonders of the world." Esther and Jean sit together in the garden and rip on H. P. Lovecraft (his "rugose tentacles"), surrounded by absurd, silent fecundity ("Beautiful little plant genitals swaying in the breeze and surrounded by vast evergreens. . . . Even the now-disgraced snapdragon bells make no noise"). Esther's mind is such a joy to live in, a rich emulsion of allusion, appreciation for the natural world, and intensely quotable riffs that simmer and grow complex, like bones melting into stock. And sometimes vulnerability, sudden, astringent, and bright: "Do you think Jean is—might be—a something-else?"

Jean shows up at Esther's house with gifts of bacon, of black cherry ice cream, of "inferior lox." Esther and Jean show up for one another against men. Jean leaves a parting curse on the faculty party where Esther has been demeaned: "a formal, balanced sentence . . . hanging in the air in front of the house. The kind of thing written in letters of fire over the portals of the Atreidae." When Jean is later accosted at a bar by a male co-op member, Esther grabs him by the shirtfront and calls him a fake radical. ("I felt sorry for him. It's that tender, humane compassion you feel right after you've beaten the absolute shit out of somebody.") In Russ's work, older women often rescue younger ones. In *The Female Man*, the traveler from another reality, Janet Evason, rescues the teenager Laura Rose from the solitary life of a teenage girl in 1970s gender-policed America. But here, rescue is mutual: both Heroine #1 and Heroine #2 "wuz pushed." Something in Russ's work is shifting.

The moment in which Esther realizes she desires Jean: "I started thinking again and the first thought was very embarrassing: I realized I had been staring very rudely at Jean . . . whose breasts were silhouetted through her blouse by the late afternoon sun." Embarrassing, rude. In 1985, Russ would famously write of Kirk/Spock slash fiction "that their subject is not a homosexual love affair between two men, but love and sex as women want them, whether with a man or with another woman."*[11] ("I used to daydream . . . that I was a man making love with another man," Esther tells us.) Russ highlights the role of shame, scruple, and hesitation in K/S: "So paralyzing are these worries and scruples and hesitations to the two characters involved that over and over again the lovers must be pushed together by some force outside themselves. Somebody is always bleeding or feverish or concussed or mutilated or amnesiac or what-have-you in these tales."[12] In other words, there are science-fictional forces bringing Kirk and Spock together. But for Esther, a character in a realistic fiction, lust can be as simple as "a permission of the will." She condemns herself for it: "nonsense, just fantasy. . . . What you do sordidly, in cellars." She makes more vows: "It'll ruin our friendship. And suppose she tells someone?" Finally, she kisses Jean on the neck. Closing her book "deliberately," Jean turns and kisses her back. "You don't ask the whole world if it's really doing what it's doing," Esther says.

Critics have been mean, even snide, about the sex in *On Strike Against God.* "The reader is left bemused," writes one, "about whether the first-person narrator is referring, in her use of the metaphor, 'rose,' to the anus or clitoris, or perhaps both."[13] Which reader, again, is *bemused*? In general, critics are mean and snide about attempts to put sex into language. (See the annual Bad Sex in Fiction Award hosted by the *Literary Review*.)**[14] This is

---

*For those not in the know: Kirk/Spock slash fiction, or K/S, is the erotic subgenre exploring sexual and romantic attraction between the two leads of the original *Star Trek* TV series.

**Its purpose: "to draw attention to the crude, tasteless, often perfunctory use of redundant passages of sexual description in the modern novel, and to discourage it"—i.e., to discourage not the effect but the attempt.

because everyday language naturally breaks down around sex—an "impalpable barrier," as Esther calls it. But Russ flings herself, laughing, straight into the aporia. "We—uh—'did things,' we—uh—'endured' and we—mm—'with our.'" In a 2011 interview, Russ reminisced: "When I was in my teens I do remember reading *Forever Amber*, which was the scandalous book of the time. And the sex scenes always ended with three or four dots. I got to the point where if I saw three or four dots, it would turn me on."[15] I think part of this book's critical neglect has to do with the deep feeling that one shouldn't try to break that elliptical silence. Some deep resistance in us wants sex to be private, allusive, removed.

But I love this book for not being removed. I love the period detail: the drawn curtains, the spaceship vibrator on the couch, the living room quilt. I love the wide-eyed, clinical wonder: the observation that "women's faces are covered with fine, almost invisible down," the "odd sort of diagonal" motion of Jean using Esther's hand to get off, the sex rash: "Utterly fascinating. You can only see it on very fair-skinned women . . . wild roses and milk." I love the awkwardness, and I love the tenderness that holds the awkwardness. I love Esther being a lowkey lech ("Back rubs are sneaky, low-level trickery," another echo of *The Female Man*.) I love how lyrical it gets: "She's a vast amount of pinkness—fields and forests." And I love how even this sequence isn't free of the war: "To me she looks beautiful but very oddly shaped; I suppose there's the unconscious conviction that one of us has to be a man and it certainly isn't me." I love how *extra* it all is, how vulnerably, too-muchly sweet. "I fulfilled a daydream of twenty years' standing and nibbled along her hairline, under her temples and around her ears." I love how the sex gets to be all the things we get to be.

From Russ's 2011 interview:

> One thing I have tried to do when I write . . . was take the
> sex in my stories and simply make it part of the whole
> fabric. It's not special, it's not sacred, it's not demonic, it
> just happens. It's as much an ordinary part of life as heat-
> ing your dinner up, or something, and I always worked
> very hard to get that over. That's the antithesis, the three
> dots, I guess.[16]

Reading the sex in this book, I keep wondering: If,
by hypothesis, this approach to sex didn't jibe with SF's
literary practices in 1973 or even 1980, what practices
did it jibe with? Another way to ask this: What lesbian
writers, at this time, was Joanna Russ reading? The book
was written in 1973 and not published until 1980 by
Joan Larkin's Brooklyn-based Out & Out Books, one
of many feminist and lesbian-focused presses that had
emerged during those seven years. Very little lesbian writing was officially available in 1973. How connected was
Russ, in Ithaca in 1973—soon to be the founding place
of Firebrand, the Moosewood Collective, the Crossing
Press Feminist Series that would one day reissue *On
Strike*—with unofficial channels?[17] Thinking of my own
experiences exchanging manuscripts with other trans
women novelists in the 2010s makes me wonder whose
privately circulated confessionals she was reading, and
how she shaped her work in response. (In *On Strike*,
Esther haunts the library, "picking out obscure references to memoirs written by bad ladies two hundred
years ago and novels by worse ladies who, though
personally blameless, wrote bad books . . . The awful
constriction, the huge skirts.") Writing sex and desire
between women—stepping away from the neon world of
science fiction, creating a new language—is work. How
alone was Russ in that work? I wish I knew.

The second time Esther and Jean have sex, Esther
draws the curtains in advance, and the two take their
clothes off and sit on the couch for tea. They compare

bodies: "I showed Jean the mole on my hip; so she lifted her hair and showed me the freckles on the back of her neck." Earlier, Esther recalls necking with a friend at summer camp at twelve: "We all did . . . A point of peculiar integration," another image that recurs in *The Female Man*. Here, with Jean, this thread continues: "We talked about the ecstasies and horrors of growing breasts at twelve, of bouncing when you ran, of having hairy legs . . . There is this business where you think people end at the neck." ("So they split me from the neck up," laments Joanna in *The Female Man*.) But as the women talk, something changes: "As we reconstituted ourselves in our own eyes—how well we became our bodies! How we moved out into them . . . until she looked—as she had felt to me before—of one piece . . . as if thirty years ago we had been interrupted and were only now just resuming."

I don't know exactly how autobiographical *On Strike* is, but it *feels* diaristic: meaning it captures the way the emotions in a diary, however transitory, feel permanent. On one page, Esther is musing on an article about George Eliot she doesn't want to write: "Waiting for Jean is useful: perceptions are sharpened." On another, she's overcome as she drives home: "The wet, cloverleaf roads twist and turn under the city lights like shining black snakes. It's just rained: brilliance and darkness . . . The world belongs to me. I have a right to be here."

And yet I know the book isn't some kind of transfigured diary, edited into shape for publication: its pace and plan are too elegant. What's more, there are all the recurring images. Picturing Joanna Russ's writing, in this book and in general, I see a storm of words circling in the air, then being grounded by lightning. Where the lightning strikes, the earth charges, and lightning becomes more likely. In *The Female Man*, Janet Evason gives a nervous Laura Rose a back rub; Esther does this for Jean. The assassin Jael Reasoner regards a male sex partner's "bananaflower" genitals; Esther recalls her former husband's with the same word. In both books, here is the sequence of declaring desire: a kiss on the neck, a bright red blush, a rupture—in *On Strike*, "reality tore itself in two, from top to bottom," while "reality tore wide open" in *The Female Man*. Strong experience heightens and intensifies memories, leaving them behind as sensory objects in the mind. And strike after strike—as the object is regarded and regarded again, from context to context, book to book, over the course of a life and work—its meaning and significance involutes, elaborates like Celtic knotwork.

This, I believe, is *On Strike Against God*'s material substrate: memories once felt, later transfigured, as lightning turns earth to fulgurite glass. Fulgurite memories are the bridge across works and genres. In science fiction, living memory has, by necessity, to be set within projected material: this is how to build a cyborg body, which the genre, to *be* genre, requires. But free of genre restriction, memory and the body, however initially divided, can knit together without seam. In *The Female Man*, the charge between Janet and Laura requires a Whileaway, an alternate-dimension feminist utopia, as catalyst. Here, it's a property of the world that reader and author share. To come out, to become radical, is something you might actually go out and do. In this way, *On Strike* isn't a lapse: it's a progression.

The final third of *On Strike Against God* accelerates into crisis: Jean flees; Esther laments. She questions whether the relationship was even real. "I can never tell anyone." Of course Jean returns, tells a furious Esther ("I don't want her") that she loves her, too. She's sorry she got scared; she was staying in Boston with "other Lesbians." Her flight from Esther, then, wasn't a flight from Esther at all, but from the strike. She lacked the courage to live up to the expected role of Heroine #2—but now she has found it. "I didn't lift a finger," says Esther of their make-up sex, "just like all those ladies in peignoirs in vampire movies"—and then Esther sits "admiring beautiful Jean, who now wanted the same things done to her." And then the two of them go out to the garden with Jean's new rifle to learn how to kill men.

With this, the question of the plot—how does one get the nerve to go on strike?—is answered: Heroine #1 and #2 meet, connect, realize they are not alone. But for me, this answer raises three more questions. The first:

(1) Who is Jean?

I mean when she isn't being a "shield-maiden," or "Heroine #2," or "one of the seven wonders of the world." We know that to Esther, Jean is everything: "I saw already what the pattern of my love affair would be: worrying each time she was away, relieved each time she came back . . . I'm a Jean-ist." Things we know about Jean: she's twenty-six to Esther's thirty-eight. She has a part-time job "checking out books or something." She lives in a co-op, has parents whom Esther sees socially. She writes, reads, makes her own clothes. She is a force.

In a 1975 review of what sounds like an awful Harlan Ellison movie, Russ writes: "According to Samuel Delany, literary characterization proceeds by means of three kinds of actions: gratuitous, purposeful, and habitual, and well-written characters perform all three."[18] Jean is purposeful, and Jean has habits, and Jean has as many gratuitous fancies as Esther. But I think what I want and do not yet get from Jean is more precisely expressed by my second question:

(2) Who is Esther, to Jean?

This I find much harder to understand. The book is so intensely inside Heroine #1's consciousness. "Without love there's nothing to bring into focus what's outside oneself," says Heroine #1. And this is the real force of this book—the "supernova" that will come of Esther's namesake star—the moment at the beginning of the love affair when you're blinded by the sudden fact of another person. Here is someone whom you respect—recognize—desire—who desires you back.

But one of the facts outside oneself is that consciousness that is not oneself—more, that is different from oneself. Jean is force—then Jean is afraid—then Jean is not afraid anymore. What is the inner context, elided or not, that connects these three dots? We don't know. And here is the issue, because Heroine #2 is structurally, in the end, the principal protagonist: I mean, she drives the plot. All Esther has to do is wait. Jean even buys her an apology watch: "A good one. Perhaps twenty-five dollars. An awful lot, for her."

I keep imagining Russ composing this novel in 1973—imagine her, also, dancing with a student in 1971—and I think of how little I know about what community she had at this moment of mapping a new world. And I think about how palpably lonely this book, and Esther, can feel. What bothers me is that this is a book about coming out and finding plurality—finding that you are not alone. But is it plurality if there are no real disagreements, just delayed affinity? Part of the genre expectation of any story with romantic relationships—whether explicitly a romance, or generally in "literary fiction"—is that the characters, whatever their affinities, will at some point face an impasse. To resolve it, one or both characters must grow. But this is not actually what happens between Esther and Jean. This book, pining and all, is a vision of lesbian heaven: once you are through the gates, once you have overcome your fear of lesbianism itself, no difficulties will remain. In heaven, are we separate?

There is a glimpse of a future beyond Heroines #1 and #2 in the finale, which makes the number of heroines suddenly infinite. "It's beginning . . . let's be us . . . For goodness' sakes, let's not be against us." Like a balloon taking off, the book moves into a direct address that transcends Esther and Jean, transcends the framework of the strike against God, transcends men altogether. "You're alone. . . . You have wonderful memories. . . . You breed cats. . . . You can't stand my mother. Sometimes you are my mother." The revolution will communicate outward, send signals: "Have you met Jean in New Zealand? Did you meet somebody you thought might be Jean? That's enough." There will be a new world, one where we talk, discover, fight: "about whether trade unionism meant feminism and feminism meant Lesbianism and Lesbianism meant trade unionism and so forth." The book transcends linearity altogether, breaks into a series of footnotes, some without referents. Like magic, the scenery flats fall, as do all walls. The last words of *The Female Man* (barring the "to my book" epilogue) are *I, myself.* The ending of *On Strike against God* is *you.**

And this is my third question:

(3) What happens next?

---

*Here is a footnote on that footnote. Because I have a fourth question to add to the three I started with, and this is the one that haunts me as I read: Is this fantasy for me? Can "you" = trans woman?

To reframe that question: what was, is, transness to Joanna Russ? On the one side, the book has many trans flags for me, most involving its vision of gender (see many, many of the quotes above). In her 2007 telephone interview at WisCon, when asked whether she retained prejudice toward trans women, Russ said no. I think about that, and I think about what I see in the image of Anna, the "half-changed" non-op transsexual in *The Female Man*, force-feminized by Manland in a way that Jeanine, the dreamy, dying-inside, eternal-1950s version of Joanna Russ, quickly recognizes.

But against these, I remember Russ praising Janice Raymond's *The Transsexual Empire*, which asserts that "all transsexuals rape women's bodies by reducing the female form to an artifact," in a letter to Alice Sheldon, or

Because the moment you signal beyond yourself, and a voice that's not yours answers, you're no longer at the end of the story, but the beginning.

More precisely, here's what I want. In 1973, Joanna Russ turned away from science fiction to find a new approach to her material, to step outside metaphors and reclaim her "real experience of life." The book she'd write would be lesbian Great Literature, and a literature about connection: "I've hung my red petticoat out on a stick and I'm signaling like mad." It would ask questions: What does desire look like among equals? And what if you didn't have to wait for a portal to Whileaway or Womanland to open in order to demand it? What if you had to be brave right now?

The book is lightning, illuminating the territory for just long enough to capture it. But love and queerness aren't only incandescence: they're what sustains burning. They look different in the daylight. Part of the power of

---

reviewing Mary Daly's *Gyn/Ecology*, which makes the case that trans women are agents of patriarchy sent to invade and destroy women's spaces, in the pages of *Frontiers* in 1979 ("I suddenly woke up a week later, dazzled, shouting: 'It's true! It's all true!'"). How much sin did Russ's final conversion and repentance actually cover? Or, and this is the more important question: If all we now have of Russ is text, which of these two Russes is speaking in the book's final footnote?

I kept hesitating about whether to ask this at all, whether this footnote spoils the party of bringing this beautiful book back into print. I'm doing it because I want to take the finale's invitation seriously. I want to believe in the vision that I think would have bridged this book and the next: of love as solidarity, of love without possession, love as teaching one another to shoot, asking about what it's like to drive a taxicab, sharing the freckles on the back of our necks. I'm here for visions of increasing curiosity, plurality, engagement. I spent a lot of time with Joanna Russ in writing this essay. I echo so many people who've read her: she is brilliant. She insists upon better treatment, refusing to pretend that it's impossible. There is no excuse for not meeting a striker's demands. The book is about how "the nerve to defy God" stems from recognition. There are trans women out there whom I recognize and who recognize me. I can't ask Joanna Russ whether I and mine get to be in the finale. But I can ask for that—specifically, I can ask *you*.

Russ's work generally—what has been so bracing as I've been writing this—is how completely uncompromising it is, how much a storm. I am very far from personally uncompromising, but when I came out as trans, I thought the possibilities of transition, as such, could transform the world. I wrote a book about it, because you have to. But what I really want to imagine for Joanna Russ is the book *after*: a book about negotiating a world that is about ambiguity and plurality (either with rifle or without). I want to see a version of this story—which many, many of Joanna Russ's daughters[19] have written in the fifty years since 1973—where Esther and Jean fight and reconcile, and where the fight is not about whether one or the other has courage enough for queerness. Assuming queerness—assuming a transformed world—the two women can instead fight, reconcile, and grow around the places where they are not identical. I want that for everyone.

Russ was headed here, I think. As the book closes, Jean and Esther have separated offstage: Jean moves to New Zealand for graduate school, leaving Esther alone beyond letters once a week. ("The marriage of [Kirk and Spock] is in many ways ideal," Russ writes in 1985: "neither has to give up 'his' work in the world; both have adventure and love; telepathy provides lifelong commitment and the means of making such a union unbreakable and extremely intimate."[20]) The last in-scene glimpse we get of Esther, she's finding happiness through sex with the kind of women that she used to be afraid to want ("A big, fat, low-income woman with a ducktail haircut. . . . I really do object to the low income, and so does she"). This scene feels unique in the book. Rather than an enemy or a self, this is another consciousness, someone to be curious about. The fulgurite glass—the charged autobiographical object—was the bridge from *The Female*

Man into this book. As she hands the twenty-five-dollar watch to Esther, Jean quotes Alexander Pope: "Tis with our judgments as with our watches, none go just alike but each believes his own." I think this curiosity would have been the bridge to the next.

But logically, a book can't be its own next book: this is exactly why fiction, as method, is so important. *On Strike* is a coming-out story, which should always be about happiness. It's about stepping through the door that thunder cuts into the air, finding through it a new world that is our world. Doors in the air had opened to Russ before—in 1966, when she shook before her type-writer for two weeks, preparing to write about a woman who rescued women—in 1971, commanding the floor of the Cornell women's dance—in 1973, discovering Esther massaging Jean's gun-sore shoulders in the garden as a maple tree "flames up—pure scarlet." ("Would you stop creating and put your rugose tentacle here?") The lava of each vision erupted, then flowed, cooled, became the stone and soil that grows the next. What would the new world of *you* come to look like? What would Russ's eyes have seen, after the lightning had struck? We can't know, and so it's still ours to imagine, to demand, to build.

NOTHING TOO FRIGHTENING

MARY ANNE MOHANRAJ

Sometimes you bend down to tie your shoe, and then you either tie your shoe or you don't; you either straighten up instantly or maybe you don't. Each choice begets at least two worlds of possibility, this is, one in which you do and one in which you don't; or very likely many more, one in which you do quickly, one in which you do slowly, one in which you don't, but hesitate, one in which you hesitate and frown, one in which you hesitate and sneeze, and so on.

—Joanna Russ, *The Female Man*

1.

I have dreams about Amirthi. Nightmares.

Amirthi lives in Negombo, Sri Lanka. She's married, of course, with four children, ages fifteen to twenty-four. The elder two went to study abroad. The younger two are still at home, but soon she and her husband will be done with the child-rearing part of their lives. She's not sure what they'll do next. There was a time when she thought she might be a professor, but the first child put an end to that; it was a difficult birth and a dark stretch afterward, and when she finally had time and heart to think again, the child needed her, and her husband was always at work.

She teaches preschoolers instead, though it turns out that she only likes children under five in very small doses— more than half an hour of their high-pitched chaos and she's desperate for the silence of a library (or a grave). This applies to her own children as well.

Amirthi's eldest daughter is in medical school now, in America; dutiful Sunday Zoom calls are full of complaints about how hard the work is, how long the hours. Amirthi is alternately proud and sick with jealousy.

Amirthi is my middle name, the name I'm known by in the Sri Lankan community, the name my parents call me, the name my husband would have used if I'd married within caste and culture instead of running off in college to date white boys and white girls and various not-white folks until I realized monogamy was not for me. I barely spoke to my parents for a decade. (Another way of looking at it: they barely spoke to me.)

I did have children, two of them, but not like my mother, not at nineteen. She didn't get to finish high school—she married and had me, and her doctor husband brought her to America. She tried to get her GED—Cintha was certainly smart enough. But Mohan was hard at work all the time, and she had two more children, and it was too difficult, all alone.

Sometimes the choices you make at eighteen (or the choices made for you) shape the course of your life in ways you couldn't have imagined. I grew up with a terror of being locked into that same little box.

When I was in high school, my parents told me they'd started sending my photo back to Sri Lanka, trying to arrange my marriage the way theirs had been arranged. They wanted to make sure I was settled, that I was safe.

In Sri Lanka, Amirthi went on with her life. The ethnic conflict rose around her and her family, then settled again. They almost fled to Canada with her cousins—but her mother had grown ill, and angry, and refused to leave. So they stayed and survived, and Amirthi kept her head down and took care of her mother, and her children, and her students, and built a life.

There was a brief affair with Sumathy-down-the-road. Sumathy smiling, hibiscus tucked in her hair. Sumathy of the small, sweet breasts, shaped nothing like mangoes. Sumathy who made small noises when Amirthi undid the button on her office pants and slid her hand inside, down to the heated core of her.

Amirthi's (nice, understanding, reasonable) husband never found out about it. Or he knew, or suspected at least, but was wise enough not to say anything. Amirthi wasn't about to leave the children, and Sumathy had two of her own, so there was never any future to it. They both knew that going in, and after a few short months, the heat subsided.

OR

Amirthi's husband found out about the affair. He started drinking, heavily. One night, Amirthi came home from the kottu shop where she'd just picked up dinner for the family and he, enraged that she spent so much of his money instead of cooking dinner herself, beat her to death with her own cast-iron pan, splattering her brains across the new-swept floor.

I convinced my parents that I needed to concentrate on my studies, which won me a few more years. "Concentrate on my studies" is a very useful phrase in the South Asian community; I recommend it to you, should you need such an escape. I didn't apply to any colleges in the same state as my family, though I didn't tell them that until the application checks were due and it was too late to change.

Halfway across the country, I found enough space to breathe.

2.

Russ was born in 1937, came to adulthood in the 1950s and '60s.

> *I wanted to take off all my clothes and step out of my under-*
> *wear. And then take off my hair and fingernails and my face*
> *and my flesh and finally my very bones. Just to step out of it.*
> *All the way out of it.*
>
> —Joanna Russ, *On Strike Against God*

I was born thirty-four years later, in 1971. When I read Russ, I think, "It's still bad, but not as bad as it used to be." I rarely feel like I don't want to be a woman, though I'm not particularly attached to being a woman in the way I'm expected to be.

I've sung the song "I Enjoy Being a Girl" (which Russ points out is never written about being a boy; why would it be?). There are times when I enjoy the feminine trappings of what girls are allowed/encouraged/required to perform. Earrings and makeup and even heels—at five-foot-nothing, it's nice to be a little taller, even if my feet are screaming after a few hours. I've kicked my shoes off to dance at a wedding, or to walk home, trying not to step on broken glass.

> *Already dainty and good, not liking to have smudges on my*
> *dress (when I remembered) and setting my dolls to school like*
> *my elementary-school teacher aunt, dressing them in appropriate*
> *costumes for the season (which practice I continue with myself,*
> *by the way . . .).*
>
> —Joanna Russ, *On Strike Against God*

I dress seasonally, too; it pleases me to have that in common with Joanna. We can play with prettiness, with aesthetics, when we feel like it; that alone doesn't make us less feminist. We don't *have* to dress up, though. It's not required.

I teach Russ's story "When It Changed" to my students. It shocked me when I first read it in the '80s, just the idea that two women might be married, might live on a planet populated only by women, could perhaps not bother dressing up to please the eyes of men.

I ask my college students what they'd do if they lived alone in the woods, if they never had to deal with anybody at all. Most of us would bathe, because if you don't, you get itchy and sticky. Clean clothes are nice, and slipping into clean sheets at the end of the night. A neat braid keeps long hair from getting tangled; chopping it short works too. That's pretty much it. The most feminine of my students, the ones who spend an hour every morning on hair and makeup (knowing if they don't they'll be penalized, especially the brown and Black girls with "bad" hair), get a far-off look in their eyes. They see a world where they could roll out of bed in their pajamas and *stay that way*.

> When Mary Anne started college, a teacher misread her name, shortened it to Mary. She didn't feel comfortable correcting him, so she let it go, and soon classmates assumed that that was what she preferred, so she became Mary.

> Mary tried to be a good daughter. She dressed in the neat outfits her mother preferred, avoiding spaghetti straps and remembering her pantyhose. She wasn't supposed to date, but she let boys feel her up sometimes at frat parties (under the blouse, over the bra). Mary *always* wore a bra, including to sleep.

Mostly, the penalties I encounter for not performing femininity sufficiently are subtle. I'll never know what jobs or promotions I didn't get. When I applied for teaching jobs after finishing my doctorate in 2005, women professors advised me to wear a skirt suit because I'd be interviewed by older men who didn't like women in pants.

> *I made myself look frail and little. "Oh, no," I said. "I just can't keep up, you know."*
>
> —Joanna Russ, *On Strike Against God*

I was going to be interviewing at the Modern Language Association annual conference in Philadelphia at Christmas, walking between four different hotels through the cold and sleeting snow. I wore pants. If getting the best job I could was my priority, that was a mistake. But maybe it wasn't a mistake. Maybe wearing a skirt for those reasons would have been the first concession, the first step into a more constrained life.

Mary dated a white boy quietly her sophomore year, but she kept it secret from her family; she wouldn't even hold his hand walking across campus for fear some other South Asian student would see and it would get back to her parents. When it ended, Mary was sad but also relieved.

Mary went to medical school and in her few free evenings had dinners with Sri Lankan men her parents suggested. She tried to like them. She convinced herself she was in love with one of them, eventually, and married him, and he let her keep working as a doctor (he liked the money) even after they had their fourth child.

Mary became a pillar of the community, active in her church, doing whatever she could to make it better for the women, the children. She started a foundation to help underprivileged women. Mary did a lot of good. She died in bed, surrounded by grandchildren and great-grandchildren, and didn't miss the husband who'd run off decades ago with his young white secretary.

OR

Mary walked into the bathroom one day when the children's screaming got to be just too much for her, when she was coming off a three-day ICU shift. She swallowed a handful of Xanax and chased it with several shots of whiskey.

That's an ending too.

I fell on Russ like a ravening beast. I don't remember when I first read Russ, but between ages eight and thirteen, I haunted the children's section of the New Britain public library and read every book with the little dragon or rocket ship symbol on the spine signaling science fiction and fantasy. I found *The Adventures of Alyx* and *The Female Man*; I read every single Russ they had. I didn't understand everything I read, but I understood what Joanna was telling me.

She was telling me that I had options—that there were a host of other lives I could live, if I dared to reach for them.

Students ask me how I could write so explicitly about sex. Wasn't I worried about what my parents would think, or what they'd do? I tell them my parents threatened to yank me out of college and send me to a convent school in Sri Lanka, but never went through with it. I tell them I'm working on a memoir, that I'm going to call it *Bad Daughter*, and they laugh. Then we get serious.

That's all the guilt I ever felt. I think I had it out somehow that night; it's like going through an electric fence where the worst point is just before you touch it and your nerves jump, but once you go through, it's O.K.

—Joanna Russ, *On Strike Against God*

I tell my students: the worst part is the first time, and you do it because you feel like you have no choice. I didn't decide to break my parents' hearts, to give my mother nightmares and my father heart palpitations. I just couldn't breathe if I kept cramming myself into that good-girl box.

You force yourself to break the rules because the alternative is unbearable.

I tell my students: it gets easier with practice.

3.

Some paragraphs back, I wrote about a young mother "desperate for the silence of a library (or a grave)," and I wanted to go back and edit that out, because that was too grim, wasn't it? I shouldn't be so morbid about raising children; it's not okay to say that stuff out loud. Other people might get the wrong idea. My mother called me once because I'd been complaining on my blog about exhaustion and lack of sleep. Amma said, "You can't talk like that about your children in public."

In 2010 I was giving a speech at WisCon, the longest-running feminist science fiction convention in the world, and partway through I said, "I hate babies." I swear, the entire room took an audible breath. Close to a thousand people, mostly women, feminists, shocked that a woman—a mother—could say such a thing.

I think Joanna would leave in the line about the grave. She'd also tell me that I don't need to tell you that I love my kids, of course, which I have typed and erased three or four times now.

I love my kids, even if I kind of hated them as babies, since neither one slept through the night until nine months had passed. They were shrieking sacks of potatoes who would only quiet down with constant rocking and singing, hours upon hours upon hours. Before I had them, I used to think singing to my babies would be nice.

Making cookies with preschoolers also sounds nice, but it turns out that I hate that too. The key to surviving, I eventually figured out, is to let them decorate one or two cookies, make a giant mess, then send them away to eat their cookies, which is all they really want. I'd have my husband clean everything up. And then, maybe a day or two later, I'd get to decorate the rest of the cookies in peace.

The cumulative lack of sleep during our children's infancy made both me and Kevin angry, resentful, and more than a little crazed. (Kevin is a committed feminist who actually split the sleepless hours with me evenly, even though I'd talked him into wanting kids—even though he'd had a much clearer idea of how much work it would be than I had. I'd bought the motherhood dream, hook, line, and sinker.) I read a study that said the brains of parents of infants looked remarkably like the brains of psychotic people.

No parent is surprised when I tell them this.

Amirthi: You make it sound so awful and hard. I had four children and three miscarriages; I would've had more children if I could. Our grandmother had nine, you know. Nine!

Mary: I had four, but I wanted just one more. We didn't have a lot of money, but we didn't care; we were rich in children. Didn't you ever want more?

Mary Anne: Yes. If I could've convinced Kevin to start sooner, if I didn't have work I loved, if we weren't so tired— then yes, yes, yes. You are so lucky.

4.

I used to volunteer with an anti-violence hotline; in the training, I learned that one of the worst times for a marriage is right after children are born. The parents are exhausted and stressed and probably not having very much sex, and one of them may be frustrated by that fact. So many men leave their wives then, or hit them. Statistically speaking, women are most likely to be murdered by their intimate male partner. What does knowing that do to a marriage?

> "Well, you can't get along without us, now can you?" says piggy, with a little complacent chuckle. This is my cue to back off fast-fast-fast. . . . I said crossly that they could all go stuff themselves into Fish Lake; it would be a great relief to me.
>
> He twinkled at me. "Disappointed in love," he said.
>
> I think he thought that I thought that he thought that I thought I was flirting. This is unbearable.
>
> —Joanna Russ, On Strike Against God

I've dated women. I could have just stuck to women and maybe that would have been safer. But nothing is actually safe. It was an LGBT anti-violence hotline. I learned that men beat men, and women beat women. I listened to those beaten people at two in the morning. I told them if they were ready to leave, there were places they could go. Places they would be safe.

A same-sex relationship isn't necessarily safe, but patriarchy weighs upon it differently—less likely to crush and twist love beyond recognition. The women of Russ's Whileaway fight duels with each other, kill each other, but it's a different kind of violence. On Whileaway, women fight, but they get to fight back.

The only man who ever laid a violent hand on me is my father, who slapped me across the face. Just once. At age twelve, I'd raised my hand to catch my mother's, to stop her caning me. *Wait until your father gets home.* That slap didn't hurt nearly as much as the cane. But it broke something in our relationship, even though he never touched me again.

And yet, maybe it was for the best; after that, I no longer automatically respected his parental authority. That slap gave me permission to step out of the box and make other choices.

I've dated many men, slept with many men, and none of them have hit me. But I know—*I know* that I've been lucky. I'm a small woman, not trained in violence or resistance. I exist unbeaten by their sufferance.

Knowing that can really mess up a heterosexual relationship.

In a relationship years ago, I lay in bed with a man I loved, not wanting him to touch me but also not wanting to say no, not out loud. It would hurt him, upset him. Anger him. I pretended to be asleep. I'm not proud of that.

Most nights, I lie in bed beside my husband and watch television. Sometimes there's a scene, one of many, where a man hurts a woman because he can. Kevin doesn't like it, but it doesn't hit him the way it does me. Sometimes I can't watch, and I close my eyes, asking him to tell me when it's over. Sometimes I ask him to turn off the television altogether. Enough.

Our son is fourteen and mostly cares about playing video games with his friends. That won't last forever. We don't know what choices he'll make around dating and sex; we don't even know his orientation yet. But we're talking to him, we're having *all* the conversations, trying to head off disaster.

Our daughter is sixteen, and her high school teaches

self-defense as a standard part of the physical education curriculum. Yet despite all our efforts to educate and shelter, to strengthen and empower, she's been frightened and hurt, more than once. We, her parents, have failed to protect her, and it's shattered us.

> *If I ever deliver from between my smooth, slightly marbled something-else thighs a daughter, that daughter will be a something-else until unspeakable people (like my parents—or yours) get hold of it. I might even do bad things to it myself, for which I hope I will weep blood and be reincarnated as a house plant.*
> —Joanna Russ, *On Strike Against God*

Kevin and I, back-to-back and side-by-side, trying to give our children knowledge and options, fighting the weight of the world. Impossibly heavy, crushing every good intention.

5.

> *What do you do when the club won't let you in, when there's no other, and when you won't (or can't) change? Simple.*
> *You blow the club up.*
> —Joanna Russ, *On Strike Against God*

Russ is often described as a radical feminist. When I was in college in 1992 I took a feminist theory class with Lauren Berlant, and in retrospect, I wish I could give her all the apologies; I was a stubborn smart aleck who argued incessantly with the teacher, and in almost every single class I raised the standard liberal feminist arguments to her radical ones.

As a professor myself now, I can hope that at least I gave her a convenient mark to tear apart. For every one of my "Can't we just make small changes?" and "Is it really that bad?" and "Won't fighting make it worse?" arguments, Berlant had a cutting answer.

That was me at twenty; I didn't know anything. Perhaps I could call myself a radical, by Russ's definition:

> Radicals are people who fight their own oppression. People who fight other people's oppression are liberals or worse. Radicalism is being pushed to the wall.
>
> —Joanna Russ, *On Strike Against God*

I did that much. In my twenties, pushed to the wall, I did what I wanted to do with my life. I wrote about sex, slept around, dated men and women and multiple people at once, blew up any chance of the arranged marriage that my parents dreamed of, and endured the burn of breaking through the electric fence. I counted the cost—my parents barely spoke to me for years—but was willing to pay it.

But that was just for me, for my life. I couldn't ask anyone else to take that kind of risk and I wouldn't dare to take it for them.

Thirty years later, I don't call myself a radical (though my parents might be surprised to hear it). I can see the system is corrupted, is broken, is failing so many people. I understand why you might want to blow it up, why incrementalists are seen as servants of the system in the end, inevitably corrupt.

"The master's tools will never dismantle the master's house," says Audre Lorde, and there's truth there. But the cost to blowing up the house—that cost would be immense. Worse, I think, than the cost that we endure living in it, improving it in tiny ways, day by day. I think.

I might be wrong.

I ran for office in 2016, when Trump was elected, when Hillary was denied her victory and so many of us had our hearts broken. I served four years on the local library board, and now four more on our high school board. America has massive discrepancies in race and education, and I work with the rest of the board on efforts like de-tracking: eliminating separate educational tracks such as gifted/honors, since research shows racism affects who is selected for such tracks, which can have far-reaching educational and career consequences. We hope to learn whether, by shifting policy and practice, we can compensate at least a little for the ongoing legacy of slavery in America.

Good work, important work, but sometimes my fellow board members and the school administration get so focused on race that they elide its intersections with gender justice. I have one more year on the board, and the last thing I'm trying to do is persuade them that we need more than a racial equity policy (currently part of our strategic plan); we need an intersectional equity policy.

We are a data-driven board, which I appreciate.

But it's easier to measure how many Black boys are admitted into honors classes (not nearly enough) than it is to measure how many girls are coerced into sex by their boyfriends, how many are assaulted and raped, how many are harassed by their coaches or teachers, how many miss school as a result, how many are afraid to walk the halls, how many have their grades suffer, how many are left with a legacy of anxiety and depression and trauma (so many).

It's particularly difficult to gather data because women, all women, are told to elide it, to hide it, to protect the men, to protect the peace. We're trained in deception for the supposed good of society. (And then they slam us for being liars.)

There is the vanity training, the obedience training, the self-effacement training, the deference training, the dependency training, the passivity training, the rivalry training, the stupidity training, the placation training. How am I to put this together with my human life, my intellectual life, my solitude, my transcendence, my brains, and my fearful, fearful ambition? I failed miserably and thought it was my own fault.

—Joanna Russ, *The Female Man*

I bring the issues up, I keep bringing them up, I'm a broken record—but I'm careful not to push too hard. Don't take too much time at the board meeting—there are important issues waiting for discussion. Don't take up too much space. I wouldn't want to be seen as a hysterical woman.

I don't blow up the house (I'm only a little bit tempted). I'm far left in my beliefs but centrist in my practice, just trying to pull the Overton window (the window defining what the public will accept as reasonable political choices at any given moment) a little further left. I think I can do more good this way, get us closer to a brighter future. I wish I could ask Joanna what she'd do in my place.

Mary Anne to Mary Joanna to MaryJo. MaryJo has fire in her eyes and a knife in her boot. She doesn't temper her language for anyone. MaryJo says *fuck!* a lot. MaryJo is the fucking mayor. When a vote goes against her, she takes to social media, she writes letters to the paper, she makes sure that every citizen of the village knows exactly what she thinks and why.

MaryJo can be convinced she was wrong—but you'd better have a damn good argument. She studies martial arts and home canning. She seizes neglected empty lots and adds four allotment gardens to the village; she's got a giant freezer in her garage, a community breast-milk bank. She runs a shelter out of her house for women who come to Illinois to get abortions now that *Roe v. Wade* has been overturned.

MaryJo has long ago figured out who among her friends and neighbors can be trusted, and, just as important, who has skills that will be useful when the revolution comes.

You're going to have to *earn* your place in her compound.

OR

One vote too many goes against the mayor—MaryJo pulls out her gun and goes around the board table full of men: *bang, bang, bang, bang, bang, bang!*

I've seen radicals in local government; they often have a tough time getting anything done. One woman I admire, whom I voted for, was elected to the local village board—and then I watched as her impassioned voice was met with dismissal. She didn't compromise and she had a hard time building coalitions. Issue after issue, she was shot down. When she argued to defund the police (instead of spending millions on a new police station), she was ridiculed by colleagues, by the press, by the public. In the end, she stepped down from office, traumatized.

Perhaps her voice made a difference, shifted people's positions, if incrementally—the current board just announced that instead of demolishing our historic village hall and building a massive new police station, they're only doing a small glass addition to the hall. They're moving the police station out of the basement and into the light.

6.

Joanna wrote stories where women blew things up. In *The Female Man*, a woman uses her steel teeth and claws to tear apart a man who ignores her clearly stated "no." Jael comes from a dimension, a timeline, where women and men are at war, and doesn't hesitate to advocate for killing men. I don't think Joanna was actually advocating for that.

But she raises the question. She states the radical position in words, at least. For Joanna, no words need be stifled and smothered; nothing is too frightening to be said out loud.

If there's someone with a position far more radical than yours, then your moderate, slightly-left-of-current position sounds far more reasonable. I'm not asking for the moon and the sun, not like *her*—just a slightly bigger piece of the earth. The loud radical position makes the quiet progressive shift possible. (I doubt that satisfies the radical, though.)

I read science fiction writer and anarchist Margaret Killjoy, whose writings frighten and provoke me. It sounds scary, building a community without police. Am I being too cautious? Could I reach for more for my students, my community, if I would only dare to be disliked and mocked? Sometimes I'm afraid Joanna would be disappointed in me. Maybe I've grown centrist in my middle age. I have children now. I have more to lose.

Still, in the end, I write. That is where I am bravest and most effective—not in bed, not at the board table. Maybe politicians do need to bite their tongues sometimes, to compromise to get things done, but writers—writers can say anything. Everything.

It's harder for me to write explicitly about sex now than it was in my twenties. I may have silenced my parents' voices, but I hear my neighbors, my fellow board members—it's unnerving, writing a scene about joyously sucking clit and then the next day going into a publicly broadcasted meeting to reevaluate the school's guidelines on sexual harassment. The two actions are not *actually* in conflict, but as Samuel R. Delany says, society will always push us toward the most conservative position it can. That pressure doesn't let up.

Still, I'm trying. I tell the truth the best I can, and when I'm scared to say something, I remember the first time I shoved my way through that electric fence. It hurt, but it was a pain I learned I could bear. I try to teach my students to do the same. Sometimes, now, they say things that shock *me*, and I know I've succeeded.

That's the legacy of Joanna for me. I started this essay calling her, respectfully, Russ, but the more I peeled away my own defenses to tell you my story, the more I wanted to call her Joanna.

Joanna, my friend, whom I never met but who would have loved me anyway, the way I love all of you. When I was young, she helped me see that I had choices, if I was willing to pay the price.

> So hello. It's beginning. I don't care who you sleep with, I really don't, you know, as long as you love me. As long as I can love all of you. Honk if you love us. Float a ribbon, a child's balloon, a philodendron, your own hair, out the car window. Let's be for us. For goodness' sakes, let's not be against us.
> —Joanna Russ, *On Strike Against God*

Now that I'm older, she's the voice in my head, pushing me to keep questioning myself. I should be fighting harder. I should say all the things, especially the forbidden ones. Perhaps my political actions must be somewhat moderated to be effective, but I can let my writerly imagination be as radical as I want, entirely untrammeled, and encourage my students to do the same.

Maybe we'll blow things up, a little bit.

I want to make Joanna proud.

She looked around her and she knitted her brow . . . and then she wrote what I think we should all follow, not to excess, of course . . . but to excess, because the Road to Excess leads absolutely everywhere. . . .

She wrote:

Let's be reasonable. Let's demand the impossible.

—Joanna Russ, *On Strike Against God*

THE OTHER AXIS: AN INTERVIEW WITH SAMUEL R. DELANY

ALEC POLLAK

Samuel R. Delany is a novelist, critic, theorist, essayist, and memoirist as prodigious as he is prolific. He is "one of the most widely read writers of modern science fiction"[1] and the "country's first prominent Black author of science fiction,"[2] not to mention a "revolutionary chronicler of gay life."[3] His purview is vast: throughout a career spanning over seven decades, Delany has authored landmark publications in science fiction, literary criticism, queer theory, social commentary, and autobiography, for which he has been awarded multiple Nebula, Hugo, and lifetime achievement awards. As he recounts in *The Motion of Light in Water*, his acclaimed autobiography set in pre-Stonewall New York, his long career has brought him into contact with an exceptionally diverse cast of characters, including his wife and collaborator Marilyn Hacker as well as Albert Einstein, Bob Dylan, Stokely Carmichael, Stormé DeLarverie, W. H. Auden, James Baldwin, Octavia Butler, Allan Kaprow, and fellow queer science fiction luminary Joanna Russ.

This interview constitutes but a part of an ongoing conversation between Delany and me, pursued since 2021 as part of my ongoing biographical work on Joanna Russ and, more recently, my editorial work on Russ and Delany's extensive correspondence. Throughout, I've sought to better understand Russ's emergence, ascent, and legacy through the eyes of one immersed in her milieu, devoted to her works, and similarly invested in science fiction's potential as "a vehicle for social change."[4] Though this perspective is widely held today, it was largely unfamiliar at the dawn of science fiction's "New Wave," when the genre was still blinkered, heavily empirical (in Susan Koppelman's words) "white boy's fiction" ("What Can a Heroine Do," page 231). Delany's admiration for Russ remains steadfast, and his memory of their shared context, values, and literary goals will be illuminating for new and present-day readers of Russ.

Delany and Russ met at a dinner party in the late 1960s and embarked shortly thereafter on a decades-long correspondence "of Victorian bulk." Delany calls their correspondence "the most important thing in [his] archive," which is high praise, to say the least. Their friendship was one of mutual respect, adoration, and incisive critique—they were each other's loyal readers, editors, and confidants. "You're still the best writer in the SF community—and tower over most outside it, too," wrote Delany in 1983. "And that's not tact; it's just the truth."[5] Behind each author's cornerstone works—*Dhalgren* and *Trouble on Triton* for Delany, *The Female Man* and now *On Strike Against God* for Russ—exists the other's editorial pen.

But if Russ and Delany hadn't met at Terry Carr's fateful dinner, they doubtless would have encountered one another elsewhere. They quickly emerged as two of science fiction's foremost innovators during the tumultuous 1970s, part of a much broader cohort of authors taking the genre by storm, wresting it from science fiction's old guard, and deploying it, in Delany's words, as an "important exercise for those who are oppressed."[6] The two labored to reconcile science fiction with their own lived experiences (Russ was a lesbian; Delany, a Black gay man), all while languages for naming identity and making sense of one's experience rapidly evolved around them. This quick evolution is borne out in each author's fiction, but also in the public's shifting reception to their fiction over the years. As Russ's friend, peer, and reader, Delany's relationship to Russ's fiction preserves a kernel of the context they shared and offers insight into how Russ has been read—and how we might read her today.

ALEC POLLAK: You and Joanna were friends for decades. How did you meet?

SAMUEL R. DELANY: I was invited over to Brooklyn Heights for dinner by Terry Carr, who was, at the time, my editor at Ace Books. This was in 1967 or 1968. And I remember Terry mentioning on the phone that Joanna Russ would be there, although I had no idea who she was at the time. The dinner was perfectly pleasant; we touched on her playwriting work and her time at the Yale School of Drama, but she never mentioned that she was a fiction writer, nor did she bring up her [first published] novel, *Picnic on Paradise* (1968), which was in production with Ace Books at that very moment as part of Terry's series of Science Fiction Specials.

And then, about two or three weeks later, I got the galleys for *Picnic on Paradise* in the mail from Terry. I was actually rather impressed that Joanna had managed to go through a whole dinner and not mention her own work, and I thought, "Maybe I should start doing the same thing." Anyway, I read the galleys in one afternoon, and the book was extraordinarily good. A friend of mine, Sue Schweers, read them in one afternoon, too. She finished them and said, "That's the realest thing that has happened to me in years," which I remember because that's how Russ's writing always made me feel. It's also a noteworthy response to have to a science fiction novel.

AP: After you met, your relationship evolved primarily through letters—you only met in person a handful of times.

SRD: That's correct. When I moved to San Francisco, we were on different sides of the country, and so I began to write her, and she began to write me back. And this became a very lengthy correspondence which continued basically right up until just before she died.

AP: I'm not sure "very lengthy" quite does it justice . . .

SRD: Our correspondence is of Victorian bulk. Both sides of it are in storage in my archive at Yale's Beinecke Library. It is thousands of pages long, and is, I believe, the most important thing in my archive, along with a far briefer correspondence with Guy Davenport.

AP: That's incredibly high praise. What did you learn from Russ? How did she influence your writing?

SRD: With all due respect, I think probably I influenced Joanna's writing more than she influenced mine. Well, I learned all sorts of things about her politics, and I was able to say, "No, no, no, no." I was the one who was constantly telling her "no"—mainly that homosexuality was not a disease that could be cured, which was a popular and persistent misconception at the time. That's the problem in *And Chaos Died*—in it, homosexuality gets cured. Again, I think *And Chaos Died* is a brilliantly written novel. I still think all of her novels are gorgeously written and they are worth reading simply because of the writing. She had some reservations about them, herself. She eventually decided that a *Picnic on Paradise* was "protofeminist," for example. Well, given what was going on, I think protofeminism is pretty good.

AP: What *was* going on at the time?

SRD: Oh, it was a terrible time for women. Just a terrible, terrible time. It's hard to imagine now. I remember when my mother needed a hysterectomy, and my father refused to pay for it, because it was a "woman's problem." One of the things I do write about somewhere is pockets—women's jeans didn't have functional pockets. I remember once when Marilyn came home out of the rain, put on my pants, and got this weird look on her face. I said, "What's the matter?" And she said, "The pockets, they are so big!" And that's when I first started thinking, "What would I be like if I had spent my entire life without pockets? Without functional pockets?" I've long thought that the model of infantilized women was the fundamental model for all other prejudice, whether Black or gay or what have you—the infantilized woman who was not, of course, a complete human being. This is why Joanna's title *The Female Man* is so revolutionary.

AP: You sing Russ's praises at every opportunity, it seems. You've been so generous with me these past few years—letting me interview you about Russ, contributing to this volume, helping me edit your letters. Why?

SRD: If I can use my name to draw attention to my friend, I want to do that. She's one of the finest stylists of American fiction. It's troubling how few know this, and I want to do what I can to help remedy that.

AP: Again, that's incredibly high praise. Why? What was Russ doing that set her apart from other science fiction writers of the time?

SRD: For one thing, she wrote incredibly sumptuous sentences. The one I always used to quote to my students is from *And Chaos Died*. She writes, "The Big One was obviously one of those epoxy-and-metal eggs produced by itself—the Platonic Idea of a pebble turned inside out, born of a computer and aspiring towards the condition of Mechanical Opera." It's densely allusive—it helps if you catch the reference to

Walter Pater, "All art constantly aspires to the condition of music." But it's also a simple pleasure to read.

AP: Not everyone felt the same way you did. Why was Russ so controversial?

SRD: Often because of what other people said about her. People would say, "Oh, she is shrill and harsh." No! If there is any writing that isn't shrill, whether in her science fiction, in her fiction, or in her nonfiction, it's hers. She was *not* a shrill writer.

AP: That sounds like bald-faced sexism to me.

SRD: Yes.

AP: I can't imagine a more methodical, stylistically tight writer than Russ. In your essay on Russ in *Starboard Wine*, you talk about how much of science fiction is "appallingly written."

SRD: Yes, I think 95 percent of science fiction was appallingly written. Take Frank Herbert—he was one of the nicest people I've ever met, but he could not write a paragraph. The fact that he and Roger Zelazny tied for the Hugo that year [1966], and Zelazny, like Russ, was a spectacular stylist, just goes to show where prose style ranked in terms of importance. Herbert was not a spectacular stylist—most people can't even remember a novel of Herbert's other than *Dune*.

AP: And yet, it only takes one, right?

SRD: Yeah, it only takes one. My regular experience with Frank Herbert, as I said, was that he was a lovely guy. He brought home my second Hugo Award back from Germany and stopped off in New York and rang my doorbell and said, "Hi, it's Frank Herbert. I've your Hugo." Which was a very sweet thing to do, and we sat up and talked for hours. But he could not write his way out of a paper bag.

AP: There are a lot of letters in which you talk to Russ with a great level of adoration and admiration, as though she is a mentor to you. You're always thrilled to receive her edits on your manuscripts. What I'm coming to understand is that you admired what an incredible stylist she was.

SRD: That's it, fundamentally, yes. She was an amazing stylist. It's really important to talk about style. I think the critical temptation is to spend one's entire time just writing about context. But taking up every criticism of Joanna ever made is a waste of time.

AP: That's helpful to hear because right now I'm grappling with a lot of these criticisms of Russ. I've found that there's a lot of ritualistic disavowal and disclaiming of Russ; there are people who love her, people who hate her, and then there is an enormous number of people who love her but can't make peace with themselves for loving her, and so spend a lot of time disclaiming about how problematic she was. It's true: we know she produced works that contradicted her earlier works, and we know she apologized for some previously held views. Of course, her various prejudices and -phobias and -isms remain preserved across her published writings. At the same time, she still makes present-day readers gasp and cry and swear to change their lives. What do we do with this tension?

SRD: It's important to remember when all these things were written. Time makes all art problematic. We don't look at Leonardo da Vinci paintings the way his contemporaries looked at Leonardo da Vinci paintings because we have lived with Leonardo da Vinci all our lives. But his contemporaries had not. And it's the same thing with Russ. Which is to say, Russ's prose stories came into existence at a certain time. And before that, they were not there. And that needs to be taken into consideration and put into context when one is discussing her work. Time moves forward around her stories, and we move forward with time.

I grew up with [George Orwell's 1949 novel] *1984*, and all of my childhood was before the year 1984. And then one evening in 1984, as an adult, I got on a bus and someone had written on a piece of cardboard and taped it to the back of the driver's seat, "What? 1984 already?" For my entire childhood, and up until that point, 1984 had meant "the future," but at that moment it meant "the present," and soon it meant "somewhere in the past." Now it's many years in the past. But while it was approaching, you thought, "Oh, it's going to be the future forever." But it wasn't.

AP: "Time makes all art problematic." I appreciate that because I think that Russ, right now, is an excellent case of tension between the language of a certain moment becoming dated but the prose itself retaining much of its potency. Because much of what was innovative, imaginative, and progressive for Russ when she was writing stories like *And Chaos Died*, *The Female Man*, and *The Two of Them* isn't just dated now, but often actually quite outdated and even regressive. Like the way she talks about sexuality in *And Chaos Died*, and gender in *The Female Man*, and Islam in *The Two of Them*. There's the question of whether context is potent enough to outweigh the visceral reaction people may have to a novel in a present moment that's very different from the moment when Russ wrote it, a present moment when that visceral reaction is the product of very frightening human rights abuses that Russ couldn't have foreseen, but that her fiction speaks to now. Can you talk about the extent to which we should be laboring to insert context into the discussion of Joanna's works versus how much her narratives should be left to speak for themselves?

SRD: I think the best way to criticize Joanna is to show your own delight in the prose and in the structure of the stories. Talk about both her style and the content of her ideas, because those things combined are what make her extraordinary, and they're what resolve the tension you describe. Where, to quote Wittgenstein borrowing from Lukács, ethics and aesthetics are one. You need descriptions that convey a sense of real critical enthusiasm, which is much more useful than detailed arguments from, if I may be so blunt, idiots.

Take *The Two of Them*. You have to read the book and get through to the very end, where Irene and Zubedeyeh are walking down the road together and they become a single mother and her child on the side of the road somewhere in Texas, hoping someone will stop and give them a ride. I think it's incredibly moving because they've gone through all this inter-stellar travel—so much has happened to them, and they've had to suffer so much to get where they are. But now, they're the most ordinary Americans you might see out of a truck window, just a single mother and her daughter. It's that shift—it's about America.

AP: That's a great prompt to turn to the text of *On Strike Against God*. I was struck by a part of your 1973 letter to Joanna about the novel where you talk about reading the scene in the garden with the narrator, Esther, and her soon-to-be lover, Jean, which I'm reproducing here so readers can see for themselves.

> *Dear Joanna,*
> *About forty-eight seconds ago, I just finished reading this novella call[ed]* On Strike Against God—*most of the time, my daughter was pulling apart the phonebook we have given her to mutilate.*
>
> *I was reading along, enjoying the writing immensely, thinking that perhaps the characters were a little vague, but*

the whole language process was so beautiful that I would just roll in it and let the words do with me what they would. Then, I suddenly got to about page 48, where Jean comes out in the garden after the narrator. And I burst out crying, had to get up and go wipe my eyes, came back and read on, and felt so good I swept my daughter up in my arms and, quite beside myself, told her, "it's going to be all right! It's going to be all right! You see, it's going to be all right. I promise you!" and then went back to reading—and she was very happy, and laughed with me and we both laughed together and I read her some pages of the story out loud, and she tried to eat one—so then I put her down again and went on reading, and she's been in such a good mood since, from time to time I have gotten up from reading to give her a hug, and by page fifty-five I felt so good, and just went on feeling better and better (with a moment for wrenching sadness when Jean left) right on until the end!

[. . .]

Arms, legs, head, feet, backbone and guts are all there!

(No, I don't think it's perfect. But I'll read it again before I go into the whys of that.) It's like the other axis of the Female Man. The two of them should be published in one volume (this one first, I think) and they would be it. It's the first piece of fiction in years I have read that has made me feel that fiction doesn't have to embody some stupidity in order to be recognizable as such.

I am all delight and joy over it; I can't wait to give it to Marilyn when she does come home, who is anxious as I to read it and, in your last letter, was all delighted at the prospect of getting a new J.R. ms to read.[7]

AP: It's a very beautiful scene—you, dancing around with your young daughter, crying and repeating, "It's going to be all right." But when you flip to the actual scene in the book, which starts on page 78 of this edition, it's honestly pretty bleak. The scene you love follows a sequence of encounters in which Esther is mocked, demeaned, and dismissed by various men at a party.

She goes out into the garden to cry, and Jean comes out to comfort her. This is the scene, the scene in the garden, that made you jump for joy. What did you find so moving about Jean coming outside to comfort Esther?

SRD: Well, I suppose it was the buildup of everything up until that point. As someone I read recently says, you don't read Russ's novels—they happen to you. And that's a combination of content and style, but mostly style. In a way, there's nothing particularly extraordinary about these scenes—they are made up of lots and lots of little details that affect the narrator and, by extension, the reader. One of the problems with dealing with the details in the book is that a book like this is nothing but a collection of details. And that's why it's so good.

AP: Can you explain what you mean by that?

SRD: Well, *On Strike Against God* isn't what you'd call a "realistic" novel. It's not. But there are passages with lists of details that you recognize, you know, like the terrible people at the party.

AP: Wait, why isn't it a "realistic" novel? It's not a well-known novel, but where it is known, it's known for being Russ's only novel-length "non-genre" work. And by that I mean "realistic," if not "realism."

SRD: Well, it's not a realistic novel because you're not going to go to a party and experience the sequence of events that Joanna lays out. What's much more likely is that you're going to go to a party and just not talk to anybody—not feel like you could talk to anybody—because you're too shy. At each party, there's one or two of the elements here, but nobody goes to a single party where all of these things happen. But all the elements have stayed with Joanna, and she's put them all in one scene, which is why it's so brilliant. She's thought, "OK, let's construct, for the sake of the novel, the worst party you can think of." And then she does it. She gives you a party scene like no party scene before. . . . The party becomes the quintessence of about twelve or fifteen parties. But you don't know that when you start the scene, because Joanna doesn't say she's going to do it. She doesn't announce, "I'm going to give you the worst party imaginable." You don't know what the scene is going to be *for*, that it is going to be about the particularly obnoxious male guest list and how miserable Esther can get. You only realize at the end, when you, the main character, has gone through it all with her and fled the house.

AP: Would you mind revisiting the scene with me?

SRD: Not at all. We have to do it together.

AP: I'm happy to.

> *The demon got up. The demon said Fool. To think you can eat their food and not talk to them. To think you can take their money and not be afraid of them. To think you can depend on their company and not suffer from them.*
>
> *Well, of course, you can't expect people to rearrange their minds in five minutes. And I'm not good at this. And I don't want to do it. It's a bore, anyway. Unfortunately I know what will happen if we keep on; I'll say that if we are going to talk about these things, let us please talk about them seriously and our fake Britisher will say that he always takes pretty girls seriously and then I'll say Why don't you cut off your testicles and shove them down your throat? and then I'll lose my job and then I'll commit suicide.*

SRD: . . . which is not funny. It's all too serious. One laughs to keep from crying.

> *I once hit a man with a book but that was at a feminist meeting and anyway I didn't hit him really, because he dodged. I have never learned the feminine way of cutting a man down to size, although I can imagine how to do it, but truth to tell,*

that would go against what I believe, that men must live up to such awful things.

SRD: The notion that there are people walking around who can just do this! Usually, the absolutely perfect comeback line falls into your head an hour after you've left the situation. I think Joanna was maybe the first person that I remember talking about the French idea of "l'esprit de l'escalier," the spirit of the back stairs, where you think of what you should have said on the way out. And this is something that everybody understands because we've all thought, "Gee! If I had only said . . ."

AP: It's funny that you say, "One laughs to keep from crying," given the fact that, according to your letter to Joanna, you begin crying for joy in just two pages.

SRD: What's wonderful is the way it's set up. It's all the things Esther has been through before and how it's set up so that you have been through them, too, and so when someone who is marked by the novel as a good person comes out to help, you just feel it.

AP: Something characteristic of Russ's work, I think, are these long sentences that bring you along for the ride—they list everything that Esther's going through, and the lists go on and on and on. They wear on you, like the events they depict wear down Russ's characters, until you join Esther at her lowest points. Like, for instance, when Esther is standing in the yard outside the party:

> *I said to my demon that there are, after all, nice people and nasty people, and the art of life is to cultivate the former and avoid the latter. That not all men are piggy, only some; that not all men belittle me, only some; that not all men get mad if you won't let them play Chivalry, only some; that not all men write books in which women are idiots, only most; that not all*

men pull rank on me, only some; that not all men pinch their secretaries' asses, only some; that not all men make obscene remarks to me in the street, only some; that not all men make more money than I do, only some; that not all men make more money than all women, only most; that not all men are rapists, only some; that not all men are promiscuous killers, only some; that not all men control Congress, the presidency, the police, the army, industry, agriculture, law, science, medicine, architecture, and local government, only some.

I sat down on the lawn and wept.

Shortly thereafter, Jean comes out into the garden to comfort her.

SRD: "I sat down on the lawn and wept." Which, again, is a recall of another great sentence, "On the banks of the Babylon, I sat down and wept." And because it has that resonance, it carries the whole Bible with it.

AP: I'm glad you point that out. That connection hadn't occurred to me! To me, that sentence, "I sat down on the lawn and wept," felt like a natural outgrowth of the despair of the previous paragraph . . . a despair that just rolls on and on and on, semicolon after semicolon after semicolon. It starts hopeful—not all men are bad, after all, she's saying—and then it discourages you, and then it mocks you, and then it keeps rubbing it in, the disappointment and the fear and the degradation, and then it spits you out, all chewed up, to weep. I'm going to be honest—when I read *On Strike Against God*, my response to that scene was definitely not, "It's going to be all right," even when Jean does come out into the garden to comfort Esther. But yours was.

SRD: And the reason mine was, is because that was the first time I had read anything like that. Well, it was the first time I had read something like that in a novel that wasn't science fiction. *On Strike Against God* is not a science fiction novel, which was what was so important about it.

AP: When you say you hadn't encountered anything like that before, do you mean you hadn't encountered somebody laying out with such painstaking detail the kind of negative experience Russ writes into the party and then pulling out of it?

SRD: Yes. Well, that somebody could put down all that despair and point it out in such a way that you could respond to it. And then pulling out of it with the help of another woman, specifically.

AP: Talk about aesthetics and politics being one!

SRD: As Wittgenstein said.

AP: So it was the fact that Jean came out into the garden to comfort Esther that moved you.

SRD: Yes.

AP: To help pluck her from that despair was a radical event.

SRD: Yeah. It's radical in Esther's life, and it's radical in literature! You'll not find it in any other piece of literature from the time—at least, not that I can think of. Other than a couple of Joanna Russ novels, which, of course, were science fiction, unlike this. She has the thing of two women getting together and helping one another, which she tackles in novel after novel. It's all quite wonderful.

AP: Why does it feel significant to you that it happened in a novel that's not science fiction?

SRD: Well, because one of the reasons I liked science fiction is because, in general, it gave women a little bit more space to be full, developed characters. They got to inhabit the world in different and more imaginative ways. This does not mean every science fiction novel does it well—certainly not. Joanna would tell

you. But in some of the best ones, the women characters are notable. That's one of the things I'd always
liked about it, myself.

AP: So it felt novel to you that Joanna wrote these women
characters, with love and solidarity between them, in
a work of fiction that wasn't science fiction.

SRD: Precisely.

AP: Joanna wrote to you in a letter, about *On Strike Against
God*, "I flatter myself that the implicit science fiction
perspective gives it much of its fun." I've really taken
that to heart, and I've tried to find where in the novel
the "implicit science fiction perspective" is at work.
What do those words conjure for you?

SRD: What people who write science fiction live with
in order to write it. "Implicit science fiction perspective" is something about the writer, not the book. I
imagine it's also slightly different for each writer. It
was different for Joanna because she's a woman, and
because she was probably smarter than I was. And it
was certainly different for writers who wrote different stories. But it's what science fiction writers live
with in order to write. I can't tell you what it is more
than that.

AP: So it's a statement about Joanna, you think, not
On Strike Against God. You know—that's not what I
thought it meant, but I think you could be right.
Because the scenes in the novel that I've identified as
having an "implicit science fiction perspective" are
tinged with fantastical elements, but they're also very
much *about* what Joanna was living with at the time—
which is what allowed her to write the story she was
writing the way she did. Take the character of the
Count, for example, Esther's undead psychoanalyst
who rides a flying motorcycle. She writes:

> *My psychoanalyst (who has in reality been dead for a decade)*
> *came out of the clouds and swooped back at me as I trudged*
> *home, great claws at the ready, batwings black against the*
> *moon, dripping phosphorescent slime. Etcetera. (All the way*
> *from New York.)*

SRD: That's a brilliant stylistic way of closing off that sentence, you know. We've got "my psychoanalyst" who's really been dead for ten years, which establishes the realm of fantasy, and then the "I"—the "I" is ordinary, someone who trudges home.

AP: Exactly! "He comes back every once in a while," Esther explains,

> *very stern and severe; then he goes back up into a cloud to*
> *clean his fangs. We get along. After a while you tame your*
> *interior monsters, it's only natural. I don't mean that it ever*
> *stops; but it stops mattering.*

SRD: You know, I always associate this scene with a conversation I had with a gay mentor of mine, John Herbert McDowell, at the old Lüchow's restaurant on Fourteenth Street. I remember saying to him, "John, does life ever get any better than this?" I was probably thirty, and John was forty-five. He thought for a moment, took a sip of his martini, and said, "No, it doesn't. But you care a lot less." And he was right.

AP: That's the insight Joanna decides to deliver here through an undead vampire on a motorcycle. Do you think that adds anything to the insight? Or is it just a pleasant gimmick?

SRD: I don't think it's a gimmick. She's right—it stops mattering, and in life, you have to learn that. Either somebody has to tell you, or you figure it out for yourself. Joanna figured it out for herself. That's what we're seeing here, with the Count—her figuring it out for herself. John figured it out for himself. I was fortunate enough to ask and actually get an answer.

AP: You wrote to Joanna, "[*On Strike Against God* is] like the other axis of the *Female Man*. The two of them should be published in one volume (this one first, I think) and they would be it." Why did you think the novels should be published in one volume?

SRD: Probably because she wrote one right after the other, and the two novels clearly approach the same autobiographical material from different perspectives. It's interesting that I said that, though, because that's not really done. Pairing science fiction and non-science fiction, that is. Recently, I've had a bunch of short stories rejected from Random House. Why? Because some of them are non-science fiction, and they're only interested in me as a science fiction writer. It's easy to get pigeonholed in one genre. They said, "There's too much non-science fiction in it." And I realized I had become a product.

AP: That definitely happened to Russ, which affected *On Strike Against God*. All her name recognition was tied to *The Female Man*, and so *On Strike*, as non-science fiction, went out of print pretty fast.

SRD: I'm sure Joanna had the experience of becoming a product much earlier than I did.

AP: Let's go back to something you said earlier. You said, "Russ's prose stories came into existence at a certain time. And before that, they were not there." That's such an elegant, almost deceptively simple way of putting it. They weren't there and then they were—a seemingly small shift, around which so much actually changed. Basically, the baseline was different—the baseline for what "radical" meant, for example.

Take Esther's confrontation with a man at a bar, who approaches and bullies her and Jean about

whether they're committed to "social revolution."
Maybe we'd call that "performative politics" today.
Anyway, Esther grabs the man by the shirt and says,

> *People who fight other people's oppression are liberals or*
> *worse. Radicalism is being pushed to the wall. . . . You're*
> *white, male, and middle-class—what can you do for the revo-*
> *lution except commit suicide?*

It's an intensely second wave diatribe—incendiary, with a call to violence, and all that. One of the
things that preoccupies me is this question of, does
the at-the-time radicalism of Russ's prose come across
forty years later?

SRD: Radicals are people who fight their own oppression. That's a wonderful description, and it couldn't
be better that it's right there. People who fight other
people's oppression are liberals or worse. At a certain
point, you have to tell people to get their foot off
your neck. And if nobody has their foot on your
neck . . . The problem is, I can't read this and not be
someone who remembers the shift in the meanings
of words like "radical," "liberal," and "conservative."
That's what I get from this—those definitions. For
Joanna and me, liberals were, by definition, the enemy.
Not the enemy—the foolish ones. They didn't know
enough to do *anything*. What can you do, for example,
but commit suicide? And the implication of that for
me is: since you're not going to commit suicide, you
just have to learn what's going on. And if you do that,
you'll probably do better. I hope that's what I did. But
we now think of Democrats as liberals and Republi-
cans as—well, nobody thinks of them as conservatives
anymore, even, it's closer to fascism. But what those
words mean today, they didn't mean then.

From the Archives

WHAT CAN A HEROINE DO?
OR WHY WOMEN CAN'T WRITE

JOANNA RUSS

The following essay was written in 1971 and published in 1972 in Susan Koppelman's Images of Women in Fiction: Feminist Perspectives, *one of the earliest pioneering anthologies in a field that was later to blossom as the rose. Although the jargon common today in so much feminist literary criticism and even in queer literary criticism did not exist then (cheers! say I), we were aware of the same issues, and we wrote about them. I do not think that now I would conclude a manifesto like this one with praise of science fiction (it can be just as good or bad as anything and just as timid, clichéd, and dull), but at the time I was, I think, getting ready to write my own science fiction and was—without being explicitly aware of it—looking for a way out of the cultural deprivation described in the essay. That so many women like myself could actually read and enjoy (or watch and enjoy) the kind of white boy's fiction (Susan Koppelman's phrase) that all of us had spent our life reading, explicating, analyzing, and assuming to be Fiction itself is, I think, a tribute to the unselfishness and empathy of the human imagination. But how much more fun it is (not to mention enlightening) to see through the assumption . . . and change it. The essay was written in the years immediately following a three-day symposium on women, hosted by the (then) School of Home Economics during the 1969–1970 intersession. No other college in Cornell University would touch the subject. The result was a ferment of talk (reflected in the attributions listed in the notes) that lasted for years. I went home feeling that the sky had fallen. One of the most immediate results was my understanding that "English literature" had been badly rigged, and out of that insight came this essay.* *

*This introduction to "What Can a Heroine Do" was written by Joanna Russ and originally published in *To Write Like a Woman: Essays in Feminism and Science Fiction* (Indiana University Press, 1995).

1. Two strong women battle for supremacy in the early West.

2. A young girl in Minnesota finds her womanhood by killing a bear.

3. An English noblewoman, vacationing in Arcadia, falls in love with a beautiful, modest young shepherd. But duty calls, she must return to the court of Elizabeth I to wage war on Spain. Just in time the shepherd lad is revealed as the long-lost son of the Queen of a neighboring country; the lovers are united and our heroine carries off her husband-to-be lad-in-waiting to the King of England.

4. A phosphorescently doomed poetess sponges off her husband and drinks herself to death, thus alienating the community of Philistines and businesswomen who would have continued to give her lecture dates.

5. A handsome young man, quite virginal, is seduced by an older woman who has made a pact with the Devil to give her back her youth. When the woman becomes pregnant, she proudly announces the paternity of her child; this revelation so shames the young man that he goes quite insane, steals into the house where the baby is kept, murders it, and is taken to prison where—repentant and surrounded by angel voices—he dies.

6. Alexandra the Great.

7. A young man who unwisely puts success in business before his personal fulfillment loses his masculinity and ends up as a neurotic, lonely eunuch.

8. A beautiful, seductive boy whose narcissism and instinctive cunning hide the fact that he has no mind (and in fact, hardly any sentient consciousness) drives a succession of successful actresses, movie produceresses, cowgirls, and film directresses wild with desire. They rape him.

Authors do not make their plots up out of thin air, nor are the above pure inventions; every one of them is a story familiar to all of us.[1] What makes them look so odd—and so funny—is that in each case the sex of the protagonist has been changed (and, correspondingly, the sex of the other characters). The result is that these very familiar plots simply will not work. They are tales for heroes, not heroines, and one of the things that handicaps women writers in our—and every other—culture is that there are so very few stories in which women can figure as protagonists.

Culture is male.[2] This does not mean that every man in Western (or Eastern) society can do exactly as he pleases, or that every man creates the culture *solus*, or that every man is luckier or more privileged than every woman. What it does mean (among other things) is that the society we live in is a patriarchy. And patriarchies imagine or picture themselves from the male point of view. There is a female culture, but it is an underground, unofficial, minor culture, occupying a small corner of what we think of officially as possible human experience. Both men *and women* in our culture conceive the culture from a single point of view—the male.

Now, writers, as I have said, do not make up their stories out of whole cloth; they are pretty much restricted to the attitudes, the beliefs, the expectations, and, above all, the plots that are "in the air"—"plot" being what Aristotle called *mythos*; and in fact it is probably most accurate to call these plot-patterns *myths*. They are dramatic embodiments of what a culture believes to be true—or what it would like to be true—or what it is mortally afraid may be true. Novels, especially, depend upon what central action can be imagined as being performed by the protagonist (or protagonists)—i.e., what can a central character *do* in a book? An examination of English literature or Western literature reveals that of all the possible actions people can do in this fiction, very few can be done by women.

Our literature is not about women. It is not about women and men equally. It is by and about men.

But (you might object) aren't our books and our movies full of women? Isn't there a "love interest" or at least a sexual interest in every movie? What about Cleopatra? What about Juliet? What about Sophia Western, Clarissa Harlowe, Faye Greener, Greta Garbo, Pip's Estella, and the succession of love goddesses without whom film history would hardly exist? Our literature is full of women: bad women, good women, motherly women, bitchy women, faithful women, promiscuous women, beautiful women? Plain women?

Women who have no relations with men (as so many male characters in American literature have no relations with women)?

Oddly enough, no. If you look at the plots summarized at the beginning of this article, and turn them back to their original forms, you will find not women but images of women: modest maidens, wicked temptresses, pretty schoolmarms, beautiful bitches, faithful wives, and so on. They exist only in relation to the protagonist (who is male). Moreover, look at them carefully and you will see that they do not really exist at all—at their best they are depictions of the social roles women are supposed to play and often do play, but they are the public roles and not the private women;[3] at their worst they are gorgeous, Cloudcuckooland fantasies about what men want, or hate, or fear.

How can women writers possibly use such myths?

In twentieth-century American literature there is a particularly fine example of these impossible "women," a figure who is beautiful, irresistible, ruthless but fascinating, fascinating because she is somehow cheap or contemptible, who (in her more passive form) destroys men by her indifference and who (when the male author is more afraid of her) destroys men actively, sometimes by shooting them. She is Jean Harlow, Daisy Faye, Faye Greener, Mrs. Macomber, and Deborah Rojack. She is the Bitch Goddess.

Now it is just as useless to ask why the Bitch Goddess is so bitchy as it is to ask why the Noble Savage is so noble. Neither "person" really exists. In existential terms they are both The Other and The Other does not have the kind of inner life or consciousness that you and I have. In fact, The Other has no mind at all. No man in his senses ever says to himself to *himself*, I acted nobly because I am a Noble Savage. His reasons are far more prosaic: I did what I did because I was afraid, or because I was ambitious, or because I wanted to provoke my father, or because I felt lonely, or because I needed money, and so on. Look for reasons like that to explain the conduct of the Bitch Goddess and you will not find them; there is no explanation in terms of human motivation or the woman's own inner life; she simply behaves the way she does because she is a bitch. Q.E.D. No Other ever has the motives that you and I have; the Other contains a mysterious *essence*, which causes it to behave as it does; in fact "it" is not a person at all, but a projected wish or fear.

The Bitch Goddess is not a person.

Virgin-victim Gretchen (see number five, above) is not a person. The faithful wife, the beautiful temptress, the seductive destroyer, the devouring momma, the healing Madonna—none of these are persons in the sense that a novel's protagonist must be a person, and none is of the slightest use as myth to the woman writer who wishes to write about a female protagonist.

Try, for example, to change the Bitch Goddess/Male Victim story into a woman's story—are we to simply change the sex of the characters and write about a male "bitch" and a female victim? The myth still works in male homosexual terms—Man and Cruel Youth—but the female equivalent is something quite different. Changing the sex of the protagonist completely alters the meaning of the tale. The story of Woman/Cruel Lover is the story of so many English ballads—you have the "false true lover" and the pregnant girl left either to mourn or to die, but you do not have—to indicate only some elements of the story—the Cruel Lover as the materially sumptuous but spiritually bankrupt spirit of our civilization, the essence of sex, the "soul" of our corrupt culture, a dramatization of the split between the degrading necessities of the flesh and the transcendence of world-cleaving Will. What you have instead, if the story is told about or by the woman, is a cautionary tale warning you not to break social rules—in short, a much more realistic story of social error or transgression leading to ostracism, poverty, or death. Moral: Get Married First.

No career woman, at least in literature, keeps in the back of her mind the glamorous figure of Daisy Faye, the beautiful, rich, indifferent boy she loved back in Cleveland when she was fighting for a career as a bootlegger. Reversing sexual roles in fiction may make good burlesque or good fantasy, but it is ludicrous in terms of serious literature. Culture is male. Our literary myths are for heroes, not heroines.

What can a heroine do?

What myths, what plots, what actions are available to a female protagonist?

Very few.

For example, it is impossible to write a conventional success story with a heroine, for success in male terms is failure for a woman, a "fact" movies, books, and television plays have been earnestly proving to us for decades. Nor is the hard-drinking, hard-fighting hero imagined as female, except as an amusing fluke—e.g., Bob Hope and Jane Russell in *The Paleface*. Nor can our heroine be the Romantic Poet Glamorously Doomed, nor the Oversensitive Artist Who Cannot Fulfill His Worldly Responsibilities (Emily Dickinson seems to fit the latter pattern pretty well, but she is always treated as The Spinster, an exclusively female—*and sexual*—role). Nor can a heroine be the Intellectual Born into a Philistine Small Town Who Escapes to the Big City—a female intellectual cannot escape her problems by fleeing to the big city; she is still a woman and Woman as Intellectual is not one of our success myths.

With one or two exceptions (which I will deal with later) all sub-literary genres are closed to the heroine; she cannot be a Mickey Spillane private eye, for example, nor can she be one of H. Rider Haggard's adventure-story Englishmen who discovers a Lost Princess in some imaginary corner of Africa. (She can be the Lost Princess, but a story written with the Princess herself as protagonist would resemble the chronicle of any other monarch and would hardly fit the female figure of Haggard's romances, who is—again—the Other.) The hero whose success in business alienates him from his family is not at all in the position of the heroine who "loses her femininity" by competing with men—*he* is not desexed, but *she* is. The Crass Businessman genre (minor, anyway) is predicated on the assumption that success is masculine and a good thing as long as you don't spend all your time at it; one needs to spend the smaller part of one's life recognizing the claims of personal relations and relaxation. For the heroine the conflict between success and sexuality is itself the issue, and the duality is absolute.

The woman who becomes hard and unfeminine, who competes with men, finally becomes—have we seen this figure before?—a Bitch. Again.

Women in twentieth-century American literature seem pretty much limited to either Devourer/Bitches or Maiden/Victims. Perhaps male authors have bad consciences.

So we come at last to the question of utmost importance to novelists—What will my protagonist(s) do? What central action can be the core of the novel? I know of only one plot or myth that is genderless, and in which heroines can figure equally with heroes; this is the Abused Child story (I mean of the Dickensian variety) and indeed many heroines do begin life as Sensitive, Mistreated Waifs. But such a pattern can be used only while the heroine is still a child (as in the first part of *Jane Eyre*). Patient Griselda, who also suffered and endured, was not a Mistreated Child but the adult heroine of a peculiar kind of love story. And here, of course, we come to the one occupation of a female protagonist in literature, the one thing she can do, and by God she does it and does it and does it, over and over and over again.

She is the protagonist of a Love Story.

The tone may range from grave to gay, from the tragedy of *Anna Karenina* to the comedy of *Emma*, but the myth is always the same: innumerable variants on Falling In Love, on courtship, on marriage, on the failure of courtship and marriage. How She Got Married. How She Did Not Get Married (always tragic). How She Fell In Love and Committed Adultery. How She Saved Her Marriage But Just Barely. How She Loved a Vile Seducer And Eloped. How She Loved a Vile Seducer, Eloped, And Died In Childbirth. As far as literature is concerned, heroines are still restricted to one vice, one virtue, and one occupation. In novels of Doris Lessing, an authoress concerned with a great many other things besides love, the heroines still spend most of their energy and time maintaining relations with their lovers (or marrying, or divorcing, or failing to achieve orgasm, or achieving it, or worrying about their sexuality, their men, their loves, and their love lives).

For female protagonists the Love Story includes not only personal relations as such, but *bildungsroman*, worldly success or worldly failure, career, the exposition of character, crucial learning experiences, the transition to adulthood, rebellion (usually adultery) and everything else. Only in the work of a few iconoclasts like George Bernard Shaw do you find protagonists like Vivie Warren, whose work means more to her than marriage, or Saint Joan, who has no "love life" at all. It is interesting that Martha Graham's dance version of Saint Joan's life turns the tale back into a Love Story, with Saint Michael (at one point, in the version I saw) inspiring Joan by walking astride her from head to foot, dragging his robe over her several times as she lies on her back on the stage floor.

How she lost him, how she got him, how she kept him, how she died for/with him. What else is there? A new pattern seems to have been developing in the last few years: authoresses who do not wish to write Love Stories may instead write about heroines whose main action is to go mad—but How She Went Crazy will also lose its charm in time. One cannot write *The Bell Jar*, or *Jane Eyre*, good as it is, forever.

A woman writer may, if she wishes, abandon female protagonists altogether and stick to male myths with male protagonists, but in so doing she falsifies herself and much of her own experience. Part of life is obviously common to both sexes—we all eat, we all get stomachaches, and we all grow old and die—but a great deal of life is not shared by men and women. A woman who

refuses to write about women ignores the whole experience of the female culture (a very different one from the
official, male culture), all her specifically erotic experiences, and a good deal of her own history. She falsifies
her position both artistically and humanly: she is an
artist creating a world in which persons of her kind
cannot be artists, a consciousness central to itself creating a world in which women have no consciousness, a
successful person creating a world in which persons like
herself cannot be successes. She is a Self trying to pretend
that she is a different Self, one for whom her own self
is Other.

If a female writer does not use the two, possibly
three, myths available to a she-writer, she must drop the
culture's myths altogether. Is this in itself a bad thing?
Perhaps what we need here is a digression on the artistic
advantages of working with myths, i.e., material that has
passed through other hands, that is not raw-brand-new.

The insistence that authors make up their own plots
is a recent development in literature; Milton certainly did
not do it. Even today, with novelty at such a premium in
all the arts, very little is written that is not—at bottom—
common property. It's a commonplace that bad writers
imitate and great writers steal. Even an iconoclast like
Shaw "stole" his plots wholesale, sometimes from melodrama, sometimes from history, sometimes from his
friends.[4] Ibsen owes a debt to Scribe, Dickens to theatre
melodrama, James to other fiction of his own time—
nothing flowers without a history. Something that has
been worked on by others in the same culture, something that is "in the air" provides a writer with material
that has been distilled, dramatized, stylized, and above
all, clarified. A developed myth has its own form, its
own structure, its own expectations and values, its own
cues-to-nudge-the-reader. When so much of the basic

work has already been done, the artist may either give the myth its final realization or stand it on its head, but in any case what he or she does will be neither tentative nor crude and it will not take forever; it can simply be done well. For example, the very pattern of dramatic construction that we take as natural, the idea that a story ought to have a beginning, a middle, and an end, that one ought to be led to something called a "climax" by something called "suspense" or "dramatic tension," is in itself an Occidental myth—Western artists, therefore, do not have to invent this pattern for themselves.

Hemingway, whom we call a realist, spent his whole working life capitalizing on the dramatic lucidity possible to an artist who works with developed myths. The Bitch Goddess did not appear full-blown in "The Short and Happy Life of Francis Macomber"—one can find her in Fitzgerald—or Hawthorne, to name an earlier writer—or Max Beerbohm, whose *Zuleika Dobson* is certainly a Bitch Goddess, though a less serious one than her American cousins. "Macomber" is the ultimate fictional refinement out of the mess and bother of real life. Beyond it lies only nightmare (Faye Greener in West's *Day of the Locust*) or the half-mad, satiric fantastications Mailer uses to get a little more mileage out of an almost exhausted pattern.

"Macomber" is perfectly clear, as is most of Hemingway's work. Nobody can fail to understand that Mrs. Macomber is a Bitch, that the White Hunter is a Real Man, and that Macomber is a Failed Man. The dramatic conflict is extremely clear, very vehement, and completely expectable. The characters are simple, emotionally charged, and larger-than-life. *Therefore* the fine details of the story can be polished to that point of high gloss where everything—weather, gestures, laconic conversation, terrain, equipment, clothing—is all of meaning. (Compare "Macomber" with *Robinson Crusoe*, for example; Defoe is much less sure from moment to moment of what he wants to say or what it means.) One cannot stop to ask why Mrs. Macomber is so bitchy—she's just a Bitch, that's all—or why killing a large animal will restore Macomber's manhood—everybody knows it will—or why the Bitch cannot tolerate a Real Man—these things are already explained by the myth.

But this kind of larger-than-life simplicity and clarity is not accessible to the woman writer unless she remains within the limits of the Love Story. Again: what can a heroine do?

There seem to me to be two alternatives open to the woman author who no longer cares about How She Fell in Love or How She Went Mad. These are (1) lyricism, and (2) life.

By "lyricism" I do not mean purple passages or baroque raptures; I mean a particular principle of structure.

If *the narrative mode* (what Aristotle called "epic") concerns itself with *events* connected by the *chronological order* in which they occur, and *the dramatic mode* with *voluntary human actions* which are connected both by *chronology and causation*, then the principle of construction I wish to call *lyric* consists of *the organization of discrete elements* (images, events, scenes, passages, words, what-have-you) *around an unspoken thematic or emotional center*. The lyric mode exists without chronology or causation; its principle of connection is *associative*. Of course, no piece of writing can exist purely in any one mode, but we can certainly talk of the predominance of one element, perhaps two.) In this sense of "lyric" Virginia Woolf is a lyric novelist—in fact she has been criticized in just those terms, i.e., "nothing happens" in her books. A writer who employs the lyric structure is setting various images, events, scenes, or memories to circling round an unspoken, invisible center. The invisible center is what the novel or poem is about; it is also unsayable in available dramatic or narrative terms. That is, there is no action possible to the central character and no series of events that will embody in clear, unequivocal, immediately graspable terms what the artist means. Or perhaps there is no action or series of events that will embody this "center" at all. Unable to use the myths of male culture (and apparently unwilling to spend her life writing love stories), Woolf uses a structure that is basically nonnarrative. Hence the lack of "plot," the repetitiousness, the gathering-up of the novels into moments of epiphany, the denseness of the writing, the indirection. There is nothing the female characters can do—except exist, except think, except feel. And critics (mostly male) employ the usual vocabulary of denigration: these novels lack important events; they are hermetically sealed; they are too full of sensibility; they are trivial; they lack action; they are feminine.[5]

Not every female author is equipped with the kind of command of language that allows (or insists upon) lyric construction; nor does every woman writer want to employ this mode. The alternative is to take as one's model (and structural principle) not male myth but the structure of one's own experience. So we have George Eliot's (or Doris Lessing's) "lack of structure," the obviously tacked-on ending of *Mill on the Floss*; we have Brontë's spasmodic, jerky world of *Villette*, with a structure modeled on the heroine's (and probably author's) real situation. How to write a novel about a person to whom nothing happens? A person to whom nothing but a love story is *supposed* to happen? A person inhabiting a world in which the only reality is frustration or endurance—or these plus an unbearably mystifying confusion? The movement of *Villette* is not the perfect curve of *Jane*

Eyre (a classic version of the female Love Story)—it is a blocked jabbing, a constant thwarting; it is the protagonist's constantly frustrated will to action, and her alternately losing and regaining her perception of her own situation.[6] There are vestiges of Gothic mystery and there is a Love Story, but the Gothic mysteries turn out to be fakery, and the Love Story (which occupies only the last quarter of the book) vanishes strangely and abruptly on the last page but one. In cases like these the usual epithet is "formless," sometimes qualified by "inexperienced"—obviously life is not like *that*, life is not messy and indecisive; we know what life (and novels) are from Aristotle—who wrote about plays—and male novelists who employ male myths created by a culture that imagines itself from the male point of view. The task of art—we know—is to give form to life, i.e., the very forms that women writers cannot use. So it's clear that women can't write, that they swing wildly from lyricism to messiness once they abandon the cozy realms of the Love Story. And successes within the Love Story (which is itself imagined out of genuine female experience) are not important because the Love Story is not important. It is a commonplace of criticism that only the male myths are valid or interesting; a book as fine (and well-structured) as *Jane Eyre* fails *even to be seen* by many critics because it grows out of experiences—events, fantasies, wishes, fears, daydreams, images of self—entirely foreign to their own. As critics are usually unwilling to believe their lack of understanding to be their own fault, it becomes the fault of the book. Of the author. Of all women writers.

Western European (and North American) culture is not only male in its point of view; it is also Western European. For example, it is not Russian. Nineteenth-century Russian fiction can be criticized in much the same terms as women's fiction: "pointless" or "plotless" narratives stuffed with strange minutiae, and not obeying the accepted laws of dramatic development, lyrical in the wrong places, condensed in the wrong places, overly emotional, obsessed with things we do not understand, perhaps even grotesque. Here we have other outsiders who are trying, in less than a century, to assimilate European myths, producing strange Russian hybrids (*A King Lear of the Steppe*, *Lady Macbeth of Mtsensk*), trying to work with literary patterns that do not suit their experiences and were not developed with them in mind. What do we get? Oddly digressive Pushkin. "Formless" Dostoevsky. (Colin Wilson has called Dostoevsky's novels "sofa pillows stuffed with lumps of concrete.") Sprawling, glacial, all-inclusive Tolstoy. And of course "lyrical" Chekhov, whose magnificent plays are called plotless to this very day.

There is an even more vivid—and tragic—example: what is an American Black writer to make of our accepted myths? For example, what is she or he to make of the still-current myth (so prominent in *King Lear*) that Suffering Brings Wisdom? This is an old, still-used plot. Does suffering bring wisdom to *The Invisible Man*? When critics do not find what they expect, they cannot imagine that the fault may lie in their expectations. I know of a case in which the critics (white and female) decided after long, nervous discussion that Baldwin was "not really a novelist" but that Orwell was.

Critical bias aside, all artists are going to be in the soup pretty soon, if they aren't already. As a culture, we are coasting on the tag-ends of our assumptions about a lot of things (including the difference between fiction and "propaganda"). As novelists we are working with myths that have been so repeated, so triply-distilled, that they are almost exhausted. Outside of commercial genres—which can remain petrified and profitable indefinitely—how many more incarnations of the Bitch Goddess can anybody stand? How many more shoot-'em-ups on Main Street? How many more young men with identity problems?

The lack of workable myths in literature, of acceptable dramatizations of what our experience means, harms much more than art itself. We do not only choose or reject works of art on the basis of these myths; we interpret our own experience in terms of them. Worse still, we actually perceive what happens to us in the mythic terms our culture provides.

The problem of "outsider" artists is the whole problem of what to do with unlabeled, disallowed, disavowed, not-even-consciously-perceived experience, experience which cannot be spoken about because it has no embodiment in existing art. Is one to create new forms wholesale—which is practically impossible? Or turn to old ones, like Blake's Elizabethan lyrics and Yeats's Noh plays? Or "trivial," trashy genres, like Austen's ladies' fiction?

Make something unspeakable and you make it unthinkable.

Hence the lyric structure, which can deal with the unspeakable and unembodiable as its thematic center, or the realistic piling up of detail which may (if you are lucky) eventually *add up to* the unspeakable, undramatizable, unembodiable action-one-cannot-name.

Outsiders' writing is always in critical jeopardy. Insiders know perfectly well that art ought to match their ideas of it. Thus insiders notice instantly that the material of *Jane Eyre* is trivial and the emotionality untenable, even though the structure is perfect. George Eliot, whose point of view is neither peccable nor ridiculously romantic, does not know what fate to award her heroines and thus falsifies her endings.[7] Genet, whose lyrical mode of construction goes unnoticed, is meaningless and disgusting. Kafka, who can "translate" (in his short stories only) certain common myths into fantastic or extreme versions of themselves, does not have Tolstoy's wide grasp of life. (That Tolstoy lacks Kafka's understanding of alienation is sometimes commented upon, but that does not count, of course.) Ellison is passionate but shapeless and crude. Austen, whose sense of form cannot be impugned, is not passionate enough. Blake is inexplicable. Baldwin lacks Shakespeare's gift of reconciliation. And so on and so on.

But outsiders' problems are real enough, and we will all be facing them quite soon, as the nature of human experience on this planet changes radically—unless, of course, we all end up in the Second Paleolithic, in which case we will have to set about re-creating the myths of the First Paleolithic.

Perhaps one place to look for myths that escape from the equation Culture = Male is in those genres that already employ plots not limited to one sex—i.e., myths that have nothing to do with our accepted gender roles. There seem to me to be three places one can look:

(1) Detective stories, as long as these are limited to genuine intellectual puzzles ("crime fiction" is a different genre). Women write these; women read them; women even figure in them as protagonists. The slang name, "whodunit," neatly describes the myth: Finding Out Who Did It (whatever "It" is).

(2) Supernatural fiction, often written by women (Englishwomen, at least) during the nineteenth and the first part of the twentieth centuries. These are about the intrusion of something strange, dangerous, *and not natural* into one's familiar world. What to do? In the face of the supernatural, knowledge and character become crucial; the accepted gender roles are often irrelevant. After all, potting a twelve-foot-tall batrachian with a

kerosene lamp is an act that can be accomplished by either sex, and both heroes and heroines can be expected to feel sufficient horror to make the story interesting. (My example is from a short story by H. P. Lovecraft and August Derleth.) However, much of this genre is as severely limited as the detective story—they both seem to have reached the point of decadence where writers are restricted to the re-enactment of ritual gestures. Moreover, supernatural fiction often relies on very threadbare social/sexual roles, e.g., aristocratic Hungarian counts drinking the blood of beautiful, innocent Englishwomen. (Vampire stories use the myths of an old-fashioned eroticism; other tales trade on the fear of certain animals like snakes or spiders, disgust at "mold" or "slime," human aggression taking the form of literal bestiality (lycanthropy), guilt without intention, the *lex talionis*, severe retribution for venial faults, supernatural "contamination"—in short, what a psychoanalyst would call the "archaic" contents of the mind.)

(3) Science fiction, which seems to me to provide a broad pattern for human myths, even if the specifically futuristic or fantastic elements are subtracted. (I except the kind of male adventure story called Space Opera, which may be part of science fiction as a genre, but is not innate in science fiction as a mode.) The myths of science fiction run along the lines of exploring a new world conceptually (not necessarily physically), creating needed physical or social machinery, assessing the consequences of technological or other changes, and so on. These are not stories about men *qua* Man and women *qua* Woman; they are myths of human intelligence and human adaptability. They not only ignore gender roles but—at least theoretically—are not culture-bound. Some of the most fascinating characters in science fiction are not human. True, the attempt to break through culture-binding may

mean only that we transform old myths like Black Is Bad/White Is Good (or the Heart of Darkness myth) into new asininities like Giant Ants Are Bad/People Are Good. At least the latter can be subscribed to by all human races and sexes. (Giant ants might feel differently.)

Darko Suvin of the University of Montreal has suggested that science fiction patterns often resemble those of medieval literature.[8] I think the resemblance lies in that medieval literature so often dramatizes not people's social roles but the life of the soul; hence we find the following patterns in both science fiction and medieval tales:

I find myself in a new world, not knowing who I am or where I came from. I must find these out, and also find out the rules of the world I inhabit. (the journey of the soul from birth to death)

Society needs something. I/we must find it. (the quest)

We are miserable because our way of life is out of whack. We must find out what is wrong and change it. (the drama of sin and salvation)

Science fiction, political fiction, parable, allegory, exemplum—all carry a heavier intellectual freight (and self-consciously so) than we are used to. All are didactic. All imply that human problems are collective, as well as individual, and take these problems to be spiritual, social, perceptive, or cognitive—not the fictionally sex-linked problems of success, competition, "castration," education, love, or even personal identity, with which we are all so very familiar. I would go even farther and say that science fiction, political fiction (when successful), and the modes (if not the content) of much medieval fiction all provide myths for dealing with the kinds of experiences we are actually having now, instead of the literary myths we have inherited, which only tell us about the kinds of experiences we think we ought to be having.

This may sound like the old cliché about the Soviet plot of Girl Meets Boy Meets Tractor. And why not? Our current fictional myths leave vast areas of human experience unexplored: work for one, genuine religious experience for another, and above all the lives of the traditionally voiceless, the majority of whom are women. (When I speak of the "traditionally voiceless" I am not pleading for descriptions of their lives—we have had plenty of that by very vocal writers—what I am talking about are fictional myths *growing out of their lives* and told by themselves for themselves.)

Forty years ago those Americans who read books at all read a good deal of fiction. Nowadays such persons read popularized anthropology, psychology, history, and philosophy. Perhaps current fictional myths no longer tell the truth about any of us.

When things are changing, those who know least about them—in the usual terms—may make the best job of them. There is so much to be written about, and here we are with nothing but the rags and tatters of what used to mean something. One thing I think we must know—that our traditional gender roles will not be part of the future, as long as the future is not a second Stone Age. Our traditions, our books, our morals, our manners, our films, our speech, our economic organization, everything we have inherited, tell us that to be a Man one must bend Nature to one's will—or other men. This means ecological catastrophe in the first instance and war in the second. To be a Woman, one must be first and foremost a mother and after that a server of Men; this means overpopulation and the perpetuation of the first two disasters. The roles are deadly. The myths that serve them are fatal.

Women cannot write—using the old myths.

But using new ones—?

NOTES

1. Number three is a version of *The Winter's Tale*; number four, the life of Dylan Thomas, as popularly believed; number five, the story of Faust and Marguerite; and number eight, a lightly modified version of part of *The Day of the Locust*. The others need no explanation.

2. I am indebted to Linda Finlay of the Philosophy Department of Ithaca College for this formulation and the short discussion that follows it.

3. I am indebted to Mary Uhl for the observation that Dickens's women are accurately portrayed as long as they are in public (where Dickens himself had many opportunities to observe real women) but entirely unconvincing when they are alone or with other women only.

4. An overstatement. The plot of *Widowers' Houses* was a gift.

5. Mary Ellmann, *Thinking about Women* (New York: Harcourt, Brace & World, 1968). See the chapter on "Phallic Criticism."

6. Kate Millett, *Sexual Politics* (New York: Doubleday and Company, 1970), pp. 140–47.

7. In comparison with the organic integrity of Dickens's, I suppose.

8. In conversation and in a paper unpublished as of this writing.

NOT FOR YEARS
BUT FOR DECADES

JOANNA RUSS

I. FACT

When I was twelve I fell in love with Danny Kaye. For almost a quarter of a century I have regarded that crush as the beginning of my sexual life. But "sexual" is a dangerous word precisely because it splits one part of experience off from the rest. It was only when I began to ask, not about "sex" or my "sex life" but (more vaguely) about my "feelings" and about "emotional attachments" that I began to recall other things, some earlier, that the official classifications of "sex" censored out and made unimportant. Perhaps that's the function of official classifications. Names are given to things by the privileged and their naming is (wouldn't you think?) to their own advantage, but in the area of sexuality women are emphatically not a privileged class. So let's ask about "friends."

At eleven I played erotic games with girl friends, acting out nominally heterosexual stories I (usually) had made up. One script (minus the kissing and touching we added to it) I showed my mother, who praised it but laughed until she cried at one stage direction, which has a lover climbing a rope ladder to his sweetheart's window, being discovered by her parents, and gloomily exiting by climbing back down the ladder. About this time I went on my First Date with a nice, plain, gentle, thoroughly dull little boy called Bill (we called him "Bill the Hill"). The necking he wanted to do bored me, but I was tremendously proud of having a First Date. At about that time, one winter's evening, one of my girl friends seductively and skittishly insisted on kissing us all good night; that night I dreamed I was being led further and further into a dark forest by an elf who was neither a girl nor a boy, rotting oranges as big as people hung on the trees, and when a storm began, I woke in terror, knowing perfectly well that I had dreamed about my friend and that I was feeling for her what ought to go on with Bill the Hill. I told my mother about it and she "handled it very well" (as my analyst said many years later).

She said it was "a stage."

That summer I was in summer camp and all the twelve-year-old girls in the bunk necked and petted secretly (with each other) but the next summer everybody seemed to have forgotten about it. Certainly nobody mentioned it. Everybody remembered the "dirty jokes" we had told every night for hours (grotesquely heterosexual or homophobic stories I thought the other children had invented) and none of my friends had forgotten the (heterosexual) serial stories I had made up and which several other little girls continued. But that whole summer of fumbling with your best friend had become invisible. Since nobody else mentioned it, I never did either.

My "best friend" was Carol-Ellen. I called her my "best friend," not my "lover." I had strong and sometimes painfully profound feelings about her and would have been miserably jealous if she'd preferred anyone else to me. Yet I never thought that I "loved" Carol-Ellen or that what we did was really "sex" (although it was somehow not only sex, but a far worse kind than the boys' panty-raids or girls staying out with boys after curfew). I never gave to what had happened between us the prestigious name of "love" (which might have led me to stand up for its importance) or the wicked-but-powerful name of "sex."

What I had begun to learn (in "it's a stage") continued that summer, that my real experience, undefined and powerful as it was, didn't really exist. It was bad and it didn't exist. It was bad *because* it didn't exist.

Simultaneously with being mad about Carol-Ellen, I read Love Comics. I believed in them. (Everybody read them and everybody, I suspect, believed in them.) Like dating and movies and boys, they were about real love and real sex. I remember disliking them and at the same time not being able to stay away from them. They demanded things of me (looks, clothes, behavior) which I disliked, and they insisted on the superiority and importance of men in a way I detested (and couldn't connect with any of the little boys I knew at camp). But they offered a very great promise: that if only I would sacrifice my ambitions and most of my personality, I would be given a reward—they called it "love." I knew it was in some way "sexual." And yet I also knew that those hearts and flowers and flashing lights when the characters kissed didn't have anything to do with sex; they were supersex or ultrasex; they were some kind of transcendent ecstasy beyond ordinary life. They certainly didn't have anything to do with masturbation, or with what Carol-Ellen and I were secretly doing together. I think now that the most attractive rewards held out by the Love Comics (and later by the movies, the books, and the psychoanalysts) was freedom from responsibility and hence freedom from the burdens of being an individual. At twelve I found that promise very attractive. I was a tall, overly-bright and overly-self-assertive girl, too much so to fit anybody's notions of femininity (and too book-ish and odd to fit other children's ideas of an acceptable human being). If anybody needed an escape from the guilt of individuality, I certainly did. The Love Comics told me that when it came right down to it, I wasn't any different from any other woman and that once love came, I would no longer have to worry about being imprisoned in my lonely, eccentric selfhood. The hearts and flowers and the psychedelic flashing lights would sweep all that away. I would be "in love" and I would never have to think again, never agonize over being "unpopular," never follow my own judgment in the face of criticism, never find things out for myself. This is the Grand Inquisitor's promise and I think Germaine Greer is quite right to see in the cult of "romance" a kind of self-obliterating religion. I didn't know that at twelve, of course. Nor did I know enough to look at the comic books' copyright pages to see which sex owned them, published them, and even wrote them. But I believed. And if I hadn't gotten the message from comic books, I would still have gotten it (as I did later) from movies, books, and friends. Later on I would get the same message from several (not even one!) psychiatrists and psychology books. Nor did the High Culture I met at college carry a different message. The insistence on certain kinds of looks and behavior, the overwhelming importance of men, and the sacrifice of personality and individuality (as well as the promised rewards) were always the same. (The only thing college added was contempt for women—which didn't change the obligation to be "feminine.")

Ti-Grace Atkinson calls this the heterosexual institution.

Time passed. Carol-Ellen went to another camp. At fourteen I felt for a male counselor of nineteen the vulnerability, awkwardness, and liking I've since learned to call "erotic tension." Somebody else asked him to the Sadie Hawkins Dance and I cried in the bathroom for three solid minutes. I didn't know him well and didn't feel for him with one-quarter of the intensity I had for Carol-Ellen, but this time I had an official name for what

I was feeling; I called it "love." I think what drew me to him was his kindness and his lack of good looks, which made him seem, to me, like a fellow-refugee. He was embarrassed at the dance (about me, I suspect) and roared about, clowning, which disillusioned me. I don't believe Carol-Ellen could have disillusioned me; I knew her too well and she was too important to me. I don't remember his face or his name, although I remember Carol-Ellen's perfectly (possibly because I took good care to get a snapshot of her). And Carol-Ellen, though of course a fellow-creature, was not a fellow-refugee; she always seemed to me far too good-looking and personally successful for that, so much so that I wondered why nobody else noticed her beauty. I always felt graced by Carol-Ellen's picking me for her best friend; after all, she could've been friends with anybody. But somewhere in my feelings about Bernie (Sidney? Joe? Scottie?) was the disheartening feeling I came to recognize later in my dealings with men: *He'll do.*

The year before that, in junior high, an older boy of fifteen (a popular person whose acquaintance I coveted) complimented me on a scarf I was wearing and I responded as we always did in my family: "Thanks, I got it at . . ." He laughed, partly amused, partly critical. "I didn't ask you where you got it! After all, *I'm* not going to get one." I knew that I had made a social mistake, and yet my embarrassment and shame were mixed with violent resentment. I knew then that the manners I had been taught (they seemed to me perfectly good ones) were now wrong, and that I would have to learn a whole new set for "boys." It was unfair. It was just like the Love Comics. I knew also that somewhere deep down I didn't believe in the absolute duality of male and female behavior (in terms of which he'd criticized me) and that somewhere in the back of my mind, in a reserve of boundless arrogance, I was preparing revolutionary solutions for such people: *That's false and I know it. And just you wait.*

Yet all of this: revolution, Lesbianism, what-have-you, took place in profound mental darkness. I wrote moody Lesbian poems about Carol-Ellen, played with the idea of being a Lesbian, a tremendously attractive idea but strictly a literary one (I told myself). I wrote a Lesbian short story, which worried my high school teacher into asking me if I had any "problems you want to talk about." I knew the story had bothered him and felt wickedly pleased and very daring. The story itself was about a tall, strong, masculine, dark-haired girl (me) who falls in love with a short, slender, light-haired girl (?) and then kills herself by throwing herself off a bridge because the light-haired girl (although a Lesbian) will have nothing to do with her. I couldn't imagine anything else for the two of them to do. A few months later I began a novel (without connecting it with the story): here the dark-haired girl has become a dark-haired young man and the two lovers do get together (here I *could* imagine something for them to do) although light-hair eventually breaks the love affair off. On what grounds? That she's a Lesbian! The young man, by the way, does not kill himself.

At the same time I began to wonder what pregnancy felt like and to write poems about Being Female, which I thought meant having no mind and being immersed in some overwhelming, not necessarily pleasant experience which was much bigger than you were (no, I didn't yet even know that D. H. Lawrence existed; it was Love Comics again). I fell in love with a male gay friend and went with him and his sister to the Village, where they adjured me to pretend I was eighteen ("For God's sake, Joanna, put your hair up and wear earrings!") so that we could drink real liquor in a real bar. I had disturbing dreams about him in which he came to the door of my family's house in a dress and a babushka. (At the time I interpreted the dream as worry about his effeminate mannerisms. Now I'm not so sure.) Later, in my first year of college, he came to visit and I teased him into kissing me; it felt so good that the next day I insisted on going farther. The only place we could use was the dormitory lounge, and possibly because of the publicity of the location, things turned out badly; he got scared, I got nauseated, and after he left I spent a wretched hour surrounded by friends, who cheerfully told me that the first time was always rotten. The housemother, a young-ish psychologist, told me the same thing, and when I told her about my feelings for women (I must've had them, although I can only remember telling her about them) she said I was "going through a stage."

Somehow, in a vague and confused way, I didn't believe that. I found *Mademoiselle de Maupin*, a nineteenth-century novel in which a woman disguises herself as a man and has a love affair with a woman and a man (I thought the man was a creep and was really only interested in the woman). I wore slacks and felt defiant and ashamed. I tried to find out about Lesbianism on campus and annoyed my friends ("This school is awful. Do you know there are Lesbians here?" "Where! Where!" "Oh, Joanna, *really*."). I acquired a "best friend" for whom I had painful, protective, profound feelings &c. without ever recognizing &c. I found another "elf" and followed her around campus at a distance, feeling embarrassed. I went out on dates, which were even more crucial than they had been in high school, and got kissed by various men, which mildly excited and not-so-mildly disgusted me. My "best friend" told me stories about Lesbianism in her high school, in which everyone was a Lesbian except her, but when I wanted to go with her to a Lesbian bar in New York (over vacation) she wouldn't, and when I desperately asked her to pretend we were lovers in front of a third person, whom I said I wanted to shock (I didn't know myself at that point exactly what I was doing) she got very angry and upset.

So I gave up. It wasn't real. It didn't count, except in my own inner world in which I could not only love women but also fly, ride the lightning, be Alexander the Great, live forever, etc., all of which occurred in my poetry. I regarded this inner life as both crucially important and totally trivial, the source of all my vitality and yet something completely sealed off from "reality." By now I had learned to define the whole cluster of feelings as "wanting to be a man" (something I had not thought of before college), and saw it simultaneously as a shameful neurotic symptom and an indication of how much more talented and energetic I was than other women. Women with "penis envy" (another collegiate enlightenment) were inferior to men but were somehow superior to other women although they were also wickeder than other women. My best friend thought so. The psychology books my mother read thought so. The movies seemed to think so. Two years later the second elf turned up one summer (we had become distant friends) and the whole business started all over again. I now recognized it as a recurrent thing. I laughed at it and called it "penis envy." It was about at that time that I began the first of a long series of one-way infatuations with very macho men (these lasted into my thirties), agonizing experiences in which I suffered horribly but had the feeling that my life had become real and intense, even super-real, the feeling that I was being propelled into an experience bigger and more overwhelming than my own dreary life, a life I was beginning to detest. The first man I picked for this was my "best friend's" fiance. I kept the infatuation going, totally unreciprocated, for almost a year. He left school, they split up. I managed to go out with him once (we necked) and felt, in immense erotic excitement, that if only he would love me I could submerge my individuality in his, that he was a "real man," and that if I could only marry him I could give up "penis envy" and be a "real woman."

It sounds just like Love Comics.

In high school I believed (along with my few friends) that college would see an end to the dating game, to the belief that women were inferior to men, and that intellectual women were freaks. But it was in college that I first got lectures about "being a woman" from boys I knew, and heard other women getting them, heard that so-and-so knew "how to be a woman," and was surrounded by the new and ghastly paraphernalia of dress rules and curfews. (My parents had been extremely permissive about where I went and with whom.)

After my twelfth summer I had gone (very early) into a high school where I knew nobody; I became depressed. In college I became more depressed. I went to the school psychiatrist, who told me I had "penis envy" and was in love with my father. I was willing to agree but did not know what to do about it (he said, "Enjoy life. Go out on dates") and became even more depressed. By the end of graduate school I no longer had problems with "feelings about women"; I felt nothing about anybody. Occasionally I slept with a short, gentle, retiring man for whom I felt affection but no desire; puzzlingly, the sex didn't work. Later, when I got into my twenties and into psychoanalysis, and began to feel again, I "fell in love with" handsome macho men who didn't know I existed; I hated and envied them. The more intense and unreal these one-way "love affairs" were, the more dead and flat my life became in between. (When the man was not inaccessible, I made sure I was.) I got married to a short, gentle, retiring pleasant man (*He'll do*) and worked very hard at sex, which I loathed. I fell in love with a male homosexual friend because he was so beautiful and his life was beautiful and I wanted to be part of his life. I certainly didn't want to be part of my own life. I acquired a series of office jobs, none of which I could bear to keep ("Isn't there anything you like about your job?" "Yes, lunch hour."). I went into analysis because I was extremely depressed and very angry, and when my analyst asked (once) if I had homosexual feelings, I said "Oh, no, of course not," without even thinking. Even if it hadn't been nonsense, everybody knew that the real problem was men, so I thought endlessly about men, worried about men, worried (with the active help of my analyst) about the orgasms I wasn't having with men, worried about my childhood, worried about my parents, all in the service of worrying about my relation to men. Nothing else mattered. When my analyst asked me if I enjoyed sex, apart from orgasm, I remember wondering mildly what on earth he meant. It's quite possible that analysis did help me with my "dependency problems," although for a man who urged me to be independent, he was remarkably little concerned at my being economically dependent on my husband; he thought that was O.K. I didn't; for one thing my husband hated his job as much as I hated mine. He told me that my relationship with my mother was bad (I agreed) but when I talked about my father I would get so enraged (about all men, not just about that one) that he would become tolerantly silent and then tell me I was showing resistance. He once said that if I'd been born a boy, I could've turned out much worse: "You might have been homosexual." He said that what had saved me from going really crazy in my childhood was my father's love. He once remarked that I had intense friendships, and I said, "Yeah, I guess," not at all interested. But apart from the two remarks I've noted we never talked about my homosexuality. We talked about my "frigidity."

I remember someone in the group (I was in group therapy for years) asking me if my husband was a good lover, and my absolute, blank helplessness before that question. I remember analytic remarks that enraged and baffled me: that getting married showed "ego strength"—I had done it partly because I was running out of money and couldn't stand working, a motive of which I was bitterly ashamed and which I never told anybody; that it was surprising that my husband could "function sexually"—I had an impulse of absolute rage, which I suppressed; that I was afraid I would be physically hurt in the sex act—"No, I'm afraid I'll turn into a 'real woman,'" "But you are a real woman"; that I could be "active" by telling my husband what to do to me; and that men and women had different social functions but the same dignity—"Yeah, separate but equal" and that one I actually said out loud.

If analysis did any good, it certainly did not do it in the area of sex. Perhaps having some stories published helped. Being invited to writers' conferences and, for the first time in my life, meeting people like myself helped. (Question: why is it so hard making friends in group therapy and so easy making friends at writers' conferences? Answer: because writers are crazy.) Years later when I heard the phrase "the iron has entered your soul" I entirely misunderstood it. I thought that when you passed a certain point in misery you could really take the misery into you and turn it into strength. Perhaps I did that somehow. I made the first genuine decision of my adult life and left my husband—I was panic-stricken, clearly a matter of "dependency problems" but also a matter of getting out of the heterosexual institution. I got a job I liked, partly by accident ("You mean they'll pay me for *that*?"). I learned to drive. I got a job in another city and left analysis. I was desperately lonely. I kept "falling in love" with inaccessible men until it occurred to me that I wanted to be them, not love them, but by then feminism had burst over all of us. I stopped loving men ("It's just too difficult!") and in a burst of inspiration, dreamed up the absolutely novel idea of loving women. I thought at the time that my previous history had nothing to do with it.

Just before I left my husband I had a dream, which I still remember. (I had begun to have nightmares every night after we made love.)[1] I was alone in a city at night, walking round and round a deserted and abandoned schoolhouse, and I couldn't tell if I was frightened because I was alone or frightened because I wasn't alone. This dark schoolhouse was surrounded by uncut grass and grass was growing in the cracks of the sidewalk. I sat down on the front steps, in a world unutterably desolate and deserted, wishing very hard for someone to take me away from there. Then a car, containing the shadowy figures of a man and a woman in the front seat, pulled up, and I got inside, in the back seat. The car began to move and somehow I strained to keep it moving, for I suspected it wasn't going anywhere; and then I looked down and there, through the floorboards, grew the grass.

There was no car. I was back on the steps, alone. And I was terrified.

It was years before the phrase "grass growing in the streets" connected itself to the dream. (I knew from the first that it was about being alone.) I think now that the deserted schoolhouse is psychoanalysis (where I am to be "taught" what to be), and that the shadowy man and woman are what psychoanalysis is teaching me; that is, the heterosexual institution. But the schoolhouse is dark and deserted, grass grows in the streets (as was supposed to happen in the 1930s here if that radical, Roosevelt, won), the man and woman are only shadows, and I'm totally alone in a solitary world. Marriage is an illusion. My "teacher" is nonexistent.

It seems to me now the only dream I've ever had, aside from (a possible) one in childhood, that's genuinely schizophrenic, with the changelessness of madness, the absolute desolation, and the complete lack of hope.

But it didn't happen. Instead I got out.

II. FANTASY

But now we reach problems. Am I a "real" Lesbian?

There is immense social pressure in our culture to imagine a Lesbian as someone who never under any circumstances feels any attraction to any man, in fantasy or otherwise. The popular model of homosexuality is simply the heterosexual institution reversed; since heterosexuality is (supposedly) exclusive, so must homosexuality be. It is this assumption, I think, that lies behind arguments about what a "real Lesbian" is or accusations that so-and-so isn't "really" a Lesbian. I have been attracted to men; therefore I'm not a Lesbian. I have few (or no) fantasies about women and do have fantasies about men;[2] therefore I'm not a Lesbian. This idea of what a Lesbian is is a wonderful way of preventing anyone from ever becoming one; and when we adopt it, we're simply doing the culture's dirty work for it. *There are no "real" Lesbians*—which is exactly what I heard for years, there are only neurotics, impostors, crazy virgins, and repressed heterosexuals. You aren't a Lesbian. You can't be a Lesbian. There aren't any Lesbians. Real Lesbians have horns.

Since we are outside the culture's definitions to begin with, most of us are not going to fit the culture's models of "sex," not even backwards. There is the Romantic Submission model for women. There is the Consumption Performance model for men. A few years ago *Playboy* came out with a cover made up of many small squares, each of which contained a picture of part of a naked woman: a single breast, a belly, a leg, two buttocks, &c. There were no faces. I had just come out at this time, and was very upset and confused because I couldn't respond to this model. Not only wasn't I relating to women that way; I hated the model itself because I had spent so much time on the other end of it and I knew what that detachable-parts business does to a woman's sense of self. Did this mean that I was not a Lesbian? Not by *Playboy*'s standards, certainly. Mind you, I was not therefore a healthy or good woman. I was merely sick, criminal, or crazy. Oddly enough, I don't think I've ever felt guilty about sleeping with women per se; I always felt that my real crime was *not sleeping with men*. After the first euphoria of discovery ("Joanna, for Heaven's sake will you lower your voice; do you want the whole restaurant to know?") what plagued me—and still does—is the nagging feeling that in not sleeping with men I am neglecting a terribly important obligation. I'm sometimes attracted to men I humanly like; when this happens I feel tremendously pressured to do something about it (whether I want to or not). When I don't act on it, I feel cowardly and self-ish, just as I used to feel when I didn't have orgasms with my husband. Women, after all, don't count. What happens between women isn't real. That is, you can't be beaten up on for more than twenty-five years and not carry scar tissue.

Unfortunately there is something we all do that perpetuates the whole business, and that is treating fantasy as a direct guide to action. Suppression doesn't only affect behavior; it also affects the meaning and valuation we give behavior. And it affects fantasy. The popular view is that daydreams or other fantasies are fairly simple substitutes for behavior and that the two are related to each other in a simple one-to-one way, *i.e.* what you can't act out, you daydream. I don't believe this. For years I did, and was sure that my heterosexual fantasies indicated I was a heterosexual. (My Lesbian fantasies, however, could be dismissed as "wanting to be a man.") I think now that fantasy, like any other language, must be interpreted, that it does not "translate" simply into behavior, and that what is most important about it is the compromise it shows and the underlying subject-matter at work in it. For example, fantasies about "sex" may not be about sex at all, although the energy that feeds them is certainly sexual. I know that in growing up I had fantasies about rescuing Danny Kaye from pirates at the same time that I loved Carol-Ellen. I couldn't find my fantasy of a gentle, beautiful, non-masculine, rescuable man in any of the little boys I knew; there was only dull Bill (*He'll do*) and the creeps I hated and feared who grabbed me at parties or came up to me in assembly and said, "Baby, your pants are showing." By the age of fifteen I was having two kinds of fantasies: either I was an effeminate, beautiful, passive man being made love to by another man or I was a strong, independent, able, active, handsome woman disguised as a man (sometimes a knight in armor) who rescued another woman from misery or danger in a medieval world I could not picture very well. The first kind of daydream was full of explicit sex and secret contempt; the second was full of emotion and baffled yearning. Whenever it came time to go beyond the first kiss, I was stopped by my own ignorance. There was a third daydream, rarer than the other two, in which I was an independent, able, strong woman disguised as a man and traveling with my lover, an able, strong man who alone knew the secret of my identity. This kind was not satisfying, either emotionally or sexually, and I think I tried it out of a sense of duty; the one virtue it had was a sort of hearty palship that I liked.

In a sexual situation there are at least two factors operating: who you want the other person to be and who you want to be yourself. If I try to analyze my own past fantasies, I come up with one theme over and over, and that is not who the Other is, but what kind of identity I can have within the confines of the heterosexual institution. What I'll call the Danny Kaye fantasy is William Steig's *Dreams of Glory* with the sexes changed: little boy saves beautiful adult woman from fate worse than something-or-other. (If you look at the early Kaye films, you find that something of the sort is indeed happening, although not nearly to the extent I thought when I was twelve.) I still think that if I had emerged at puberty into a female-dominant culture in which little girls could reasonably dream of rescuing handsome, gentle, sexually responsive (but non-initiating) men from peril, I could have made an uneasy peace with it. I would probably have ended up the way a good many men do within the heterosexual institution: homosexuality for them remains an area of profound uneasiness, although their outward behavior and what they allow themselves to feel matches the norm.[3] However, even the cultural artifacts that turned me on in my youth all took it back in the end, just as Mae West's wooing of Cary Grant in *She Done Him Wrong* is shown up as a fake in the end of the film; he's really a tough cop. In fact, though this model of sexuality is not totally inconceivable and unspeakable, it turns up rarely and is explicitly disallowed. The sixties produced it in grotesque form in Tiny Tim; it took the seventies to produce David Bowie. But the heterosexual institution is wary of this model; it's politically very dangerous. And heterosexual men are trained to avoid it like the plague. Even as a fantasy it disappeared early in my adolescence.

Fantasy Number Two was cued off at age fifteen or thereabouts by something I read, and later on there were movies about Oscar Wilde and so on. (I have never ceased to be amazed at the fact that works about male homosexuality can exist in libraries, quite respectably bound, some even minor classics. They're few enough but Lesbian works are far fewer.) The one film I hoped would be about Lesbianism (*Maedchen in Uniform*) wasn't and disappointed me very much. This fantasy got more and more important as I got older, more depressed, *and more outwardly conforming to the heterosexual institution*. There were years in my twenties when this was the only way I could daydream about sex at all. I had, by that time, put into this fantasy all the explicit fucking that never got into the others, I'll give you all the passivity and charm you want . . . if only I'm not a woman.

Number Three (woman/woman) began early; it was modeled on a (totally sexless) parodic little story by Mark Twain about a woman disguised as a man, entitled "A Medieval Romance." At fifteen I added material from *Mademoiselle de Maupin*. For close to a decade my knowledge of Lesbianism was limited to these two fictions, one of them a parody (I was too naive to spot this at twelve), and although the emotional tenacity of this fantasy has been awesome, I never put much "sex" into it. I did not, after all, know what women did with each other.[4] And since the only way I could get near a woman was to disguise myself as a man, I had to protect my disguise (otherwise she wouldn't want me). So it was all impossible. Also, I was uneasy about wanting anybody else to "be the girl," since I knew what a rotten deal that was; I couldn't imagine anybody choosing it voluntarily. And how dull she was! But because I was a sort-of-a-man I couldn't very well love anybody else. Lesbianism modeled on the heterosexual institution didn't work and I had not the dimmest social clue that any other form of it could exist. And in my heart I think I would infinitely have preferred the reality of loving a woman to any fantasy; the very fact that it was a fantasy used to make me cry (in the fantasy). So this daydream also dies eventually.

The woman-disguised-as-a-man with a man was a pale one; it was too close to the reality of the heterosexual institution. Male attire is a flimsy protection for the culturally harassed female ego. I used this one rarely.

A fantasy that appeared sporadically through my teens and (like the male homosexual fantasy) got heavy in my twenties was explicit heterosexual masochism.[5] It was physically exciting, erotically dependable, and very upsetting emotionally. I never connected this one to Love Comics and never imagined that it might have social sources; I thought I had invented it, that it meant I was a "real woman" and "really passive," and also that I wanted to be hurt and that I was crazy.

There were two situations I never used in any of my fantasies: a woman loving a man and a man loving a woman. That is, I could never imagine myself in either role of the heterosexual institution. I think now that the heterosexual-masochistic fantasy was a way of sexualizing the situation I was in fact in, and that one of the things it "means" (in translation) is that I was being hurt and I knew that I was being hurt *because* I was a woman, that it was not sexual at all (as I had been promised) but that I wished to goodness it would be; then at least I would get something out of it. I also suspect that sado-masochism is a way of preventing genuine involvement;

either he wasn't emotionally there and present or I wasn't, and anyhow *the only thing* I can get from all of this is an orgasm.

The one cultural cue I had in abundance was the Dominance/Submission model of the heterosexual institution. The one cultural cue I barely had at all was Lesbianism (there is no cultural vocabulary of words, images, or expectations in this area). Oddly enough, for someone who thought she "wanted to be a man," I never imagined myself a man at all; by what sheer cussedness I managed to resist that cue, I'll never know.

What do people do with their sexuality? Whatever they can, I think. I think fucking can "work" within a wide variety of physical conditions. And the head-trips may not be connected to what one responds to in real life at all. In a fine essay on female sexuality Linda Phelps says that female sexuality is "schizophrenic, relating not to ourselves as self-directed persons, not to our partners as sexual objects of our desire, but to a false world of symbols and fantasy. . . . It is a world whose eroticism is defined in terms of female powerlessness, dependency, and submission. . . . In a male world, female sexuality is from the beginning unable to get a clear picture of itself." She says also that many women "have no sexual fantasies at all" and those who do "often have the same sadomasochistic fantasies that men do."[6]

Yeah.

Looking back, I think my fantasies were desperate strategies to salvage something of my identity, even at the expense of any realistically possible sexuality. There was, of course, this behavior with women that I wanted but I couldn't talk about that; it was the most taboo of all. (My first incredulous words at thirty-three: "You mean that's *real*?" Yes, I knew it happened, but . . .) I recognized my Lesbian feelings at age eleven; less than a year later I could no longer even recognize *what I was actually doing*, let alone what I later wanted to do. The only remotely positive encouragement I got, as well as the only analysis or naming, was the "stage" business. So partly I hung on in a muddled way and partly I gave up; after sixteen I gave up completely. The non-verbal messages were too strong. I think that anyone trying to maintain behavior important to them in the face of massive social pressure can only do so in a crippled and compromised way (especially in isolation), whatever form the crippling takes, whether it's guilt or an inability to fantasize or an inability to act. Or perhaps a constant re-shuffling of the roles prescribed by the heterosexual institution. As I got older things got worse; in my twenties I began to have occasional night dreams in which I was physically a man. I dreamed that a bunch of men were running after a bunch of women with felonious intent. I dreamed that I was being unmasked as "not really a man" and that everyone was laughing at me. As I had progressed from college to the less sheltered graduate school and from there to the not-at-all-sheltered job market my situation became worse and worse. I wasn't a man (let alone a homosexual man). I certainly couldn't love women, I was a *woman* and *women* loved men and dull, gentle men weren't "really" men, and if I liked them I wasn't "really" a woman (and anyhow I didn't like them except as friends; sex with them was no good). I was out of college now, I had to earn my own living, I had to get married, I had to shape up and have orgasms, this was the *real world*, dammit.

So I read Genet and Gide (I scorned *The Well of Loneliness* which I came to much too late anyway) and believed that art and life were totally separate. By then I really did want to be a man (for one thing, men didn't have such horrible lives, or so the heterosexual institution informed me). I was married. I was frigid. I couldn't earn my own living. I wasn't sure I was a writer. Psychoanalysis seemed only to prove more and more that the impossibility of my ever being a "real" woman was my own fault. I was hopelessly crazy and a failure at everything. My analyst, in the kindest possible way, pointed out to me that my endless infatuations with inaccessible men were not realistic; I tried to tell him that for me nothing was realistic. My maneuvers for retaining some shred of autonomy within the iron-and-concrete prison of the heterosexual institution were getting desperate; they now involved wholesale transformations of identity or the direct translation of my real situation into "masochism," which terrified and disgusted me. (I only brought myself to write about these fantasies many years later, by which time they had lost much of their glamor.) I knew that I did not really want to sleep with men. But that was sick. I did want to sleep with men—but only in my head and only under very specialized circumstances. That was sick. In short I had—for close to twenty-five years—no clear sexual identity at all, no confidence in my own bodily experience, and no pleasure in lovemaking with any real person. I had to step out of the heterosexual institution before I could put myself back together and begin to recover my own bodily and emotional experience. When I did, it was only because the women's movement had thoroughly discredited the very idea of "real" women, thus enabling me to become a whole person who could then pay some attention to the gay liberation movement. (My most vivid feeling after my first Lesbian experience: that my body was well-put-together, graceful, healthy, fine-feeling, and above all, *female*—a thought that made me laugh until I cried.) Whenever people talk about the difference between politics and personal life, I'm dumbfounded. Not only were these "political" movements intensely "personal" in their effect on me; I can't imagine a "political" stance that doesn't grow out of "personal" experience. On my own I would never have made it. I can still remember—and the institutional cruelty behind the incident still staggers me—telling my woman-disguised-as-man-with-man fantasy to my psychoanalyst, and this dreary piece of compromise (which did not, in fact, work erotically at all) met with his entire approval; he thought it was a real step forward that I should imagine myself to be a "real" woman being made love to by a "real" man. Then he said, smiling:

"But why do you have to be disguised as a man?"

There's a lot I haven't put in this story. For example, the years of limbo that followed my first Lesbian affair ("What do I do now?"), the overwhelming doubts that it had happened, which attacked me when I had to live an isolated life again in a world in which there exists absolutely no public sign that such things happen, or the self-hatred and persisting taboos ("Women are ugly" "Vaginas are slimy and strong and have horrible little teeth") or the terror of telling anyone.

As I said, by the time I read *The Well of Loneliness* I had learned that the whole business was absurd and impossible. (The book's gender roles also put me off.) I never dared buy one of those sleazy paperbacks I saw in drugstores, although I wanted them desperately. I was terrified to let the cashier see them. (Mind you, this didn't mean I was a Lesbian. It only meant that if I read all of the arousing scenes I glimpsed in them, I might become so aroused that I might go to a bar and do something Lesbian, which would be awful, because I wasn't one.) I suppose not reading about all those car crashes and suicides was a mild sort of plus, but I don't think it's a good idea to reach one's thirties without any cultural imagery for one of the most important parts of one's identity and one's life. So I've made some up. I hope that in filling the fantasy gap for myself, I've helped fill it for others, too.

I would like to thank various literary women for existing. Some of them know me and some do not. This is not an exhaustive list. Among them are: June Arnold, Sally Gearhart, Barbara Grier, Susan Griffin, Marilyn Hacker, Joan Larkin, Audre Lorde, Jill Johnston, Marge Piercy, Adrienne Rich, and too many more to put down here.

POSTSCRIBBLES

1. Overheard at a gay conference, Lesbian to gay man, nearby a woman minister in "minister suit" trying not to smile: "We're *all* in drag."

2. A common way to cloak one's hatred of and dismissal of an issue is to snot it, *i.e.*, the outraged ignorance of the reviews of Marge Piercy's *Woman on the Edge of Time* and the more sophisticated (and more hateful) reviews of Adrienne Rich's *Of Woman Born*.

3. The paralysis of the "open secret," everyone reassured about their generosity and your safety . . . *except you*. Or the (even worse) open secret which everybody knows *except you*, a closet so vanishingly small that it's collapsed into a one-dimensional point and extruded itself (possibly) into some other universe, where it may be of use but not in this one. A well-meaning woman friend, upon learning that I was a Lesbian, "That's all right. It's nobody's business but yours."

4. Some white male reviewer in the *New York Times* speaking slightingly of the *irredentism*[7] of minority groups in our time. The Boys never cease to amaze me.

5. That isn't an issue.

That isn't an issue *any more*.

That isn't *really* an issue any more.

Therefore why do you keep *bringing it up*?

You keep *bringing it up* because you are crazy.

You keep *bringing it up* because you are destructive.

You keep *bringing it up* because you want to be annoying.

You keep *bringing it up* because you are greedy and selfish.

You keep *bringing it up* because you are full of hate.

You keep *bringing it up* because you want to flaunt yourself.

You keep *bringing it up* because you deliberately want to separate yourself from the rest of the community.

How do you expect me to support a person as crazy/destructive/annoying/selfish/hateful/flaunting/separatist as you are?

I really cannot support someone as *bad* as that.

Especially since there is no really important issue involved.

6. Vaginas do not have sharp little teeth! Pass it on.

NOTES

1. And only *if* we had made love.
2. Up to about a year ago.
3. I don't mean that such men are "really" homosexual. That's going back to the model of the heterosexual institution again. They've suppressed a good deal of themselves, although what is allowed to exist isn't necessarily false.
4. I have only recently become aware of the extent of my own woman-hating and my own valuing of male bodies as more important, valuable, strong and hence "beautiful" than female bodies. Even a Lesbian wouldn't want an (ugh) *woman*! Even if she loved her. Feelings of inferiority climb into bed with you.
5. I'm talking of "masochism" as most women I know understand it: *i.e.* humiliation, shame, embarrassment, impersonality, *emotional misery*. Physical pain was not part of it; oddly enough, physical pain is what most men I know assume to be "masochism."

6. "Female Sexual Alienation" by Linda Phelps, reprinted in *The Lavender Herring: Lesbian Essays from "The Ladder,"* eds. Grier and Reid, Diana Press, Baltimore, MD, 1976, pp. 161–170. Ms. Phelps does not address herself exclusively to gay women. I think in this area she's probably right not to, as I suspect the mechanisms are the same for both, though one would suffer more symbolic distortion and the other more total obliteration.

7. Italian radicalism of the later 19th century, calling for a unification of all the Italian-speaking peoples, *i.e.*, nationalism: by extension, fighting for the rights of a group which perceives itself to have common interests. How wicked.

CORRESPONDENCE BETWEEN MARILYN HACKER AND JOANNA RUSS

JOANNA RUSS TO MARILYN HACKER, 23 OCTOBER 1973

23 October 1973

Dear Marilyn,

Your letter is lovely—esp. since now I can write two letters where formerly I would've written one, one to you, one to Chip.

Your book business is rather like my teaching, except teaching does leave more time & more ways one can cut corners, and so on. And you are beginning to sound just like Chip about London—I have this feeling that the two of you will turn up in NYC again—or I guess I should say the three of you.

And goodness knows, you BOTH need separate rooms. And the baby ought to have a velvet-lined cell where it can be put when both grownups have other things to do. Mind you, a *nice* cell, and a nest, too, but having seen your flat, I agree that it's crowded.

God, it seems we all end up in the same place. A very close friend of mine, who used to get upset when I went on & on about MEN is now divorced; another came back from Canada more militant than I've ever been, and here you are saying just what we're all thinking.*
I can't read modern novels any more (unless they're by women), I can't *bear* the conventional Didion sort of

---

*And what you were not saying 2 summers ago.

stuff, the usual Young Enraged Man simply seems to be writing from the other side of the moon or something. And I am worrying endlessly over the aesthetics of propaganda/polemic/didactic writing, trying to figure out (the worst problem currently) *whom* one is writing to. I think we both went through the business of I'm Not A Girl I'm A Genius, only they really won't let one do that; it just won't work. George Eliot is the most heartbreaking cop-out I've been able to find: every book I've read (tho' I haven't read Romola) breaks about halfway through. Her courage falters, her plot switches in mid-track like a locomotive suddenly on a switchback, and the scheme of the book crumples up. And it's always where she comes to the conventional limits of femininity. Maggie changes into a different character in mid-book in MILL ON THE FLOSS (so does Tom, by the way)—Daniel Deronda is really two books—poor Gwendolen is left hanging in mid-air in the damnedest way while Daniel takes off for Zionism—and in MIDDLEMARCH Dorothea's first problem (what to do with her self) somehow vanishes in the middle of a Love Affair. You can just see the book fall to pieces in each case. Only ADAM BEDE holds together—and there's no stand-in for the author there. Bronte, seems to me, simply stuck to her own experience and let it dictate to her: she writes the Great Romance once (Jane Eyre, naturally the book everyone reads), lets her book split in two in *Shirley*, and breaks into the most bitter, passionate kind of subversion in *Villette*. Which is why, I am beginning to suspect, George Eliot (with her male world view) is considered a Great Writer and Bronte isn't. Or aren't (both).

I don't think it's a matter of space but of fear. There's Daniel's mother in DERONDA, the Jewish opera singer who hacked her way out of the ghetto and a ghastly father, even gave away her son so (1) she wouldn't have to bother about him & didn't want to and (2) so he wouldn't be raised a Jew: it's all there, the freedom, the ruthlessness, the price, the transcendent necessary arrogance—and the author takes it all back by saying she isn't LOVING. (!) Her life could be written, even in the 19th century, but Eliot didn't. Bronte could have. I think Lucy Snowe is magnificent, tho' I suspect some of the loose ends in the book might just come from Bronte's early death. Was it published after her death?

[...]

I'm happy with my teaching now, loathing my colleagues more than I can say (it wasn't Cornell; it's just the Type) and have just finished a 38,000 word novella in which my 2 Lesbian heroines end up practicing shooting a rifle in their back yard. I want to call it "On Strike Against God", this being what some judge said in the 19 cent. to a group of striking women workers: that they were on strike not just against their employers, but against God.

I would imagine you'd know by now—has Chip mentioned it to you?—that I've just about decided heterosexuality is, for me, the worst mistake I could make with the rest of my life. I was itching to tell you when I saw you in London but was too craven. And—not that I think you will immediately broadcast the news—do not tell anyone. I am not sure yet how I want to become publicly branded or by whom. And certainly if by chance any news of this should seep back to the academic community in which I live, that would most likely be IT.

The labeling still bothers me. I don't feel like an anything sexually—and am quite capable of watching Christopher Lee on the Late Late Show (when I don't have class the next day) and mooning about him all night. But I have more and more the feeling that my attraction towards men is compounded of a real witch's brew of bad things—adoration, self-contempt, nostalgia, negativity—there's something not-real about it, very imaginative and all that but still all in the head. While what I have felt for women has always been real, concrete, hooked to a concrete situation and person, and quite freeing. And very sexual. I keep trying to tell myself that the sex of the person I'm attracted to doesn't matter, but that's nonsense. It matters tremendously. Because all the power differentials, all the politics, all the pain & despair and God knows what of the past 34 years (by the age of two I was already being made into a sexist mess) simply can't be wiped away. Maybe they could if the world around me did not constantly and endlessly reinforce them. (Which is a point I often tried to make to my analyst, without the slightest success.) I suspect you are right, and that we are all involved in very complex gender games, that people become hetero- or homosexual for very different, individual, and complicated reasons, and that men and women do so for extremely different reasons. But somehow all this has to be shoved into two labels. As a character says in that wonderful WHAT THE BUTLER SAW: "there are only two sexes, Preston, only two! This attempt at a merger will end in catastrophe."

So I have fantasies (when I do) about men, but seldom. And none at all about women (except willful ones). And am not sleeping with anybody. And keep losing the memory of my one rather pitiful and disastrous Lesbian affair, which was *nonetheless* magnificent, freeing, sensuous, beautiful, mind-bending, and real. I suppose the problem is that even with a Lesbian mind or soul or personality, I still walk around with a head full of heterosexual channeling. But it doesn't seem to get below the head.

Of course there seems to be no way of making friends with any of the men here without getting my toes trampled on constantly. I try to turn a lot of it aside, or laugh at it, or ignore it, not wanting to fight a dozen battles a day, so eventually I explode and *they* are all amazed. I'm told I'm "over-sensitive"—a quantified view of existence that has always puzzled me immensely! And alas there are so few people to talk to. And I'm tremendously gregarious at work. That is probably a writer's problem: one can be either alone-and-working or gregarious, but switching takes time.

That may be why you've been so caught up in buying books—get into one head and you can't get out into another.

My former lover and I are still very good friends, by the way. She has simply run shrieking from any sexual contact with anybody, apparently feeling so overwhelmable by people that she won't sleep with anyone. And I do think feeling herself to be a (gasp, gulp) Lesbian did freak her out. But my goodness, I don't feel any different.

Chip's preface to Hogg impressed me a lot as you know, if you saw my letter to him—because of the connection it suggests—absolutely bedrock connection—between aesthetics and ethics. Aesthetics IS ethics,* in another key, one might say. I find myself worrying endlessly over my novel and the new novella that somehow the structure isn't right, isn't tidy, isn't "dramatic" or "good"—because indeed once you get outside the accepted values, everything changes, including one's ideas of narrative. So the long long short story (I think it's really a short story

---

*Like "The political is the personal!" *Propaganda is an appeal to the future.*

in motion, if not in length) has no proper "ending"—it ends with a leap into the future, so to speak. Either one must leave that up in the air, as it were, (VILLETTE!) or end in defeat, which is a beautifully aesthetic ending, but hateful morally. Both the novel and the story end by, in a way, dumping themselves into the reader's laps. And my OWN aesthetic sense, nurtured by unities and conclusiveness and dramatic resolutions which, in fact, are embodiments of accepted moral ideas, stirs uneasily and says No, no, no. But (responds the other lobe of the brain) *that's what happened.* How can one write about success in a situation in which success and the implications of it are still unrealized and fluid in actuality?

Suppose, for example, in THE LEFT HAND OF DARKNESS, Estraven *hadn't* died? What a bloody moral mess LeGuin would have on her (I almost wrote "his") hands! Here we have an alien hermaphrodite and a male human (who's not quite real) *in bed* together. Worse still, *living* together. Could they live happily ever after? What would the real quality of their feeling for each other be? Could they get along? (Probably not.) Would they end up quarreling? (Their heat periods don't match, let alone culture shock.) So the great old Western Tragic Love Story is called in to wipe out all the very human, very real questions, and we can luxuriate in passion without having to really explore the relationship. You see what I mean.

It just struck me that my 2 pieces, like INVISIBLE MAN, like RUBYFRUIT JUNGLE, like even ISABEL AND SARAH (which is cute but not that good) have no "endings"—the story ends either by saying: Here I Am—i.e. burning into you an image of the protagonist's predicament* (like Ellison and like my novel) OR by saying not

---

*which is always a double-bind, a no-win situation.

"We succeed" but "We are now ready to attempt" or "We begin to attempt." Which, studied by traditional criticism, is all very unimpressive, and "badly-structured." Villette, it seems to me, ends with a Here I AM. You either end with "Now we actually begin" (or "It's up to you, reader") i.e. the rallying cry to the barricades—or we end with sheer lyricism, the power of one image, like the man in his room lined with electric light bulbs. One is a double-bind; the other is a promise or an appeal. And promises and appeals are certainly suited to propaganda. There have been lots of Unhappy Housewife novels in which (if she doesn't go mad) the woman abruptly "solves" her predicament by denying it; I have 5 paperback books that do this, inc. Up the Sandbox, which is the worst. Also Diary of a Mad Housewife. They won't make the leap. Polemics ought to end with a kind of prayer. I found myself writing at the end of my novel "Go, little book" etc. and last line "For on that day, we will be free." (Schmalz, I tell you!) And in the novella, "I never challenged Daddy—til now." But these are beginnings, not endings. So the aesthetic of polemic is going to be very very different from the aesthetic of either comedy or tragedy. (Isn't there something in German romantic writing that has this odd, "unfinished" quality? Because, in fact, it hasn't yet happened? Shelley's Prometheus ends with the lyrical faith-leap into The Image.) Oh tragedy is so *beautiful*. Jeez. Ugh. In my novella I said "You want a reconciliation scene? *You* write it."

It really is aesthetically different. I suppose to poets it's just as hard, but I envy you—you don't have to produce PLOTS, you bastards.

[…]

Here I am, hung up on explaining to my friend here why I loathe and wish to destroy paternal middle-aged white men who tease me by flirting with me.

And a former Cornell colleague saying airily that Gilman et al are silly people and why get angry at them?

Anyway, just came to me that in the novella, the process is as clear and plain as can be: (1) heroine has happy Lesbian love affair, after lots of initial worrying and reluctance (2) heroine "tries out" her feminism—integral to the affair and in fact what produced it—on 2 sets of friends (3) is repulsed by both (4) is radicalized (5) gets lover back (who has been going through same process) (6) prepares for Ultimate Revolution by learning to shoot rifle. Says her one wish is to "kill someone." Not in hatred, but to make a change, a difference, a dent in the world. Could it be more dramatically/narratively put? Problem is that the ending is ethically the wrong sign—it shocked me as I wrote it. And what it will do to my colleagues if they ever read it is best left unimagined!

The pressure of the endings I didn't write—the suicide, the reconciliation, the forgetting of the feminist issues (which I think far outweigh, or rather include, the Lesbian ones) kept trying to push me off my seat as I wrote. I kept saying to myself "That's banal. That's propaganda. That's *obvious*." (Oh how subtle failure can be!) But there was simply nothing else to do—anything else would have been false. In a vague way I remembered Frantz Fanon's bit about having to shoot the oppressor just to make the tremendous discovery that The Man *is* vulnerable. But it was pure Russ, I assure you.

The aesthetic problem, as I see it, is that the "prepare to succeed" is itself tentative and complex—it's not like an already settled issue, i.e. the Knights of Malta marching off to the Crusades. The real uncertainty of real issues comes in.

Goddess knows, it's also the only kind of live literature now. All the old solutions have turned to fuzz & lint, as far as I am concerned. For women it was always (1) failure (2) the love affair which settles everything. Look at George Eliot, WANTONLY drowning Maggie so she can rehabilitate her. Oh, it kills me. This, from a talent as good as (or even better than) Tolstoy! *Wuthering Heights* gives us both the old tragedy and the new tentative hope-of-success—which is why, of course, all movie adaptations leave out Part II and no critic up until College English 1970 has spent any time at all on Cathy #2 and Hareton Earnshaw, except to say that the novel "declines."

I am getting so that the very name "tragedy" or phrases like "the beauty of tragedy" make me grind my teeth. What excuses! Ah, one learns from suffering. Go tell it to Ralph Ellison.

And the happy ending of The Exception.

Still, it's good to be writing now (if not living). All these beautiful pathetic heroines drowning & dying & getting poisoned or going interestingly mad. And all these heroes dying nobly, feh. Feh, feh, feh.

I must stop now—I haven't yet got my rugs and my downstairs neighbors (who get up at 6 AM) come hallooing up the stairs if I type past 11. This spring I shall try to get a house.

Tell Chip that my new novella ends where he thought FEMALE MAN should end. (Actually I was getting there at the end of CHAOS, when I had someone say "Just life" i.e. not a settlement or solution, just things going along.)

Oof! If you have time, tell me what kind of poetry you've been *thinking* of. The whole business of propaganda is utterly fascinating to me.

It is the only live stuff.

Joanna

MARILYN HACKER TO JOANNA RUSS,
28 SEPTEMBER 1975

28 Sept. 1975

Dear Joanna,

[. . .]

I had just gotten to the part in the letter where I was going to say, and now, about intelligent attractive power-ful Lesbians conquering the world, & talk about On Strike Against God. I picked it up to remind myself of what I was going to say, and read it, again, all the way through, which is why this is Sunday afternoon instead of Sunday morning. What a good book. I'm glad you wrote it. I'm glad *somebody* wrote it, and especially that it was you. (I've never gotten to say that I found The Female Man even better on second and third readings, that all the minor changes were right, that I can't wait to see it in print.) Not to finish a book with anger or disap-pointment or disgust. Thank you. I would like to write a letter to Ted Solotaroff at the *American Review*, sending him a copy, and saying I think this novella is great, and I'm sending it to you in the hope that you will agree & accept the privilege of publishing it. And what a good antidote to the sexist claptrap you usually present as fiction. In fact, if you (Joanna) agree, I will do just that—perhaps a slightly more diplomatically phrased letter, copy to you of course. They would give you (compara-tively) lots of money. And lots of people, lots of *women* would read it, instead of being insulted by Philip Roth or collaborating in the cheerful hopelessness of the Catho-lic convert woman short-story writer with eight children and a sexy but unsympathetic husband. (but Nature is beautiful, isn't it?)

May I indulge in a few very small bits of lit-crit? I will.

Until the party scene, I was confused about Jean's age & status (job). On second reading, I noticed that she is said to be considerably younger than her friends, who are later said to be in their mid-thirties. But on first reading I assumed she & Esther were coevals until the party, when I found out she was 25. Somehow things would have clarified themselves much more quickly (in terms of visualizing the characters &c) if she was said fairly early to be a 25-year-old graduate student (because I kept picturing her to myself as 35, profession to be revealed, simply, I guess because one assumes that people described first as my friend X are the same age as the speaker. The narrator's past experiences given in the first pages place her in her thirties pretty definitely.

I'm probably not entitled to say this, but Stevie's reaction, though perfectly believable seemed to me pretty atypical of what the average gay male reaction would be (Relieved? Congratulatory?) Which is not to exonerate gay males of sexism, or to want the episode changed.

Very minor point—when Esther goes back home, & describes having been attracted to a girl she saw walking in front of the library, this girl seems to be wearing the same outfit, or at least the same top, as Leslie was at Ellen & Hugh's, though it isn't said to be the same or similar. And it just made me stop a moment. I mean, if it *was* the same blouse, Esther would have noticed it. And if it wasn't, its description made it seem so.

And last. The last pages are good, well-written, occasionally brilliant, threatening, strong, &c. But why are they addressed to *men*? I wanted this one to be for us, women. I can see the problem, that the book must end on a note of challenge, and you're not looking to go out & shoot *women*, but there is still the implication that The Man is still so important that even *this* book, even in defiance, in hatred, in challenge, is addressed to *him*, that the person you see reading it is not a woman or a girl thinking here is something at last, but a *man* being Affronted.

Chip & Whiffles came back. Chip out again to see if an ambulance comes for a man who had a heart attack or epileptic fit in the park next door. Whiff is sitting on the floor at my feet, tearing a telephone book in half. Page by page, admittedly, but she'll work her way up to more impressive feats. Trying to crawl these days, and obsessed by the problem. Betting (straight light brown) hair.

Will close now and post this.

Love,
Marilyn

ALTERNATE ENDINGS TO
ON STRIKE AGAINST GOD

JOANNA RUSS

1973 (I)

Just as I never challenged him again.
Until now.

I don't kill for pleasure. I don't kill for sport. I don't kill for cruelty.

I don't play fair—because I don't play.

I'll kill if I have to, if I'm pushed—and I must have the capacity to kill in this secret guerilla war in which we're punished for not giving in, punished for not having weapons, punished for using weapons, and (above all) punished for ever ever naming in public (except in joke) the real name of the real game.

We may joke about it—while lying on our backs.

128

again. Just as I never challenged him again.

Until now.

    I don't kill for pleasure. I don't kill for sport.

    I don't play fair - because I don't play.

    I'll kill if I have to, if I'm pushed - and I must have the
capability to kill in this ~~xxxx~~ secret guerilla war in which ~~women~~ we're
~~are~~ punished for ~~x~~ not giving in, ~~we're~~ punished for ~~not having~~
weapons, ~~we're~~ punished for using weapons, ~~we're~~ punished *and (above all)* for ~~naming~~
~~the name of the game, ever admitting x in public that there is a~~
~~war - though we may joke about it. While lying on our backs.~~
   ever   in public
ever/naming/(except in joke) the real name of the real game.

    We may joke about it - while lying on our backs.

293

1973 (II)

Just as I never challenged him again.
Until now.

I don't kill for pleasure. I don't kill for sport. I don't kill for cruelty.

I don't *play fair*—because I don't play.

I'll kill if I have to, if I'm pushed—and I must have the capacity to kill in this secret guerilla warfare in which we're all engaged, this war in which we're punished for not giving in, punished by giving in, punished for using weapons, punished for not having weapons, and above all punished for ever, every [*sic*] admitting in public (unless we giggle and cover our lying mouths with our delicate little hands) that we know the real name of the real, wicked, deadly, ghastly losing game.

We are allowed to joke about it—on our backs.

You let us laugh at your jokes.

Am I going to kill you? That depends on you. (What a wicked animal! When one attacks it, it defends itself.) If I need you out of the way, if you stand in my way, if it's necessary, if I feel nothing for you. (Don't try to play on my affections; you no longer know how.)

If you're my enemy.

Are you?

128

again. Just as I never challenged him again.

Until now.

I don't kill for pleasure. I don't kill for sport. I don't kill
for cruelty.

I don't <u>play</u> <u>fair</u> - because I don't play.

I'll kill if I have to, if I'm pushed - and I must have the capability to kill in this secret guerilla warfare in which we're all
engaged, in this war in which we're punished for not giving in, punished by giving in, punished for using weapons, punished for not having weapons, and above all punished for ever, every admitting in public (unless we giggle and cover our lying mouths with our delixate
little hands) that we know the real name of the ⅹ real,/deadly game.
                                        wicked, deadly, ghastly *boei*

We are allowed to joke about it - on our backs.

You let us laugh at your jokes.

Am I going to kill you? That depends on you. (What a wicked
animal! When one attacks it, it defends itself.) If I need you out of
the way, if you stand in my way, if Ixfeelxnathingx it's necessary,
if I feel nothing for you. (Don't try to play on my affections; you
no longer know how.)

If you're my enemy.

Are you?

1974

Just as I never challenged him again.
Until now.

I don't kill for pleasure. I don't kill for sport. I don't kill for cruelty.

I don't *play fair*—because I don't play.

I'll kill if I have to, if I'm pushed—but I have, and will have, and must insist upon having (whether I use it or not) the capability to kill in this secret guerilla war in which we're all engaged, a war in which we're punished for not giving in, punished by giving in, punished for using weapons, punished for not having weapons, and above all, punished for ever, ever admitting in public (unless we blush and giggle and cover our lying mouths with our delicate little hands) that we know in our bones the real name of this real, wicked, deadly, ghastly, losing, murderous folly you so genially, so cheerfully, and so jokingly insist on.

We're allowed to joke about it—on our backs.

And you thought the Civil War was something. Innocent! Do you know who this war divides? If I need you out of the way, if you stand in my way (and you have stood in my way for ten thousand years, I think), if it's necessary, if I feel nothing for you (don't try to play on my affections; you no longer know how)—

I'll kill you.

If you're my enemy.

Are you?

128

again. Just as I never challenged him again.

Until now.

I don't kill for pleasure. I don't kill for sport. I don't kill
for cruelty.

I don't play *fair* - because I don't play.

I'll kill if I have to, if I'm pushed - but ~~one thing I must~~
~~insist on is my~~ *have, and must insist upon having (whether I use it or not) the* capacity to kill in this secret guerilla warfare *a war* ~~in~~
~~which we're all engaged~~, in which ~~we're~~ punished for not giving in,
punished by giving in, punished for using weapons, punished for not
having weapons, and above all, punished for ever, ever admitting in
public (unless we blush and giggle and cover our *lying* mouths with our *delicate*
little hands) that we know in our bones the real name of ~~the~~ *this* real, wicked,
deadly, ghastly, losing, murderous folly you so genially, so ~~k~~
cheerfully, *and* so jokingly insist on.

We're allowed to joke about it - on our backs.

And
You thought the Civil War was something? Innocent! Do you know
who
~~what~~ this war divides? If I need you out of the way, if you stand in
my way (and you have stood in my way for ten thousand years), *I think* if it's
necessary, ~~if you don't get out of my way,~~ if I feel nothing for
you, (Don't try to play on my affections; ~~or my compassion;~~ you no
longer know how,) —

I'll kill you.

If you're my enemy.

Are you?

297

NOTES

Introduction: I'm Not A Girl I'm A Genius

1. Gwyneth A. Jones, *Joanna Russ* (Urbana: University of Illinois Press, 2019), 3.

2. "Readercon: Guests," accessed March 1, 2020, http://www.readercon.org/previous/r26.htm.

3. Larry McCaffery, *Across the Wounded Galaxies: Interviews with Contemporary American Science Fiction Writers* (Urbana: University of Illinois Press, 1990), 178.

4. Julie Phillips, praise for Joanna Russ by Gwyneth A. Jones, "Joanna Russ," University of Illinois Press, accessed April 16, 2023, https://www.press.uillinois.edu/books/?id=p084478.

5. Julie Phillips, "'I Begin to Meet You at Last': On the Tiptree-Russ-Le Guin Correspondence," *The Cascadia Subduction Zone* 6, no. 2 (2016): 5.

6. B. D. McClay, "Joanna Russ, the Science-Fiction Writer Who Said No," *New Yorker*, January 30, 2020, https://www.newyorker.com/books/under-review/joanna-russ-the-science-fiction-writer-who-said-no.

7. Philip K. Dick, *The Selected Letters of Philip K. Dick* (Nevada City, CA: Underwood Books, 1991), 48.

8. Samuel R. Delany, "Joanna Russ and D. W. Griffith," *PMLA* 119, no. 3 (2004): 500.

9. Jones, *Joanna Russ*, 86.

10. Kathy Hovis, "Alumni Share Career Paths after FGSS Degree," March 19, 2019, https://as.cornell.edu/news/alumni-share-career-paths-after-fgss-degree.

11. McCaffery, *Across the Wounded Galaxies*, 178.

12. Joanna Russ, *How to Suppress Women's Writing* (Austin: University of Texas Press, 1983), 127.

13. Joanna Russ to Samuel R. Delany, 25 September 1974, box 78, folder 23, Samuel R. Delany Papers, James Weldon Johnson Collection in the Yale Collection of American Literature,

Beinecke Rare Book and Manuscript Library (hereafter cited as Delany Papers).

14. Joanna Russ to Samuel R. Delany, 7 October 1974, box 78, folder 23, Delany Papers.

15. Paul Walker, "Joanna Russ," in *Speaking of Science Fiction: The Paul Walker Interviews* (Luna Publications, 1978), 247.

16. Russ, *How to Suppress*, 127.

17. Joanna Russ to Samuel R. Delany, 4 October 1974, box 78, folder 23, Delany Papers.

18. Susan Koppelman to Joanna Russ, 26 November 1979, box 6, folder 20, Joanna Russ Papers, Special Collections and University Archives, University of Oregon Libraries (hereafter cited as Russ Papers).

19. Jaqueline Lapidus to Joanna Russ, 6 December 1977, box 7, folder 28, Russ Papers.

20. Anne Hawthorne to Joanna Russ, 1 February 1975, box 6, folder 4, Russ Papers.

21. Samuel R. Delany to Joanna Russ, 19 September 1974, box 3, folder 8, Russ Papers.

22. Joanna Russ to Samuel R. Delany, 4 September 1974, box 78, folder 23, Delany Papers.

23. Joanna Russ to Samuel R. Delany, 4 October 1974, box 78, folder 23, Delany Papers.

24. Joanna Russ to Samuel R. Delany, 4 September 1974, box 78, folder 23, Delany Papers.

25. George J. Sullivan, "Dear Ms. Wallace," *Feminist Bookstore Newsletter* 2, no. 1 (1978): 9.

26. "Strategy Session: Getting Books Re-Issued," *Feminist Bookstore Newsletter* 1, no. 9/10 (December 1977): 13.

27. Kristen Hogan, *The Feminist Bookstore Movement: Lesbian Antiracism and Feminist Accountability* (Durham, NC: Duke University Press, 2016), 51.

28. McCaffery, *Across the Wounded Galaxies*, 195.

29. McCaffery, *Across the Wounded Galaxies*, 195.

30. Florence Howe, "Lost and Found—and What Happened Next: Some Reflections on the Search for Women Writers Begun by The Feminist Press in 1970," *Contemporary Women's Writing* 8, no. 2 (July 1, 2014): 136–53.

31. Alison Bechdel to Joanna Russ, 10 June 1986, box 1, folder 9, Russ Papers.

32. Imogen Binnie, afterword to *Nevada* (New York: Farrar, Straus and Giroux, 2022), 267.

33. Amal El-Mohtar (@tithenai), "I'm so tired of not knowing women the way I know Coleridge or Tolkien, discovering them in my thirties instead of having them shape my childhood. It's a kind of mourning in the celebration of finding them at last. It's not fair," Twitter, July 1, 2019, 8:48 p.m., https://twitter.com/tithenai/status/1145856829034942465. For more commentary from El-Mohtar on Russ, specifically *How to Suppress Women's Writing*, see Amal El-Mohtar, "Why Are There so Many New Books about Time-Travelling Lesbians?," *The Guardian*, August 9, 2019, https://www.theguardian.com/books/booksblog/2019/aug/09/why-are-there-so-many-new-books-about-time-travelling-lesbians.

34. Carmen Maria Machado, "How to Suppress Women's Criticism," *Electric Literature*, October 14, 2016, https://electricliterature.com/how-to-suppress-womens-criticism/.

35. Joanna Russ to Samuel R. Delany, 10 November 1980, box 70, folder 3, Delany Papers.

36. Russ to Delany, 10 November 1980.

37. Patricia Romney, *We Were There: The Third World Women's Alliance and the Second Wave* (New York: Feminist Press, 2021), 3.

38. Samuel Delany, "The Legendary Joanna Russ Interviewed By Samuel Delany," in *The WisCon Chronicles*, vol. 1, 2007, 162.

39. Breanne Fahs, ed., *Burn It Down!: Feminist Manifestos for the Revolution* (London: Verso, 2020), 5.

40. Monique Wittig, "The Straight Mind," in *The Straight Mind and Other Essays* (Boston: Beacon Press, 1992), 32.

41. Andrea Dworkin, *Intercourse* (New York: Free Press, 1987), 154.

42. Radicalesbians, "The Woman Identified Woman," in *Burn It Down!: Feminist Manifestos for the Revolution*, ed. Breanne Fahs (London: Verso, 2020), 41.

43. Fahs, *Burn It Down!*, 5.

44. Joanna Russ, *The Female Man* (Boston: Beacon Press, 1986), 151.

45. Johanna Fateman, "Andrea Dworkin," in *Icon*, ed. Amy Scholder (New York City: Feminist Press, 2014), 38.

46. Johanna Fateman, introduction to *Last Days at Hot Slit: The Radical Feminism of Andrea Dworkin*, by Andrea Dworkin, ed.

Johanna Fateman and Amy Scholder (South Pasadena, CA: Semiotext, 2019), 38.

47. Fateman, "Andrea Dworkin," 65.

48. Fateman, introduction to *Last Days at Hot Slit*, 38.

49. Sophie Lewis, "Shulamith Firestone Wanted to Abolish Nature—We Should, Too," July 14, 2021, https://www.thenation.com/article/society/shulamith-firestone-dialectic-sex/.

50. Fahs, *Burn It Down!*, 5.

51. Sam Huber, "Risk, Originality, Commitment," *New York Review of Books*, accessed August 14, 2023, https://www.nybooks.com/online/2023/01/26/risk-originality-commitment/.

52. Susan Griffin, "The Way of All Ideology," *Signs* 7, no. 3 (1982): 648.

53. Griffin, "The Way of All Ideology," 648.

54. Sam Huber, "Risk, Originality, Commitment."

55. Fateman, introduction to *Last Days at Hot Slit*, 20.

56. Joanna Russ to Samuel R. Delany, 1 February 1974, box 78, folder 21, Delany Papers.

57. Joanna Russ to Samuel R. Delany, 4 September 1974, box 78, folder 23, Delany Papers.

58. Joanna Russ to Samuel R. Delany, 26 October 1980, box 70, folder 3, Delany Papers.

59. Joanna Russ to Samuel R. Delany, 25 September 1974, box 78, folder 23, Delany Papers.

60. Joanna Russ to Samuel R. Delany, 7 October 1974, box 78, folder 23, Delany Papers.

61. Lee Mandelo, "Reading Joanna Russ—On Strike Against God (1980)," *Reactor*, October 14, 2011, https://reactormag.com/reading-joanna-russ-on-strike-against-god-1980/.

62. Joanna Russ to Samuel R. Delany, 1 February 1974, box 78, folder 21, Delany Papers.

63. Joanna Russ to Samuel R. Delany, 6 October 1975, box 78, folder 24, Delany Papers.

64. Sarah Schulman, "Books in Brief," *New York Native*, no. 156 (April 14, 1986): 38.

65. Joanna Russ to Samuel R. Delany, 4 October 1974, box 78, folder 23, Delany Papers.

66. Joanna Russ to Samuel R. Delany, 25 September 1974, box 78, folder 23, Delany Papers.

67. Marilyn Hacker, unpublished review of *On Strike Against God*, box 5, folder 27, Russ Papers.

68. Joanna Russ to Samuel R. Delany, 7 October 1974, box 78, folder 23, Delany Papers.
69. Russ to Delany, 7 October 1974.
70. Russ to Delany, 7 October 1974.
71. Joanna Russ to Samuel R. Delany, 4 October 1974, box 78, folder 23, Delany Papers.
72. Marilyn Hacker, "The Rest of Our Lives: New Lesbian Fiction," *Christopher Street* 5, no. 5 (April 1981): 46–49.
73. Hacker, "The Rest of Our Lives," 49.
74. Joanna Russ to Marilyn Hacker, 10 October 1974, box 78, folder 20, Delany Papers.
75. Fahs, *Burn It Down!*, 5.
76. Hacker, "The Rest of Our Lives," 46–49.
77. Fahs, *Burn It Down!*, 9.
78. Joanna Russ to Samuel R. Delany, 25 May 1976, box 78, folder 25, Delany Papers.
79. Fateman, introduction to *Last Days at Hot Slit*, 39.
80. Fateman, introduction to *Last Days at Hot Slit*, 12.
81. Joanna Russ to Samuel R. Delany, 7 October 1974, box 78, folder 23, Delany Papers.

On Lightning, and After Lightning

1. Keridwen N. Luis, "Les Human Beans? Alienation, Humanity and Community in Joanna Russ's *On Strike Against God*," in *On Joanna Russ*, ed. Farah Mendlesohn (Middletown, CT: Wesleyan University Press, 2009).
2. Jennifer Breen, "Alternatives to Marriage," in *In Her Own Write: Twentieth-Century Women's Fiction* (New York: St. Martin's Press, 1990), 73–87.
3. Samuel R. Delany, "Joanna Russ and D. W. Griffith," *PMLA* 119, no. 3 (May 2004): 501.
4. Gwyneth Jones, *Joanna Russ* (Champaign: University of Illinois Press, 2019).
5. Joanna Russ, author's note to *How to Suppress Women's Writing* (Austin: University of Texas Press, 2018 [1983]).
6. Joanna Russ, letter to Samuel R. Delany, November 10, 1980. This information per Alec Pollak.
7. This information also per Alec Pollak!
8. Joanna Russ, letter to Samuel R. Delany, September 4, 1974, again courtesy of Alec Pollak.

9. Again, courtesy of the impossibly helpful Alec Pollak. From Russ's letter to Marilyn Hacker, October 9, 1974.

10. Delany, "Joanna Russ and D. W. Griffith," 503.

11. Joanna Russ, "Pornography by Women for Women, with Love," in *Magic Mommas, Trembling Sisters, Puritans and Perverts: Essays on Sex and Pornography* (Trumansburg, NY: Crossing Press, 1985), via a somewhat dubiously transcribed copy I found at https://web.archive.org/web/20140405044924/https:// sites.google.com/site/evalangui/translations-traducciones/ pornographywithlove/.

12. Russ, "Pornography by Women for Women, With Love."

13. Breen, "Alternatives to Marriage."

14. BBC News, "Third Time 'Lucky' for Bad Sex Winner," December 3, 2022, http://news.bbc.co.uk/2/hi/entertain-ment/2540197.stm.

15. Joanna Russ, "My Hair Stood on End!: Talking with Joanna Russ about Slash, Community, and Female Sexuality," interview by Consuela Francis and Alison Piepmeier, *Journal of Popular Romance Studies* 1, no. 2 (March 2011), https://www.jprstudies.org/2011/03/interview-joanna-russ/.

16. Russ, "My Hair Stood on End!"

17. The generous, impossible-to-be-grateful-enough-to Alec Pollak quotes Russ in a 1974 letter on Judy Grahn's "Common Woman" poems: "I wish I could meet her." Joanna Russ, letter to Marilyn Hacker, October 9, 1974.

18. Joanna Russ, "'A Boy and His Dog': The Final Solu-tion," *Frontiers* 1, no. 1 (Autumn 1975): 156, https://doi.org/10.2307/3346428.

19. See, for example, Jessa Crispin's incredible foreword to the 2018 edition of *How to Suppress Women's Writing* (Austin: University of Texas Press).

20. Russ, "Pornography by Women for Women, with Love."

The Other Axis: An Interview with Samuel R. Delany

1. Samuel R. Delany, "Samuel Delany, Settling Future Limits," interview by Pat Califia, in *Occasional Views* by Samuel R. Delany (Middletown, CT: Wesleyan University Press, 2021), 40.

2. Julian Lucas, "How Samuel R. Delany Reimagined Sci-Fi, Sex, and the City," *New Yorker*, July 3, 2023, https://www.newyorker.com/magazine/2023/07/10/samuel-r-delany-profile.

3. Lucas, "How Samuel R. Delany Reimagined Sci-Fi, Sex, and the City."

4. Joanna Russ to Samuel R. Delany, 4 October 1974, box 78, folder 23, Samuel R. Delany Papers, James Weldon Johnson Collection in the Yale Collection of American Literature, Beinecke Rare Book and Manuscript Library.

5. Samuel R. Delany to Joanna Russ, 6 June 1983, box 4, folder 17, Joanna Russ Papers, Special Collections & University Archives, University of Oregon Libraries (hereafter cited as Russ Papers).

6. Samuel R. Delany, "Samuel R. Delany, The Art of Fiction No. 210," interview by Rachel Kaadzi Ghansah, *Paris Review*, no. 197 (Summer 2011): https://www.theparisreview.org/interviews/6088/the-art-of-fiction-no-210-samuel-r-delany.

7. Samuel R. Delany to Joanna Russ, 19 September 1974, box 3, folder 8, Russ Papers.

ACKNOWLEDGMENTS

Sam Huber, Carol Stabile, and Mahinder Kingra encouraged this project from its earliest stages. Margaret Homans and Amy Villarejo read drafts of the introduction when it was unwieldy and unfit for other readers. Joan Lubin helped me tell my own story, excruciating as it was.

This volume is enormously indebted to Linda Long—to her intimate familiarity with Joanna Russ's archive at the University of Oregon, and her willingness to locate and verify archival documents at a moment's notice. Thanks also to Casper Byrne, who saved this project from apocalyptic missed deadlines at least twice.

Joanna Russ's stewards, Madelyn Arnold and Winifred Eads, inspired, reminisced, and grieved with me and granted permission at crucial stages. Diana Finch's facilitation has been tantamount.

At the Feminist Press, Lauren Hook, Nick Whitney, and, of course, Margot Atwell's editorial visions (and patience) have been invaluable. Annamariah Knox agonized with me over the cover, and Ewa Nizalowska introduced the inimitable Sasha Staicu, who graciously and expertly contributed her beautiful art.

Madelaine Taft-Ferguson brought Joanna Russ into my life in 2013 and has singlehandedly kept this project on track. Thank you, Madelaine, for never missing the forest for the trees and reading this entire volume at least a dozen times. If it owes its existence to anyone, it's you.

ABOUT THE CONTRIBUTORS

JEANNE THORNTON is the author of *Summer Fun*, winner of a Lambda Literary Award, as well as *The Dream of Doctor Bantam*, *The Black Emerald*, and *A/S/L*. She is the coeditor, with Tara Madison Avery, of *We're Still Here: An All-Trans Comics Anthology*, as well as the copublisher of Instar Books. Her writing has appeared in *n+1*, *WIRED*, *Harper's Bazaar*, smoke and mold, and other places. She lives in Brooklyn. Her website is jeannethornton.com.

MARY ANNE MOHANRAJ is author of *Bodies in Motion*, a finalist for the Asian American Books Award, as well as ten other titles, including *Without a Map* (coauthored with Nnedi Okorafor) and *The Stars Change*. Mohanraj founded the Hugo-nominated magazine *Strange Horizons*. She serves as executive director of both DesiLit and the Speculative Literature Foundation, and editor in chief of *Jaggery*, a South Asian literary journal. Mohanraj lives in a creaky old Victorian in Oak Park with her partner, Kevin, two small children, and a sweet dog.

SAMUEL R. DELANY is a retired novelist, critic, and professor who lives in Philadelphia. He is the author of *Dhalgren* (Bantam Books, 1975), *Hogg* (Black Ice Books, 1995), *The Mad Man* (Voyant Publishing, 1995), *Times Square Red, Times Square Blue* (New York University Press, 1999), and the four books collectively known as Return to Nevèrÿon (Wesleyan University Press, 1993). In 2023, he was profiled in the July 10 & 17 issue of the *New Yorker*.

JOANNA RUSS (1937–2011) was a Hugo and Nebula Award-winning author of feminist science fiction, fantasy, and literary criticism. Born in New York City, Russ graduated from Cornell University in 1957 and held teaching appointments in English and creative writing across the country until settling at the University of Washington in 1977. A historic, groundbreaking writer of feminist science fiction, she is best known for her novel *The Female Man* and now for her darkly funny survey of literary sexism, *How to Suppress Women's Writing*.

ALEC POLLAK is a writer, academic, and organizer. She is the winner of the 2023 Hazel Rowley Prize and the 2018 Ursula Le Guin Feminist Science Fiction Fellowship for her work on a biography of Joanna Russ. Her writing appears in the *LA Review of Books*, the *Yale Review*, and various academic publications. She is a PhD candidate in the Department of Literatures in English at Cornell University.

The Feminist Press publishes books that
ignite movements and social transformation.
Celebrating our legacy, we lift up insurgent
and marginalized voices from around the
world to build a more just future.

See our complete list of books at
feministpress.org

THE FEMINIST PRESS
AT THE CITY UNIVERSITY OF NEW YORK
FEMINISTPRESS.ORG